We asked readers to describe

Danielle Steel

'Danielle's books always make me feel **strong, inspired and happy** – truly a page-turning experience' *Liz*

'She has a remarkable ability to write different stories at an **amazing pace**. Every time I pick up a book I know that I'm going to be taken through **highs and lows**' *Gillian*

'I feel like I've **travelled the world** through her descriptions of the places in her books' *Ann*

'Every book **gets you hooked** from page one' *Julie*

'Danielle Steel takes me to another place with her masterful story-telling ... **Absolute reading pleasure** from the first page to the very last' *Holly*

'I have **drawn immense strength** from the characters in many of her books' *Sarika*

'I love how she puts **her whole heart** into her writing' *Corina*

'I just love getting lost in her books. I can **stay up all night reading one**, just to know how it ends' *Kimmy*

'Danielle is such **an inspirational writer**, whose experiences are carried into the books. When I read each book, I feel as though **I am there with the characters** . . . They have gotten me through some very tough times and I would be lost if I didn't have one of her books in my hand' *Katie*

'Danielle Steel's books are **the perfect escape** from reality. Every time I read her books I'm transported to another place, ready for a new adventure' *Kelly Ann*

'I have been reading Danielle Steel books for fifty years or more and have kept every one – she is **my favourite author**' *Christine*

'**Gripping** reads that you **can't put down**' *Joanne*

'Her stories are **beautiful** and **gut-wrenching** and **totally unforgettable**. She has to be one of the best in the world' *Linda*

Against All Odds

Danielle Steel has been hailed as one of the world's most popular authors, with nearly a billion copies of her novels sold. Her recent many international bestsellers include *The Right Time*, *Fairytale* and *Past Perfect*. She is also the author of *His Bright Light*, the story of her son Nick Traina's life and death; *A Gift of Hope*, a memoir of her work with the homeless; and the children's books *Pretty Minnie in Paris* and *Pretty Minnie in Hollywood*. Danielle divides her time between Paris and her home in northern California.

Danielle Steel

AGAINST ALL ODDS

PAN BOOKS

First published 2017 by Delacorte Press, New York

First published in the UK 2017 by Macmillan

This paperback edition published 2018 by Pan Books
an imprint of Pan Macmillan
20 New Wharf Road, London N1 9RR
Associated companies throughout the world
www.panmacmillan.com

ISBN 978-1-5098-0023-0

1 3 5 7 9 8 6 4 2

A CIP catalogue record for this book is available from the British Library.

Typeset by Palimpsest Book Production Ltd, Falkirk, Stirlingshire
Printed and bound by CPI Group (UK) Ltd, Croydon, CR0 4YY

Visit **www.panmacmillan.com** to read more about all our books
and to buy them. You will also find features, author interviews and
news of any author events, and you can sign up for e-newsletters
so that you're always first to hear about our new releases.

To my beloved children,

Beatie, Trevor, Todd, Nick, Sam,
Victoria, Vanessa, Maxx, and Zara.

May you be forever blessed,
wise, and greatly loved,
as much as I love you!

with all my love,
Mommy/ds

Foreword

Dear Reader,

When my nine children were very young, I used to say that my concerns for them were safety first, and happiness (a close) second. But first, you want to be sure they don't bump their heads, fall down the stairs, burn a finger or run into the road. Accidents happen to everyone, but if you watch your young children carefully, you can usually keep them safe. And then you can focus on their happiness – the birthday parties they want to go to, the movies they want to see, the fun things they want to do, the doll they want for Christmas – and making sure that they feel safe and loved and happy.

As they get older, the mission of their safety and their happiness becomes much more complicated. The jobs they choose, the people they fall in love with, the exciting travels they want to do (to places that really frighten you). You have less control, if any, less influence than you'd like – sometimes watching them grow up is like watching a scary movie you may have seen before. You know where all the dragons are lurking, and when they're going to jump out, and you can't do a thing to stop the dragons, and there is very little you can do to convince your children that you know what you're talking about. (Sound familiar yet, if you're a parent?) One of my friends said that having adult children is like seeing what they're doing with a glass wall between you, so you can see them but they can't hear a word you say. All too true.

And one thing I have learned in my life is that you can't beat the odds. If the chances are that something is going to be a disaster, you're not likely to be the lucky winner who can beat the odds. Someone wins the $100-million lottery, but I've never known anyone who did. Very few people can beat the odds of an impossible situation and come out a winner. And I am terrible at watching my children get hurt, at any age. It's what I dread most, and most of us do. I don't want them to be sad or injured in any way.

All of those life lessons inspired *Against All Odds*, because at some point all of our children, or most of them, try to beat the odds, no matter what we say – just as we did when we were young. (I shudder at the foolish things I did! Fortunately, my own children are much more sensible than I was!) But young is young, and we all take chances, and so do our kids. And that's very hard to watch, as a helpless observer who loves them and wants to protect them, whatever their age.

Against All Odds depicts just those situations that we all worry about, that give us sleepless nights, for our children. And somehow, miraculously, most of the time there is a guardian angel somewhere who manages to help them turn things around (or our kids are smarter than we think), and most of the time they escape the dire fates we fear. Being a parent is the greatest joy on earth, a roller-coaster ride, and can be scarier than any movie. So this is fiction, but the situations in the book could be all too real. May the guardian angels keep your children and loved ones safe, whether children or grown up – and hang on for the ride! It's all worth it, but they certainly do keep us busy and on the edge of our seats some of the time. Good luck! And I hope you enjoy the book!

Love, Danielle

If Ever There Is Tomorrow

If ever there is tomorrow when we're not together,
there's something you must remember:
You're braver than you believe,
and stronger than you seem,
and smarter than you think.
But the most important thing is, even if we're apart,
I'll always be with you.

> —from *Pooh's Grand Adventure,*
> Walt Disney Pictures

Chapter 1

On a hot sunny day in June, Kate Madison drove her ten-year-old Mercedes station wagon through Greenwich, Connecticut, until she reached Mead Point Drive, and followed the directions she'd been given until she arrived at tall iron gates. She pressed a buzzer and said her name when a male voice answered. A moment later the gates swung open, and she drove slowly onto the property. The grounds and gardens were impressive and there were beautiful old trees lining the driveway. She had been in the area many times before, though never to this particular estate. The woman who had owned it was a well-known society figure who had only stopped going out shortly before she died, at ninety-two. Before that, she had been one of the grande dames of New York society, a generous woman who was best known for her philanthropy. She had no children, and had been on the best-dressed lists for years, mostly for her vast collection of French haute couture, which looked fabulous on her even at her great age.

The woman's clothes were being disposed of by two

nieces, who were finding the project far more tiresome than they had expected. Both were in their sixties and lived in other cities, and their husbands were executors of the estate.

They had already made arrangements with Sotheby's to sell the jewelry, had consigned the furniture to Christie's to auction, and were keeping some of the more important art. The rest was either being donated to museums or sold privately through a dealer in New York. And all that remained to deal with now was their aunt's wardrobe, which filled three enormous rooms that had previously been bedrooms in her spectacular house. The deceased had been a small, very thin, elegant woman, and her nieces couldn't imagine who her clothes were going to fit. The coats maybe, many of which were voluminous, and she had some magnificent furs, but the dresses were minute.

They had contacted Kate's store, Still Fabulous, after reading about it on the Internet, when a friend in New York recommended it to them. Kate had disposed of the friend's mother's wardrobe too, and she'd been very pleased with the results. Kate herself and Still Fabulous had a golden reputation in New York as the best, most elegant resale shop in the city, located in SoHo. She sold clothing that she bought outright occasionally at auctions, or she sold things on consignment, so she had no initial investment. She only sold clothing which was in impeccable condition or brand-new. She had some wonderful vintage pieces, but most of what she sold was current and still fashionable. Her customers loved her store.

Opening it had been a dream Kate had had for many years before she finally could. She was adept at combing resale stores herself, out of necessity, and she loved the hunt for beautiful things. When Kate's husband died when she was twenty-nine, leaving her with four young children, she had worked at Bergdorf Goodman for five years, first as a salesgirl, then as a buyer of designer clothes. She was well versed in new designer clothing too, but the thrill for her was in finding unique pieces, some vintage, some recent. And in the eighteen years she had owned Still Fabulous, she had gone to Paris many times to buy exceptional items at auction that others often overlooked. She bought only the most pristine items, in perfect condition, and they had to be still wearable and look chic. She liked older, more historical vintage pieces as well, but she bought them judiciously or took them on consignment, in case they didn't sell. If they looked ridiculous, were out of style, or in poor condition, she didn't want them in her store. She remembered many of the really beautiful and exceptional pieces she had sold, where they came from, and kept meticulous records of who she had sold them to. Her prices for important designer clothes were high, but fair.

Kate got out of the car in Greenwich, pounded the heavy brass knocker smartly, and a moment later, a butler in a starched white jacket opened the door. Kate felt a blast of cool air from inside, and was relieved to realize the house was air-conditioned. It would have been too hot to go through the closets otherwise, examining heavy winter clothes and furs along with the rest. It was obvious that she was expected, and she was respectfully led into a wood-paneled library by the butler. She could see at a glance that the walls were lined with rare leather-bound books, many of which were probably first editions and worth a fortune. The family was selling them at Christie's too. They were keeping very little of their aunt's estate. Kate was enjoying looking around discreetly, and was standing at the open French windows, with a view of the exquisitely manicured gardens. It was not the first time she had been in a home like this to evaluate and buy items from an estate.

A secretary appeared a few minutes later, apologized for being late, and led her to the locked rooms that were the woman's closets. They were any woman's dream, and a sight to behold, as the young woman turned the lights on. There was row after row of impeccably hung garments, many of them in individual cloth bags, and several racks of fabulous furs. And there were specially built cupboards for hats, handbags, shoes, and drawers for her custom-made underwear, satin nightgowns, scarves, and gloves. There was one entire closet of evening gowns, many of which Kate knew she couldn't use. Nowadays most of her clients, even the most social ones, led more informal lives. She might be able to take a dozen or so of the beautiful gowns, but there were at least two hundred there, in black, pastel, and brilliant colors, and always with evening bags and shoes to match.

One of the closets contained mostly French haute couture, from important designers, many of whom no longer existed. The collection was worth a fortune, and had cost an even bigger one when the woman bought the clothes hanging on the racks. It was a treat to see such magnificent pieces. Kate asked the secretary for permission to take some photographs. She agreed without a problem, and told Kate she was welcome to stay as long as she liked. Kate smiled as the secretary said it. She would have loved to spend a week there, not just a few hours, but she couldn't indulge herself just for the fun of it. She had to single out the items she could sell, and think about her more important private clients, as well as what she wanted in the store. Her shop was also a valuable archive for famous designers, who came to do research sometimes, when they were looking for inspiration for their next collections.

Kate had another segment of clientele as well. She had long attracted movie stars and celebrities who borrowed and rented evening gowns to wear to press events, premieres, and award ceremonies like the Oscars. The evening gowns would work well for them. And she had rented clothes as costumes for several movies over the years.

On a more human scale, while she still worked at Bergdorf's, she had acquired clients she consulted for, helping them to build their wardrobes or finding special items for them. It had given her extra money she needed for her children and inspired her to open a store of her own. The steady additional income she made from fashion consulting had given her the seed money to open Still Fabulous, along with loans her best friend, Liam, helped her obtain at the bank where he worked. Still Fabulous had produced beyond expectations, and within three years she had repaid all the loans. She started her business on a shoestring and watched her budget closely, and it grew rapidly in a relatively short time.

Kate was strikingly chic, and always dressed simply. She had worn a black linen Chanel suit, with white piqué collar and cuffs and matching white camellia on the lapel. She looked trim and elegant as always, and had an innate flair for fashion, for herself as well as others. She was tall, slim, and had long straight blond hair she wore in either a sleek ponytail or a bun. At fifty-three, she looked ten years younger than she was, and went to a gym five times a week to maintain her figure. The secretary in Connecticut was impressed when she saw her, but not surprised. Kate Madison had been highly recommended as the best in the resale business, and supposedly had an unfailing eye for what would sell, and women would still want to wear. She never picked the trendy pieces that were a flash in the pan and had gone out of style almost as soon as they were made. Her clients loved finding things they could wear forever, some of them iconic pieces from the designers who had made them.

Kate carried a lot of Chanel at the store, Yves Saint Laurent from Paris, and Dior from the days when Gianfranco Ferré designed it in the eighties and nineties. She also had Balmain from when Oscar de la Renta had done their haute couture, and Christian Lacroix before they closed, both haute couture and ready-to-wear. And Givenchy, from both the days of the great designer himself, and its more recent incarnations by Alexander McQueen and Riccardo Tisci. There were designers others had forgotten, the many young designers who had died in the seventies and eighties, and some later, at the height of their talent, Patrick Kelly and Stephen Sprouse among them. And she sold the American brands of ready-to-wear that everyone loved, Donna Karan, Calvin Klein, Michael Kors, Oscar de la Renta, Carolina Herrera, and here and there a nameless brand that she bought not for the label, but because it had style, or *gueule* or *chien,* as the French called it. That ephemeral something you couldn't really describe but that made a woman look special when she wore it, if she had the guts to pull it off. Kate also found wonderful basics like simple little black coats, pea coats, expertly cut Prada, and skirts and pants and sweaters that were timeless.

The secretary came in to check on her as Kate was photographing several beautiful evening gowns from Paris. She had made her way through the first closet, with two more to explore.

By three o'clock, Kate had seen all she needed to of the woman's collection, and had photographed the most important pieces. Kate thanked the secretary and promised her a list of the prices she would suggest in the next few days. With many of the pieces, she had to guess what they sold for originally, but she knew the market well. The rule of thumb was that she charged clients half of what the items had originally cost, and Kate split what she made fifty-fifty with the seller. So the seller got 25 percent of the original purchase price, and so did Kate. And in the case of exceptional items, or something truly iconic, she might charge more, and the price she sold it for was always negotiable. It was a very fluid business, and with rare and important pieces, she recommended donating them to museums for a tax deduction for the donor. She loved finding special things for her clients, and her merchandise often came to her in unusual ways, sometimes from estates like the one in Connecticut. What she had seen that day was a remarkable collection, and Kate knew just what she wanted from it, which pieces she felt her clients would want to wear and would sell well. There was an editor at *Harper's Bazaar* who was always anxious for beautiful furs, and there were great ones in that estate. The elegant dowager in Connecticut was going to make some people very happy with the treasures she had left.

The success of Kate's business was legendary, from a tiny little storefront when she first opened in SoHo, before it was as fashionable as it became later. In time she had taken over a bakery on one side of her and a small restaurant on the other, and her shop was a good size now. She rented three apartments above it to use as storage for the items she either didn't have space for in the store, or chose not to display to random clients, and saved for special people and events.

An editor of *Vogue* had discovered her in her second year, which had helped her a lot. And little by little her reputation grew, through magazines and by word of mouth. She became one of the best fashion finds in New York.

In the years since she opened, she had put four children through college with scholarships and without student loans, and had put them in private schools also on scholarships before that. Her mother had been a high school English teacher, and helped her obtain the scholarships, and tutored the kids when needed. Kate had always been adamant that she wanted her children to have a good education that would give them a great foundation for life, and they had all done well in school and had good jobs now.

Kate had dropped out of college herself in her junior year to marry Tom Madison. Her parents had objected vehemently to no avail when she gave up school. Kate was headstrong and determined and sure of what she was doing, and madly in love with Tom. He was twenty-six and in law school at the time, they had no money to live on, and Kate went to work at Bergdorf's for the first time, selling designer clothes. She worked right up until the day she delivered Isabelle, their first child, a year later, when she was twenty-one, and was back at work four weeks later. Her salary just barely fed all three of them, paid the rent and daycare for Izzie while Kate worked. She had begun combing resale shops then for clothes she could wear to work.

Two years after Izzie was born, she gave birth to twins at twenty-three, Justin and Julie. She gave up her job at Bergdorf's then, to stay home with them, and eked out what they needed by consulting with private clients. Tom graduated from law school when the twins were born, and got a good job with a major law firm. He supported the family then, after Kate's three years of hard work, and the consulting money she continued to earn helped make ends meet. They didn't live lavishly, but they managed, and somehow with some juggling they always had enough. Kate knew how to stretch their money and was creative and resourceful, and Tom worked hard and did well at the firm. They lived in a cramped apartment in the

Village, with the three children in one room, and Tom and Kate in the second bedroom, which was tiny, but they were happy and felt blessed.

They had another baby, William, six years after the twins were born, when they were a little less strapped. But halfway through Kate's pregnancy, Tom developed mysterious symptoms no one could figure out for several months. He was diagnosed with a rare, exceptionally aggressive form of pancreatic cancer a week before Willie was born. He lived the agonies of the damned for three months, and died when Willie was three months old, the twins six, and Izzie eight. Tom's death had blindsided them completely, they had remained hopeful to the end, and Kate was suddenly a widow at twenty-nine with four children. Tom was thirty-five when he died, and the insurance money he left had kept them going for a year, and then Kate had to go back to work full-time at Bergdorf's, as a salesgirl. She rose to buyer quickly by working many extra hours while her mother babysat for the children, and the rest was history.

After five years at Bergdorf's, she took a chance and opened Still Fabulous. She was thirty-five and very brave, and with her consulting jobs and salary at Bergdorf's, had saved enough to start out on next to nothing, with loans. She only took items on consignment then and couldn't afford to buy anything. Looking back on it at times, she didn't know how she'd done it or had the guts, but she had and it had worked. She never forgot those hard years when she was building her business and bringing up her children at the same time. But somehow, they always had what they needed, and now they were all adults, had been well educated, and had good jobs. As far as Kate was concerned, her real success had been her kids. They were all still very close, and she was proud of them.

Izzie had followed in her father's footsteps. She had gone to NYU on a full scholarship and lived at home then, because they couldn't afford the dorms, followed by Columbia Law School, and now, at thirty-two, she worked at a prestigious Wall Street law firm.

Justin had gone to Brown, on a scholarship as well, and was a freelance writer, doing magazine pieces and writing a novel. He was thirty and living in Vermont. Both he and Izzie had held jobs all through school. Julie, Justin's twin, had had a harder time in school than her siblings. She had moderate dyslexia, and her grandmother had tutored her for her entire school career, and helped her keep up her grades. Julie had a remarkable artistic talent and her mother's love for fashion, and had gone to Parsons School of Design. She was working for an up-and-coming young designer now who paid her well. She got none of the glory for the clothes she designed, but she earned a decent salary she could live on. In her early years after Parsons, she had had four roommates, but at thirty she could finally afford a loft she loved on her own.

And at twenty-four, Kate's youngest, Willie, was the family techie they all teased and called a geek. He'd gone to UCLA but came back to New York when he graduated. He had a great job with an online start-up that they hoped would become a big success.

None of Kate's children were married. Izzie had suffered a broken engagement two years before. Her fiancé had dumped her for a debutante from a fancy New York family, and they had recently gotten married. Izzie hadn't gotten over it yet, and had an edge to her now that she'd never had before, which Kate hoped would dispel in time. She hadn't dated anyone seriously since, and worked hard at the law firm. She was hoping to become a junior partner soon.

Justin was gay and lived with his partner, who taught history and Latin at a local high school in the town where they lived in Vermont. Richard was thirty-six, and they had met at a writing workshop four years before. Kate had realized that Justin was probably gay when he was eleven, and was supportive when he came out at sixteen. Richard's family was still in denial. They were a conservative family in the South, and disapproved of everything about his life, in contrast to Kate's loving acceptance of both of them.

Julie had had a series of relationships, though none serious. She said most of the men she met in the fashion world were gay, and she worked too hard to date much.

She had always been shy, and didn't mind spending time alone. She was a gentle soul, with a huge talent. She put all her time into designing four collections a year, not romance. And at thirty, she wasn't worried about getting married.

Willie, the "baby," was unofficially the family "slut," according to his sisters. He went out with one girl after another, and as many as he could at the same time. At twenty-four, he just wanted to have fun, and didn't want a serious relationship, and was honest about it with the girls he dated.

Justin and Willie had both suffered growing up without a father, despite Kate's efforts to be both parents to all of them. But it was harder with the boys. Once in a while she heard from teachers that the boys lied about their father being dead, and pretended to their friends that he was working in another city or on a trip. Justin suffered from it less than Willie, and always had Kate take him to the father-son dinners at school. He still remembered his father, though the memories were dim now. Willie didn't, since he'd been only three months old when Tom died, but they had photographs of him in their rooms when they were growing up, and Kate talked about him frequently to keep his memory alive.

Kate had made her peace with being a widow, the children had kept her busy for many years until they grew up and left for college. She'd had some romances but was too frantic trying to keep their collective heads above water and provide for them to get seriously involved with anyone for a long time. Most of the men she met didn't want the burden of four children not their own. And the few who seemed to like the idea were never the ones Kate was drawn to. She always said that she and the children were doing fine, and for the most part she was right. But it was lonely for her at times now, not having a husband or partner, with her kids on their own, with busy lives. She made the best of it, and in recent years there were only casual dates from time to time. She often thought it was ironic that now that the children were grown up and doing well, she would have had time for a man but never met anyone who appealed to her. The men she met now were either married or commitment phobic. And she was busy with her store, and loved what she did.

Days like the one she had spent going through the estate in Connecticut were still fun for her. It was exciting to find beautiful clothes, often knowing their provenance and who had worn them. Clothes like the ones she had seen and sold in the course of her business were pieces of fashion history, and it still thrilled her to make special discoveries.

Her family mattered more than anything to her and her children were the joy of her life. And Still Fabulous gave her tremendous satisfaction, was something to be proud of, and had fed them well.

She could hardly wait to get back to the store now and figure out what she was going to agree to sell for the estate, and which pieces she wanted to buy outright and keep to offer special clients.

*

Isabelle Madison was in a hurry as she left her office. She'd had to reorganize all her appointments for the afternoon in order to accommodate the pro bono assignment she'd been given. She always thought that it was inconvenient that attorneys in her firm had to accept pro bono work as part of their giving back to the community. She had done an internship in the district attorney's office years before, when she was in law school, and had discovered how much she hated criminal work. She was a business attorney who specialized in mergers and acquisitions, but she was conscientious, and would do the best she could with the case. She knew only the bare bones of the charges. The defendant, Zach Holbrook, was accused of possession of a large amount of marijuana and cocaine with intent to sell. He had no previous arrest record, and his last name was that of an illustrious family in New York, but she had no idea if he was related or if it was just a coincidence. And whatever his name, the defendant sounded badly behaved to her. He had been drunk and disorderly and had resisted arrest. She had to remind herself to keep an open mind as she got out of the cab in front of a seedy bar where he had offered to meet her. She didn't want to have him come to her office, so had agreed to meet him at the bar. She'd had no idea how bad he'd look.

Holbrook had already been arraigned, and was out on his own recognizance because he wasn't considered a flight risk, and Izzie met him at the bar he had suggested. A public defender had attended the arraignment before she was assigned to the case. She was already planning to ask for a continuance of the proceedings, so she could do some research into the case. But according to the police report, he had been caught red-handed with a fairly large amount of cocaine, and he was clearly guilty. It was going to be difficult to come up with a credible defense.

She arrived five minutes early for the appointment, and her client showed up half an hour late, and was not what she had expected. She'd expected him to look slightly derelict, and maybe like a drug addict, despite the fancy family name. He was thirty-five years old, strikingly hand-some, and was wearing a clean white tee shirt, black jeans, a black leather biker jacket, and motorcycle boots. The jacket had obviously been expensive, and he was covered with tattoos, including on the backs of his hands and crawling up his neck. His hair was shoulder length but clean, and he had several days of beard stubble. He looked sexy and stylish and was friendly and relaxed when he sat down at her table. He could guess immediately that she was his attorney. She looked the part. She was relieved to see that there was nothing ominous about him. If anything, he was charming, which annoyed her as he explained that he was sorry he was late, he had just flown in from Miami, where he'd spent the weekend, which concerned her, since she wasn't sure he was allowed to leave the state. What if the flight had been late or canceled? He seemed very casual about the charges he was facing. She didn't think the marijuana charges would be hard to beat, but the large quantity of cocaine in his possession would be. She told him that he could go to prison, and he insisted that was unlikely since he'd never been arrested before. He didn't seem worried at all as he sprawled in the chair across from her, and drank a beer, while Izzie drank water.

She wondered if she could get him to show up in court in a suit for future appearances, even a sport coat, instead of like a rich boy's version of a Hells Angel in a movie. He had a very studied "bad-boy" look. There was something theatrical about him, and much too smooth. He joked through the meeting, which Izzie didn't find amusing. He admitted to her within the client-attorney privilege that he had, in fact, sold cocaine and marijuana. It wasn't the first time but he'd never been caught before. She was not pleased to be representing him. It seemed like a waste of her time. She had better things to do than defend the black sheep from a wealthy family. He had told her immediately that he was part of the family whose name she had recognized, not that it mattered.

"Why did you ask for a pro bono attorney?" she asked him bluntly, "instead of just paying for one?" She was surprised he qualified as indigent. He seemed like he could pay for his own, and his family surely could have. The district attorney's office had exercised their right to ask the judge for a pro bono attorney in order to move the case along, since all the public defenders were currently overworked, and the judge had agreed.

"I'm dead broke. I have no money," he said easily. "My family cut me off when I turned thirty. They don't approve of my lifestyle." He smiled broadly, seemingly undisturbed by it. Further conversation with him told her that he had never had a job and didn't want one. He didn't see why he should work, since no one else in his family did. He had dropped out of high school after being kicked out of all the best boarding schools in the East. "I deal coke sometimes when I'm broke," he said with an ingenuous look, as though that were an acceptable form of part-time employment. And he said he thought it served his family right for not supporting him. He explained that all of his relatives lived off a family trust, but the trustees would no longer disburse funds to him, at his father's request, since he had dabbled in drugs when he was younger. So he had no money, but didn't work. Isabelle wondered how he lived, other than occasional coke deals. From what he said, he was living hand to mouth but had just gone to Miami. She wondered how he had paid for that. He was obviously resourceful.

Holbrook volunteered that his father was married to his fifth wife, who was twenty-two years old, and his mother to her fourth husband, and lived in Europe. He said his parents had divorced when he was five, and had been marrying other people ever since. His mother lived in Monte Carlo and he never saw her, and his father alternated between various homes in Aspen, L.A., and Palm Beach, and he ran the family investments from wherever he was.

"I'm the black sheep," Izzie's client said proudly. He had a sister who had been in and out of rehab and was living in Mexico, and a flock of step- and half siblings Izzie couldn't keep track of and he wasn't close to. He was the proverbial rolling stone from a dysfunctional family with money but no stability. He seemed to be without anchor or foundations, acted more like a kid than an adult, and had clearly never grown up. And what bothered Izzie most about him, other than his obvious irresponsibility, was that he was so appealing and occasionally funny that even she smiled several times at what he said. He was totally without remorse but not without charm, by any means. And he was obviously intelligent. It was hard not to be somewhat seduced by him, and despite her best efforts not to be, she was, but gave no sign of it to him.

She was trying to think what defense she could use for

him, and was hoping there was some improper technicality about the arrest or the charges that she could use to
have the case against him thrown out. Otherwise he was
screwed and would go to prison. She told him not to ever
wear the leather biker jacket for court appearances, to put
on a proper shirt, and get a haircut and shave before they
went to court. He laughed at what she said, and obviously
didn't take it seriously, while she tried not to notice his
broad shoulders, and how toned his body was in the tee
shirt under the leather jacket. He was visibly amused by
her instructions and intense look.

"You're cleaning me up?" he asked her.

"Trying to," she said tersely. "Judges don't like that
look."

She didn't want him appearing and acting like a juven-
ile delinquent, or wasting her time, if he expected her to
win his case. He had pleaded not guilty at the arraignment
and got a three-month continuance while he waited to be
assigned a pro bono attorney, and she intended to extend
it so she could research the case. She had made all the
notes she needed to at the bar, and he smiled at her as
they stood on the street for a minute. She found his cocky
attitude irritating. He was arrogant, although the family
history he had given her sounded pathetic. She almost felt
sorry for him, in spite of herself, and he clearly wasn't
doing anything with his life and never had. He was one of
those people where everything had gone wrong right from

the beginning, and still was. He seemed foolish and imma-ture, not evil.

"Can I take you to dinner sometime?" he asked her with a mischievous look, and Izzie frowned. She was his attorney of record, not a date.

"No, you cannot. You're facing very serious charges here, Mr. Holbrook, and I strongly advise you not to do anything foolish before we get this resolved. Where are you staying, by the way? Do you have an apartment?"

"I was staying with friends, but I got kicked out," he said, grinning sheepishly, which made him look younger than he was. "My grandmother lets me stay at her summer house in the Hamptons when I'm in New York. But I'm going back to Miami tonight."

"I am fairly certain you are not allowed to leave the state with this case pending." She was also wondering how he was going to pay for the plane fare if he had no money, but she didn't ask.

"Probably not, but my grandmother has a house in Palm Beach too, so I can stay there if I need to." He didn't seem to be without comfortable lodgings in posh places, only without a work ethic and a conscience about what he'd done to get arrested. It was trivial to him. And justi-fied by lack of family financial support, which he felt was his due.

"I'll be in touch," Izzie said soberly. He had given her his cellphone number and email address to contact him. "I want to review some of the details of the arrest and see if we can make a deal, or even get you off on a technicality." She thought it was her only hope of keeping him out of prison.

"I'm sure you'll find something," he said, seeming relaxed and confident. "I'll call you when I'm back in New York." She had given him her business card and planned to see him at her office next time. She hadn't wanted to bring a criminal to her office, but he looked respectable enough despite the biker jacket and tattoos. They would have three months before the next court appearance. And she hoped to get another continuance then too, to drag it out and give her time to prepare their case. "We'll do lunch," he said, and hailed a cab.

She stood staring after him as he rode away, still stunned by how nonchalant he was. She had never seen anyone as cavalier, but the details he had told her about his early life, divorced parents, many remarriages, no stable family, growing up in a series of boarding schools, with no parental involvement in his youth, and no work ethic as an adult, probably explained his attitude. It was a recipe for disaster, which he was heading for now and didn't seem to know or care. She couldn't imagine him surviving in prison. He was much too spoiled. And he was obviously used to getting whatever he wanted, or somehow making his life work. It didn't bother him how haphazard it was. He had practically undressed her with his eyes, and yet there was an innocence to him too. But she had no intention of having lunch with him or falling prey to his charm. She was much smarter than that, she thought, as she took a cab back to her office, relieved to be returning to the real world. The world of Zach Holbrook disgusted her. Wasted lives.

Two hours later, her paralegal staggered into Izzie's office with an enormous vase with three dozen long-stem bright pink roses and a card that said "Thanks for everything. See you soon. Love, Zach." Izzie almost groaned when she read the card. This was not the relationship she wanted with him. She was angry instead of pleased.

"New admirer?" her paralegal asked her with a smile, as Izzie frowned and shook her head.

"No. New client." She offered no further explanation, but she wasn't happy about it, and her paralegal left the room with no comment after depositing the roses on a table behind Izzie's desk. Izzie went back to work without glancing at them, annoyed at Zach Holbrook all over again. He was completely inappropriate in every way, no matter how beautiful the flowers were, or how attractive he was. All she wanted was to get rid of the case. And she hoped she'd be lucky enough to get him off or make a deal so she didn't have to keep seeing him over the next few months. He was a headache she didn't need. There was no room for a charming, unruly black sheep in her life.

Chapter 2

The two nieces of the deceased dowager in Connecticut were delighted with the prices Kate suggested for the items she wanted, and the clothes were delivered to Still Fabulous the following week. Kate was there when they came in, dropped off by a chauffeur with a van. She and Jessica, her assistant, checked them again, entered them in their inventory, and put them upstairs to show their most favored clients. Kate had already contacted several of them, and the editor from *Harper's Bazaar* had said she wanted two of the fur coats. They were Revillon and in perfect condition. One was a shaved dark blue mink that had been worn only a few times, and the other was an incredibly chic skunk. She was picking them up in a few days. Kate had chosen a whole rack of Chanel suits, several items of haute couture, some Oscar de la Renta cocktail dresses, and a dozen alligator bags in different colors that looked brand-new. The dowager had kept her clothes impeccably, and it always excited Kate to bring in items of such high quality. She was sure it would all sell very fast. It was one of the best estates she had seen in years.

Kate's daughter Julie came to visit a few days later, after work. She loved seeing what her mother found. They shared a passion for exquisitely made clothes, especially haute couture, and Julie had learned much about designing from what she had seen in her mother's store since she was twelve years old. Her own style was modern and more extreme and fashion forward, but she always said that she'd been heavily influenced in what she designed by what her mother had shown her and taught her over the years. They spent an hour going over everything, and Kate invited her to dinner at a restaurant nearby. The neighborhood had improved a lot since Kate had opened the store. The shops and restaurants around her were trendier and more elegant now, and there were many places to eat well with her children when they had time to drop by.

They went to a nearby restaurant best known for its wholesome food, fresh vegetables, homemade pasta, and salads, where Julie liked to have lunch, and they talked about the latest collection she was working on. She was frustrated at times, because she would have liked to do more exciting clothes for their line, but the designer she worked for wanted her to maintain the image and style of the house. But she enjoyed her job and the people she worked with, and she was making a healthy salary now. It was an excellent job, and prestigious, as the head designer for an up-and-coming firm. Her learning disability had caused her problems in school with reading and math, but she had enormous talent with anything involving art or design.

"You should have been a designer, Mom," she said to her mother with a warm smile, as they shared a Mediterranean salad. Julie looked nothing like her. She had her father's dark eyes and dark hair, and was smaller than her mother and older sister, who were both tall, thin, and blond and looked more like sisters than mother and daughter.

"I'm better at appreciating other people's designs," Kate said with a smile in response. She loved spending time with Julie. She was a gentle person, and they always got along. Izzie had a stronger personality, and was sharper and more critical at times, particularly since her broken engagement, which had left her bitter about men, and often harsh in the past two years. Kate hoped it wasn't permanent, and that she'd mellow again when she met a man she cared about, but it hadn't happened so far. "I'm a better shopper," Kate said honestly, laughing at herself.

"What's Grandma up to?" Julie asked her. "I haven't talked to her in weeks. Where's she off to now?" All of the children enjoyed their grandmother, who was a fiercely independent woman. She loved to travel, and had a widowed friend close to her own age, whom she dragged halfway around the world at every opportunity. She loved going to exotic places, and Frances tagged along. They had been schoolteachers together before they both retired. Grandma Lou, as they called her, had taken each of her grandchildren on an adventure trip when they turned twenty-one. She and Julie had gone on a fabulous trip to India nine years before, which Julie had never forgotten. It had influenced the fabrics she was drawn to for several years. And three years ago, she and Willie, her youngest grandchild, had gone to Dubai. Izzie had insisted on going to Scotland and Ireland, which Grandma Lou thought was too tame. She had added four days in Venice and a weekend in Paris before she brought her home, and Izzie had loved the trip. And she and Justin had gone on a walking trip in Nepal, which was more her style. She had been an important person for them ever since they'd been born, adding spice and adventure to their lives on a weekend trip to Quebec, a tour of the battlefields of the South, and visits to Yellowstone National Park and the Grand Canyon when they were small. She brought them interesting books and told them tales of her own trips to Africa and Asia. She was always open to learning new things, and had recently started taking Mandarin lessons, in preparation for a trip she was planning to Beijing in a year. It was hard to keep up with her.

"I think she's going to Australia this summer, on some kind of museum tour. She's already planning a trip to China next summer. She's taking Mandarin lessons to get ready for it. And she's going to Argentina after Christmas." She already spoke Spanish. Kate's mother was an exciting person to have in their lives, and at the same time, a solid, stable one. She had been invaluable to Kate, bringing up four children alone. They didn't have a father, but they had a grandmother who added immeasurably to their lives. She had a thirst for knowledge and wanted to see everything firsthand. Nothing daunted her. She was a remarkable woman, and at seventy-eight she didn't seem to be slowing down. Her traveling companions always had trouble keeping up with her. She stayed in remarkable shape, and was an expert in yoga. She had tried to convince Kate to try it for years, but Kate was less athletic than her mother and insisted she didn't have time. Kate went to the gym and took a spinning class once a week, which was exercise enough for her.

The two women had an enjoyable dinner before Julie went home to her apartment. Kate didn't ask her if she was seeing anyone, because she knew the answer to the question. Julie hadn't gone out with anyone in months. By the time she got home from work late at night, she was too tired to go anywhere, and she was content to stay home in her loft in the East Village. Her siblings were far more social than she was. Julie never minded being at home, and felt no pressure to meet a man. When she had time to spare, she went to Vermont to stay with her twin brother and his partner for a few days, usually between collections. They were a happy threesome whenever they were together. Kate was pleased that her children were all close, even more so to one another than to her, although they liked spending time with her too. And Grandma Lou was welcome at any family meal or plan. The best times they all shared were on holidays when they were all together, and Justin's partner Richard had been a happy addition to the group for the past four years.

None of Justin's siblings had significant others for the time being, nor did Kate, although her longtime friend Liam, her best friend since college, sometimes joined them. He was like a brother to Kate and an uncle to the kids. He was married to a quiet woman who didn't like to go out at night, and he had two daughters who were in college in Europe, so he was always happy to be with Kate and her kids. He worked for a bank and led a serious, circumspect life, and had been a big support to her when Tom died. They had been good friends now for more than thirty years.

Liam had advised her in setting up the financial foundation of her business, and helped her get loans a couple of times in the beginning. She said she couldn't have done it without him, and he was always available to counsel her, even about the kids. He said he had a good marriage, but as much as Kate loved him like a brother, she had never warmed up to his wife, nor Maureen to her, so her friendship with Liam flourished separately from the rest of his life. Kate always invited them as a couple when she gave cocktail parties, or invited them as a family to events with her children, but Maureen rarely came. She was a shy, retiring woman and preferred to let Liam see Kate on his own. She wasn't jealous of Kate. She just had nothing to say when they were together. Maureen was from Maine, and spare with words. Kate's lively family, and her own style and enthusiasm about life, had always been too much for Maureen. But she was a solid support for her husband, and a good mother to their kids. And for the spice and fun in his life, Liam had Kate and her busy tribe. And he always said that he had been in love with Grandma Lou since the day he met Kate. He called her sometimes just to see how she was, and ask what she was up to. The answer to that question was always interesting and unexpected. Louise was the only world traveler he knew who was almost eighty years old.

Grandma Lou had spent her seventy-fifth birthday on safari in Africa, and had returned with incredible photographs. It embarrassed Kate sometimes how much more adventurous her mother was than she was herself. Kate was happier staying closer to her home, her business, and her kids, even now that they were grown up. Her mother had always been fiercely independent, even in her youth and during her marriage, and her husband had admired her for it and encouraged her. She grew even more so once she was widowed, and had the chance to do all the things she had dreamed of for years but never could do while she was married. And she had opened the world as a learning experience for her grandchildren. They loved spending time with her and hearing about her travels. They confided their secrets to her, and asked for her advice. She was always candid with them, even if she didn't agree with their mother. She thought Kate was a terrific mother, even better than she herself had been with her only child, but at times she thought she protected them too much. Grandma Lou believed they needed to learn their own lessons about life. Kate didn't want them to get hurt, but as their grandmother pointed out, sometimes that was the only way to learn. It was the subject of many discussions between Kate and her mother, to what extent one could shield one's kids from the hard lessons in life. It was an age-old question to which there was no answer, only different opinions.

When they talked about it, Liam was more inclined to think as she did, and had a tendency to overprotect his two girls. It had taken every ounce of self-restraint he'd had to let them both attend college in Europe. And having been so sheltered at home, they were hungry for the world. Penny was at the University of Edinburgh, and Elizabeth was in Madrid. He had already been to visit them several times, although Maureen didn't like to travel and hadn't gone with him. The girls were ecstatic to be where they were, and far from home, although they loved their parents.

*

Kate's mother dropped by to see her at the store the day after she had dinner with her younger daughter. Grandma Lou had been on a walk in SoHo on her way home after yoga.

"Hi, Mom," Kate said, happy to see her. "I have something for you." It was a beautiful navy blue Chanel suit from her latest intake, and was the perfect size for her mother, and Kate thought it would be useful for her. It still had the tags on it from the woman in Connecticut, and had never been worn. She brought it out of a locked closet with pride. She kept special finds there, waiting for clients she had promised them to or had called them about. She had saved the suit for her mother. Grandma Lou stood staring at it for a minute, and squinted. Her straight gray hair was cut in a bob like she had worn all her life. Her hair was thick and full, her blue eyes bright and alive. She was wearing leggings, a pink Lacoste shirt, and the running shoes she wore on her hikes. Her figure was still trim and her face surprisingly unlined, and she had the stride of a much younger woman, particularly when she picked up speed when she was walking. She hadn't bothered with a handbag, and had her keys and wallet in her pocket. She hated to be encumbered, and she didn't care if she looked chic or not. She thought of clothes as functional, unlike Kate, who'd had a passion for fashion all her life.

"Do you really think that's me?" Louise asked, seeming worried, and her daughter smiled. "It's awfully serious looking, isn't it?" She was less excited about the suit than Kate had hoped.

"You can wear it out to dinner, Mom, or if you go to the theater." Louise looked dubious at the thought. She was more comfortable in jeans and the easy clothes she wore to travel. She thought comfort was more important. And Kate always looked stylish, whatever she wore, even in jeans. She would never have left her house without a bag, usually a Chanel or a well-seasoned Hermès that had come through the store. And Kate loved high heels. Louise had always preferred flats.

"Why don't you try it on?" Kate encouraged her about the navy suit. It was a classic, and she knew her mother would look great in it, if she could convince her to wear it. "Humor me." Her mother laughed, disappeared into a fitting room, and emerged a few minutes later with her Lacoste shirt under the jacket, her leggings showing under the skirt, in her beaten-up old running shoes, as Kate laughed. "Now that's a look, Mom." They both considered her image in the mirror, as Kate's mother stuck her arms out like a kid in an outfit her mother had forced her to wear but didn't want to.

"I'm not sure it's me," she said cautiously. In fact, it

wasn't. But Kate hoped it could be, if her mother was willing. "Where would I wear it?"

"Out to dinner with me sometime." Kate tried to inspire her and her mother laughed.

"Do I have to? I will if you want me to. I always knew you wanted a mother who dressed like this." Her mother had worn jeans for as long as Kate could remember, when other mothers were wearing wraparound skirts and cute dresses and high heels. Kate's mother hated dressing up, and it had never mattered to her father, who thought she was gorgeous whatever she wore. They had had a terrific marriage, and accepted each other as they were. He had owned a successful contracting business, and they had a good life, and Kate had been happy growing up. She had always felt safe and protected in her parents' world, and wanted her children to have the same sense of security with her, even without a father, after Tom died.

Kate's financial situation had been far less secure than her parents', once she was the children's sole support, but she had always managed, and something had always happened to help her pull a rabbit out of the hat when she needed it most. And when she was in dire need, her mother had helped her, although she didn't have a fortune either. But they had never known serious lack thanks to Kate's ingenuity about providing for them, and her willingness to work hard. And she had conveyed the same work ethic to all her children, with good results. All her children worked hard at their jobs.

"So what do you think about the suit?" Kate asked as her mother wandered around the store in the chic navy Chanel with her running shoes and pink shirt, and Kate could see she didn't like it and didn't really care, which was a waste. Someone should have it who really loved it and for whom it would be a fantastic find. For her mother, it looked more like a punishment than a prize. "You don't have to take it if you don't want to," she said, gently letting her mother off the hook, and Grandma Lou laughed and was relieved.

"I don't think you'll ever make me into a respectable-looking mother in a Chanel suit. What I really need are new hiking boots before my summer trip. You wouldn't have any of those, would you? We're going to do some hiking after our museum tour," she said earnestly and her daughter laughed. Hiking boots were definitely not the look Kate had spent almost twenty years cultivating at Still Fabulous.

"I'm afraid we're fresh out," she said and gave her mother a hug, and a few minutes later, Louise took off the suit, handed it to Kate, and left, delighted to have escaped the Chanel suit, although she appreciated the thought. Once in a while, Kate actually found something her mother liked, but this recent attempt was definitely not her look. She had given her mother a wonderful lamb and suede coat she had worn two years before on a trip to Tibet, and some fun Chinese pajamas she wore at home. But for the most part, despite her daughter and granddaughter being steeped in fashion, Grandma Lou had no desire to be chic, and was content to dress as she chose.

*

Grandma Lou was in Australia with Frances in August, the week after Izzie returned from a weekend in Vermont at her brother's, when Zach Holbrook called Izzie at her office to discuss his case. She had sent him several emails to which he hadn't responded, and she was about to report it to the court and attempt to get excused from the case, but hadn't gotten around to it yet. If he didn't care about his court case and the felony charges against him, why should she? She took the call as soon as her paralegal said he was on the phone.

"Hello, Isabelle," he said, sounding relaxed and friendly, far more so than she felt about him. "How about our lunch?"

"How about your pending case that could send you to prison? Do you have any interest in talking about that?" she responded tartly, and for an instant he was silent on the other end.

"Did I catch you on a bad day?" He sounded like a chastised child.

"Not at all," she said coolly. "You haven't answered

my emails, and I was planning to resign from the case. I can't deal with a client who won't respond. If you're not interested in your own defense, why should I be?" He was startled by her bluntness and chilly tone.

"I've been busy. I kept meaning to answer you. My grandmother had a stroke in Palm Beach, and I was staying with her." Izzie didn't know if it was true or not, but suddenly she felt sympathetic toward him. Despite her resistance to him, and disapproval of his lifestyle, he somehow made her feel as though she should be nice to him, because life had handed him some tough breaks.

"I'm sorry to hear it," she said quietly. "Is she okay?" It made her think of her own grandmother, and how grateful she was that she was in good health. She had talked to her on Skype a few days before. Her grandmother was proficient with computers and Willie was always showing her something new. She had a state-of-the-art computer at home, a laptop for when she traveled, and she always carried an iPad in her purse. She had taken several classes and had even mastered Excel.

"She's better now, thanks for asking," Zach said. "She's a plucky old girl. I love her a lot. She's the only member of my family who ever gave a damn about me. I've been staying with her for the past two months. So where are we with my case?" he said warmly.

"I've looked over all the details of the arrest, and I can't find anything wrong with it. I think the only thing we can do is try for a plea bargain, have you plead guilty, and ask for probation."

"Won't it go on my record then?" He sounded disappointed that she couldn't get him out of it, but she was an attorney, not a magician, and he had been arrested with the drugs in his possession.

"Yes, it will," she said honestly. "But if you don't plead and you push it to trial and are found guilty as charged, you could go to prison for a few years. I'd like to try to avoid that for you. How do you feel about a plea bargain?"

"If you think that's the only choice, I guess there's nothing else to do. I don't want to go to prison," he said, sounding anxious finally.

"You'll have to behave if you're on probation, though. If you get caught with drugs again, and arrested, they'll send you right to prison for probation violation. We have a shot at probation this time because it's your first arrest."

"I know," he said soberly. "I get it."

"Let me talk to the assistant DA assigned to the case, and see what I can do." She had very little to bargain with. He wasn't gainfully employed or a solid citizen. He was from a well-known family, which no one cared about, and had been caught with drugs.

"What about our lunch?" Zach asked before she could hang up.

"I never agreed to lunch with you," she reminded him.

"Yes, you did," he teased her, putting the charm on her

full blast. "Or you should have. Come on, let's go to lunch. We can discuss my case if that will make you feel better."

"I'll call you after I speak to the assistant DA," she said coldly, ignoring his invitation, and ended the call.

It took her two days to reach the assistant DA assigned to Zach's case, and he didn't sound interested in making a deal with her.

"Why should I make a deal with you?" he said bluntly. "We got the guy cold. We both know he was selling or planning to. The guy's a jerk, he's some spoiled boy who never grew up, he's probably been dealing on a small scale for years and just never got caught. And you know he's going to do it again."

"Then you can put him in prison next time. The prisons are full of guys a lot worse. You said it yourself, he's small-time. You're not putting away some danger to society. You've taught him a lesson. He gets it. I doubt he'll do it again."

"You're lying to me, counselor, and you know it. He's probably been dealing again since he got out of jail on this arrest." She hoped it wasn't true, but knew it was possible.

She decided to try another tack. "You and I have more important things to do than waste our time on a case like this. You have real criminals to put away, and I need to do my job. Why spend months going to trial when he's willing to plead for probation?" There was silence on the other end because the assistant DA knew she was right. He did have bigger fish to fry. And Zach Holbrook wasn't really a danger to anyone but himself.

"I'll think about it and let you know," he said, and called her a week later, after the Labor Day weekend. He had just gotten three big cases, and he knew Izzie had a point. He didn't need a small-time case like this. It was easier to just plead it out. "Okay. If he pleads guilty, we'll reduce it to a misdemeanor and give him probation. Two years. And if he screws up again, we'll send him away."

"Sounds like a deal to me." And if Zach did screw up again, it wouldn't be her problem, and they could assign him to someone else.

"I'll have the papers drawn up and you can bring him in to plead."

"Just say when, and I'll have him there." She hoped she was telling the truth and that Zach would have the brains to show up. If not, the DA would be pissed and so would she, and the deal would be off.

"Sometime next week," the DA said. "We'll let you know."

"Thank you," Izzie said sincerely. They were both happy to get rid of the case. As soon as she hung up, she called Zach on his cell. He said he was in the Hamptons, and she told him not to go anywhere until the plea bargain was complete. He promised not to and didn't mention lunch again. He sounded busy when she called, and she didn't care.

The following week, as soon as she was notified by the DA's office, she called Zach and told him to meet her there, and on what day. He thanked her for doing a good job, and this time when he met her, he was on time, and wearing a suit, a white shirt, and a tie, he'd cut his hair, and he had shaved. He looked more like an attorney than a defendant. The meeting was over quickly. The plea bargain and probation were confirmed by the judge after Izzie entered the guilty plea for Zach. They didn't assign him to drug rehab, because two random drug tests had come out clean. They assigned him a probation officer, whom he had to check in with once a month. The PO was a woman, and she was a little flustered when Zach turned the charm on her. He couldn't help himself. It was how he related to women. And she was flattered by the attention. He was such a good-looking guy. Other than that, Izzie was impressed by how circumspect he had been this time, and they shook hands outside the court. She was in a hurry to get back to her office for a meeting with her boss, and delighted that the case had been disposed of. Zach looked serious and appropriately chastened when he thanked her again.

"You did a great job," he said seriously.

"There wasn't much I could do. You need to stay out of trouble now, or they really will send you away," she warned him.

"I know. I'm not crazy, and I don't want to go to prison.

How about lunch?" he asked her, cautiously this time. She was one of the few women he'd met who was impervious to his charm.

"I'm late for a meeting, I can't. But thank you anyway."

"What can I do to thank you?" he asked gratefully. She realized then that he had actually been scared, although it never showed. There was something vulnerable about him, which made her feel sorry for him again.

"You don't owe me anything, Zach," she said kindly. "I just did my job. I'm glad it worked out okay," despite the guilty plea, but at least he wasn't going to jail. And maybe he had learned a lesson from it. For his sake, she hoped that was the case.

"Would you ever have dinner with me?" he asked wistfully. It was hard for him to imagine that she would, and she seemed like she was about to say no. "You're a nice person, and I'd just like to thank you."

"Stay out of trouble," she said, smiling at him. "That's all the thanks I want." And he looked so sad as he gazed at her like a big forlorn puppy that she didn't have the heart to turn him down. "Sure, maybe we can have dinner sometime." She didn't really mean it, but didn't know what else to say.

"How about tonight?"

She didn't want to, but thought it might be easier to just do it and get it over with. Reluctantly, she said yes, and felt foolish as soon as she did.

"Sure. I have to make it early. I have a brief to write tonight," she said sternly, to remind him that this was a business dinner and he was a client, not a date.

He suggested a restaurant she knew and liked close to her office, at seven-thirty, and after agreeing to meet him there, she jumped into a cab and went back to work. She felt faintly stupid for accepting the invitation, but it was two hours out of her life. And she forgot about him as soon as she got to the office, until she was ready to leave at seven o'clock, and then remembered her appointment with Zach. She brushed her hair and put on lipstick before she left her office, and walked to the restaurant carrying her briefcase with the work she had to do that night. It felt more like a nuisance to her than a date. And he was still wearing the suit and had taken off the tie when she arrived. He had a deep tan after the summer, and she couldn't help but notice again how handsome he was.

She ordered a glass of wine, and he ordered a scotch and water after they sat down, and he was predictably adept at drawing her out in conversation. He was at ease with people, especially with women.

"Married?" he asked her as they sipped their drinks, and she shook her head. She didn't tell him about the broken engagement, and the guy who'd broken her heart and married someone else. But she looked serious for a moment and then took another sip of her wine and relaxed.

"No, single," she confirmed. She knew he was single from the court papers and probation report.

"I lived with a woman for two years. She had a kid who was like my son. We broke up and she moved to L.A. She's married now. I haven't seen the boy since she left. It was nice for a while, though." Everything in his life was transitory, and she suspected he didn't want the responsibility that went with a solid life. "Why is a beautiful woman like you single?" he asked her with a dazzling smile as he nursed his scotch, and changed the subject back to her.

"I'm not the marrying kind," she said easily. It had been her pat answer for the last two years, and made getting dumped seem better.

"You just haven't met the right guy," he said confidently, as though he might be it, which seemed laughable considering how they'd met. "My guess is you work too hard."

"Probably. I enjoy what I do," and then she laughed. "When I'm not doing pro bono criminal work, which doesn't happen too often. I'm a corporate lawyer, which is more interesting to me." It wasn't his idea of fun, but it clearly was to her. She was wearing the dark gray suit she had worn for court, and it looked like a uniform she was comfortable in.

"I'd love to get you out to East Hampton sometime," he said. "It's so relaxing there at my grandmother's place."

"How is she, by the way?"

"She's better. She's staying in Palm Beach for the winter. She's going to let me stay in East Hampton this year. It's great there in the winter. I can walk on the beach and think. I go fishing every day. And I love to sail." It sounded like a wholesome life to her, unlike the felony charges against him, which were a different story. But maybe that had been an aberration and what he was describing was the real guy. He was a man of many facets, not just the criminal she had represented.

She was surprised by how pleasant dinner was, talking to him. He was easygoing and relaxed, respectful and funny, and incredibly smart. It seemed too bad that he had never gone to college, found work he wanted to do, or had parents who cared about him when he was young. He might have done more with his life than being a beach bum at his grandmother's house and dealing drugs. He insisted on paying for dinner, and was polite and considerate when he put her in a cab, and he looked at her through the open window and thanked her for having dinner with him.

"I'd really like to see you again sometime," he said and looked as though he meant it, and for an instant, she felt the same way. She nodded and then the cab drove away, while she remembered things he had said during dinner. He seemed like such a reasonable person and a kind man. And it was a strange twist of fate that their paths had crossed. She was glad she had kept him out of jail. He surely didn't belong there, and as the cab took her to her apartment, she couldn't help thinking that Zach Holbrook was a guy who deserved a real chance, and she hoped he'd get one, and turn his life around. If he'd had a caring family, like hers, his life could have been so different. She was still thinking about him when she walked into her apartment, turned on the lights, took off her jacket, and sat down at her desk. She pulled her files out of her briefcase. She had hours of work ahead of her, but she couldn't help thinking about how surprisingly pleasant and intelligent Zach had turned out to be. It had been the best evening she'd had in two years. And then she buried herself in the brief she had to write. But strange as it was, her dinner with Zach Holbrook had been a breath of fresh air, and gave her hope that there were still nice men in the world. He made it easy to forget his foolish mistake.

Chapter 3

Izzie heard from Zach a week later, and she knew she'd been thinking of him more than she should have been. Something about their evening together had made her feel human and like a woman again. He was handsome and sexy, but his gentleness and honesty were what had appealed to her. Being with him was so much less complicated than with the men she knew, who were always in competition with her. Zach had no ax to grind, and he was so open and real about everything that she couldn't imagine him running off with some debutante, like her fiancé. Nothing impressed him because of where he came from, and he had nothing to prove. He didn't care about any of the status symbols other men his age were chasing. All he wanted, he had said at dinner, was a good woman who was the real deal. As she was, he was fed up with phonies and fakes. Izzie had been engaged to a man who had turned out to be both, and was in hot pursuit of all the trappings of success. The girl he had married had been just another step up on the ladder he was so desperate to climb. Zach didn't care about any of it. And when he invited her to East Hampton for the day, Izzie accepted. They had spoken on the phone several times by then, and she liked him, and his texts made her laugh. His arrest seemed so completely not a part of who Zach was that she didn't care about it anymore. And no one had to know. She had seen at their second meeting how respectably he could behave. And when he picked her up at the train station in East Hampton, she was happy to see him. He had come to the station in a beautiful old Buick his grandmother kept in the garage. It was in mint condition.

They had a fantastic time swimming in the ocean. He took her fishing off a point near his grandmother's home, which was an elegant old house. He was healthy and athletic. There were a caretaker and housekeeper at the house, but they were off for the weekend, and Zach had made her lunch himself. They walked along the beach at sunset, and he wanted to take her out on his small sailboat, but the sea was rough. Instead they went to Montauk and explored the lighthouse and had dinner at a noisy restaurant where the food was delicious. She had never had as good a time with any man in her life, or felt as at ease. And although she was usually cautious and somewhat distant on first dates, he kissed her before she left, and she had never felt as hungry for any man in her life. Maybe because it had been two years since she'd liked or trusted a man. Zach melted her ordinarily cool reserve with the searing, white-hot force of his kiss. He was very sensual and stirred something in her that she had never felt before. All the pent-up emotions of the past two years came rushing out, and she could hardly bring herself to leave his arms. He stood waving at her as the train pulled out of the station on its way back to the city, and he called her as soon as she got home.

"Wow, what happened right before you left? I felt like an avalanche had hit me." He sounded as shaken by it as she was, and he went to New York to see her the following night. They were going to go to dinner and a movie, and wound up in her bed instead, and he never left. She went to work the next morning, feeling like she'd been reborn, and he was waiting for her at her apartment when she got home. He cooked her dinner and they could hardly wait to get back to bed. He was the most powerfully sexual man she had ever known. He spent the week with her, and they went back to East Hampton for the weekend.

Justin called her on Saturday morning, when she and Zach were about to go out on his boat. Her brother wanted to know how she was, because he knew that weekends were lonely for her. She told him she was in the Hamptons. He was surprised, since she had seemed down when she'd visited him in Vermont.

"Well, that's good to hear. How did that happen?"

"I'm staying with friends." She sounded happy and relaxed, and promised to call him on Sunday night when she got home. After they hung up, Justin commented to

Richard that it was the best he had heard her sound in two years, and maybe she was coming back after all her anger and bitterness over the broken engagement. He felt like the sister he knew and loved was back.

"Maybe she's in love," Richard suggested, though he didn't really believe it. Justin's sister had been so shut down for so long that he thought it would take a long time for her to come alive again. But if she was happier now, for whatever reason, he was glad, and he knew Justin worried about her. They both agreed that it would take a remarkable man to make Izzie trust someone again.

For the next several weekends, Izzie went to East Hampton with Zach. They cooked together and walked on the beach, sailed his boat, and spent quiet nights by the fire in his grandmother's luxurious home. It was all like a dream, and a new experience for her to abandon herself to a man, even her ex-fiancé. And as an added bonus, their passion for each other seemed to be limitless. He came into the city to be with her during the week, and hung around at home or met up with friends while she worked. Even her mother noticed a new lilt in her voice when they talked. She didn't want to pry but said something to Julie when she dropped by the store.

"Is anything happening with Izzie?" Kate asked discreetly. She knew she wasn't privy to all her children's secrets anymore, and she didn't try to be. They had a right to their adult lives.

"No, not that I know of. Why?" Julie didn't know about Zach either. Izzie hadn't told anyone, and didn't want to yet. She wanted to keep the magic of their relationship to herself, and the circumstances surrounding it would be hard to explain. She wanted to protect it for now, since it was so new.

"She sounds great," Kate said, looking pleased, and mentioned it to her mother when they had lunch.

"I hope it's not some rebound romance," Grandma Lou said wisely. "She's been so locked up and down on everyone for so long, she's liable to go off like a rocket for the wrong guy."

Kate shook her head. "That's not Izzie's style. She's too sensible for that." Kate had faith in her children and knew them well. And Izzie was the most levelheaded of the four.

"Those are the ones it happens to. She was hit so hard when Andrew walked away and married that girl. And it's taken her a long time to come back. I hope you're right and she's finally thawing out. I just hope it's with the right guy," Louise said with a determined look.

"I don't even know if it is a guy. Maybe she's just happy at work. But she sounds terrific, and she said something about going to East Hampton for the weekend," Kate explained. "She said it was to visit friends."

"I'm sure she's fine," Grandma Lou said, trying to reassure them both. She had great faith in Kate's children, but she was also realistic about the pitfalls of life. Their mother still worried about them all the time, and some-times forgot that they were grown up. She was concerned about Julie working too hard and not having a boyfriend, and about Izzie not getting over her broken heart. She was happy about Justin and Richard and thought they were a good match and a great couple. And she was mildly con-cerned about Willie's flock of girlfriends and overactive sex life and hoped he didn't get one of them pregnant. They were all on the right path with their careers, but with the exception of Justin, none had settled their per-sonal lives yet, and it sometimes kept her awake at night, worrying about them, just as it did Kate.

"Maybe it's time for you to think more about yourself than about your kids. You don't put any more effort into finding someone than either of your daughters, and if you don't want to end up alone, maybe you should. You're too young to be on your own for the rest of your life, Kate. And it's been a long time since you had anyone in your life. At my age, it doesn't matter, but at yours it does." Her mother looked at her seriously as she said it.

"There are lots of people your age and a lot older who find someone and get married," Kate reminded her and served it right back to her, but Louise was unimpressed.

"I had a good marriage for a long time, and I don't need another one. I couldn't travel as much as I do if I had to take care of someone, or be here to keep him company. I don't want to be tied down at this point in my life, except to you and the kids. And you can all manage fine when I'm away. I don't want some man complaining every time I get on a plane. Or to be a nurse. I took care of your father, and he would have taken care of me. But we had a lot of great years before that. I don't want to start at that part at my age. I'm having fun. I don't want to screw that up." It sounded sensible to Kate, and her mother didn't seem to mind being alone. She was always busy doing something that interested her, taking a class or seeing friends, or planning her next trip. It was hard to find fault with that. And Kate knew that her mother was right about her. Kate hadn't made any real effort to meet a man in several years. She would have liked to have someone to share her life with, but she was set in her ways too, and it wasn't as easy to meet men as it used to be. They were all married or seemed strange, and she had no desire to put up with someone else's quirks. She was still very involved with her kids, and the men she had dated earlier had always resented that. In those days, she had been a mother first, since she had to be both mother and father to her children. Now she was less engaged with them, but they would still be someone else's children to any man she met. Her life seemed almost complete, with her friends, family, and work. It was hard to imagine how a new man in her life would fit in.

She brought it up to Liam the next time they met at one of their favorite haunts, Da Silvano, for a glass of wine and a plate of pasta. She always loved seeing him. They could tell each other anything, and had for years.

"Your mother's right, as usual. She always is. You're too young to be alone, Kate. I worry about you too," Liam admitted as they finished lunch.

"What do you want me to do, stand on a street corner and whistle for a guy, like a cab? They don't fall out of trees, you know." He laughed at what she said. He was a good-looking man, and was aging well. He was a year older than Kate. He still looked the same as he always had, with a little distinguished gray at the temples, and most important, he was intelligent and kind. It always intrigued her that he didn't demand more of Maureen. But instead of insisting that she join him for every social occasion, he let her do her thing. He was willing to let her lead the retiring life she preferred, and he saw many of their friends on his own. It was an arrangement they had agreed to many years before, since he was more gregarious than she was. It wouldn't have suited Kate, but it worked for them.

"You could go to more parties, or places where you'd meet men," he scolded Kate, since she'd brought the subject up herself. He knew she'd been too busy with the kids to focus on romance for a lot of years, but it was different now, even though Kate thought it was too late, which he said was absurd at her age. She was fit and trim, youthful in her appearance, and beautiful and as appealing as ever.

Men always looked at her admiringly and she seemed not to notice.

"Like go to bars?" She looked horrified.

"You know what I mean. You don't try." They both knew it was true, and she didn't deny it.

"I'm happy the way I am." There was truth in that too, but she did miss having a man in her life at times. "And whenever I meet single guys now, they're weird."

"They can't all be weird." He laughed at her. He always loved talking to her. He could never banter with anyone the way he did with Kate.

"Maybe they can all be weird," Kate said thoughtfully. "There are a lot of strange guys out there. There's a reason why they're single. No woman wants them."

"What about a widower?" he said helpfully.

"Are you suggesting I read the obituaries and start stalking them?" She had read the obits to find estates for clothes for her store early in her business, but she didn't do that anymore. It was too awkward and embarrassing writing to bereaved relatives about buying their loved ones' clothes.

"It can't be as hopeless as all that," Liam commented.

"I just figure if it's right, someone will come along, and if not, I'm fine the way I am." She was at ease about it. It wasn't high on her list of things to worry about. She was far more concerned about her kids finding good partners than herself. They had lives to live ahead of them. She had already been married, had children, and had a busy life and career. Her children all had that to look forward to.

They lingered for a long time over lunch, as they always did, and since it was already October, Kate asked him about his Thanksgiving plans. Liam reminded her that European schools didn't have time off for Thanksgiving so his daughters weren't coming home.

"We're going to my father-in-law's house." Kate knew he didn't enjoy it, but was doing it for Maureen since the girls would be away. His own parents had died many years before. "What about you?"

"Same as every year, they're all coming to me for Thanksgiving. That and Christmas are my favorite times of year. I get them all at the same table for a big meal."

"Will Justin stay with you?"

"No, they stay with friends, but they come over for Thanksgiving dinner. And of course my mother comes too. She's planning some big trip again in January. Argentina, I think. But she'll be home for the holidays. She's going to China next summer. She's been studying Mandarin all year."

"She's amazing," Liam said with admiration. "I hope I have half her energy at her age."

"I think you just have to keep moving, and doing, and learning. There's always something new she wants to do. She's a role model for us all," Kate said with a warm smile at her friend. Kate knew how lucky she was to have such a terrific mother.

They left the restaurant reluctantly after two hours of easy conversation and laughter. Liam went back to his office and Kate returned to the shop. The store was busy in the fall before the holidays, with customers looking for dresses to wear to parties and holiday events. Her most recent acquisitions, and some old ones, were flying out of the store. And an article in the Sunday *Times Magazine* had mentioned Still Fabulous, which always brought in new business, with people who hadn't heard of them before. And after Thanksgiving, they kept the store open two hours later at night to make it easier to shop.

*

By November, Izzie and Zach had been deeply involved for almost two months. They were still spending weekends in the Hamptons at his grandmother's house, despite the cold weather, which made it even cozier at night. The housekeeper and caretaker were used to seeing her, and Zach had keys to Izzie's apartment in the city by then, and came and went while she was at work. They had settled into a regular life, but she was still concerned that he didn't work, and had no regular plans in the daytime, and nothing to do with himself. His grandmother gave him some money from time to time, which wasn't enough to live on, but with a roof over his head and food provided by his grandmother's employees, all he needed was enough to take Izzie out to dinner occasionally, and pay for movies and cabs. Izzie didn't expect him to contribute to her home, but he needed more to do than just wait for her to come home at night.

Zach didn't seem to mind not having a job, or not doing something constructive with his time. It didn't even occur to him. He read, he went for walks, he met up with his friends. She had signed him up at her gym, but he was a grown man, and she thought he should have an activity and a purpose in life. But when they saw her friends, or had dinner with lawyers she worked with, he didn't appear to mind saying that he didn't work. It made him seem prosperous and like a trust fund baby, which he had been, but a very meager one, and it bothered her for him. She tried to bring the subject up gently, and he laughed whenever she did.

"You don't have to be embarrassed about it," he told her. "I'm not. My father doesn't work either." But his father also had control of his own money. Zach didn't. He negotiated with his trustees for a pittance, and they thought he should be working too, and then they would have been freer with the money if they thought he was responsible. They didn't want to encourage him to stay indolent and unemployed. But even having too little money didn't inspire him to get a job.

"Is there anything you like to do?" Izzie asked him, trying to guide him in the right direction.

"Yes, make love to you," he said, and the topic would be brushed aside while he made love to her. No matter what she did, she couldn't get him interested in a job. Their sex life took precedence over all else, except her work.

She still hadn't said anything to her family about him, and didn't want to do so prematurely, although their relationship seemed solid, but it was still early days, and she was savoring the secret. He didn't answer her phone at the apartment, so no one ever knew he was there. She had toyed with the idea of inviting him to her mother's for Thanksgiving, but he wanted to visit his grandmother in Palm Beach so she wouldn't be alone for the holiday, so Izzie didn't have to make a decision. He called her frequently and was always nice to her. He was surprisingly well behaved for a self-declared black sheep, although he never called his parents, and she noticed that they never called him. Her own mother called her every few days, and Izzie called Grandma Lou once or twice a week to check in with her. Most of the time, she was doing something and too busy to talk.

"What's your family going to think about us?" Zach asked her in bed one night before Thanksgiving.

"They'll be intrigued, and want to meet you. And they'll be happy for me." She smiled at him, her head close to his on the pillow. But she also knew that they would want to know what he did as a job. In her family, everyone worked. Not working was not an option, nor even a remote possibility, for any of them. And they all liked what they did. Living as Zach did, doing nothing, on money he begged from his grandmother or his trustees, would be inconceivable to them, and would make them suspicious of him. And given how little money Zach could eke out of any of them, she couldn't understand his not wanting to work. It wasn't fun being broke. She had taken to leaving a couple of hundred dollars in a drawer in the kitchen, without comment, so he would have pocket money. She didn't want to just hand it to him, but he knew where it was, and she replenished it every few days. He was spending a few hundred dollars a week of her money. And it occurred to her frequently that it would have been nice for both of them if he'd had even a small job. But he thought that beneath him, and he had no skills to sell, and no education. He was smart and charming, and gorgeous to look at, but you couldn't get a job with that, not a decent one. And he would never have considered working as a waiter or something he considered menial, like being a salesman, although he might have been good at it. But she knew his not working would be a major stumbling block with her family, and Zach wasn't shy about saying he didn't work and almost seemed proud of it. She had no idea how to explain it to her family. They were all going to disapprove of that, and of him as a result, no matter how happy she was.

Izzie had never gone out with anyone like him before. He still loved dressing like a "bad boy." He had all kinds of motorcycle gear and leather jackets, which he wore with jeans and biker boots. It made him look sexy to her, but she couldn't see her brothers dressing like him. She suggested modeling to him once, or acting, but he laughed at that too. He was perfectly happy as he was, and didn't mind being broke or getting cash from her. She didn't want to support him, although she was well paid at the law firm. That was a pattern she didn't want to establish in their relationship. He mentioned a few times that his trustees might give him money if he was married, depending on who he married, but she didn't want to marry him for that reason alone, and they hadn't been together long enough to consider marriage. She didn't know how to handle his complete lack of work ethic, and it was hard to discuss with him since he wasn't bothered by it. But other than that, they were ecstatically happy and got along. It was a unique relationship in her life, and maybe for that reason, she found it exciting. She kept telling herself that sooner or later she'd convince him to go to work, but there didn't seem to be anything he could do. It was not an easy problem to solve. And Zach wasn't worried about it at all. He liked having free time to do what he wanted and had no shame about Izzie supplying his financial needs. And being gainfully employed seemed dreary to him.

He "borrowed" three hundred dollars from her when he left for Palm Beach the day before Thanksgiving, and had no way to pay it back. The trustees had paid for his airfare, since it was to visit his grandmother.

Izzie thought about it after he left, and she knew it would have to change, or eventually it would impact their relationship, even if it hadn't yet.

He called her from the plane before his flight took off and told her he loved her. He was so sweet and affectionate with her that he was irresistible. He had brought her back to life, and given her faith in the human race again. He had healed her broken heart and made her happy. And after they hung up, she wondered if that was enough. Maybe the rest didn't matter. Maybe black sheep never got jobs, and weren't supposed to work. But if so, it was going to put a heavy burden on her. And she noticed when she went to make herself a cup of tea that the cash drawer in the kitchen was empty. He had taken what was there along with the three hundred dollars she gave him. It was expensive loving a black sheep.

Chapter 4

Kate's children arrived at her apartment around three o'clock on Thanksgiving Day every year. They talked and laughed, happy to see one another, and they sat down to an early dinner at six, after her daughters helped her with the final touches in the kitchen. Grandma Lou came early to help cook the turkey, and Richard loved to help and was a fabulous cook.

Everyone was in high spirits, talking at once and teasing each other, very much as they had when they were children. Kate said grace before the meal, and then they brought in the food from the kitchen and passed it around. She prepared a traditional Thanksgiving dinner, and other than Christmas, which was equally festive, it was everyone's favorite day of the year.

They all noticed immediately how happy Izzie looked this year, and they were halfway through dinner when Justin pressed her about it. She finally admitted that she was seeing someone, and she said demurely that it was going well.

"Okay," Justin said, smiling at her, "tell us what that

means. Who is he? What does he do for a living? How did you meet him? And is it serious? Let's get the cards on the table," he teased her. "We all want to know."

"Oh, for Heaven's sake," she said, blushing. "Don't be so nosy. He's very nice, his name is Zach Holbrook, and we've only been dating since September." They were a lot more involved than just dating—they were basically living together—but she didn't think they needed to know that, even if they wanted to. She wasn't ready to tell all yet.

"How did you meet him?" Justin was relentless.

"He was a client," she said truthfully, but she didn't describe how she had defended him on felony charges in a pro bono criminal case. That wouldn't have occurred to any of them, and they would have been horrified, and so was she initially, but it didn't matter anymore. She knew now what a decent person he was. He was also incredibly sexy, and she was in love with him.

"What does he do?" Justin persisted, and she hesitated for a fraction of an instant.

"He has a trust fund," she said in a soft voice. And that was true too. They just didn't happen to give him much money from it. Almost none in fact.

"Does he work?" Willie asked her. It was a reasonable question. He might have, but the answer was no.

"Not at the moment," she said vaguely.

"Why didn't you bring him?" Grandma Lou asked her, watching her carefully. She could sense that there were things that Izzie wasn't sharing with them, and didn't intend to. Kate had that feeling too.

"He's with his grandmother in Palm Beach for Thanksgiving."

"He sounds very fancy," Julie said quietly. "Is it weird being with someone who has so much money he doesn't have to work?"

Izzie nodded in answer to the question. "Sometimes." She was dodging their questions artfully. They wouldn't have liked the truth.

"What did he do before?" Justin chimed in again, assuming that he must have worked at some time.

"His father manages their investments," she said vaguely, and tried to change the subject by commenting on how good the food was.

"When are we going to meet him?" Kate asked her daughter. "Would you like to bring him for Christmas?" She wanted to lay eyes on him and judge for herself. She could tell that he was important to Izzie.

"I don't know yet. We're still getting to know each other." That wasn't entirely true, but she didn't know what else to say.

"You're welcome to bring him anytime you choose," Kate said, grateful to see her oldest daughter so happy. She was smiling about it and looking warmly at Izzie when Justin startled them all with news of his own.

"Richard and I have been interviewing surrogates since

August, and we think we've met the right one. We found her through friends in New Hampshire. She's done this once before. She's twenty-nine years old, married, and has two children. Richard and I have decided to go ahead with her. And a friend of Richard's that he grew up with is giving us her eggs. They're going to harvest her eggs next week, and with any luck, if it works, the surrogate will be pregnant and we'll have a baby on the way by Christmas." He beamed at Richard as he said it, and the two men exchanged a smile. There was silence at the table for a moment as everyone stopped eating and stared at them, and Kate looked upset.

"A baby? Why do you want a baby? Why don't you just get married, since it's legal now? A baby is an enormous commitment." And she wasn't convinced they were ready for that. "And what if the surrogate won't give it up?" Kate could see all the pitfalls instantly, and Izzie nodded.

"She gave up the last one she gave birth to without a problem," Richard said quietly. "We feel confident that she's reliable and honest. And she won't get the final payment until she signs off. We've been talking about it for a long time, and we don't want to adopt. We'd rather have our own. And to answer your question, Kate, we've talked about marriage too, and it's not important to either of us. But a baby is. We know it's a big commitment. We both feel ready. We want to have a family of our own, and this seems like the right time. We've been meeting with doctors and lawyers for months." Justin nodded, and his mother was fighting back tears. She knew that Justin's income was decent but irregular, and Richard's salary as a teacher wasn't large. How were they going to afford a baby? And what if they broke up? All she could see ahead of them were the risks, and none of the appeal of starting a family.

"Why would you want a baby now, when you're both so young?"

"I'm nine years older than you were when you had Izzie, Mom. And Richard is thirty-six." Justin spoke in a calm voice, but no one at the table looked enthused at the idea.

"From a legal standpoint, surrogacy is very risky business," Izzie said in a disapproving tone. "There are a great many cases where the surrogate won't give the baby up once it's born. Why take a chance on that kind of heartbreak? If you want kids, why don't you adopt?"

"That's not without risk either," Justin said quietly, "and for a number of reasons, Richard and I feel that surrogacy is the right choice for us." They hadn't made the decision impulsively, but no one else knew that, and they had both put some money aside. Enough to move ahead now.

"How do you know she's healthy, and not a drug addict, or she won't drink while she's pregnant? You don't know who this woman is," his mother said, looking anxious.

"We know enough, Mom, to be comfortable about her. And our friends got a wonderful baby from her. The baby is healthy, and she was honest and reasonable." Justin was visibly disappointed by his family's reaction. He had hoped they'd be happy for them. It had been a huge decision and they'd put a lot of thought and research into it, and soul searching, and it was what they both wanted more than anything. They had no doubts.

"I really feel you should rethink it," Izzie said firmly.

"Izzie's right," Kate said definitively.

"I think it's wonderful," Julie said, beaming at her twin brother and Richard. "I hope you have twins." They both laughed at that. It had occurred to them too. "We'd be fine with twins. But we're hoping for one this time," Richard answered for him.

"I think you're crazy to want kids," Willie added. "They're messy, they smell, they keep you up all night. Why would you want a baby?" Richard and Justin both laughed at his reaction, which was appropriate for a twenty-four-year-old who couldn't imagine why anyone in their right mind would want children.

"Be careful you don't wind up with one," Justin warned him.

"I think it's an excellent idea," Grandma Lou said in a strong voice, and Kate stared at her mother.

"How can you say that?" Kate challenged her. "They have no idea of the responsibility or the commitment.

What if something happens to one of them, God forbid?" She looked straight at Justin and then at Richard. "What if you break up?"

"Straight couples break up," Grandma Lou said sensibly. "Tom died and you survived it, and did a great job bringing up the children. Children survive divorces and the death of a parent. And no one understands the commitment one has to children until they have their own. That's never stopped anyone. And Justin and Richard aren't children. It sounds like they put a great deal of thought into it, and are doing it responsibly," Grandma Lou said in an approving tone, with a smile at her grandson, which he was grateful for.

"You can't send it back if it's too much for you to handle," Kate warned them.

"That's not going to happen, Mom. We want this baby, and we've put a lot into it, time and money. We met seven surrogates before we chose this one. The legal term is 'gestational carrier,'" he said, educating them all to what was already familiar to them.

"Can you afford it?" Kate asked them, looking panicked. She knew what it was like raising children with very little money, and the strain it would put on them. More than they could imagine.

"We can," Justin assured her. "Not easily, but we can. We've been saving up for it, and when I sell my book, we'll have more."

"You and Tom couldn't afford Izzie when you had her," Kate's mother reminded her. "Or the twins. People do it all the time, and find the money as they go along. Your father and I weren't making much money when we had you either. If everyone waited until they were rolling in money, most people wouldn't have children. You work it out, just as you and Tom did, and your father and I did. Justin and Richard will work it out too. Congratulations." She beamed at them. "We should all be celebrating," she said, with a pointed look at her daughter. "And next year on Thanksgiving, I'll be a great-grandmother. I couldn't be more pleased," she said firmly, and the table exploded in chatter after that with a million questions about the egg donor, the surrogate, and how the process worked. Kate was noticeably silent for the rest of the meal. Justin had a quiet word with her before they left.

"I'm sorry you're upset about it, Mom," he said sadly. He had wanted her support and for her to be pleased, and she very obviously wasn't, which was a blow to him.

"I'm not upset. It's not that I don't approve. I'm just worried for you, for both of you. Having a baby is huge. I want to be sure you know what you're getting into. I think it's so much responsibility for you, financially, emotionally, and in every other way."

"We do know what we're getting into, Mom. Trust me. I want you to be happy for us, and excited about the baby," he told her honestly. "We're not children. We know what we're doing." He sounded very sure.

"No one knows what they're doing before they have children," Kate said bleakly.

"Are you sorry you had us?" he asked her bluntly.

"Of course not," she said, shocked by the question. "It's the best thing your father and I ever did."

"Were you sorry you had us after he died?" Justin asked more gently.

"Certainly not. I was happy I had you, and such a big part of him."

"Then why would it be different for us?"

"You don't know how the child will feel one day to have two fathers and no mother. What if they give him or her a hard time in school?"

"They give the children of straight parents a hard time in school too. And we'll be there to support him or her. And we'll explain it to him as soon as he's old enough to understand."

"It's a little too modern for me," Kate said, looking deeply worried for them. But she hugged them both and told them she loved them when they left. Grandma Lou stayed to chat with her, and the others went home to bed.

"You have to back off on this," Grandma Lou told her seriously. "You can't control what they do. It's important to them, and they're trying to go ahead with it in the best way they know how. You have to be supportive of them,

Kate. I understand your concerns, and I'll worry about it too. But for the sake of your relationship with Justin, you have to at least pretend to be pleased. He'll never forgive you if you don't. We owe it to him to be on his team now, and endorse their decision. You don't have any other choice, unless you want Justin to distance himself from you, maybe forever. They're going to do it no matter what we say. You need to get on board, Kate. Don't lose your son over this. It's not worth it. They'll have the baby anyway." They were wise words, and Kate knew she was right, and she remembered how worried her parents had been when she dropped out of school to get married and got pregnant immediately, and with Tom in law school, they had depended on her salary, which was far less than Justin and Richard made. But she didn't like the surrogacy idea at all. It sounded fraught with risk to her. Yet she also knew that Justin wasn't going to change his mind and suddenly give up the notion of their having a child. Grandma Lou was right, and there was no choice but to get on the bandwagon, or Justin would never forget it or forgive her. She had asked him if Richard's parents knew, and they didn't. The boys hadn't told them since his parents weren't even willing to acknowledge that their son was gay.

"You're the only grandparent this child is going to have," her mother reminded her. "So you'd better get used to it, for your son's sake," she told Kate sternly. "And I

honestly think they'll handle it well. I think it's very exciting, and brave. Having a baby is always a courageous
thing to do. You never know how it's going to work out.
But you managed four on your own, I'm sure they can
handle one with the two of them. They're sensible,
responsible young men. Have faith in Justin's judgment.
He's a smart boy, Kate. And he'll be a good father. And
however you feel about it, this is what he's going to do.
You can't let him down."

There were tears in Kate's eyes as she nodded. Her
mother was right, but she was worried about it anyway.
It seemed too difficult to her. Grandma Lou left a little
while later, and Kate was left to ponder everything that
had happened that night. Izzie was in love, and Justin was
having a baby.

In the cab going home, Izzie was grateful that Justin's
news had gotten them off the subject of Zach and the fact
that he didn't work. And God help her if they ever found
out how they'd really met. She almost shuddered at the
thought.

And once back at their friends' apartment, Justin
talked to Richard about his mother's reaction to their
news.

"Does she think we're idiots, or children?" he said
angrily about his mother. "She acts like we're the first gay
men to ever do this. She's usually so cool." But she hadn't
been that night. Richard was far more willing to forgive

her than Justin, who felt cut to the quick by what she'd said and her negative response.

"She's worried for you, that's all," Richard said soothingly. "To our parents, we're always kids. And in this case, kids having kids. And surrogacy shocks a lot of people. It's not 'normal,' and Izzie's right, there have been problems with it in some states, particularly when it was first legal. Give her time. She'll adjust."

"She worries about us all too much," Justin complained to his partner.

"She's a mother, that's what she's supposed to do," Richard said and Justin laughed ruefully.

"Then let's agree now not to be like that with our kids," Justin said and then remembered what Izzie had said. "And by the way, what do you think about Izzie's trust-fund-baby boyfriend?"

"It better be a big trust fund or he'll be a heavy weight on your sister. As ambitious and hardworking as she is, I'm surprised she wants to be with a man who doesn't work."

"He must be great in bed," Justin said, laughing, but it had bothered him when she said Zach didn't work, and he thought she looked embarrassed by it too. It had been a night of big news and startling announcements. He and Richard were especially touched by his grandmother's reaction to their baby, and they had a lot to look forward to in the next few weeks. They were both excited and stressed about it. Their friend's eggs were going to be harvested in a few days, and mixed with their sperm. They both wanted to be sperm donors for their baby. The sperm and eggs would be fertilized in the laboratory, and then the two most viable ones put into the surrogate's womb, and hopefully one would take. They could both hardly wait. It was an incredible process and the culmination of a dream for them. They fell asleep talking about it that night, as they had for weeks. And all they could do now was pray that they would be fathers soon. It would prove to both of them that if cherished long enough, dreams do come true.

Chapter 5

Before Justin and Richard drove home to Vermont on Sunday, they stopped in to see Kate again for breakfast. She seemed to have calmed down and didn't mention their baby plans again. She had had a long discussion about it on the phone with Izzie on Saturday, and she shared her daughter's concerns, but she thought it best to be diplomatic with Justin and Richard, and they avoided the subject too. This was a wrinkle Kate hadn't expected. They had no interest in getting married, although it was now legal, and it had never occurred to her that they would want to embark on fatherhood in lieu of marriage. It didn't sit well with her values, whether they were gay or straight. In Kate's mind, you got married and then had babies, and not the reverse, and did not have babies instead of marriage. Their relationship seemed solid, but who knew what the future would bring? A baby just seemed premature to her. Justin was still establishing his career, living on a shoestring, depending on writing articles for magazines, and he was working on his first novel. At thirty, financial stability was still several years away, and

Richard's salary as a schoolteacher was barely enough to support them, let alone a child. And with the surrogacy, she could see trouble on the horizon. Why couldn't they?

It was all she could do not to mention it again when they came to see her to say goodbye. But, following her mother's advice from Thanksgiving, she kept things light. And she doubted that she could dissuade them anyway. They said they'd had a nice weekend with their friends, and had had a dinner party at their home the night before. The two boys had always had a nice social life, and were an established couple. They preferred to hang out with other gay men like them, who had solid relationships and serious domestic lives. Justin had never liked the promiscuous side of the gay scene in New York. His home life was important to him, just as theirs had been when they were growing up. Family was all important to them. In light of that, their wanting a child was no surprise. But it seemed like an added burden on the relationship to Kate—a financial one they couldn't afford—and the legal aspects of surrogacy seemed terrifying to her.

She had breakfast with them, and then they left for the six-hour drive back to Vermont.

"Well, that was nice. Your mom seems like she's calmed down," Richard commented as they got in their battered Volvo station wagon. He seemed relieved. He had always gotten on well with Kate, more so than with his own parents, who were narrow-minded and critical of them. Kate was much more open in her thinking and accepting of her son, and had always been warm and affectionate with Richard and respectful of them as a couple. He liked her, and she called him her son-in-love.

"Don't believe everything you see," Justin said tersely as he got behind the wheel and started the car. He knew his mother better. "My mother doesn't want a battle with us, and my grandmother probably told her to cool it and calm down. But you saw how upset she was on Thanksgiving. That doesn't just disappear with her when she wakes up the next morning. We haven't heard the last of this yet. And Izzie is going to get her even more wound up about the legal pitfalls. We know what they are. I think we've made a good choice with Shirley, but we'll never convince my mother of that. She always sees everything that can go wrong. I think my father dying so young, and leaving her with four kids to support and very little money, taught her that life can go to shit in a minute. She doesn't like anything high-risk for any of us. And I guess having children is risky, they can get sick, something can go wrong, and, who knows, maybe Shirley will go nuts and try to keep the baby. But you can't live in the basement with a blanket over your head either, waiting for the roof to fall in. We have to lead our lives. I'm just sorry she isn't happy for us. I hoped she would be, but I was wrong." He looked unhappy as they drove through SoHo and headed out of New York.

"Don't be too hard on her," Richard said quietly. "She's always been great about us. My parents would go crazy at the idea of our having kids and using a surrogate. It's a lot for parents to absorb."

"I don't think my mother would like the idea of a surrogate even if we were straight. I don't think this is about our being gay," Justin said fairly. "It's about her thinking we're too young and we don't have enough money to support a child, which is something she knows about, and we're relying on a total stranger to hand over our baby when it's born."

"At least she's accepting of us," Richard reminded him.

"When are you going to tell your parents?" Justin asked, glancing at him.

"How does never sound to you? Or maybe when our son or daughter goes to college, or gets married. We can invite them to the wedding. Our kid's, not ours." Justin laughed at the idea. They both knew how hostile Richard's parents were about his being gay. They had wanted him to go to a psychiatrist for "treatment" to cure him of his "deviant behavior." It was unbearable to them that their son was gay. And they acted like Justin didn't exist. A baby would put them over the edge. Richard's siblings, a brother and sister, were no better. Both were married and had children, and he hadn't heard from either of them for several years, and it had been made clear to him that he wasn't welcome to come home for holidays, "until he cleaned up his life," i.e., was no longer gay. They were convinced it was a bad decision he had made, and they had had their pastor talk to him about it too. Kate found it hard to believe that there were still parents in the world who behaved that way, and she had always been extra loving to her son's partner because of it. But a baby via a surrogate seemed to be too much even for her.

They got back to their home in Vermont at six o'clock, after stopping for gas and a sandwich along the way. They had agreed to a meeting with Shirley, their surrogate, that night, before Richard's friend Alana's eggs were harvested the next day. Both Justin and Richard planned to be there for that, but they wanted one last meeting with Shirley before she signed their agreement at the attorney's office the next morning.

They unpacked their bags from New York, Richard made them some soup and a salad, and they were just putting the dishes in the dishwasher when Shirley and her husband arrived. They had left their two kids with her mother. Her parents were aware of the project. Shirley had done it before, and she had told them that offering herself as a surrogate served a dual purpose, it made someone else truly happy, and it gave them money they needed for their own kids. Her husband had no problem with it. He was a carpenter, and she worked at a local supermarket and would keep her job unless she had a problem with the pregnancy. But she was young and healthy, and there was no reason why she would. Her three previous pregnancies had gone smoothly, and she had delivered all three babies naturally in record time.

As he had been each time they met him, Shirley's husband, Jack, was taciturn when he walked in. But he had never objected to what she was doing, and he liked the two men. The two fertilized ova were going to be implanted in her uterus later that week at her most receptive time. Her own ovulation cycle had had to be halted chemically as they wouldn't be fertilizing her eggs, so she was making no genetic contribution to the pregnancy. She was merely an incubator for the fetus for nine months, and biologically not its mother. Everything was clear.

"Would you like coffee or tea?" Richard offered when they sat down. "Or a last glass of wine?" He smiled at Shirley. From the time Alana's eggs were inside her, she had agreed not to drink any form of alcohol, use drugs except those prescribed medically, or smoke cigarettes or marijuana. She had no problem consenting to that. They looked like healthy, responsible people. Shirley wasn't attractive, but she seemed wholesome and intelligent. She and Jack had come up with the idea of surrogacy three years before, after the birth of their second child, when they realized they couldn't make ends meet. She had had such easy pregnancies that they agreed, as long as she didn't have sex with the baby's father, which the doctors had assured them was not necessary. She could have had in utero fertilization, but after considerable research, Justin and Richard had opted for in vitro fertilization, where the eggs would be fertilized outside of her womb and then implanted in her uterus. It was more complicated and more expensive but a surer process, so they chose IVF.

Shirley was looking forward to being pregnant again, and said she felt great when she was. And nine months didn't seem long to her, though it felt like an eternity to Justin and Richard to wait to have their baby in their arms.

They both accepted coffee and chatted for a while. She had agreed to meet with both men every two weeks and give them full reports on her medical visits and sonograms, and details on the baby's progress. And they had chosen the obstetrician they wanted her to see, supposedly the best one in town. Shirley's fee was to be paid half at the outset and half after the delivery, with a check for her expenses sent to her once a month. She would be getting the first check the next day when she signed the agreement. No money changed hands that night. It was just a friendly meeting to confirm that everything was a go on both sides, and that no one was having second thoughts or regrets. They left after an hour, and Justin and Richard had a glass of wine when they did.

"It's hard to believe it's all starting tomorrow, finally, isn't it?" Justin said, as they sat in their small, cozy living room by the fire. They had one bedroom and a small study Justin used to write. They were going to give up the study to the baby, and Justin said he'd write in the kitchen after that. It was the best they could do, since they couldn't afford to move to a bigger house. They were willing to make all the sacrifices they had to for their child.

They went to bed after that, and were both too nervous and excited to be amorous. Justin was up at six, and Richard shortly after. They were meeting Alana at the hospital at eight, and she arrived right on time. Alana and Richard had known each other since his childhood, and they had remained good friends once they grew up. She was a nurse herself, so she was familiar with the process, and she liked Justin too. She was a bright, vivacious, pretty woman, and both men were grateful for what she was doing for them. She had a boyfriend and he knew about the plan. She had volunteered her eggs when she heard what they wanted to do, and she was relinquishing all rights to the baby. She was thirty-six, like Richard, but all her hormone tests had shown her to be still fertile and her eggs healthy, and Richard loved her like a sister. They were both happy to have her be the biological mother of their child, or twins, if both eggs survived.

She didn't want them in the room with her when her eggs were harvested, and it was supposedly a painful process. But she came through it bravely. The doctor came out to talk to them an hour later, and told them that everything was fine, as Justin and Richard waited nervously in an area for family and visitors. They had both provided the necessary sperm when they arrived. Everything had gone according to plan. And the threesome left the hospital two hours after they'd arrived. Alana was slightly woozy from the pain pills they'd given her after the harvesting, and they took her home and promised to check on her later. And then Justin dropped Richard off at the school where he worked, and went home to his computer to write. All he could do was stare at it for a while and think about what was happening. Somewhere in a laboratory, his and Richard's sperm were meeting Alana's eggs, and nine months from now their baby would be born. It made Justin cry as he thought about it, from the sheer enormity of the moment. He had never wanted anything so much in his life.

*

When Zach came back from Palm Beach the Monday after Thanksgiving, he couldn't wait to see Izzie. She rushed home from the office at six o'clock, and they were in bed five minutes later. They were still breathless afterward, when he looked at her and smiled.

"I missed you so damn much. My poor grandmother sleeps all the time now, but it was nice for her to have me there. No one else ever goes to visit her anymore." She was eighty-nine, frail, and in failing health. And Izzie thought it was nice that he'd gone, although she had missed him too. "So how was your family when you told them about me?" he asked with interest. She had told him that she had admitted to them that she was seeing someone, but her brother hiring a surrogate to have a baby had pre-empted all other subjects immediately after.

"They were fine," she said quietly. "Curious. Intrigued." She didn't want to tell him too bluntly that they wouldn't have understood why he didn't work, even if he'd had money. And they would have understood it even less since he didn't. She was having a problem with it herself. "Mostly, they were upset about my brother Justin wanting to have a baby with a surrogate. I think it's pretty crazy too, given all the legal risks."

"He's the gay one?" he asked casually, and she nodded. "So when am I going to meet them?" She had been think-ing about taking him to dinner with them on Christmas Eve or Christmas Day, since they celebrated both, but she still wasn't sure. He could see her hesitate and looked hurt. "Are you ashamed of me, Izzie?"

"Of course not." She was instantly embarrassed. "But they're very square and normal, and you're pretty racy for them," especially if they knew the truth, that he had been recently convicted for dealing drugs, and that was how she'd met him. "I don't want them to interrogate you or give you a hard time."

"I'm a big boy, I can take it," he said calmly. "And they

can't be too square or normal if you have a gay brother who's having a baby with a surrogate. That's a little 'racy' too."

"Not really. It's just legally stupid. At least I think so. My mother's not happy about it because they won't get married. Maybe she's worried about their relationship being solid, and the financial burden it will put on them. But no one wanted to listen to either of us. And my sister and grandmother thought it was great. They'll do what they want anyway."

"They have to make their own mistakes," Zach said philosophically.

"My mother doesn't see it that way. She worries about all of us. And in this case, I agree. I don't see why they need to have a baby, and surrogacy can be a mess. But my brother seems very determined. We're all pretty stubborn." She smiled at Zach. "I was thinking about taking you home for Christmas, if you really want to. If not, it can wait." But their holiday get-togethers were the only time that everyone was there. And her relationship had gotten so serious so quickly with Zach that she felt as though she should introduce him to her family before much longer.

"I'd like that," he said, looking pleased, and he kissed her. "Thank you."

"You'll have to play it pretty straight," she warned him. "I don't think the sexy biker look will go over well with them on Christmas."

"I think I can manage a coat and tie for your family," he said. He had done it for their second court appearance, although she hadn't seen that look since. But at least she knew he was capable of it, and it would matter to them. What was going to matter to them even more was the fact that he was unemployed. It would please her family if he got a job, would make them like him better, and it would certainly help her with expenses. But she had no idea if she could talk him into it, or convince him that it would be good for him too. She had a month to try, but when she got up for work the next morning, and he lay happily sprawled across her bed like a sleeping giant, with no sign of waking and nothing to get up for, she realized again how different his life was. And as she left a hundred dollars in the kitchen drawer for him, she wondered how long this could last, unless he decided to get serious and grow up. There was no sign of it yet. And she knew she was enabling him by giving him money, but she didn't know what else to do.

*

On Friday afternoon, as Justin was struggling with an article about chemical risks to the environment, which bored him, but he needed the money, the fertility doctor called him. Justin's heart skipped a beat when he answered, and he wondered if there was a problem.

Maybe all Alana's eggs had died, or their sperm hadn't fertilized them.

"Is something wrong?" Justin asked, holding his breath for an instant.

"Not at all," the doctor said warmly to reassure him. "I just wanted to let you know that we put two fertilized eggs in Shirley's uterus today. We had five good ones, but we had agreed on two." Justin and Richard had said that they wanted a single child, and could handle twins if they had to. They couldn't imagine triplets, and didn't want to risk it. So the doctor had used two of the fertilized eggs, but no more. And if it didn't work this time, Alana was willing to do it again, as was Shirley. "Everything went smoothly. She's fine. We told her to stay in bed today, but she can be up tomorrow. And we'll check her hormone levels in about ten days to see where things stand. It's looking good." Justin could hardly contain himself until Richard got home, and gave him the news as soon as he walked through the door. They were jubilant at the prospect, and had dinner with Alana that night. She was fine after having her eggs harvested four days before, and proud that two fertilized eggs had been implanted.

"I almost hope you have twins," she said to them over wine at dinner, and they groaned, although Justin wouldn't have minded having twins if they could afford it. He loved having a twin sister, and they had had a ball growing up. He was closer to her than to anyone else on the planet except Richard. She had called him several times that week to see what was happening and if they'd done it yet. He hadn't heard a word from his mother, which Justin knew meant she was still upset but not saying anything.

The next call they got from the doctor was the following week, to tell them that Shirley's hCG levels were high in her blood test, which meant that at least one of the fertilized eggs had taken. Technically, she was pregnant, but they needed to keep checking now to see if her hormone levels continued to rise, or dropped if she lost it. If they rose higher than normal, it would mean that both embryos had implanted. All they could do was check her hormone levels now. And in a few weeks they could do a sonogram to make sure that one or both of the embryos were still there. But for the moment at least, Shirley was pregnant.

Justin let out a scream when he hung up the phone, and Richard came running to see what had happened.

"She's pregnant! It worked! They have to keep checking to make sure it holds, and they don't know how many there are yet. But she's pregnant!" The two men danced around the room like children, and Richard opened a bottle of champagne he'd been saving, although it was still early days, and a little premature to be celebrating, but at least the first phase of the process had worked. They called Shirley after that, giddy from the excitement more than the champagne, and she sounded fine. She said it had all been easy so far and she felt good. She had just come home from work at the supermarket, and they could hear her kids in the background. They hoped that would be them one day.

Five days later, Shirley's hormone levels were still high, though not excessively so, and the doctor guessed that she was carrying one implanted embryo, not two, but she was definitely pregnant. There was nothing more to do now except continued blood tests and a sonogram in two weeks. The boys were beside themselves at the news. Shirley sounded almost nonchalant about it, she had expected it to go well. Her pregnancies always had. She didn't feel pregnant yet, but she was in good health, and it would take a few weeks for her body to catch up with the elevated hormone levels, and give her the early signs of pregnancy. She had a doctor's appointment in three weeks, and agreed to let them come to the sonogram with her. She smiled when she heard how excited they were. It reassured her that she had done the right thing.

For the next few weeks it was all Justin and Richard could talk about, although they hadn't told anyone yet. They wanted to wait until the first sonogram before they did, just to be sure that everything was fine. But so far so good. They had a baby on the way. Its due date was August 25, which still seemed like a lifetime away. Justin wanted desperately to call his mother and tell her, but given how upset she had been on Thanksgiving, he didn't dare. It made him sad not to be able to share it with her. He didn't even call Julie. They had decided to wait, until Christmas at least. He felt like a kid waiting for Santa Claus, as he counted the days till Christmas to tell his family. The details about the baby's sex would come later. For now, all they knew was that their surrogate was pregnant, and no matter how artificially it had been conceived or who gave birth to it, it was their baby, and it seemed like a miracle to them.

Chapter 6

Justin and Richard went to the sonogram with Shirley on December 23, which was the earliest possible date the obstetrician would give them, and they saw the fetus clearly on the screen, in the right place, the right size. There was only one fetus. The other egg had fallen away and disappeared, so it would be a single birth. The technician measured the size and gave them the computerized due date. And both men burst into tears when they saw it on the screen, and the technician handed them a printout of the baby's image on the sonogram. It was too soon to see the heartbeat, but the fetus looked fine, and Shirley said she was feeling pregnant by then. The two men left the room for the internal exam, and the doctor said everything was great when they came back in. Their baby was due on August twenty-fifth. Richard was going to request paternity leave for the first month of school, and Justin could hardly imagine getting through the next eight months. They had so much to look forward to.

They drove to New York that afternoon, to stay with the same friends they always did, and Justin dropped by to see his mother at the store the next day, but she was out doing last-minute shopping. He had wanted to tell her the news alone, but since she was out, it would have to wait until their family dinner that night. They had dinner together on Christmas Eve, and those who wanted to went to mass. Justin and Richard were planning to go this year, to give thanks for the miracle happening to them. And they always got together informally for lunch the next day, on Christmas Day.

Izzie had invited Zach to lunch on Christmas Day, because Christmas Eve was more intimate and even more of a family event, and she thought his introduction to the family might go better the next day, although she wasn't sure.

Justin could hardly wait for dinner that night, and he and Richard arrived looking handsome and well dressed in suits, right after both his sisters showed up in black cocktail dresses. Julie's was one of her own designs. And their mother was wearing a black velvet hostess gown with golden sable on the cuffs that was vintage Givenchy, and made her look like a queen with her long blond hair in a simple French twist. She was very stylish as always, and the dress looked brand-new. Grandma Lou was wearing a red velvet pantsuit that she wore for Christmas every year. Willie was the last one to arrive, in a black suit and black shirt with a black tie his mother had given him. He looked very handsome and young and trendy. Everyone was in good spirits as they kissed each other, and dinner smelled delicious. It was turkey with a new recipe for stuffing Kate had found in a magazine. It was the same dinner as Thanksgiving, with yule logs for dessert, and Christmas pudding, just like when they'd been children.

Kate served them all champagne and smiled as she admired her handsome family. They were a good-looking group. They all loved Christmas, and there was a tall Christmas tree in the corner of the room, covered with lights and ornaments, with all their presents under it. The apartment was decorated with lights her assistants had helped her put up, and the table looked festive. It looked like a magazine spread, and reminded them all of how wonderful their Christmases had been while they were growing up. And Grandma Lou was excited about her trip to Buenos Aires. She was leaving in two days, on the day after Christmas. Her friend Frances was going with her, and Grandma Lou had talked her into taking tango lessons, which didn't surprise anyone.

They made it through the first course of dinner with lively conversation, and by then Justin couldn't stand it any longer. He had to share their news. He rapped his wineglass with a fork as soon as Willie had carved and carried the turkey in for their mother, and the rest of the meal was on the table waiting to be served. Justin was beaming as he looked at his partner and then his family.

"Richard and I have something to tell you," he said in a

choked voice as they watched him raptly. "Our surrogate is pregnant. Our baby is due on August twenty-fifth," he said with tears in his eyes that he couldn't hold back, and his twin put her arms around him and was crying too.

"I'm so happy for you! Congratulations." And then Julie got up to hug Richard, and the whole family burst into animated conversation. Willie laughed and told them he still thought they were nuts to want a kid, but he was good-natured about it and loved teasing them. Grandma Lou was beaming. And Izzie and Kate were more subdued. The best Izzie could do was say that she hoped everything turned out all right and there weren't any problems. And Kate hesitated for a long moment and then went and put her arms around her son, with all the love she felt for him in her embrace, and all her worry for him in her eyes. Justin saw it too.

"I just want you to be happy, and for life to be easy for you. Having children is a huge step, but if you both feel ready for it, then you have my blessing." It was too late to say anything else with the surrogate already pregnant. Kate still thought it was a foolhardy, risky thing to do, and a burden they didn't need, but it wasn't her decision to make, and all she could do was be supportive and worry about them now. The baby didn't seem real to her yet.

There were tears rolling down Justin's cheeks when he hugged his mother as she gave him her blessing, and his younger brother teased him about it immediately.

"You're such a girl!" Willie loved razzing him about being gay, but he didn't mean it, and Justin laughed as he wiped the tears away.

"I'm man enough to kick your ass," Justin warned him and gave him a brotherly shove.

"No, you're not. You're pregnant. Sit down and don't hurt yourself," Willie said and they all laughed. "I hope the baby's a boy, we need more men in this family." He rolled his eyes as he said it, and the food was passed around with lots of friendly chatter, while Grandma Lou talked about her trip to Argentina.

"I hope I'll still be able to take my great-grandchild on his or her first adventure trip when they turn twenty-one. Let's see, I'll be ninety-nine then, that should work." They all laughed and Justin assured her that he was counting on it.

They were all in good spirits, and only Kate seemed quiet. It always made her nostalgic to share holidays with them. They were so grown up now, and it made her think of Tom and how proud he would have been of them. She couldn't help wondering what he would have said about his grandchild, but after twenty-four years, he was a gentle memory now. The responsibility for the family had rested on her for a long time.

They played charades as they always did after dinner, and Julie had brought a new game for them that had everyone laughing hysterically, and midnight came quickly, for those who wanted to go to midnight mass. Kate always went. Grandma Lou never did and wasn't religious. Justin and Richard wanted to go and the two girls joined as well. Willie was meeting friends at a nearby club where someone he knew was giving a party.

"What about your guy?" Justin asked Izzie. He'd been mildly surprised that he wasn't there, but grateful too since he could make his announcement about the baby without strangers present. It was a very emotional moment for him.

"He's coming to lunch tomorrow," Izzie said, sounding slightly tense about it. She was defensive about Zach, and wasn't looking forward to hearing everyone's opinions, but she didn't want to wait much longer to introduce him.

"I can't wait to meet him," Justin said sincerely, and Izzie turned and snapped at him.

"Are you being sarcastic?"

"Of course not. Why would you say that?" She didn't answer, but he sensed that she was annoyed that he hadn't heeded her advice about the surrogate. Izzie liked playing the role of older sister, and on legal issues thought everyone should listen to her, but her brother and Richard had their own ideas.

They walked to the church they always went to on Christmas Eve, and then disbanded to their own homes after the service. Justin and Richard dropped Kate off in a cab. And Julie and Izzie shared one to go to their respective homes, and talked about Justin's baby.

"I think they're crazy," Izzie reiterated to her sister. "Can you imagine what a mess that's going to be if she refuses to give the baby up?" Izzie said angrily. "They're fools to trust her," she said glumly. It was her mantra now.

"Maybe it'll be fine," Julie said gently. She always thought her twin could do no wrong, and she loved Richard too. She wanted everything to go smoothly for them.

They were all back at Kate's apartment at noon the next day, for turkey leftovers, stuffing, cranberry sauce, smoked salmon, quiche, prosciutto, cheese, and sliced roast beef. It was a casual feast served as a buffet, and they sat at the dining table. They arrived dressed nicely, but less formally than on Christmas Eve. Izzie had told Zach that he didn't have to wear a suit since he was coming Christmas Day, but she was slightly unnerved when he emerged from their bedroom after he dressed, wearing a black cashmere sweater, leather pants, and his biker boots, with the leather jacket he always wore. She seemed uncomfortable but didn't want to say so. The suit might have been better after all.

"Am I okay? You look worried." He had seen her expression immediately. "You said casual, so I took you at your word." And he had shaved. But his hair was even longer than it had been a few months before and he was wearing it in a ponytail, like her mother's. He looked handsome and sexy as he always did, but not quite the way she knew her family would look on Christmas Day.

"They're not as jazzy as you are," she said discreetly. But he had a right to be his own person, and she didn't want to cramp his style.

"Too much leather?" he asked as he kissed her.

"I love you, you're fine," she answered and kissed him back. With the long hair and the tattoos, the leather wouldn't make much difference and she didn't want to be critical of him. It was Christmas, after all, and she wanted to share the blessing of her family with him, since he practically had none of his own. He had called his father in Aspen and hadn't reached him, and said his mother was probably skiing in St. Moritz or Gstaad, but he never heard from her and didn't know how to find her. So at least, Izzie thought, she could share her own family with him.

Justin and Richard saw Zach first as he walked through the door. Justin's eyebrows shot up, and Richard smiled, thinking that Zach was the best-looking man he'd seen in years, and was in fantastic shape. His muscles rippled under the tight cashmere sweater, and his legs looked powerful in the tight leather pants.

"Calm down," Justin whispered to him, and Richard laughed.

"Too bad he's not one of us," Richard whispered back, and Justin laughed as Zach and Izzie walked into the living room. She was wearing slacks and a sweater, a red coat, and high heels, and looked very pretty. And Julie's eyes grew wide as Izzie introduced her to Zach. She couldn't imagine Izzie going out with someone like him in a million years. All her boyfriends had been doctors or lawyers or corporate executives. Zach seemed like a rock star in their midst. Izzie introduced him to her brothers and Richard, and Grandma Lou, who seemed fascinated by him. Kate was in the kitchen getting another platter of food and nearly dropped it when she walked into the room and saw him. She had the same reaction as Julie. She couldn't even remotely imagine her oldest daughter with him, although he was polite when he greeted her, and obviously well brought up. He just seemed totally different from the rest of them.

"I think he's cool," Willie whispered as they went to sit down at the table.

"More like hot," Richard added, and Justin shoved him playfully.

Zach sat between Izzie and Grandma Lou, who engaged him in a lively conversation, and after a while Zach seemed at ease and talked to all of them. He definitely looked like the odd man out, but it didn't appear to bother him. He was comfortable in his own skin. They had all been told about his not working on Thanksgiving, so no one asked him about his job. Richard asked him where he'd gone to school, and Zach listed all the boarding schools he'd been thrown out of, laughing, and added that he hadn't gone to college.

He was lively and funny and loved talking to Grandma Lou and it was obvious that he was crazy about Izzie, and she was equally so about him. But all of them were slightly shocked that they were together. They were a most unlikely pair. He was deep in conversation with Justin and Richard, when Grandma Lou commented to Izzie.

"He's a bright young man," she said admiringly, "and he's obviously well brought up, but how does he fit into your life?" she asked quietly. "You have important demands on you as an attorney in a very traditional firm. How does that work?"

"Everybody likes him," Izzie said with a look of determination.

"I can understand why. But with no career of his own, will he be a problem in yours?"

"I have a right to date who I want to," she said stubbornly.

"Of course you do," her grandmother agreed. "But some people are harder to blend into one's life than others. There's a bit of the wild boy about him." The leather pants and jacket, tattoos and biker boots were not lost on her. "That's fun when you're alone, but it could prove difficult over time. Where's his family?" she asked with interest.

"His mother is in Europe, and his father is all over the

place. He doesn't see them. He has a sister in Mexico, and a grandmother in Palm Beach."

"He's a bit of a rolling stone," Grandma Lou commented dryly.

"He's never had a family he could rely on. I thought he might enjoy being with us today. He hasn't had a family Christmas since he was a kid," Izzie said compassionately, and her grandmother nodded.

"That could be hard for him to adjust to now. You may think that would be a blessing in his life. He might not agree, particularly if he's used to doing whatever he wants. There's a price to pay for being in a family like ours. To some extent, you have to play by the rules. He doesn't look like he's had many in his life." She was surprisingly accurate in her assessment of him, but Izzie remained convinced that what he needed now was stability and a loving family. And a job, of course.

"He's wonderful, and very loving to me," Izzie assured her. "That's enough."

"Not always." Her grandmother gazed at her pointedly. "It should be, but it isn't always. It's difficult when you come together from very different places in life. Your world might be hard for him to understand." Izzie knew her grandmother wasn't wrong, but she hoped that Zach would adjust to a more traditional life. It was a bit like hoping a wild horse would become a show horse. It was a nice dream, but the reality could be difficult to achieve.

And Izzie hadn't tried to break him in yet. A job for him was her first goal.

Zach came to sit with them then, and talked about Grandma Lou's tango lessons with her. He had spent time in Argentina himself, playing polo when he was younger. He admitted to being a proficient rider, and said his father played polo too.

Izzie and Zach were the first to leave, and you could almost feel everyone exhale when they left.

"Wow!" Justin said, a few minutes after they walked out. "I can't even imagine Izzie going out with someone like him. He looks like a hot number, and he's fun to talk to, but that bad-boy look is so not Izzie. What happened to her?"

"She got dumped by her fiancé, and he married a society debutante," his grandmother responded without hesitation. "Her ego took a hard hit as well as her heart. And Zach may be the first man to go after her seriously since then. She's been miserable for two years until now," she reminded him.

"Do you suppose he has tons of money?" Willie asked, curious about him.

"Possibly. It's hard to say. From families like his, he could be set for life, or have to live off Izzie if he's cut off for some reason. He would have that spoiled rich-boy style even if he were dead broke. Lovely manners, though." She didn't say it, but it was obvious that Grandma Lou was not

104

impressed with Zach as a choice for her granddaughter, and Kate was thinking the same thing but didn't want to criticize him to the others, in case Izzie heard about it from them later. They all talked to each other frequently, and expected it. There was no malice to what they said, but abundant interest in each other.

"He's certainly good-looking and very personable," Justin added, "and easy to talk to. But I can't see Izzie with him. He's a total departure from the kind of men she goes out with."

"Maybe that's the whole point," Grandma Lou said thoughtfully. "It didn't work with her Harvard Law School boyfriend, so she's gone the other direction. He said he never went to college, but he's very bright. Unfortunately, I think your sister thinks she's going to tame him. That may not be what he has in mind."

"What difference does it make?" Julie said blithely. "She's not marrying him. Why can't she have fun with someone different?"

"Don't be so sure about her not marrying him," Kate chimed in finally. "People do crazy things sometimes. They date someone they shouldn't, then they fall in love and want to get married, and think they're going to change. And most of the time they don't."

"Izzie always says she's not the marrying kind," Justin reminded them reasonably.

"That's only since Andrew dumped her," Kate said bluntly. "She never used to say that."

"I don't know why you're all getting so worked up. He's a nice guy. And he's just a date. Izzie's not stupid," Willie said casually and then stood up, ready to leave too. He kissed his mother and siblings, and hugged his grandmother and wished her a wonderful time in Argentina. "You can teach me the tango when you come back." He grinned at her and she laughed.

"I would love that."

One by one they left. It had been a lovely Christmas, and a momentous one after Justin and Richard's announcement about the baby. Kate was exhausted when she sat down next to her mother on the couch, after her children were gone.

"So what do you think about Izzie's new beau, Mother? Should we be concerned about it?"

"That won't change anything," Louise said with her usual practical perspective. "I assume it's more serious than she's telling us, or she wouldn't have brought him here today. I think it bears watching. I think she has illusions that she can turn him into someone like us, and that's never going to happen. He's a wild thing, and he loves it. And I think she does too, for now. She'll never tame him. That's not what he wants or who he is."

"It would never work," Kate agreed with her, but she thought her daughter was more sensible than that. "I think she's just having fun with him, and infatuated," Kate said sensibly. She was far more concerned about Justin's big decision. A child was something you couldn't undo, unlike a romance. It was forever.

"Let's hope you're right about Izzie," Kate's mother said and then stood up. "I have to pack. I'm leaving tomorrow."

"Can I do anything to help?" Kate offered and her mother smiled and hugged her.

"Just take care of yourself while I'm gone. I'll miss you."

"I'll miss you too. And you be careful gallivanting all over Buenos Aires." She felt sorry for Frances. She knew how exhausting her mother was to travel with. She was relentless about wanting to see and do everything. She never stopped.

They hugged again in the doorway and Louise thanked her for a wonderful Christmas, as always. Kate had given her some sweater sets, and a lightweight jacket to travel with, since it would be summer in Argentina, and a cashmere shawl for the plane, which would be useful.

"Don't run off with any tall handsome strangers," Kate admonished her with a smile.

"If I find one, I'll bring him home to you," she said to her daughter.

"I wouldn't know what to do with him or have the time, but thank you anyway."

"Keep an eye on Izzie," were her mother's parting words.

"I'll try," Kate promised, but she knew how difficult it was to influence any of them, or keep them safe from dangers of their own making, or ones they were still too naïve to see lurking. Her children never believed her when she warned them of trouble ahead, or saw the signs. Justin and Richard were having a baby now, with no idea what that entailed or all the things that could go wrong. And Izzie was involved with a self-indulgent man who appeared to be totally irresponsible, and she was sure that her daughter would be furious if she said that to her. She decided not to for a while, and to see where it went. Hopefully nowhere, and for once she agreed with her usually casual, unflappable mother, who worried far less than she did. If Izzie tried to turn her romance with Zach into something permanent, there was no question in Kate's mind it would never work. But, fortunately, Izzie didn't seem to have any long-term plans at the moment. In Kate's opinion, that was the best news of all.

Chapter 7

Kate had lunch with Liam two days after Christmas, and told him about Justin's baby and Izzie's new man. She always kept him abreast of what her children were up to and valued his advice. Sensibly, he told her that she had to make her peace with Justin's child, and he advised her not to get too worked up about Izzie. Hopefully it was just an aberration of some kind, and a hot romance, and it would blow over. His own daughters were home from Europe. Penny, his oldest, was madly in love with a boy in Edinburgh, and Elizabeth had three different men she was dating in Madrid. But they were both young enough that he didn't take any of it seriously, and he said that Maureen was a nervous wreck keeping track of the girls. They were in and out of the house every five minutes, and their friends were dropping by at all hours. Hearing about it made Kate realize how much she missed those days when her kids were younger and still at home. She had loved it when their friends came over, and her small apartment was jammed to the rafters with young people.

"Maureen doesn't know how good she has it," she commented nostalgically. "It's so lonely when they're gone."

"She's sad when they leave, and all the coming and going drives her crazy when they're here. Personally, I like it. It's too quiet when they're gone, and very lonely," he said honestly and smiled at Kate.

"Once they're in college, it's over. As soon as they graduate they're gone. It all happens so quickly." It had for her, and she'd been trying to adjust to it ever since. She was grateful she had the store to keep her busy.

Business had been fantastic during the holidays, and she needed to replenish her stock. She was considering going to Europe in January. Liam loved hearing about it. The success of her business was a source of personal pride to him, since he had advised her and helped her get it off the ground. She was making a very decent living from it.

They lingered over lunch and went for a walk afterward. They compared plans for New Year's Eve. Liam and Maureen were staying home, and their girls wanted to have friends in, to have dinner and dance. Kate said she'd been invited to a party by one of her celebrity clients, but she said she hated going out on New Year's Eve, and was thinking of staying home too.

"Everyone tries too hard that night. I'd rather watch old movies." She had a collection of them that he always said he wanted to watch with her, but never did. They saw each other at lunch, and only rarely in the evening. It always gave Liam a new lease on life and new energy when he saw her, and she gave him good advice about their girls, since she had been there not that long ago when her kids were the age his were now, in college.

She kept the shop open till seven on New Year's Eve, because it was always a busy day for them, when women hadn't found a dress for that night anywhere else, and showed up at Still Fabulous in desperation, and often found something perfect for whatever party they were going to. They made their last sale at six-thirty that night, an exquisite Dior gown in white satin and black velvet that looked as though it had been made for the woman who bought it. And shortly before, they had sold a gold Oscar de la Renta cocktail dress that Kate had been tempted to buy herself when it came in. It was pure glamour, and looked like melted gold on the woman who took it home, with a white fox jacket from Revillon. She was young and looked like a movie star from the fifties. Kate loved selling clothes to women who looked magnificent in them. It was like matchmaking, to find the right clothes for the right woman.

When she locked up the shop and turned the alarm on, she felt like she'd done a good day's work. She walked home as it started to snow, and she was suddenly glad she had declined the dinner party she had been invited to. She was delighted to be staying home. And she already knew which movies she was going to watch. She wanted to see

Rear Window again, and there was an old Cary Grant movie, *To Catch a Thief,* she wanted to watch too. They were perfect for New Year's Eve.

Julie had said she was having a few friends from work over for dinner, mostly her interns who were young designers. Justin had told her that he and Richard were staying home or maybe going to a neighbor's for dinner. And she knew that Izzie and Zach were going to East Hampton. God only knew what Willie was doing, but she was sure he'd be with a pretty girl to see in the New Year. And her mother would probably be dancing the tango in Buenos Aires. Her plans were always the most fun of all. She never spent New Year's Eve in New York and always managed to be someplace fun. She had been in Brazil the year before.

*

Zach and Izzie drove out to East Hampton in the afternoon on New Year's Eve, just before it started snowing. And an hour after they got to his grandmother's house, there was already a light blanket of snow on the ground. It looked beautiful and made the house seem even more inviting. They had decided to cook dinner at home, and Zach found a bottle of Cristal in the wine cellar, which he put on ice for them. Izzie had brought a small tin of caviar to surprise him. He had luxurious tastes, and it was fun to indulge him. Despite his unconventional look, he still had a fondness for the luxuries of his childhood. They had the caviar and champagne before dinner, and Zach made steaks. Izzie set a pretty table for them with his grandmother's linens and china. The housekeeper was away for the weekend, and the caretaker was in his separate cottage, so they were alone in the house. It was a perfect New Year's Eve, which suited them both, and far different from the last two she had spent alone in her apartment, crying in front of the TV as she watched the ball fall in Times Square. It was amazing how life could change. For the past four months, her life with Zach had been like a dream.

They were tucked in bed at midnight, after they had made love. And Zach poured them each a glass of red wine. It was a very old Château Margaux he had brought up when he found the Cristal they'd had before dinner.

"Should we be pillaging your grandmother's wine cellar?" she asked him guiltily, as he handed her the glass and laughed.

"She'll never know the difference. There's a lot more downstairs," he said easily. The house she was letting him use for the winter added a whole other dimension to their life. Izzie had never had a country house before, and they spent every weekend there.

He kissed her after they took a sip of the wine, and gently took the glass from her hand and set it down on the bedside table. She thought he was going to make love to her again. He was tireless, and a very skilled lover. But instead he kissed her and looked into her eyes with a serious expression.

"I have something to ask you," he said gently. "You make me so happy, Izzie. I've never known anyone like you, and I've never felt like this in my life."

"Neither have I," she said honestly. She had a wonderful time with him, whatever they did. At times, she felt like they were living in a bubble, and she hoped it would never burst.

"I love you so much," he whispered. "Will you marry me?" For a moment she thought she had dreamed the words, but when she looked at him, she knew that what he had said was real.

"Are you serious?" she asked, feeling dazed. She had never expected that.

"Yes, I am. I wish I could give you a ring, but I can't right now. All I have to give you is my heart, and the rest of my life with you."

"That's all I need," she said in a husky voice filled with emotion. "I love you too."

"Let's get married soon. I don't want to wait." It was almost as if they were already married. They hadn't been apart in four months, except when she went to work. Every other moment they were together.

"I don't want to wait either," she said, smiling, as she lay back against the pillows, and then he made love to her to make it all seem real to both of them.

She fell asleep in his arms that night, dreaming of the life they would share. When she woke in the morning, he was still sound asleep, holding her in his arms. And it was a winter wonderland outside. He opened an eye as she looked down at him and stroked his hair. She had never seen a man as beautiful in her life, and now she belonged to him. She had never been happier.

"Were you drunk last night?" she asked, grinning at him, feeling as though she was about to float away with joy.

"Why? Did I say something weird?" He looked blank as he asked the question, and then they both laughed.

"Very weird. I think we're engaged, Mr. Holbrook." He rolled over on his back with a self-satisfied expression when she said it.

"As a matter of fact, I think we are. Are you going to call your mother and tell her?" He looked as though he liked the idea.

"I think I'd rather tell her in person when we go back to the city."

"What do you think she'll say?" He looked vaguely concerned, but not very. He had liked her family when he met them, although they were as square as she said, but they had their little individual quirks too.

"I think she'll be happy for me," Izzie said about Kate. "She knows how unhappy I've been." Izzie was suddenly glad that her previous engagement hadn't worked out. If it had, she would never have met Zach and fallen in love with him. Or she might have met him anyway, but he would have been a client and nothing more. And now that she knew him, she realized how ideally suited they were to each other. They were a perfect match, although she would have never expected it, given how different their early lives were. His in the lap of luxury, hers working her way through college and law school, to help her mother. But her childhood had been a lot happier than his. And she wanted to make that up to him now. She wanted to make him ecstatic and feel loved for the rest of his days.

Zach called his grandmother and told her the news, and he reported to Izzie that she was delighted for him. And he called his father and found him in Aspen. They talked for only a few minutes and Zach looked disappointed when he hung up. His father said he was busy, congratulated him briefly, and said he was rushing out to meet friends and would call him soon. It was the usual short shrift he was used to, and he didn't call his mother, since he had no idea where she was.

They spent an idyllic weekend, and threw snowballs at each other when they went for a walk. They played like children, and much of the time, Zach acted like an overgrown boy. Izzie got serious for a minute when they were making dinner, and asked him what he was going to do now.

"About what?" He looked confused.

"Zach, you really need to find a job. It's not good for you not to work." She wanted to make it clear that he needed to contribute to their life too. She was keeping the cash drawer full and paying for everything else. It was a lot. He spent money like water.

"I'm not sure what I can do. Other than play polo and bridge. I play tennis and ski. I was a race car driver for a while, but I don't have a car. I don't have any marketable skills. I could be a tennis teacher, but you don't want me to do that, do you?" he said disapprovingly. "And I'd feel like an idiot going back to school. It's a little late for that at my age."

"You need to figure something out, just so you have something to do." It was the most honest conversation they'd had about it. But it mattered now, if they were getting married. While they were just dating, she'd felt awkward spelling it out to him.

"Is it that important to you?" he asked her and she nodded.

"I think it's important for you too. You'll feel uncomfortable being around people who work, when you have nothing to say about what you do."

"I don't care. I told you, no one in my family has ever worked."

"Everyone in mine does," she said directly. "And I think it would impress your trustees."

"Oh, that." He laughed at her. "How will I keep my role as black sheep if I get a job? They'd be worried about me."

"They might actually let you have some of your money. That would be nice for you."

"I guess it would," he said as though it was a novel idea. "I've kind of stopped thinking about it." But she couldn't keep funding their cash drawer, although it was awkward to say so. "I'll think about it," he said vaguely. And then dinner was ready, and he changed the subject, and they talked about their plans to get married. "Do you want a big wedding?" he asked her, and she shook her head immediately.

"Just my family, and a few friends. I've never wanted a big wedding. Just a husband I love, and who loves me."

"We're all set then." He beamed at her.

"What about you?" Izzie asked gently.

"Not my family. My grandmother is too frail now after her stroke. My mother wouldn't come. She gave up on me years ago. And my sister is too screwed up to go anywhere. Maybe my father would, but I don't know. And I've moved around a lot, and I'm not sure you'd like my friends." She hadn't met any so far. All he wanted was to be with her. He was a man without possessions, encumbrances, or deep ties to anyone. Everything he owned fit into two suitcases, one of which was in East Hampton, and the other in her apartment in New York. The blending of their two lives would be very simple. "I'd like to take you to

Palm Beach to meet my grandmother soon, though. She'll love you, and think I've finally done something right."

"I'd love to meet her," Izzie said sincerely. They spent a quiet night, and talked about when they wanted to get married. Izzie liked the idea of the first of May. Zach was disappointed that it wasn't sooner, but a four-month engagement would give her time to plan a small wedding with her mother. They made a list of who they wanted to invite, and it came to about thirty people, which seemed like enough to both of them. They didn't want more.

When they got to the city, Izzie dropped him off at her apartment, and went to see her mother. She was at the shop, going through one of the storerooms, trying to make order out of chaos after the holidays. She couldn't believe how much they'd sold.

Jessica told Izzie where to find her, and she went upstairs to locate her mother. Kate looked surprised to see her.

"What are you doing here?" She smiled broadly at her oldest daughter.

"We just got back from East Hampton a little while ago. I have something to tell you, Mom." She said it with a serious expression, and Kate emerged from the racks of clothes to take Izzie to her office so they could talk.

"Is something wrong?"

"No." Izzie smiled at her. "On the contrary. Zach and

I are getting married. He proposed to me on New Year's Eve." She looked ecstatic, and Kate felt her heart sink.

"Isn't that a little soon? How long have you two been dating?" She knew it hadn't been long, since sometime in the fall, which Izzie didn't tell them until November. And now she wanted to get married.

"Four months. I know it's short, but we're both old enough to know what we're doing. And I've never loved anyone as much in my life. We want to get married in May, so that would be an eight-month courtship." She was trying to sell it to her mother. Kate was so stunned she didn't know what to say for a moment. And Izzie was right, they were old enough to make their own decisions. But this seemed like a bad one to Kate. They were too different. He was a spoiled rich boy, and he had no education, and no career. In Kate's opinion he was not the kind of man Izzie should marry. The odds weren't great for success.

"How is he going to support you?" Kate asked her quietly. "He doesn't have a job."

"He has to work that out. He said he would."

"Why don't you wait until he does?" Kate said, as her heart slipped further into her shoes. This wasn't the kind of man she wanted for her oldest daughter, or for any of them. Izzie needed a man who was her equal. But the one who seemed to be her equal had betrayed her and broken her heart. And just as Izzie's grandmother had said, Zach was a rebound. But a very dangerous one, in Kate's opinion. And Izzie couldn't make it up to him for his unstable childhood. You couldn't replay history about things like that.

"We don't want to wait. We know we love each other. That's all we need to know, Mom. We'll figure out the rest as we go along."

"That's a hard way to start out." Kate felt like she was fighting for air as she said it. "You need to have some real plans. And he needs to have a job, or you'll lose respect for him."

"My respect for him is based on who he is as a human being, not what he does for work." She had almost forgotten by then how she had met him, and that he'd been dealing drugs. But fortunately her mother didn't know any of that.

"Why don't you wait awhile, and see what he does? Why the rush?"

"Why wait at our age? He's staying with me now. It's like being married."

"No, it's not. It's like dating. There's a whole lot more to marriage than meets the eye. You both need to be on firm footing when you start out. You have a solid career, but he needs a job."

"He's going to get one," Izzie said, looking irritated. "Is that all you care about?" She made it sound trivial, although his lack of a job bothered her too.

"I care about your happiness, Izzie, you know that. But I also want to see you married to a stable person, who is going to help you build a solid life. I don't want all the responsibility on you."

"It won't be. He's a strong man, Mom, and he wants to do his share. He just doesn't know yet how he'll do it."

"Well, he'd better start figuring it out. And why the big rush to marry in May?"

"We want to be married so we can start our life together. We'd get married sooner, but I figured you'd want the time to plan a wedding. We only want a very small one," she reassured her. She didn't expect her mother to create miracles in four months. "We're going to do it whatever you say," Izzie said stubbornly, "so will you give us your blessing?" Izzie's eyes pleaded with her and Kate wanted to say no. The last thing she wanted to give her was her blessing. But Izzie had spelled it out very clearly. She was going to marry him no matter what her mother said. But Kate believed it wouldn't work. Every ounce of her being was silently screaming "No! Don't do it!" But Izzie was giving her no leeway. She had made up her mind. And she didn't want to hear anything her mother had to say. Kate wondered what her own mother would think. They had been in agreement before she left that Zach wasn't the husband for Izzie, only a hot date. And now she wanted to get married.

Kate waited a long moment before she answered. "You

have my blessing, but I really think you should wait, and not rush into marriage. What's your hurry? He won't run away."

"Obviously. But why wait? I'm thirty-two years old, I'm old enough to know what I'm doing and who I want to marry." She wouldn't listen to reason, and other than forbid her, which Kate didn't want to do, and lose her relationship with her daughter, maybe permanently, she didn't know what to say.

"I think you and Zach should discuss it again. Why not be engaged for a year?" She hoped that by then Izzie would be fed up with him, or come to her senses. Kate had the strong suspicion that they were on a sexual high, and Izzie wasn't thinking clearly.

"We don't need to discuss it, and we're not waiting a year," she said firmly. "We're getting married in May. You don't have to give the wedding," she said with tears in her eyes. She was angry at her mother for the position she was taking.

"Of course I want to give the wedding. I just want you to have the best possible chance for it to work."

"It will. He's a wonderful person. He just had a lousy family and some bad breaks. He needs the stability of marriage, and so do I. I want that for both of us." But Kate knew all too clearly that Izzie had picked the wrong man, Zach would never be stable. He didn't have it in him.

They walked out of the office together then, in silence.

The decision had been made. Izzie was getting married. And Kate had no voice in it whatsoever, not one Izzie was willing to hear. "We can talk about the wedding later," she told her mother. "I just wanted you to know our plans." Kate nodded miserably and kissed her daughter before she left the store. And then Kate went back to her office and cried. After Justin's shocking announcement that they were using a surrogate and having a baby, Izzie marrying Zach, and throwing all caution and reason to the winds, was one blow too many.

*

"How did it go?" Zach asked her when Izzie got back to the apartment. Izzie looked nervous and irritated, and he saw it as soon as she walked in.

"All right, I guess. Typical of my mother, all she ever sees is what could go wrong, not what's right. She's always on some kind of witch hunt."

"And I'm the witch?" He looked worried.

"No, I am. But I should have expected it, I guess. She thinks we're rushing into it, getting married in May."

"Would she prefer June?" He was willing to wait another month if it would mollify her mother, but Izzie knew it wouldn't. A month's delay wouldn't satisfy Kate.

"She suggested we wait a year. I'm not going to do that, and she has no right to ask it of us. What difference would that make? We're practically married now. We might as well do it right and make it official." He looked pleased by what she said. "I don't want to wait any longer than we have to." A year sounded too long to him too. He saw no reason to delay, and neither did she. "She gave us her blessing, so it's a done deal. And I'm not going to argue with her about the date. I think she got that message loud and clear." He looked pleased by what she said, and that she was standing up for him. And after she unpacked, she climbed into bed with him, and he held her close. He loved the way she fought for what she wanted. And he loved knowing that she wanted him. He felt like a little boy who had finally found a home, and she was it.

Chapter 8

Kate called Liam the next day, and he came to the store to see her. She had sounded upset, and he wanted to know what was going on. She told him about Izzie, and he was dismayed.

"Can't you refuse to do it? You can tell her you'll only give her a wedding in a year." It sounded simple to him, but he hadn't been there yet with his own daughters, and didn't know how stubborn Izzie could be.

"She doesn't care. They'll get married anyway, and then not speak to me for ten years. I don't want to lose all communication with her. She's going to need me when it falls apart," Kate said pessimistically.

"Is he really that bad?" Liam asked her, and she nodded.

"He's probably not an evil person, and I'm sure he loves her. He's just spoiled and irresponsible. He's never had a job, and she admits he has no money. She'll have to support him until he goes to work, if he does."

"How does he live now?" Liam was as worried as she was, and he didn't understand why Kate didn't just forbid it. He was sure Izzie would wait then.

"There's some kind of trust fund, and I think he gets a pittance from the trustees, when they're willing."

"They must know he can't be relied on with money, if they do that at his age. By thirty-five, they ought to be able to trust him."

"Apparently not," Kate said unhappily. "They must know him better. I just can't see her married to someone like him. He's covered with tattoos. His hair is longer than mine. Everything about him is counterculture. That's not Izzie. And she has no idea how unromantic it is to carry a guy as dead weight, who doesn't contribute his share. And he has nothing to add to her life. He has no education, and no career. For a woman like Izzie, that just doesn't fit."

"What's the attraction?" Liam was puzzled. Izzie was a smart girl. It was unlike her to make such a foolish decision.

"What do I know? Sex probably, at this early stage. He's very good-looking and he's crazy about her. She was very hurt when Andrew broke the engagement, and she's been lonely for two years. And now Mr. Wonderful comes along and sweeps her off her feet, until it all comes down like a house of cards. But she doesn't see that yet. Love really is blind, I guess. But I hate to see her do this to herself. I don't see how it can work. She's trying to make it up to him for a bad childhood. He's a poor little rich boy with indifferent parents. This has all the makings of a bad movie," she said miserably. And a bad marriage.

"Do you think there's any chance it could work?" he asked, trying to be objective. Kate was very emotional about it, so perhaps not the best judge.

"None."

"Then she'll get divorced later, if you can't stop her now," he said, practically fatalistic about it.

"After three kids and ten years of a bad marriage. I hate to see her throw her life away, and you don't get those years back after you waste them. One day you wake up and you're forty-five or fifty, and you wonder where your life went."

"There's nothing you can do to change it," he said as he looked at his friend. "You can tell her what you think, and what you're afraid of happening to her. But no one listens to those warnings. If they did, there would be fewer divorces. And who listens to their parents? I didn't. Did you?"

"No," Kate admitted. "My parents had a fit when I dropped out of college to marry Tom. They wanted me to wait too and I didn't." Liam remembered, and he had thought it was a bad idea too at the time, but she hadn't listened to him either. "But at least we were happy, he wasn't a deadbeat, and he was a great guy. I took the chance—they wanted me to play it safe. No one knew he would die and leave me a widow with four kids at twenty-nine. That wasn't a character defect on his part. It was shit luck."

"True," Liam agreed. "But it doesn't sound like Izzie's going to listen to you, Kate. Maybe you just have to bite the bullet and watch her do it." He couldn't think of any other solution.

"It's like watching her go over a cliff."

"Some people have to do that, and you can't spare them, if that's what they want to do."

"I hate having kids these ages," she said with a pained expression. "They don't realize the consequences of their actions, or how high the stakes are. You can't win against the odds."

"She'll have to figure that out for herself," he said sympathetically. He put an arm around Kate's shoulders as she walked him out of the store, and he hugged her on the sidewalk. "Don't let it drive you crazy, if there's nothing you can do." She nodded, but it was already doing that. It had made her feel better to vent to Liam, but it didn't change anything. Izzie was still willing to take an enormous risk. And Kate was certain she wasn't going to win. Every fiber of her being told her that was the truth.

Kate was sitting in her office, staring into space after Liam left, thinking about what he had said, when Jessica stuck her head in the door and told her a man with a French accent was on the phone and wanted to talk to her. She had no idea who it was and took the call, out of curiosity if nothing else.

The Frenchman on the phone said his name was Bernard Michel, and he wanted to come to see her with a proposition he would like to make to her, and he was in New York for two days. She thought it sounded odd, and she wondered if he wanted to buy the store or her inventory. She wasn't in the mood to see him. She was too upset about Izzie, but he sounded pleasant and intelligent, and serious about whatever he wanted to propose to her, and she decided it might be a distraction from her anxieties about Izzie. Whenever Kate was unhappy, she took refuge in her work. It had served her well. They made an appointment for four o'clock the next day.

When he showed up at the store, he was wearing a dark suit, a white shirt, and a good-looking tie, and she noticed that he was wearing John Lobb shoes by Hermès. He looked prosperous and businesslike, in a heavy cashmere coat, and carrying a black alligator briefcase. He was tall and attractive, impeccably dressed, had salt-and-pepper hair, and looked about sixty years of age. He told her that an associate in New York had told him about her store. He asked some questions about the shop, what she sold, and how she found it, and looked around. She showed him into her office, and they sat down. Her office was very small, since she didn't want to take space away from the store. They needed every inch they could get for the clothes. And she told him they had three apartments in the building that they rented as stockrooms, and they were full as well. She was curious about why he was there.

"What can I do for you, Mr. Michel?" she asked politely. She still had no idea what he wanted. He had given her his business card, but all it told her was the name of the company, which meant nothing to her.

"What kind of business do you do on the Internet?" he asked her.

"Some, but not a lot. I have clients who email me to tell me what they're looking for, but if they're in New York, they generally prefer to come into the store and see the item in person before they buy it."

"Do you have your inventory online?" She shook her head.

"Some of what we sell moves too quickly to put it up."

"And the rest?"

"I don't have time." She was not computer savvy and had never developed her business online. It wasn't a big feature when she started, and she was doing well without it, well enough. They had a website, but only sold at the store.

He explained what he wanted to do for her then. He wanted to set up an Internet component to her business, an online shop.

"That's the business that I'm in," he said quietly. "I help people like you set up their business online. It could increase your sales considerably within a few months."

But she knew it would take a large initial investment to photograph everything, set up a website, and pay for a system and someone to run it. But Bernard Michel told her how it could work. What he said was intriguing, but a little over her head. They talked about it for a while, and she said she'd like to discuss it with her son. It was right up Willie's alley, and she wanted to know what he thought of the idea.

"I'm staying a day longer than I originally planned. Why don't you talk to your son, and we'll meet again tomorrow?" She asked him then why he had singled her out. "A woman friend of mine in Paris told me about your store and raved about it. And my associate here brought it to my attention after that. I wanted to come and see it for myself. I think this could be a very lucrative project for us both, and you could see very rapid results." Kate was fascinated by what he said. And as soon as he left, she called Willie to ask what he thought.

He was quiet for a minute, absorbing what she had said. "Honestly, I think it's brilliant, Mom. And he's right, it could double your business, almost overnight. As soon as you improve your website, photograph what you want to put online, and set up a payment system, you're good to go. I think it's a fantastic idea. Who's the guy?" She told him, and he Googled him immediately, and reported what he found to his mother. "He owns a huge company, from the sound of it, and he seems to have some fairly large holdings in the States as well."

"Do you want to come to a meeting with him tomorrow?"

"I can't, Mom. I wish I could. I have to work. Just find out what he has in mind, and we can talk about it tomorrow night over the phone. You don't have to rush into it."

She had the meeting with Bernard Michel the next day, and told him honestly that her son thought it was a great idea.

"Of course it is." He smiled seductively at her. But he didn't need to do that to convince her. She was already interested in the project. It was enormously appealing. "Let me send you a formal proposal when I get back to Paris. You can show it to your business advisors, and your son." He smiled at her. She walked him through the store again, and then he turned to her before he walked out. "Would you like to have dinner to talk about it some more tonight?"

"I'm not very good with the Internet," she confessed with a smile.

"I'm sure you'd understand. The concept is really very simple. And once you're set up to sell online, your sales will increase exponentially. It's the best way to do business today." She liked talking to him and she wanted to hear more about it, so she agreed to meet him at La Grenouille uptown, which was one of the best restaurants in New York. He said he was staying at the Hotel Pierre nearby.

Kate arrived promptly, wearing a very chic black Chanel suit and high heels, with a black sable coat over it that she had gotten at the store and looked brand-new.

They were led to one of the best tables by a headwaiter who spoke to Bernard in French and seemed to know him. They concentrated on the menu at first. And once they had ordered, Bernard explained his idea to her in greater detail. The more she heard about it, the more she liked it, and he had a simple way of explaining it to her that made sense. Once she was set up to do business online, his company would take a percentage, and would monitor sales and handle the technical details for her. The percentage wasn't huge and sounded reasonable to Kate. She realized selling online could increase the volume of her business and turn it into a giant moneymaker.

Bernard talked about his children then, and said he had a son who was an attorney, and a daughter in medical school. She told him about her children, leaving out her worries about Izzie and Justin. He seemed to be close to his children from the way he spoke about them, and was very proud of them. And in the course of conversation, it came out that she'd been widowed since her children were very young and she had brought them up alone.

"You never remarried?" He seemed surprised.

"I was too busy, with them, and the store," she said,

smiling at him. She told him about the history of Still Fabulous, and how it worked, and he was visibly impressed that she had built it from nothing and made it a success. He said it was ventures like hers that excited him, because turning it into an online store as well would take it so much further than she was able to do now. And everything he said sounded exciting to her. He offered tremendous growth potential with his plan to take Still Fabulous to a whole other level.

They had a very pleasant dinner in elegant surroundings, with wonderful food and a great bottle of wine. And when he put her in a cab to go back downtown, he promised to be in touch with her soon with his proposal, she was anxious to see it. He waved as the cab pulled away and he walked back to his hotel. It was a cold night, but he said he loved walking in New York.

The next day she called Liam and told him about it, and it sounded interesting to him too.

"How did you get to this guy?" Liam asked her with interest.

"He called me at the store." Liam Googled him and was impressed as well. He ran a major business in France, and had set up similar ventures to hers in England and other countries in Europe, and several in the States, all of them currently very successful.

Two weeks later, Bernard Michel sent her the proposal he had promised, and she emailed a copy of it to Liam and another to Willie. She printed hers out, and spent the night poring over it. It sounded brilliant and exciting, was relatively easy to set up, and had potentially impressive results. It was hard to find a reason not to do it, and Liam suggested she meet with him again when he was in New York, and he would come along. She wrote to Bernard, and he responded almost immediately that he would be back at the end of the month and welcomed the prospect of exploring the idea with her further. They made an appointment two weeks later. Kate was very excited about it, and told Justin about it when he called her to see how she was. It sounded appealing to him too. And Willie was as enthusiastic as she was. He thought it was a fantastic opportunity.

"How's the baby doing?" she asked Justin, sounding subdued. She still wasn't thrilled about it. She had to get used to the idea.

"Everything is fine so far. She'll have another sonogram in four weeks, and we'll see a lot more then." They talked about Izzie too. "I wish she wouldn't rush into this marriage," Justin said unhappily. "I just can't see them together long-term. Why doesn't she just have an affair with him and forget about marrying him?" Justin was not a fan of marriage, straight or gay, and he had been shocked when his sister called to announce her engagement.

"I told her the same thing," Kate said unhappily. "But she doesn't want to hear anything I have to say."

"Where are you going to do the wedding?" Justin asked her.

"She was going to give me some ideas. She's checking out locations with Zach. They want it very small. I'd rather be giving one for you," Kate said in a wistful tone. She liked Richard a lot better than Zach, whom she barely knew, and she still couldn't see Izzie with him.

"We don't want to get married," Justin said, as he had before. "When's Grandma coming home, by the way?" He hadn't heard from her since she left on her trip. They never did.

"Tomorrow. I haven't told her about Izzie yet. I don't think she'll be happy about it either."

"It's hard to be optimistic about a mismatch like that." Kate didn't say she was worried about him too, and their upcoming child. It seemed like all of a sudden she had two children going offtrack and taking serious risks. She had encouraged her children to be independent, but she wanted them to play it safe as much as they could.

They talked for a few more minutes and then hung up. And the next day when her mother returned from Argentina, she told her the news that Izzie was planning to marry Zach.

"I had a feeling she'd do something like that. She had that look in her eye on Christmas Day that she used to get when she was a teenager and was planning to do something she knew she shouldn't but was determined to do anyway. You can't stop her when she gets like that."

"I know. I tried. Maybe you can reason with her and get her to wait awhile."

"I'm sure I can't," Grandma Lou said, sounding resigned. "She'll just have to go through it, and learn the lesson the hard way. I don't think there will be an easy way with him. He's going to be a great disappointment to her before it's all over. I just hope she doesn't get badly hurt." It was what Kate feared most, a marriage that would end badly and take Izzie years to recover from. But they couldn't seem to stop her.

"How was your trip?" Kate asked her, to change the subject from the depressing prospect of Izzie's marriage.

"Perfect."

"Did you do the tango?" Kate asked with a smile.

"Of course. I took Frances to tango bars every night."

"She must have loved that!" Kate said, laughing. Her friend Frances was a meek, demure woman who followed her more adventuresome friend faithfully without complaint.

"No, she didn't. But she was a good sport and went anyway. She's an excellent traveling companion." Louise had learned the samba in Brazil the year before. She was tireless, and loved to dance. She sounded like she'd had fun, which was the whole point of the trip. Seeing new places, meeting new people, and broadening her world. She had tried to teach that to her grandchildren, but they were more interested in work and careers, understandably. Willie liked to have fun and loved traveling with her. The girls were more like their mother and all about work, although they enjoyed their grandmother too. "What's new with you?" her mother asked her, and Kate told her about the business proposal she'd had from Bernard Michel in France.

"Why don't you go to Paris to meet with him?"

"He's coming here in two weeks," Kate told her.

"A trip to Paris would do you good," her mother suggested. After they hung up, Kate realized she was right. A trip to Paris would be fun. She wanted to go on a buying trip anyway. Maybe if the new project panned out, she'd go for a week or two. It sounded like a plan. Her mother always broadened her horizons too. Grandma Lou was good for all of them, and Kate was happy she was home and would talk to Izzie. She wondered if Izzie would listen to her grandmother, since she listened to no one else.

Chapter 9

Izzie called her mother at the store the week after Grandma Lou's return, in late January, and told her she had located several possible venues for her wedding reception. Two were restaurants, one was a small boutique hotel in Tribeca, and the fourth was a townhouse the owners rented out on Washington Square Park. The last one sounded like the most interesting, although it was slightly more expensive, but not excessively so. Kate was planning to pay for the wedding, and could afford to, but Izzie said she was more than willing to help. Kate would have preferred no wedding, but Grandma Lou hadn't been able to slow Izzie down either. She had tried. Izzie had made up her mind and nothing would stop her.

They made a date for that Friday afternoon to see all four locations. Kate normally loved having an excuse to spend time with her children, but she wasn't feeling enthusiastic about their mission. She wished there was something she could do to bring Izzie to her senses. But she seemed to be in high spirits and excited about finding a location for her wedding, no matter how disastrous Kate thought the groom.

They started at the hotel in Tribeca and agreed that it was gloomy and dark, although the food was reputed to be excellent. Kate thought it would make everything seem somber, and she was relieved that her daughter thought so too. And the two restaurants seemed banal to both of them. They were pretty but commercial, and only one of them had a private room. For the second one, they'd have to take over the whole restaurant, and the room was too large for only thirty guests. There were seven members of the family, including Richard, Grandma Lou, Kate, and the four siblings. Liam and Maureen would be there, of course. Zach had only two friends he thought he might invite and still wasn't sure. He considered it unlikely his father would come. And Izzie wanted to invite about fifteen or twenty people from work, and not everyone would attend. They might end up with only twenty wedding guests, so a private room seemed best. They didn't like anything they'd seen as they took a cab to the house on Washington Square. It was a pretty brick townhouse from the outside, with white trim and a shiny black door. It was one of the historic homes on the square from the time of Henry James.

A property manager was waiting for them when they arrived. The owner was a movie producer in California who rarely came to New York but loved the house, and rented it out for parties and special events. It was small once they stepped inside, like many of the turn-of-the-century townhouses on the square. There were two parlors on either side of the house on the main floor, and a study at the rear that was lined with books. The living room was on the second floor, a beautifully appointed room with lovely art and a view of the park. It occupied a full floor of the house, could apparently accommodate fifty, and was comfortable for twenty-five. And on the top two floors were the bedrooms. The master suite was above the living room, and it was a lovely romantic room where the bride could dress. The kitchen and formal dining room were downstairs, and the table could comfortably seat twenty-five, or stretch to thirty with additional leaves. It was perfect for the purpose they had in mind. The walls were painted in pastel shades, the furniture was antique, the window coverings done in exquisite silks, and there was a fireplace and chandelier in every room. Izzie could instantly imagine her wedding in a place like that, although Kate thought Zach would look completely out of place in his leathers, tattoos, long hair, and biker style, but she didn't say so to Izzie. She had fallen in love with the elegant little jewel box of a house, and Kate signed the contract for May first before they left. So they had a place for the wedding. The house came with a party chef and staff, so that was taken care of too, and they could provide a florist if they wished it. It left nothing more to arrange except the invitations and Izzie's bridal gown.

And although Zach and his family were supposed to organize and host the rehearsal dinner the night before, since he had no family to do so, Kate had already agreed to have the rehearsal dinner at home. It was going to be a casual evening, and she was planning to have it catered by a Mexican restaurant nearby, which was what Izzie said they wanted. Everyone could hang out informally, and sit on the floor. It would be a nice contrast to the small, elegant location for the wedding, and since it was for such a limited group, the price was not excessive. But for an intimate wedding, put together at short notice, with only a few months to plan, it was very elegant and just what they needed. Kate wanted to give Izzie a pretty wedding, even if she was unhappy about the marriage. If they couldn't stop her, Kate felt she should have a special day to remember nonetheless, and Izzie was pleased.

They went back to Kate's apartment, feeling victorious and satisfied with their successful mission. Izzie had found a gem with the location. The invitations weren't going to be complicated. And Kate looked lovingly at her daughter as she poured them both a cup of tea in her small tidy kitchen that was as immaculate, as stylish, and as organized as the rest of her apartment. Kate was a meticulous person in all things. "Now you need the gown," she said as they sat down at the table where they had all their holiday meals. "Any thoughts?" She was being a good sport about her daughter's wedding, despite her qualms.

Izzie had already said that she didn't want a wedding dress from her mother's shop. She didn't want anything vintage, she wanted something new and exciting that Zach would love. They looked at some dresses online on Kate's laptop as they sipped their tea. Oscar de la Renta, Marchesa, Herrera, Vera Wang, and Monique Lhuillier. They were all more elaborate than what Izzie had in mind. She wanted something totally simple and pure, with flowers in her hair, no veil. She had very definite ideas on the subject, as Kate knew most brides did. She had heard it all before at her store, and in many cases, the bride ended up picking something completely different from what she said she wanted. But Izzie was as stubborn about it as she was about everything else related to the wedding. Kate suggested she go to Bergdorf Goodman, have a look around, and try some gowns.

Izzie followed her advice but saw nothing she wanted. She was stumped about where to go next so she called her mother to tell her she had found nothing at Bergdorf's. Kate was doing an intake when Izzie called her, and told her she was busy but would give it some thought and call her later. Maybe a white dress from Armani or Calvin Klein would do the trick. Even if they weren't made as bridal gowns, they would be clean, simple, and modern, and Izzie had the right figure for their designs. Kate went back to work on the collection she was checking in then. She liked to see the items herself and be sure they were up to her standards. The one she was looking at was from a family in San Francisco, who had sent her all of their mother's couture gowns, some really beautiful Chanel pieces in perfect condition, and some other family pieces no one wanted, including their grandmother's wedding gown. Kate was sure it would be too old and fragile to sell, since it was from the 1920s and almost a hundred years old, but she had promised to take a look at it, and had already suggested before she saw it they donate it to a museum. They said the dress had been carefully preserved, and it arrived in a white box, having been heavily wrapped in tissue paper since its first and only use. No one had ever worn it since, because it looked too dated and out of style.

Kate was curious to see what it would look like when she took it out of the box and unwrapped it. The box it came in was huge, and it took her and Jessica several minutes to strip away all the tissue paper, which had yellowed with age, but miraculously the gown had not. It was still a delicate ivory color, with lace arms, minute beaded embroidery covering the entire dress, and a seemingly mile-long train and veil in the same lace. The gown was exquisite when they laid it out on a clean white sheet on the floor.

"Oh my God," Kate said, looking at it. It really did belong in a museum, and Jessica touched the delicate beading with reverence. The entire dress had been handmade by a designer of the time that Kate had never heard of, apparently a local woman in San Francisco. She wondered how many hundreds of hours had gone into making it for the society bride who wore it. There were even matching white satin shoes with the same beading on them. And she could see from the gown that the bride it had been made for must have been a tall girl. It had a dropped waist that was typical of the 1920s when it had been made.

Kate knew it was entirely wrong for Izzie and not what she wanted, but she couldn't resist calling her as they stood looking at it, and she described it to her.

"It's not for you, it's really a piece of history and it belongs in a museum, but it's one of the most beautiful wedding gowns I've ever seen. Do you want to come and look at it? It would be fun for you to see it, maybe it will give you some ideas." Izzie sounded halfhearted about it, and didn't want an antique dress, but she didn't want to be rude to her mother, since she was being nice about the wedding and helping her with the plans. They still had to find a judge who would perform the ceremony, since Zach refused to be married in a church, and said that anything religious brought back bad memories of his parents, since they had taken him to church every Sunday and he had hated it. So there would be no hint of religion at their wedding, which upset Kate too. But it was their wedding, and she was trying to help make it memorable for her daughter.

Izzie agreed to come by on Saturday after the gym, and Kate left the gown laid out on the sheet on the floor of the storeroom and told everyone not to go in, so they wouldn't step on it by mistake.

She was busy again the next day with one of her best clients, the editor from *Harper's Bazaar,* when Izzie came by. Kate asked the woman to wait a few minutes, and had Jessica take over for her. She apologized and explained it was a very special mission for her daughter, even though she knew she wouldn't wear the gown, but she wanted her to see it.

They went upstairs together. Kate unlocked the door and turned the lights on, and led Izzie to where they'd left the dress, carefully spread out on the floor. Izzie frowned when she saw it, and then knelt down to touch the lace and the beading. The gown itself was satin, except for the see-through lace arms, and the train and veil looked endless. There was a white satin cap under the veil with the same beading. Seeing it again, Kate knew she had never seen such a magnificent gown, and even Izzie looked impressed when she turned to look at her mother.

"Do you think it would fit me?" Kate was surprised by the question.

"I held it up to myself yesterday, and I think it would fit me. We're the same size, so I think it probably would. The bride it was made for must have been pretty tall."

"Could I try it?" Izzie asked with a shy look, and her mother smiled.

"Of course." When her daughters were much younger, she used to bring bridal gowns home from secondhand shops so they could play dress up. This was a much fancier version of the same idea.

They lifted the gown carefully and Kate noticed again that it was in excellent condition—nothing had yellowed, nothing was stained. It had obviously been cleaned before it was put away, and the fabric wasn't brittle. It had minute white satin buttons all the way down the back, which took forever to do up, but as soon as she did, she and Izzie both saw that the gown fit her to perfection. It looked as though it had been made for her, and once on a human form and not on the floor, the impressive artistry of the seamstress showed even more. It molded exactly to Izzie's tall, lean body, but not too much so. And the beading was even lovelier and subtler when the dress was worn.

There was a full-length mirror at the end of the storeroom, and Izzie walked toward it on tiptoe, as Kate remembered the shoes and put them on the floor for her. They fit perfectly too. The bride had been a clone of Izzie's body. And she and Kate both gasped as they saw her image in the mirror. It looked like a piece of history in its workmanship, and yet the style was modern too. The train was regal behind her, and when she settled the satin cap and veil on her head and spread the veil out, it brought tears to Kate's eyes. No matter what she thought of the marriage, the dress was one of the most beautiful she had ever seen. And Izzie thought so too. It occurred to Kate immediately that it would look perfect in the late-nineteenth-century house where she was getting married. It was pure Henry James, right out of one of his novels.

"Oh my God, Mom," Izzie said, looking at her mother in awe. "Can I have it? Will they sell it to us, or is it going to a museum?"

"I told them it should, but I'm sure I can talk them out of it. I'll see what I can do." Any other dress would have seemed paltry and second-best next to this one. There was no modern dress made that would compare to it, except perhaps haute couture, but this one had the patina of history and the craftsmanship of another century.

Izzie took the dress off carefully with her mother's help and they folded it back into the box, with the shoes and veil and all the tissue paper, and then they went downstairs to Kate's office. The editor from *Harper's Bazaar* was gone by then. She had bought two Chanel suits and a Balenciaga dress Kate had put aside for her from a recent intake. And then Kate called the family in San Francisco. It was still early there, and the woman who had sent her the shipment was at home. Kate explained that her daughter had fallen in love with her grandmother's wedding gown, and was getting married on May first.

"I really didn't think anyone would want it," the woman said honestly. "Girls wear much sexier dresses now, although the beading is beautiful, isn't it?"

"It certainly is. And I have to admit, it looks spectacular on her. She must have the exact same figure as your grandmother, even her shoe size."

"She was tall for the time," the woman confirmed, and when Kate asked how much she wanted for it, the woman hesitated for a long time. Kate wondered if she was going to come up with a shocking price, since Kate had told her it belonged in a museum. And finally, the woman answered, "It's been sitting here useless for nearly a hundred years. It would be nice to know that someone who really loves it has a chance to wear it. I'm sure my grandmother would be pleased. What about five hundred dollars, and my best wishes to the bride?" she said, and Kate's eyes filled with tears again. It was the kind of luck she had always had with her shop, meeting lovely people who shared their stories with her, and blessings that fell into her lap.

"That would be truly wonderful," Kate said, sounding thrilled. "I can't thank you enough. What good luck for us that you sent it."

"I hope your daughter enjoys it!" Both women hung up feeling touched by the hand of fate, and Kate turned to her daughter with a broad smile as she wiped her eyes.

"It's yours," she said, beaming at her as Izzie's eyes

grew wide and she threw her arms around her mother's neck.

"Oh my God, I love it! Wait till Zach sees me in it. I didn't think I wanted a vintage gown, and it doesn't get more vintage than 1920, but it's the most beautiful dress I've ever seen." She felt like a queen in it . . . and a bride. And it looked as though it had been made for her. It was Izzie's dream dress. And all Kate could wish as she looked at her daughter's radiant face was that she were marrying a different man in the spectacular dress. But this was what her daughter wanted, and she had to accept her choice of both, the man and the dress.

*

A week after they chose Izzie's wedding dress and the location for the wedding, Bernard Michel came back to town, with a more detailed proposal. Kate met with him and Liam to discuss it. Because of Liam's expertise, she always relied on him to advise her on financial matters, and she trusted him completely.

The meeting was serious and took place at Bernard's hotel, in his suite. He was staying at the Four Seasons this time, on the forty-eighth floor with a dizzying but amazing view. Liam was very pleased with their discussions, and so was Kate. Everything Bernard was suggesting to enhance her business and expand it made sense. It would never have occurred to her on her own. And as soon as someone had mentioned her remarkable shop to him, he had known that an online store would develop it exponentially, and be profitable for all involved. As they left the meeting, Liam told her that she had a good chance of making a great deal of money from the plan.

"A *lot* of money," he said as they shared a cab to go back downtown. Liam didn't live far from her, in Tribeca. It allowed them to take walks together sometimes, to catch up on news, when they hadn't had lunch together for a while, if either of them were too busy. They talked animatedly about the new project, and Bernard was sending the proposal to her lawyer. If all went well, she would be able to sign it soon, and move ahead. She was going to call their online shopping business Fabulous on the Net.

She was surprised to hear from Bernard that night after she got home, when she was reading over her notes from the meeting. There were a couple of points she wanted to ask him about and had forgotten, so she was pleased he'd called. She went over them with him, and then he lingered on the phone, asking her what she was doing and how she spent her time when she wasn't working. She laughed and said she worked all the time, and occasionally saw her mother and children when they had time. And she was delighted that the Internet component to her business was going to keep her very busy while she set it up.

"Would you like to have dinner tomorrow night?" he asked her casually. She had enjoyed their meal at La

Grenouille before, but didn't expect him to take her out to fancy dinners as part of the deal, and said so. He laughed. "Don't be so American, Kate," he chided her. "Everything in life isn't about business. Can't a man take a beautiful woman out for dinner, without it being about work?" She was surprised by what he said.

"I suppose so," she said pensively, but she couldn't see why. He lived in Paris, she lived here, and the deal was almost done. They had nothing crucial left to discuss, until the papers were signed and she got started setting it up. "That's very nice of you." She sounded almost shy. She hadn't had a real date in years, and didn't think of him as one. She didn't like mixing business with romance, and never had. She had clear boundaries about things like that, just as she did with Liam, and so did he. They were friends. And Bernard was now a business associate, although he had brought her a terrific proposal and she was grateful for that.

"Is there someplace casual you enjoy? It would be nice to have a relaxed evening." She knew he had other meetings planned while he was in New York, and he had said as much to her.

She suggested Da Silvano, if he liked Italian food. It was easy, relaxed, downtown, and the pasta was great. And the owner was always there himself, which kept everyone on their toes.

"Perfect. I'll make the reservation and pick you up at

eight, if that works for you." He sounded warm and friendly, and she couldn't tell if he considered it a date. She hoped not. But there was no harm in being friends if they were going to have a business alliance. She was planning to keep it to that, in case he had any other ideas.

He was wearing slacks and a blazer and a heavy coat when he picked her up at her apartment the next day, in a town car with a driver. At the restaurant, they were shown to a table, and Bernard ordered wine for both of them. He looked happy to see her, and was funny and good company as they chatted and ordered dinner. He wasn't overtly seductive with her, but she had the feeling all night that he was courting her as a woman, not trying to get to know a business colleague better. And then he startled her with what he said as they ordered coffee and agreed to share a dessert.

"I don't know if it matters to you, Kate, but I want to be open with you. Technically, I'm married. Legally. But not in any real sense anymore. We haven't been for years. We have an arrangement which is fairly common in France. It's too complicated to get divorced and separate investments and properties that have been entwined for so long. So she leads her life, I lead mine. We're cordial when we meet. We see the children separately, we have different friends. She's like my sister now." Kate had heard of those arrangements and wouldn't have wanted one herself. But whatever worked for him was his business, and not hers.

He didn't need to explain it to her, and she had noticed immediately that he didn't wear a wedding band, which most European men did, if they were married. "I just wanted you to know," he continued, "so you don't feel awkward if we spend an evening together. I enjoy your company. I'd like to see more of you while I'm here." He was so direct about it that she was startled. No one had said anything like it to her for a long time, and never with a Continental flavor, explaining that he and his wife had an "arrangement," and that even if he was legally married, he actually wasn't in any real sense. He certainly had made his situation clear.

"She doesn't mind that you go out with other women?" Kate asked him as directly as he had been with her.

"We don't ask each other those questions," he said discreetly. "It's not my business what she does, nor hers what I do. We stayed married for the children, and now because it's less financially complicated. The spirit of our marriage died years ago."

"How sad for both of you," Kate said sympathetically, and meant it. She had been madly in love with Tom. And her parents had loved each other to the end.

"Not really," Bernard said comfortably. "It happens. In the States, people get divorced when the love affair is over. In France, people are more practical. We try to keep the family intact, in form anyway, and divorce is less familiar to us. It's a Catholic country, and divorce came very late.

155

Most of our friends have the same arrangement we do. Some have mistresses who are almost like wives." He made it sound normal and acceptable, and almost desirable, as Kate listened.

"I'm not comfortable dating a married man," she said clearly, while he nodded and appeared to agree.

"Most Americans aren't. But I would like to see you for dinner when I'm here. Would you be amenable to that? Like tonight?" She felt silly objecting to it. He had been totally proper and good company and she smiled at him as the waiter brought their dessert.

"That's fine," she said, and he made her laugh with stories about his children, work, and life in Paris, and some of his travels around the world. "You'd love meeting my mother. She loves to travel and she's a character. She just got back from a month of tango lessons in Argentina. Last year she learned the samba in Brazil. And she's been studying Mandarin for a year, for a trip to China this summer. She makes the rest of us look boring by comparison."

"I'd love to meet her, and your children," he said enthusiastically, and then she told him about Izzie's wedding and how unhappy she was about it, since tonight was personal not business and he had told her so much about himself and his marriage. "We can't control our children. My daughter in medical school has a boyfriend we all hate. He's a dreadful, rough, uncivilized person, and she's been with him for five years, with no sign of marriage fortunately. And my son lives with a woman we don't like either. They have two children, but have no plans to marry. The children are very sweet, two boys. That's common in France too, particularly now. Many of my friends' children have children but don't marry. I try not to say too much to my children, but it upsets me too at times." Listening to him, Kate wasn't sure what was better, staying married and cheating on your wife, or never marrying and having children out of wedlock. Both sounded dubious to her, and less than ideal. And then she thought of Justin and Richard, who were doing the same thing, with a surrogate no less.

"My son is having a baby too, in August. And he's not married." She didn't mention that he was gay, and didn't know how Bernard would react to two unmarried men having a child. Despite their sometimes loose morals, the French were fairly conservative, although normally in the States she never hesitated to say she had a gay son who lived with his partner.

"I can't see you as a grandmother," Bernard said with an appreciative look, and she laughed.

"Neither can I. I'm not sure I'm ready for that." She hadn't even thought of it that way yet. For the moment, it was Justin's baby, not her grandchild. It was a somewhat daunting prospect.

They continued to chat long after they finished their

coffee and he paid the check, and then he drove her home, and looked at her warmly before she got out of the car.

"I really enjoyed tonight, Kate. Even more than last time. I can't wait to see you again when I come back, in about a month."

"I'm hoping to come to Paris sometime in February, on a buying trip."

"Be sure you let me know before you come. I would love to see you there." As he said it, she remembered his "arrangement," and assumed his seeing other women really wasn't a problem. He had a totally free and easy style, and clearly didn't feel married. And he felt single to her too that night. None of his stories and anecdotes included his wife. He was a free agent, except on paper, and she felt totally at ease with him.

He kissed her on both cheeks then, and she got out of the car, and let herself into the building. He watched until she was safely inside, waved, and then they drove away, as she went back to her apartment, thinking about him. He really was a nice person. He had done something wonderful for her business, was great to work with, and now she had a new friend. Thinking about all of it gave her a new lease on life. And she was smiling to herself as she took a bath, and went to bed. She had had a lovely time with Bernard.

Chapter 10

On the night before Valentine's Day, there was a huge snowstorm in southern Vermont. Justin and Richard had invited friends over for dinner, and canceled at four o'clock when the roads became nearly impassable. And when the snow stopped and the temperatures dropped later that night, there were sheets of black ice on the road, and warnings on TV for people to stay home.

They went to bed early, and were sound asleep when the phone rang at three A.M. Justin answered, and was groggy at first when he listened, and then sat bolt upright in bed.

"How is she? Is she all right? What happened?" Richard came awake as he listened, and thought instantly of Justin's grandmother in New York. They had had heavy snows there too, and all the way down the Eastern Seaboard to Washington, D.C. "Can we see her?" Justin asked in a shaking voice. "When will they know? Is she bleeding heavily?" Justin's eyes were closed, and Richard gently touched his shoulder to reassure him. A moment later, Justin hung up, and turned to Richard with a look of panic.

"Grandma Lou?" Richard asked and Justin shook his head.

"Shirley. They were in a car accident. Jack's mother fell at home and broke her hip, and they drove to the hospital to see her, and their truck skidded on the ice. They hit a tree, they're okay, but she has a concussion, and she started bleeding a little while ago. It's too soon to know what's going to happen." She was two and a half months pregnant, the most vulnerable time for miscarriages, and it didn't sound good to either of them. "They're doing a sonogram now, but they can still hear a heartbeat. The nurse said she can bleed and still not lose it. Shirley told her to call us."

"Can we see her?" Richard asked as he got out of bed and grabbed his jeans on the chair where he'd left them.

"Yes," Justin said, looking devastated. "Do you want to go? It's dangerous as hell out there." The night was freezing and the air crisp, the temperature was below zero, and the ice on the road would be lethal.

"I'll drive slowly. Do you want to stay here?" he offered and Justin looked shocked.

"Of course not. Are you crazy?" They both dressed in five minutes, put on their warmest clothes, and walked gingerly out to their car, praying it would start. Justin shoveled a path while Richard tried to warm up the car. It failed to turn over a few times, and then sputtered to life, and they let it warm up for a few minutes, and then drove slowly out of their driveway. Richard was at the wheel, and they inched along, barely going five miles an hour, and trying to avoid the patches of ice they could see. They skidded once, but Richard regained control of the car. It took them half an hour to get to the hospital, which should normally have taken five minutes, and Shirley was still in the emergency room when they got there. She looked pale and shaken, and had thrown up from the concussion. She smiled wanly at them when they arrived and then started to cry.

"I'm really sorry, guys," she said as Justin's heart nearly stopped, thinking she had already lost the baby.

"Did you? . . . Is it . . ." he asked in a choked voice, and the nurse intervened.

"Nothing's happened, and the sonogram was fine. The fetus is fine, and the heartbeat is normal. Shirley is just a little shaken up." She put a warm blanket on her, and the two men retreated to the waiting room, not to disturb her. She told them that Jack was being treated for a broken nose he had sustained from the air bag. The one in the passenger seat had hit Shirley hard too.

Justin and Richard sat in the waiting room for four hours until seven-thirty in the morning. Shirley had been taken to a room by then, they said she was still spotting, but nothing further had happened. They were still there at noon, waiting for news, when a female resident came to see them. She was smiling, which they took as a good sign.

"She's doing fine. The bleeding stopped, but we're going to keep her till tomorrow, just to be on the safe side. I think the baby will be okay. We told her to stay in bed for a few days, until everything settles down again. She got a hell of a jolt, but babies come through worse than that sometimes and make it."

"Thank God," Justin said as he exhaled. They went to see Shirley in her room then. She looked tired and pale, but she said she felt better, except for a headache. She had no cramping, and as the resident had told them, the bleeding had stopped, and had never been major.

"I'm so sorry. My mother-in-law broke her hip, and I thought I should go to the hospital with Jack. He was driving really careful too, but we hit a patch of black ice he didn't see, and hit the tree."

"I'm glad it wasn't any worse for either of you," Justin said generously, relieved about the baby. "Can we do anything for you?"

"I'm fine. I was just scared for the baby when I got here and started bleeding."

"So were we." Justin smiled at her, and then left her to sleep. They went downstairs to the gift shop and bought magazines and a teddy bear for her. And they stopped at the florist on the way home and sent her flowers. And then they went home and climbed back into bed, and lay talking to each other. It had been a terrifying night, and they had both been sure she'd lose the baby, and were grateful she didn't. Justin called Julie that afternoon and told her about it, and as always she was sympathetic. She couldn't wait to be an aunt. And she was still disappointed they weren't having twins.

They drove Shirley home from the hospital the next day, since Jack's truck was in the shop, badly damaged from when he hit the tree. Shirley seemed much better than she had the day before. Her sister-in-law had taken her children, and she promised to stay in bed for a few days, although the doctor had said she didn't have to, if she felt all right and took it easy. But she promised to humor Justin and Richard. And Jack was staying home from work too.

And more than anything, it had reminded Richard and Justin how fragile life could be, and how much they wanted the baby.

*

Kate went to Paris, as she had told Bernard she would, in February. She treated herself to a room at the Meurice, and set out to explore all her favorite haunts to find top-quality vintage and used clothes, among them the auctions at the Hôtel Drouot, and all the little shops she had been visiting for years all over Paris. She found a few interesting items on the first day, went for a walk along the Seine, and had a cup of tea at a café. She called Bernard the day after she arrived. They had signed the final papers on their deal the week before, and when she called him, he insisted they had to celebrate. He suggested dinner at Le Voltaire, which was one of her favorite restaurants in Paris. The small, elegant bistro had been the favorite place for chic Parisians and members of the fashion elite for many years. He picked her up at her hotel and drove her there in his Aston Martin. He had looked very dashing when he stopped and got out of the car at her hotel. He seemed more subdued in New York. He looked delighted to see her when he hugged her, kissed her on both cheeks, and helped her into the car. They sped off a moment later. The weather was beautiful, and felt almost like spring, which was unusual at that time of year.

They had a wonderful time, and he invited her for a fancy dinner at Apicius the next evening, after she foraged around the resale shops and went to an auction. She had a ball going to her favorite places, and when he picked her up at the end of the day, he was wearing a dark suit. She had put on a short black cocktail dress under a dark mink coat, and it felt more like a date than their evenings out before. They went to the restaurant in the beautiful old Rothschild home, where all the headwaiters knew him and made a big fuss over them.

"I give dinner parties here sometimes," he explained to her. "In a private room they have. It's an easy way to entertain as a single man." He had almost convinced her that he was, since he lived like one. The food at Apicius was incredible, the restaurant elegant, and the service fabulous. It was one of the nicest evenings she'd ever had. And when he dropped her off at the hotel, Bernard offered to take her for a drive in the country the next day.

They drove to Deauville, in Normandy, in the morning, and walked along the boardwalk. They had lunch at a small fish restaurant he knew, and they drove back to Paris after dark and had a drink at her hotel.

"What are we doing tomorrow?" he asked her, as they relaxed at the bar. It had been a perfect day.

"You're spoiling me," she said, enjoying every minute of it. It was a wonderful experience sharing Paris with Bernard.

"Why don't we have lunch at Les Cascades, and then there's a very good art show at the Grand Palais." She agreed to the plan, and he looked regretful when she finally left him and went upstairs to her room. She called her mother to see how she was, and Louise was delighted to hear from her, although Kate didn't mention Bernard. It didn't seem appropriate to report to her mother, or relevant who she was dining with in Paris. Kate told her she was in Paris to restock the shop. She described some of the auctions she'd been to, and stayed off the subject of who she was spending her evenings with. Even at her age, she didn't want to tell her mother that she was being wined and dined by a married man. She knew her mother wouldn't approve. Nor would she, Kate realized, if one of her children were doing the same. And she couldn't help wondering what information her own children were withholding from her. It was a game every generation played to escape their parents' disapproval and not cause them concern. After a few minutes, her mother told her to have fun, and they hung up.

And at noon the next day, Bernard picked her up. It was Sunday, and lunch at Les Cascades was relaxed, looking out at the gardens, and the art show at the Grand Palais afterward was fun. They left the car there and went for a long walk, and went to the hotel George V for tea, where there was a small orchestra playing, and lots of good people-watching as they sat at a table in the gallery. They never stopped talking, and Kate enjoyed Bernard's company, more than she had expected to, and perhaps more than she should, she realized, when they retrieved his car and he took her back to the Meurice. She was about to thank him for a lovely day as they stood outside the hotel for a few minutes, when without saying anything to her, he pulled her gently into his arms and kissed her. She was startled at first, and then melted into his arms, and loved it, and then she gently pulled away.

"Should we be doing that?" she asked him softly. She was suddenly torn between thinking of him as married or single. With his status in limbo, according to French tradition, it was confusing.

"Why wouldn't we?" he answered and kissed her again.

"I'm a free man in all the ways that matter," he reminded her and he seemed so sincere that she kissed him, and then they walked slowly into the hotel. He didn't ask to come upstairs, but she sensed that he would have liked to. Doing so would have been more than she could handle for now. She needed time to absorb what was happening and what it meant, if anything. Maybe he was just an inveterate flirt and woman chaser, and if so, he was good at it, because he seemed so earnest and caring, and so interested in her. He kissed her one last time before she got in the elevator, and he called her that night when she was relaxing in her room.

"I can't stop thinking about you," he said, and she smiled. She was thinking about him too, and trying not to. She wasn't sure she wanted a romance, particularly with a married man she was doing business with. That was confusing too, but he was so appealing and so much fun. And no one had ever been as attentive to her as he was. American men were different, and Frenchmen were so adept at the art of courtship and seduction that it was hard to resist, whatever his status.

He had to work the next day, and she had things to do for the store, and there was the online store to buy for now too. He didn't invite her to dinner that night, but he showed up at her hotel and asked her to come down to the lobby for a drink. It was ten o'clock at night, and he said he had been in meetings until then, with some Chinese businessmen he was cultivating. She hesitated because of the hour, and he finally convinced her to come down in jeans and a sweater with her hair loose, while he told her about his meetings, and they drank champagne at the bar. No man had wooed her as ardently in years, if ever. And she was beginning to look forward to seeing him at the end of every day.

He came up with new plans for them every night, went to an auction with her once, and was impressed by how adept she was at bidding, and what she bought. She had a great eye for fashion. They even went to the movies one night. He seemed to have nothing to do with his nights except spend them with her. More and more, she was realizing that he was as free as he said, and it made her feel more comfortable with him. She didn't care as much that he was married legally as long as she wasn't poaching on someone else's turf, and clearly she wasn't, if he was never with his wife, and always with her.

He said he wanted to introduce her to his children, but they were having too much fun alone. And on her last weekend in Paris, they drove to Versailles and walked around, and then had dinner at a little bistro on the way home. She still had two more days, and it had been a magical trip for her thanks to Bernard, who had entertained her every night, spent the weekend with her, took her to exhibits, and saw to it that she had a wonderful time for the two weeks she was in Paris.

"I'm going to be very sad when you leave," he said wistfully, as they drove back to the Meurice after their day at Versailles.

"So am I," she said honestly. "I've always loved Paris, but it's never been like this before, thanks to you," she said, looking gratefully at him as he drove. She had grown completely comfortable with him, and it was going to be strange when she left, not to see him every night. "I've been totally spoiled."

"You deserve it," he said warmly. "It's going to be lonely here without you." He was going to New York in March, which wasn't far away. They pulled up in front of the hotel, and the doorman recognized them both, they were a familiar sight. Bernard left the car with him and walked slowly into the hotel with her, lost in thought. She had her hand tucked into his arm, and he leaned closer to her to ask the question he had wanted to ask her for two weeks but hadn't dared. He didn't want to scare her off. "May I come upstairs?" he whispered. She hesitated for a long moment as she looked into his eyes. She hadn't planned to do that, and had promised herself not to, for all the obvious reasons, the uncertainty of his "arrangement" with his wife, but what she saw in his eyes melted her resolve and she nodded, and a moment later he followed her into the elevator without a word. He walked down the hall with her, and she unlocked the door to her room and stepped inside, and he swept her instantly into his arms and held her with the force of his desire that had been building since he met her and for the past two weeks. He couldn't stop himself anymore, and in less than a minute they were on her bed with their clothes off, overwhelmed with passion like two people half their age.

He was like a tidal wave that overtook her and swept her along with the force of everything he felt for her. They were both breathless when they stopped and he looked at her and smiled.

"Oh my God, I'm so in love with you, Kate. What have you done to me? I feel eighteen years old." He made love like it, and she was just as enamored with him. "What are we going to do?" he asked, as he rolled over on his back with a broad grin, and she was smiling too. "You can't move to Paris, you have a business to run. And I can't move to New York. How am I going to live without seeing you every day?" He looked genuinely bereft at the thought.

"We'll figure it out," she said as she rolled onto her side and kissed him again. And she suspected that not being together all the time would make the time they did share even more exciting, which wasn't entirely a bad thing. He was more possessive than she was and wanted her at his side constantly. They were together every minute while she was there. For now, it was enough. And if things became serious between them, they could discuss the rest. She had no complaints, and no demands to make.

He slept at the hotel with her that night, which made it all even better and seem more real. They had breakfast together in her room in the morning, and then he left for his day, after kissing her and promising to make plans with her that night. She had two more nights left in Paris, and they were going to spend them together, and enjoy each other until she left, and then they had to go back to their own lives until they met again in March.

He took her to one of his favorite bistros that night on the Left Bank, and then they walked along the river and wound up in front of Notre Dame under a full moon. It was an idyllic scene that she knew she would never forget, and then they went back to the hotel and he spent the night with her again. And on her last night, they had room service and had a quiet evening, talking about her business and their plans.

Bernard drove Kate to the airport on the morning she left. He felt terrible that he couldn't stay with her until her flight, but he had an early meeting. He kissed her tenderly before he left her, after she had checked in her bags, and then she watched the Aston Martin disappear onto the highway, as he waved at her. It had been exactly what Paris should be, and the most perfect two weeks of her life.

She was smiling, thinking about him as she boarded the plane two hours later, and he sent her a text from his meeting. *"A bientôt. Je t'aime."* See you soon, I love you. It was all she needed to know.

Chapter 11

It was hard for Kate to get back to her usual routine when she came back from Paris. She was floating on a cloud. Every day had been perfect, every night had been fun and exciting with Bernard. She felt like a woman again. And he sent her three dozen red roses when she got home.

She caught up at her desk on the first day, and he sent her several texts. He said he didn't want to interrupt her if she was working, so didn't call. And Kate had dinner with her mother that night. Louise was in good spirits, busy as usual, and asked Kate about her trip to Paris. Although she thought about it, she still didn't tell her mother about Bernard. She was sure she wouldn't understand the "arrangement" he had with his wife. After two weeks in Paris, it had appeared to be everything he had originally said. He had total freedom to lead his own life. It was almost as though his wife and marriage didn't exist. But she knew her mother would worry that Kate would get hurt. Kate realized she would have been concerned if one of her daughters fell in love with a married man. It was precisely the kind of high-risk situation she wouldn't have wanted for them. But, she told herself, she was an adult, and he had been totally honest with her. The amount of time he spent with her clearly indicated that he was as free as he said.

She checked in with Izzie the day after, and all she wanted to do was talk about the wedding. She had ordered the invitations, and met with the florist at the house on Washington Square Park, and she had found a judge to perform the ceremony. The wedding was two months away, and hearing Izzie talk about it made it a reality, which still upset Kate. Izzie was moving full speed ahead, heading off a cliff as far as Kate was concerned. She could easily imagine her daughter in the spectacular antique wedding gown, marrying the wrong man. And she was torn between wanting to scream and forbid her to do it, and going along with it because she felt she had no other choice. She was being carried along on the tides of maternal devotion, but she knew they would be going over a waterfall in dangerous currents, and plunging to the depths below. It was an alarming thought, and she steeped herself in work in order not to think about it. And she had a lot to do before the launch of the new online business. Bernard's company was making sure that they got press to bring attention to it. And Julie offered to come in and help her organize the clothes to photograph.

They worked together all weekend, getting everything ready. They had fifty pieces that mother and daughter agreed would be showstoppers and sell quickly. She had a range of prices on the items they would be displaying on their website, and Kate was thrilled when she saw the photographs. And on Monday she asked Julie to join her at an event she had accepted at the Metropolitan Museum and had forgotten about.

"I have nothing to wear, Mom," Julie said plaintively, and her mother laughed.

"You have closets full of your own designs, and I have a store full of anything you could want. What do you want to wear? A little black dress?" She had them from at least two dozen designers, and could have outfitted an entire village in chic black dresses.

"That's so boring. Do you have anything red?"

"I'll look," Kate promised, and found three dresses she thought Julie would like. She had Jessica take pictures of them and send them to Julie on her phone. She had found a sexy Hervé Léger, a striking Dior, and a nameless brand that Kate had liked when she bought it.

Julie called back an hour later, still trying to get out of going to the event. "Do I really have to go?"

"Yes, you never go anywhere and I don't want to go alone."

"Why can't you take Willie? He loves to go out."

"He would hate the event at the Met, and I'll look like a child molester if people don't know he's my son." She had talked to him that morning, and he said he was fine.

She saw less of him than her daughters, because he was always busy, and had an active dating life, and no time for his mother. But she expected that from him at his age. At twenty-four, no man wanted to hang around with his mother, and Willie was no exception. "Did you like any of the dresses?" Kate asked her as she ate a yogurt at her desk. It was all that she had time for.

"The Hervé Léger doesn't look too bad."

"Thanks a lot, I'm selling it for two thousand dollars and it's never been worn. It was nearly five when the woman bought it, but it's so small it won't fit anyone but you." You had to have a wraithlike figure to wear it, and Julie did. Kate thought the dress would look incredible on her. "Do you want me to send it over to your office so you can try it?" The design firm where she worked wasn't too far away, and Jessica could take it to Julie in a cab.

"Maybe," Julie said, still hoping to get out of the event, but her mother wasn't letting her off the hook. She wanted Julie to get out more, and there would be a mixed crowd at the Met, many of them her age.

"I'll have it to you in half an hour." She put Jessica in a taxi with it a few minutes later, and called Julie two hours after that. "How was it?"

"I have to admit, it's pretty cool." She laughed as she said it. "You have an eye."

"That's a compliment coming from you." Her daughter was a talented designer, and had great taste. And Kate had suspected the dress would be smashing on her. "I'll pick you up at your place at seven-thirty." The event started at eight and it would take them time to get uptown in evening traffic.

And for the rest of the day, Kate didn't stop. Their new expanded website was launching in two weeks, and she had to go over the final details.

Liam called her that afternoon and complained that she hadn't called him since she got back from Paris. She felt guilty about it, but she'd been avoiding him. She didn't know what to say. She didn't want to tell him about getting involved with Bernard. She knew he wouldn't approve of her dating a married man. Liam had very rigid ideas about people cheating, and he never had. And French "arrangements" were not something he would find charming. Kate didn't want to have to explain, so she just said she had had a great time in Paris, and bought some wonderful things for the store. He said he had been busy too, and inquired about the wedding.

"Is she still going ahead?" He was hoping for Kate's sake, and her own, that Izzie would come to her senses, but Kate knew he was dreaming about that.

"Full steam, from what I can tell. I'm taking Julie to an event at the Met with me tonight. It'll do her good to dress up and meet some new people for a change." Liam always admired the time Kate spent with her children, and how connected she was to them all, whether she saw them or not. She called each of them every few days, no matter how old they were now. Her own mother was far more nonchalant, and always had been. Although she loved Kate and her grandchildren too, she called them all less often.

Kate promised to have lunch with Liam when things slowed down a little, and then rushed home to dress. She was going to wear a black velvet Dior evening suit that she had been saving for a special event, and with press expected to be there that night, this was it. With her new website about to launch, she wanted to make an elegant splash in the press. She was a discreet presence on the fringe of the fashion scene, but people knew who she was.

When Kate picked her up, Julie emerged from her building on the Bowery in the red dress. Her figure looked amazing. She was wearing a black fox jacket Kate had given her for Christmas five years before, with a splash of red lipstick, her jet-black hair pulled tightly into a bun at the nape of her neck, and staggeringly high heels that were perfection with the dress. Kate beamed as soon as she saw her.

"Wow! You are a knockout!" her mother told her proudly.

"You look pretty good yourself." Kate was wearing a black sable coat over the Dior suit, with heels almost as high as Julie's. Together they made an impressive pair, and photographers from *Vogue* and *Women's Wear Daily*

177

took their photograph as they walked in. All heads turned for an instant, and every man in the area stared at Julie. She looked sexy and young and chic.

Julie helped herself to a glass of champagne as a tray was passed around, and observed the scene shyly. She had always been less confident than her mother and older sister, and it had comforted her growing up to be a twin. She had relied on Justin to protect her and speak for her. And being dyslexic made her less sure of herself than her siblings. And socializing without Justin as an adult was still hard.

Kate introduced her to a few people she knew, and half an hour later they went in to dinner, which had been set up in the Egyptian wing. There were smoky gold tablecloths, and Tiffany had provided gold china, which looked striking on the tables. And with Julie's exotic look with her tight red dress, dark hair, and bright red lipstick, she fit right in.

They were seated at a table of ten, with two fashion editors Kate knew vaguely across the table. There was a well-known curator of the Met seated next to Kate, and a younger man next to Julie who had come with a date. He seemed to have no interest in his companion once he spotted Julie, and engaged her in conversation as soon as he sat down. He worked for a large corporation, and said he had moved to New York two years before. He had lived in Chicago and Atlanta before that, and was really enjoying

New York and the people he had met since he arrived. His date was pale and blond, and was talking to a man on her other side.

"My name is Peter White," he said with a warm smile, a few minutes after they sat down, and Julie introduced herself. She was so deeply engaged in her design work in the fashion world, he was the kind of man she normally never met. She seldom went out, and when she did it was with people she worked with, or other designers or artists. She never had a chance to meet young corporate men, and she wasn't sure what to say to him. He carried the conversational ball for her, and had her laughing after half an hour. She was enjoying the evening, and drank just enough wine to relax, but not too much. She didn't mind an occasional evening of excess, but not when she was out with her mother at a major event, and this was just that.

By the time dessert was served, she and Peter felt like old friends.

"Do you come to the Met a lot?" he asked her. He was very well dressed and very polished, and seemed like he'd be comfortable in any setting, and he looked strong and athletic. He had told her he was a big sports fan, and loved going to football and hockey games.

"I only come here with my mother," Julie said honestly, in her soft smoky voice that men thought was sexy and enchanting. She was striking and exotic-looking with her dark hair, white skin, and big brown eyes. "I don't go out a lot. I work long hours."

"That sounds intriguing." He smiled at her and she laughed.

"Not very. I'm a designer." She mentioned the brand and he looked impressed.

"You must be very talented."

"Not really. I've been drawing clothes since I was a kid. I liked drawing better than school, so I did it as a job as soon as I could. I went to Parsons School of Design."

They were still talking animatedly when the dinner ended, and he lingered to chat with her for a few more minutes until his date finally turned her attention to him again, and Kate turned to Julie. She had noticed Peter talking to her all evening, and didn't want to interfere. He was good-looking and seemed intelligent, and was mesmerized by Julie.

He said goodbye to Julie as his date pulled him away to introduce him to someone. She had a strong southern accent and seemed cloying as she slipped her hand into his arm and glued herself to him, and Julie whispered to her mother.

"Can we go yet?"

"In a minute. You looked like you were having a good time with your dinner partner."

"He was fine," Julie said noncommittally. She didn't

want to get her mother started about her needing to meet men.

"What does he do? Did he tell you?" Kate asked her.

"I don't know. He's some kind of corporate executive. He's lived in New York for two years, and he likes hockey games." Kate laughed as Julie summed up two hours of conversation in two sentences. He had disappeared into the crowd by then with his date. And a few minutes later, Kate and Julie left. The party was winding down. But in spite of her resistance to evenings like that, Julie looked like she'd had a good time and so had Kate. The curator she sat next to had been fascinating. And they talked about the evening on the way downtown.

"You should keep that dress. It looks terrific on you," Kate complimented her.

"Thanks, Mom. I like it a lot. I might even wear it again sometime."

"You should. And it made a big hit with your dinner partner. He couldn't keep his eyes off you."

"I think he was just bored with his date. He didn't talk to her all night." Kate had noticed that too.

"Maybe he liked you better," Kate said, and Julie smiled.

She dropped Julie off at her apartment and watched her go in, and then had the cabdriver drop her off in SoHo. She had a message from Bernard when she got home, but it was too late to call him. It was five in the morning in

Paris. And by the time he got up, she'd be asleep. The time difference was hard to manage sometimes, so he sent her a lot of emails and texts. He was due in New York in two weeks, and Kate was looking forward to it. She missed him. She was pleased that the evening had been a success, and that she had gotten Julie to join her. It was good for her self-confidence to have a man riveted by her. And Peter White certainly had been.

*

Julie was startled when Peter White called her at the office the next day. She had mentioned the firm she worked for but was surprised that he remembered.

"They told me you're the head designer," he said when she answered, flustered. She hadn't expected him to call her.

"Well, I guess I am . . . sort of . . . we all do the work here," she said modestly. The designer who owned the brand got all the glory and acclaim, but Julie and her design team did all the work.

"Don't be so humble. I really enjoyed the evening last night because of you. I'm calling to see if you would like to go to a hockey game with me tomorrow night. It won't be as glamorous as last night, but hockey games are a lot of fun, if you've never been to one."

"I went to a couple with my brother. He used to love them too."

"Older brother or younger?" He was curious about her.

"Neither. Well, older, technically, by five minutes. We're twins."

"How fascinating. I always wished I had a twin brother."

"It was great. I hated it when he went to college, and we didn't go to school together anymore. We're still best friends."

"Does he live here?" Peter asked her.

"No, Vermont. I go to see him whenever I can, when I'm not working." She was much more timid on the phone than she had been the night before. Being dressed up and out with her mother was like playacting. Now he had entered her real life, which was different.

"So how about the game tomorrow? Any interest?" He sounded hopeful.

She thought about it for an instant while he waited for her answer. "I'd like that. Thank you very much."

"Dress warm," he said, seeming protective of her.

"I know." She giggled and sounded very young.

"Where should I pick you up?" She gave him her address, and told him she'd be waiting outside. She never had strangers to her apartment now that she lived alone. "Where is that?" he asked, puzzled. The street didn't sound familiar to him.

"On the Bowery, downtown." It was the kind of seedy,

arty, eclectic neighborhood she liked. "Where do you live?"

"East Seventy-ninth Street, uptown, near the East River." It was where most successful people like him lived, on the Upper East Side. All of her family and friends lived downtown in SoHo, Tribeca, the East and West Village, the Meatpacking District, and her artist friends in Chelsea, and many in Brooklyn. It was a whole other world from his.

"Do you mind coming downtown?" she asked, feeling guilty for making him come so far to pick her up. "Or I could meet you at Madison Square Garden. I'll just take the subway uptown."

"Of course not." He was shocked at the suggestion. "I'm happy to pick you up." And then he asked her for her cell-phone number and email, in case he needed to get in touch with her when he was on the way. "See you tomorrow, Julie," he said, excited to see her again. She wondered what had happened to his date of the night before, and if she was important to him. But it didn't look like it, and he had spent the whole dinner talking to her and was taking her to the game. She called her brother and told him about it, and Justin was happy for her. He couldn't remember the last time she had a date, and he assumed Peter was an appropriate person if she had met him at the Met with their mother. He told her to have fun before they hung up.

Julie was smiling to herself about it as she went back to work.

*

When she went to the game with Peter, Julie had even more fun than she'd had at the Met. She wore black jeans and her favorite combat boots, a black parka, and a big white angora sweater, and her dark hair was down and framed her face. She wore very little makeup and looked even younger than she had on Monday night. They ate hot dogs and popcorn and ice cream at the game, and she asked for cotton candy when the vendor walked by and Peter laughed.

"Okay, I have to ask you. How old are you? Will I go to jail for being out with you?" He was laughing when he asked the question. She looked like such a kid, and had put a white knit cap on at the game. And her face was covered with cotton candy when she answered, with a pink spot on her nose and chin.

"I love cotton candy." She grinned at him. "I'm thirty. Why?"

"You look a lot younger. Especially tonight without the sexy dress and high heels." He teased her about her combat boots, which were her favorite shoes, and he said he loved that she could go from one extreme to the other and was totally at ease at a hockey game, and screamed as loud as he did when the Rangers scored a goal. They were playing the Bruins, there had been several fights on the ice already, and it was a heated game. He told Julie that he loved being there with her, and that his date from Savannah, his companion at the Met, had always refused to go with him. He seemed delighted Julie had come, and fit right in.

"How old are you?" she asked him, equally interested. She liked him. He was smart and respectful and fun to be with. She felt safe and at ease with him. And he had old-fashioned manners, the way he treated women.

"I'm thirty-four," he said, as the Rangers scored another goal and they both stood up and screamed. The Rangers won the game, and neither of them were hungry afterward after all they'd eaten, but he took her to a bar he knew that looked like an English pub, and they had a glass of wine, and talked for a long time.

The conversation was more relaxed than it had been at the Met. It made a difference that they were wearing jeans, and had been eating hot dogs and screaming for two hours. This was much more real. He told her that he came from a small town in Iowa and had two brothers. His parents were still married, and his father was the CFO of an insurance company, and his mother had stayed at home with them. He was the oldest child, had gone to the University of Iowa, and business school at Northwestern, and had been in the corporate world ever since. His brothers had remained small-town boys, and were both married and had kids. Although they were younger, they had been married for years. "I prefer a big city. My brothers think I'm crazy. They came to visit me here and hated it. I know that's hard to believe. How can anyone hate New York? I love it here."

"So do I," she said with a broad smile. "My brother moved to Vermont and I thought he would hate it, but he loves it. He lives there with his partner."

"Male or female partner?" he asked boldly, but she didn't mind.

"Male," she said simply. "They're having a baby in August."

"Are your parents okay about it?"

"My father died when I was six," she said matter-of-factly. "And my mother is worried. She thinks it's a lot of responsibility for them. I can't even imagine having kids yet." It was a lot of information for Peter to digest at once, but he had asked and she was candid with him. She was very much her own person, and even though she was shy, she was totally open about who she was, and he liked that about her too.

"It must have been hard growing up without a father," he said sympathetically.

"I think it was harder for my brothers. But my mother always made it okay for us. It bothered my twin brother sometimes. But my mom is terrific. She was a very hands-on mother, even though she had to work."

"What does she do?"

"She runs a high-end resale shop. And actually she just started an offshoot of it on the Internet. I think it's going to do really well," Julie said proudly. Peter could tell how close she was to her family—far more than he was to his. He only went home now once a year, if that, for Christmas. And if he had a good excuse, he skipped it entirely.

They had a second glass of wine and then he took her back to the Bowery in a cab, and she apologized for taking him so far out of his way. But he insisted he wanted to, and sounded as though he meant it. He kept the cab while he walked her to the door of her building, and she was glad he didn't pressure her to come up. She wouldn't have liked that. It was much too soon, and apparently he thought so too.

"Let's do it again soon," Peter said before he left her. "Not necessarily a hockey game, but dinner . . . something . . . I'll call you. Tonight was great." She thought so too.

She thanked him and he hugged her, and once she was through the door, he hopped in the cab, and they drove off.

She took the stairs two at a time in her combat boots, and let herself into her apartment. She had a text from Justin as soon as she walked in. She answered him even before she took off her hat and coat.

"How was your date?" he asked her.

"Teriffic," she wrote back, and as always she wrote it

with one "r" and two "f"s. Spelling was not her forte. Justin smiled when he saw it. And he was pleased she'd finally met someone she liked and had fun with on her date. He wanted her to be as happy as he was.

Chapter 12

When Bernard returned to New York, he stayed for ten days this time. He took a room at the Four Seasons, as he had before, but he stayed with Kate. It was fun doing things with him in New York, and they were both busy. He went to meetings with firms he was interested in investing in. And she was swamped with online sales, and she had to add items to their website almost every day. Their brand-new Internet business was already a huge success, and she could hardly keep up with their sales.

They ran into Liam one day when they went to a farmers market in the West Village, and he looked surprised to see them together. He called Kate about it the next day.

"Is something going on with you and Bernard?" he asked her, seeming confused and surprised, and she decided to be honest with him. She never lied to Liam, she just hadn't been ready to tell him yet. But their romance was as successful as her online business. And she and Bernard both felt as though they'd been together for years.

"Yes," she confessed. "We had dinner here a couple of times. And it started in Paris. I was going to tell you. It's still kind of new." Although it didn't feel it. And Liam cut to the chase.

"Is he married?" He had assumed that he was, wedding band or not.

"What makes you ask that?" She was startled by how astute he was, and wondered why he had asked the question.

"Frenchmen his age usually are. Unless they're widowed. They never get divorced. Or very, very few." Bernard had said as much himself.

"So he says. And yes, he's married, but he and his wife have an 'arrangement.' They're legally married, but lead separate lives, and have for years."

"That's what they all say," Liam said skeptically. "And then you find out that they're more married than you thought. Kate, be careful. I don't want you to get hurt." It sounded like a bad idea to him.

"Neither do I. But it seems to be true in his case. We went out every night in Paris, and he stayed with me. He didn't go home to her."

"Maybe she was away."

"Or maybe he's telling the truth. That's a possibility too." She was mildly annoyed at Liam for being such a cynic and raining on her parade. "Can't you be happy for me? I haven't had a man in my life in years."

"I just want it to be the right one. Not some smooth

operator who breaks your heart. Would you want this for one of your daughters?"

"Of course not. But I'm not a kid. And I think he's an honest man," she said defensively.

"In business, I'd agree with you. I don't know about the rest."

"We'll see." But she was having a great time with him. And she introduced him to Julie when she came to the store to help Kate upload merchandise photos to her website.

"I like him, Mom," she said when he went uptown for a meeting, and promised to be back in time to take her to dinner that night. "He's nice."

"I think so too," Kate said, smiling at her.

"Is it serious?" She wanted her mother to be happy too. She was seeing a lot of Peter White. He was the kindest man she'd ever met, and the most polite. He had kissed her, but she hadn't slept with him yet. He was very respectful of her and didn't want to rush.

"It's not serious yet," Kate answered. "He lives there. I live here. But for now it seems to work." But there was no question in Kate's mind. She was falling in love with him rapidly, more so every day.

"Would you ever move to Paris?" Julie looked worried when she asked her, and Kate shook her head.

"I couldn't live that far from all of you, and the store." Julie looked instantly relieved. She stayed for a while to help her mother but left before Bernard came back. He complimented her on her daughter that night.

"She liked you too," Kate said, smiling at him. And unlike Liam, Julie hadn't asked if he was married. It hadn't even occurred to her. And Kate wouldn't have admitted it to her, if she had. It was no one's business but theirs, especially here where no one knew him. As he put it, his legal status was an "administrative detail." She had told Liam and was sorry that she had. He had been so skeptical about Bernard after that.

By the time Bernard left, things were heating up before Izzie's wedding. Kate was organizing the final details. The invitations had gone out, and twenty-six people were going to be there. It was exactly what Izzie had wanted, and the perfect number for the house they'd rented. The first serious problem arose when Izzie asked Justin to give her away, and he refused.

"Are you kidding? You're my brother," she said, sounding deeply hurt. "Why not?"

"Because I think you're making a mistake and I don't want to help you do it." She was livid the moment she heard what he had to say.

"You're gay, not married, and having a baby with a surrogate, which is an even bigger mistake, and you're judging me?"

"I'm not judging you. I don't want to hand you over to a guy who has never had a job, and will probably never have one, and is completely out of place in your world. How can you think that's going to work?" He was being honest with her about what he thought.

"What business is it of yours who I decide to marry?" She didn't even care about his walking her down the aisle anymore, but she was furious about everything he'd said. Justin was a purist and always had been. He was true to himself, and wouldn't do something he believed was wrong, just to please her.

"If it works, I'll be happy for you, and I hope it does. But I don't know any other way to tell you that I'm worried about you except to refuse to give you away."

"Who made you Lord of the World, and so righteous? You're such an asshole. I think Mom is worried, and she's paying for the wedding and gave me the dress."

"I'm not your mother. And she doesn't want to lose you. I think anyone with a brain and eyes in their head would be worried about you and Zach." She wanted to tell him not to come to her wedding, but the truth was she wanted him there, and she knew that if she caused a rift in the family, it would break their mother's heart and she didn't want to do that to her. "I'm sorry, Izzie," he added, with regret.

"Don't give me that mealymouthed bullshit. And I think you're crazy to have a baby with a woman who may never give it up. You can't afford to spend ten years fighting her in court. And what if you and Richard break up?"

"That could happen to anyone. We'll deal with that if it happens. But we've been together for almost five years. You've been with Zach for six months. That's foolish right there. I don't care how hot and sexy he is, you don't marry someone you hardly know."

"I know enough." She had her own concerns about Zach, and she knew his history better than her brother did. But there had been no sign of drugs or bad behavior since his arrest in June, nine months before. And her family knew nothing about it. If they had, that would have been the last straw. It was hard enough selling them on the fact that he didn't work. When she talked to Zach about it, he kept promising to do something, but he hadn't yet.

After her rejection from Justin, she hung up and called Willie. He sounded surprised that she had asked him, but his answer was immediate.

"Sure, I'll give you away, if that's what you want. But why me? Why not Justin?" He didn't want to piss off his brother.

"We have a difference of opinion, about his baby and my future husband. You know what a prig he can be at times."

"Well, if you change your mind at the last minute, and you want him to do it, that's fine." Willie had no investment in who walked her down the aisle. He hated confrontation, but if Justin didn't mind, he was perfectly happy to give his sister away. He thought she was making a mistake too, but he would never have said it, and he figured it was her life. She was eight years older than he was, and she was a grown woman with the right to marry whom she chose. He hoped no one would ask him to choose sides between his brother and sister if the battle continued.

The next surprise happened a week before the wedding, when Julie called Izzie and asked if she could bring Peter as her date. They had been dating for six weeks by then, and were seeing a lot of each other. She was having a great time with him, and she was out with him almost every night.

"Is it important to you?" Izzie asked her. "Zach and I have never met him." Which felt a little odd to her, to have a stranger at their wedding in such a small group, but it was obvious Julie wanted him there.

"I'd like to have him with me if you don't mind too much." Her sister was so nice about it that Izzie agreed quickly.

"We'd love to meet him, and I guess my wedding is as good a place as any," she said warmly. Julie was such a gentle soul and asked for so little, she didn't want to disappoint her.

"Is there anything I can do to help you? I've been crazy busy at work, and spending time with Peter. I'm sorry I haven't asked before this." Julie had poor organizational skills and time got away from her, except at work. In her personal life, she was very fey.

"Don't worry about it. Mom and I have taken care of everything. Just come and have a good time, with your friend." Julie knew about Justin's refusal from him, but she hadn't said a word about it to Izzie. She didn't want to get caught in the middle, especially over something as sensitive as this.

*

Kate spent the day before the wedding at the house on Washington Square Park with Jessica, making sure that every detail had been attended to. A calligrapher had done the place cards and menus. Izzie and Zach had gone there a month before for a tasting of the meal and cake. Zach had brought remarkable wines from his grandmother's cellar, which he said were a gift from her. Zach's father had confirmed that he wasn't coming. He and his wife were in South Africa, going on safari and visiting friends. And Zach's mother had never responded to his calls or emails. Kate felt sorry for Zach. His family truly wasn't there for him, even for his wedding. It made her feel more sympathetic to him.

Izzie's dress was carefully put away in her mother's closet. And they were having the rehearsal dinner at her apartment that night. Everything was organized. And they were spending their honeymoon in Aspen. Zach's father had agreed to let them use his house, and Izzie had paid for the plane tickets, which her mother didn't know. And she had paid for a new tux for Zach.

The wedding wasn't extravagant, but it was going to be very pretty. She was going to carry a bouquet of lilies of the valley. And Kate had bought a brand-new navy satin Oscar de la Renta tea-length dress, and a very nice-looking beige silk suit for Grandma Lou. Julie was planning to wear a dress she had made herself. The ceremony was going to be at seven o'clock, the dinner at eight-thirty, and there was going to be dancing after dinner, in the second parlor, and Zach had hired a DJ he knew.

Kate would have loved to have Bernard with her, but Izzie had never met him, it was too soon in their relationship for him to meet her family, but she was planning to introduce him to them in the near future.

Kate got home at six o'clock, in time to bathe and dress for the rehearsal dinner. Kate was wearing a colorful Mexican top with jeans, with big turquoise earrings and gold sandals. They were expecting twenty people, and everyone had been told they could wear jeans. It was going to be an easy, relaxed evening, which was what the bridal couple wanted, and Zach was going to stay with a friend that night, so he wouldn't see the bride the next day before the wedding. Izzie was going to dress at her mother's, not at the rented house. A hairdresser and makeup artist had been arranged for Kate and both girls, and there were two cars to take them to the wedding. All the details were in place.

At eight-thirty that night, they were all helping themselves to the Mexican buffet and drinking margaritas. Izzie looked lovely in a simple pale peach dress. Everyone had fun and Julie had invited Peter for that night too. He was incredibly polite, and had kept a watchful eye on Julie all night, anxious to meet her every need. It seemed unusual to Kate. She had liked him better at the Met and he had seemed more sincere. He was trying too hard. He made a point of meeting everyone in the family, and spent an hour talking to Grandma Lou. He was a big hit, but as Kate watched him, she had an odd feeling when she saw him talking to her mother. He seemed determined to do the right thing and make a good impression, maybe too much so. She said something about it to Izzie when they met at the buffet.

"What do you think of Julie's friend?" she asked her in a whisper.

"He's perfect," Izzie said with unreserved approval.

"Too perfect?" Kate asked with a look of concern, and Izzie rolled her eyes.

"Oh, for God's sake, Mom. No one is ever going to be good enough for any of us, according to you." She wasn't joking. If she could find fault with someone as exemplary as Peter White, it was hopeless. She thought that their mother was obsessed with their well-being to an absurd degree.

"That's not true." Kate's antennae were up and she didn't know why she had a strange feeling. "I've been watching him talk to my mother for the last hour. That's a long time for a guy his age." And he had come in a suit, although he'd been told he could wear jeans. What was he trying to prove?

"We all love talking to Grandma Lou. She's telling him about her trip to China this summer. Maybe he just can't get away." Kate nodded, hoping that was true. She glanced at her future son-in-law then, who was the opposite extreme. He had come in torn jeans and a sleeveless undershirt with his biker boots, and he had refused to get a haircut for the wedding. But even looking like he'd been shipwrecked, he was a handsome man, and Izzie was wrapped around him like a snake all night.

The only tension all evening was between Izzie and Justin. She still hadn't forgiven him for not giving her away, and maybe never would. Everyone had a lot to drink, and they stayed till after midnight, and then Kate sent them all away. She didn't want them to be too hungover for the wedding. And Zach had had more margaritas than anyone at the party. Willie left with him in a cab, and dropped him off at the friend's house where he was staying, and Izzie went home alone for her last night as a single woman. She thanked her mother for the lovely evening before she left.

Kate tidied up after they had all gone home and the caterers had left, and she sat quietly in her living room, thinking about Izzie marrying Zach. She still didn't feel comfortable about it, and she hoped that Izzie was right and knew what she was doing. All of Kate's alarm bells sounded every time she saw him, and she thought her daughter was heading for disaster. The only thing Kate wanted as she headed to bed that night was not to be right about him. She prayed that she was wrong and Izzie would be happy.

Chapter 13

Izzie arrived at her mother's apartment at two o'clock the day of the wedding, and Julie shortly after. The two girls chatted quietly in the living room, and Kate sat with them. The makeup and hair people arrived at three, and at five-thirty Kate got the dress out, and carefully lifted it over Izzie's head with Julie's help. It took ten minutes to do up the buttons, and Kate put her own string of pearls around her daughter's neck as her "something borrowed," and one of Izzie's friends had given her a lace garter with a pale blue ribbon on it. So she was all set with the bridal traditions.

Kate and Julie went to get dressed while Izzie waited, and twenty minutes later they put her cap and veil on, and Kate stood back breathlessly to look at her. She had never seen such a beautiful sight as her daughter in her wedding gown. With her hair and makeup done, the dress looked even more spectacular on her than it had when she tried it on in the store.

Willie arrived at six-fifteen, and got into the first limousine with his sister to take her to the wedding. He looked very handsome in his dinner jacket and patent leather shoes, and Kate was proud of him. He seemed very grown up and manly as he helped his sister into the car. And then Kate and Julie got into the second car, and picked up Grandma Lou on the way. She was ready and waiting downstairs in her new beige suit, and had had her shimmering white hair done and cut for the occasion. Justin and Richard were meeting them at Washington Square Park, since Justin had no official function. And as previously planned, Izzie entered the house down a narrow alley through a back door, so Zach wouldn't see her when he arrived.

The guests arrived promptly, and were led into the living room on the second floor, where chairs had been placed for the ceremony. The judge was already waiting. Everyone was there by a quarter to seven, except the groom. Zach arrived looking harried and hungover at seven-thirty, half an hour late. Izzie was a nervous wreck by then and Kate was furious.

"I couldn't find my damn tie," he muttered to Justin, making his excuse. His friend where he had stayed had come with him, wearing a tuxedo jacket and jeans, and a heavy beard. Zach introduced him as Justin tied Zach's tie for him, since he didn't know how. They were just inside the front door on the main floor, while the wedding guests waited upstairs.

"At least he shaved," Justin whispered to Richard about Zach, as Zach went to stand beside the judge. He had no best man and had said he didn't need one. He had wanted to ask Willie, who was now giving the bride away, and Izzie had ordered him not to ask Justin, and didn't explain why, but Zach could see that she meant it. She didn't want Justin turning him down too. It was bad enough that he had refused her.

Izzie was waiting in a bedroom upstairs with Willie, and when the three-piece orchestra began to play classical music, she came down the stairs on her brother's arm, and Kate felt tears fill her eyes as she watched her. She knew she was crying as much for her fears for her, as for her beauty, and for the first time in a long time, she wished that Tom was at her side to see his daughter. Zach looked speechless as he watched her come down the stairs. His hair was in a long ponytail with his tuxedo, and his tie was crooked, but he had a look of innocence and wonder as he watched his future wife come down the stairs toward him, and there were tears in his eyes too. Willie handed her off to him with a solemn expression and Julie took her bouquet, and then they all took their seats for the brief ceremony. The judge made a very short wedding speech, and very rapidly pronounced them husband and wife, since there was nothing religious in the ceremony. And Zach looked like he was going to tear her clothes off when he kissed her.

"That's what this is all about," Grandma Lou whispered to her daughter, and Kate nodded, and had the feeling her mother was right, that it was all about sex between Izzie and Zach, although it was ironic to hear a woman her age say it. It was clear to both women that Izzie and Zach had a passionate physical relationship that had brought them to this point, but it didn't seem like a foundation for marriage.

When the judge introduced them to the assembled company as Mr. and Mrs. Holbrook, a cheer went up in the room, and champagne was poured and handed out, and the reception began.

It all went off impeccably, as Kate stood off to one side, chatting with Liam while observing everything that was going on. Maureen was there in an elegant navy silk suit. And a few minutes later Izzie came to thank her mother for the generous wedding. It was small, but every part of it was perfect, and Kate was pleased about that, and that her daughter was happy. But the evening was not without its concerns. Zach was visibly drunk before dinner, made an incoherent speech after they cut the cake, and was rowdy on the dance floor. He was the wild man on the floor, glued to his wife, and fortunately didn't know that he was supposed to dance with his mother-in-law. No formalities were observed since it was so unusual for the groom to have no family there to support him. Justin danced with his mother instead, and growled in her ear the entire time about how foolish Izzie was.

"She loves him," Kate said calmly, hoping for the best since Izzie had gone through with it.

"That's no excuse to marry someone like him," Justin said sternly. He looked somber and strained throughout the evening, but after a few glasses of champagne, Izzie came over and kissed him, which softened him a little.

"I'm pissed at you, but you're still my brother," she said, wanting to forgive him, and he set his glass down and danced with her.

"I just want you to be happy," he said to her and meant it.

"Then be nice to Zach. We're the only family he has here," she said sadly and Justin nodded. It was a depressing thought. And before they sat down to dinner, Kate had a text from Bernard, hoping that all was going well. It was two in the morning for him, and he said he had stayed up to text her, and didn't want to interrupt her during the ceremony or at dinner. She texted him back gratefully that everything was fine and she missed him.

The food was delicious, and after dinner, once the dancing started, Zach had taken off his coat and tie and unbuttoned his shirt, and then he did a lewd dance with Izzie. And when they cut the wedding cake, he planted his face in it. Everyone laughed, but they were a little shocked as well. And his speech was mostly slurred allusions to their sex life, which Izzie cut short. He was like a big exuberant boy going wild, not a man taking on the responsibilities of marriage, but Izzie didn't seem to mind. She was willing to forgive him everything, as Justin looked green, and Kate's heart ached for her.

The festivities ended at two A.M. as the contract required, and Izzie and Zach went back to her apartment in the limousine, after she kissed all of her family good-bye. Zach was almost too drunk to walk by then, and had to be helped into the car. And after they left, Kate found his jacket, tie, and one shoe that he had left behind. It made her sad as she folded the jacket and put it and the shoe next to her bag, with the tie. It was not the marriage she would have wanted for Izzie, or the man. His friend had left hours earlier, drunk in a cab. And the rest of the family climbed into the remaining limousine to go back to Kate's apartment for more champagne. At Grandma Lou's request, they dropped her off on the way. She said she'd had enough celebration and was tired.

"You did a terrific job, Mom," Justin said and put an arm around her, but he looked sad. This wasn't what he wanted for Izzie either, and he wondered what would come next, what surprises would be in store for her. There were sure to be some with Zach, or even many.

Willie kept the conversation from becoming morose, and Peter told Kate that it was the best wedding he'd ever been to, which they all knew was a lie. But Julie looked happy with him, and he'd been pleasant to everyone all night, which was a relief while Zach misbehaved.

Justin and Richard left at three, and Peter took Julie home, to spend the night with her. Willie fell asleep on the couch, and his mother left him there. It had been a long night for them all. And when she finally got to bed, she lay down and let out a sigh of relief. It was over. She had done the best she could, and hoped it was enough to give her daughter memories she would cherish, of a night Kate thought should never have happened.

*

Zach was sound asleep on their bed by then, still dressed. He had passed out the instant they came home, and Izzie carefully unbuttoned her dress herself, and laid it over a chair with her veil. She had felt like a princess all night, and she didn't really mind that Zach had gotten out of hand, as long as he was happy and had enjoyed their wedding. She noticed then that he was wearing only one shoe and wondered what had happened to the other one. She hadn't seen it in the car that drove them home. And then she lay down next to him, and set their alarm for the next morning. They were flying to Aspen on a noon flight and had to leave the house by ten. She hoped that Zach would make it. And then she closed her eyes and fell asleep. She was Mrs. Zach Holbrook. She smiled as she drifted off to sleep with her arms around him.

*

Zach was surprisingly fresh in the morning, when Izzie woke him at eight to get ready for the plane. He hadn't packed yet, and she helped him, as he poured them each a glass of champagne for breakfast. She had a headache from the night before, but he said it was bad luck to refuse so she drank it, and then he pulled her back into bed.

"Wait a minute . . . you're my wife now . . . you can't refuse me any time I want to make love." She laughed at what he said.

"What if we miss the plane?" she said sensibly.

"Then we'll take the next one. There is always another plane." They were flying to Denver, and then switching to a smaller flight into Aspen.

He made love to her, and they were both happy and sated when it was over. Izzie noticed that it was nine-thirty by then, and they had half an hour to get ready. She dragged him into the shower with her, and he wanted to make love to her again, and this time she wouldn't let him.

"We have two weeks in Aspen. We can stay in bed the whole time," she said, and he liked the idea.

Miraculously, she got him dressed, packed, and into the cab by ten-fifteen. She had packed her own bags two days before, and they got to the airport at eleven, just in time to check in.

He slept on the plane all the way to Denver, and by then her family was having lunch at Da Silvano, and Peter was still with Julie. He was exceptionally nice to Grandma Lou again and attentive to Kate. He talked to Justin about their baby, and to Willie about football and hockey. And everyone tried to stay off the subject of Zach and his performance at the wedding. He was family now, and out of respect for Izzie, they had to at least try to like him.

All Kate could think of to say to her mother when the others had all left after lunch was that she thought Peter tried too hard. It gave her an odd feeling.

"We must be a daunting group to come into. Everyone has their opinions. You can't blame him for trying," Louise said benevolently, but he had been nicest to her. "And he's good to Julie." It was true, but Kate hadn't liked it when he laughed when Julie read something wrong on the menu, and he had teased her. He obviously didn't know she was dyslexic and sensitive about it, but Julie hadn't said anything and laughed with him. Justin had noticed it too and stared at him, and then they changed the subject.

"Is it always going to be like this," Kate said sadly, "with people we don't like marrying the children? Do you suppose any of them will marry someone decent?" She looked seriously disheartened.

"We all like Richard," her mother reminded her, "and I think Peter could be wonderful for Julie. He's the best man she's ever gone out with."

"Maybe you're right," Kate said, trying to still her fears. Her nerves were just jangled.

"And Zach's not evil, he's just unruly and badly behaved, and he enjoys it, like a poorly trained dog." Kate laughed at the colorful image. Grandma Lou was right.

Maybe he was harmless, but also boisterous and embarrassing. The only one who didn't seem bothered by it was Izzie.

"And God knows who Willie will come home with." Kate sighed.

"A whole chorus line at some point, I suspect. I don't think we have to worry about him for a long time. And he'll probably settle down with a lovely girl we'll all like."

"That would be a pleasant change," Kate said to her mother wryly.

"All parents worry," Grandma Lou reminded her. "I worried about you too. We loved Tom, but he was in school, you had no money, you got pregnant instantly and kept having babies. I didn't see how you were going to make it. But you managed, even when he died. Sometimes it works out despite the odds. All you can do is hope once they're in it and be there for them. You can't change it." Her mother's words were wise as they left the restaurant.

"What are you doing today, Mother?"

"I'm going to a movie with Frances this afternoon, and then we're going to dinner."

"You're a better man than I," Kate said, looking exhausted. "I don't know where you get the energy. I'm going home to bed."

"You worry about them more than I do," Louise said, smiling at her. "That's exhausting. It's normal, they're your children. I'm just their grandmother. I get the fun part." But Kate knew she worried about them too, but not as much. She just didn't admit it. "And don't get yourself worked up about Peter now. I think he's a very good man, and good for her." Grandma Lou seemed confident about him, which reassured Kate.

"He made fun of her when she read the menu," she said, with a muscle clenching in her jaw at the memory. Julie had been teased in school for years when she couldn't read, which nearly broke Kate's heart for her. And Justin had gotten in countless fights in school on her behalf.

"He doesn't know, and Julie didn't look upset. Don't borrow trouble." Grandma Lou looked stern as she said it.

"I won't. You're right. I just don't want them getting hurt," she said with tears bright in her eyes. It had been painful for her watching Izzie marry Zach the day before, fearing how it would turn out.

"You can't stop them from getting hurt," Grandma Louise said sensibly. "Life will hurt them. Hard things will happen to them, as they have to all of us. And they'll survive it. You can't protect them forever." It was good advice, but as Kate walked back to her apartment alone a few minutes later, she wished that she could protect them from the painful things that would happen to them. And even more so from their own bad choices. But she knew it didn't work that way. She only wished it would. And now they were all adults, or so they said.

Chapter 14

Bernard suggested that Kate meet him in St. Bart's the week after the wedding. They hadn't seen each other in five weeks and had been missing each other. She had a mountain of work to do at the store, especially with their online business now, and they had just hired another assistant whom Jessica was training, and Kate thought she should be there too. But she wanted to see him, and agreed to go. She had been feeling down ever since the wedding. And after St. Bart's he had business in Miami and he wanted her to join him.

She told her mother she was leaving and meeting a friend and Louise thought it was an excellent idea. Kate looked exhausted, and her mother didn't ask who she was meeting, since Kate didn't volunteer it. Louise never pried, but she hoped it was a man. She thought it would do Kate good if it was.

She took a plane to St. Martin two days later, and a tiny puddle jumper from there to St. Bart's. The second flight was bumpy and the landing frightening, but she was so happy to be meeting Bernard that she didn't care how bad the trip was. He was waiting for her at the airport and held her tightly in his arms. He could see all the strain and sorrow of the past month in her eyes. And all he wanted to do now was make it better. He took her to the hotel where he had booked a villa with a private pool, and half an hour after she got there, she was in a bikini in the pool and he was with her. And it was as though they'd never been apart. They picked up right where they'd left off, talking and laughing and sharing confidences, and she told him all about the wedding, her fears for Izzie, and her qualms about Peter. He was not only her lover, but Bernard was becoming her confidant and best friend.

"I don't think you need to worry about Julie's new man. He sounds like he's just trying too hard to impress you."

"He's so perfect he unnerves me, and he crawls all over my mother."

"She probably enjoys it." He laughed and Kate visibly relaxed from his reassurance. She needed that desperately. She had been carrying all the heavy burdens alone, as always. "I'd like to meet her one day," he said about her mother.

"You will," she promised him. "All in good time."

"Does she know about me?" he asked, looking serious for a moment, and Kate shook her head.

"No, not yet. I thought it was too soon."

"And I'm married." He read her mind and finished the sentence for her. "She might not be as shocked as you think, from everything you've told me about her. She might just be fine with it." But Kate thought it unlikely, knowing her mother. There were some things she didn't tolerate and would never approve of, unfaithful husbands being one of them, and top of the list. And she was still Kate's mother and worried about her too. It was instinctive.

"I'm not ready to find out," Kate said. He nodded and didn't argue with her.

The vacation in St. Bart's with him was just what Kate needed, and by the time they left four days later, to fly to Miami, she felt like a new woman, or the old woman in better shape, emotionally and physically. She was no longer so upset about Izzie. Bernard was right. The deed was done. Now it was up to Izzie. And if she'd made a mistake, she would either have to live with it or correct it. It made Kate realize again that men were so much more pragmatic than women.

When they landed in Miami, they went directly to the Eden Roc hotel where he had taken a palatial suite, and she left him to go shopping while he worked. She had a good time at the high-end shopping mall at Bal Harbour, and enjoyed cruising all the stores, until she met him back at the hotel for dinner that night. And afterward they swam in the pool on the way to their room. The next day it was hot and sunny, and she lay on their terrace to soak up the sun. He came back to the suite at lunchtime to make love and have lunch with her. It was a piece of heaven whenever she was with him.

After four days in Miami, he flew back to New York with her and spent another week there. It was late May by the time he had to leave, and on their last night, Kate asked him what he was doing that summer.

"We rent a house in Sardinia every year for August," he said casually. "The children come and go with friends."

"You and the children?" she asked, trying to understand what the plan was, although she wasn't trying to intrude.

"The family," he said vaguely.

"How many of you?" she asked more specifically.

"It varies."

"Will your wife be there?" Kate finally asked what she wanted to know and he hadn't told her.

"Some of the time. And I'll be there some of the time, with the kids."

"Do you take turns, or are you there together?" She was frowning as she asked him. A cloud had just passed in front of the sun.

"What difference does it make? We're not together even when we're under the same roof. We're separate people."

"You still take vacations with her?" Kate asked, looking unhappy. "You never told me that before."

"I don't even think about it. We hardly speak to each other. It makes no difference to either of us."

"It makes a difference to me. I don't like the idea of your going on vacation with her." As she said it, something Liam had said rang in her ears. That married men never seemed married, until you realized that they were more married than they claimed. It was beginning to sound that way, for the first time, and a shiver ran through her.

"We do it every year," Bernard said again, as though that made it okay. But it didn't for Kate.

"But you didn't have me. Now you do," she said pointedly, and he didn't look pleased.

"You can't expect me to give up time with my children. You of all people know how important that is. That's one of the reasons I love you, because you're such a good mother." It sounded like bullshit to her.

"Do your children know about your 'arrangement' with your wife?"

"We don't need to discuss it with them. They live it, and have for many years. They understand." But how much could they understand if their parents still took vacations together every summer? Maybe they just thought he was busy the rest of the time, for work.

"Since you lead such separate lives, wouldn't you rather have separate vacations with the children? It must be stressful being together."

"We're very polite." He smiled at Kate. And very

French, she thought. It was the first time he had seriously upset her, and she was quiet for the rest of the evening, which disturbed him too. He didn't want to spoil the time they had together, especially right before he was leaving, and he had no plans to return until late June. "Don't think about it. What are you doing this summer?"

"Working."

"You don't go on holiday with your children?" In France everyone had five weeks off, by law, either in July or August. In the States, most people worked, except for a week or two, just as she did.

"I used to go away with them, when they were kids, until they finished college. Now, none of them have time. They can't get time off from their jobs. And they have their own plans, for a few days here and there, over long week-ends, like on the Fourth of July and Labor Day, which they don't spend with me."

"How sad," he said sympathetically. "Maybe we could meet somewhere in July." Because he went to Sardinia in August with his wife. That was clear to her now, and she didn't like it.

"I don't want to be part of a shift, Bernard," she said pointedly. She had never felt that way before, but they had only been together for three months, since February. She had never been through Christmas with him, or a summer. She wondered if he spent Christmas with his wife too, and suspected now that he did. It was part of the "arrangement." He could do what he wanted and lead his own life as long as he came home for major holidays and summer vacations. It was an arrangement she didn't like.

"You're not part of a shift," he insisted. "You're the woman I love."

"And she's your wife," Kate said with a determined look, and there was anger in it.

"Why are you making trouble about this now when we're so happy?" He looked like an innocent victim as he said it. And she was the culprit and attacker. He seemed wounded.

"I'm not going to be happy in August when you're with her." In fact, she was going to be miserable and she knew it.

"I can arrange to be away for a few days when the children aren't there," he said, trying to mollify her.

"I can't get away then, and that's not the point. I don't want to share you with her. This isn't joint custody."

"I have to do the best I can in the circumstances," he said firmly. And it was obvious that he was not going to change his plans for her. He was going to do what he did every year, and vacation for a month in Sardinia with his wife and family. And there was no part for her to play in that. His wife had the upper hand in August. That was her time with Bernard, not Kate's. "We'll work something out," he said placatingly, but Kate had understood, and it did not work for her. She was chilly with him for the rest of the night, and they did not make love before he left. She couldn't. She was too upset about his plans for August.

He kissed her when he left for the airport the next day, and neither of them mentioned their conversation of the night before, but it had taken a toll, and she was still mulling it over after he left. She didn't tell Liam when she saw him. She didn't want to admit to him that he was right. But in her heart of hearts, she knew he was, unless something changed. Bernard was still more married than he admitted. And that changed things for her. She loved him, but not enough to share him with another woman. Maybe his wife did, but she didn't. And she wasn't French, she was American, and the theory that half of someone else's husband was better than none didn't work for her. She had been a willing participant until now, but he hadn't explained the situation to her accurately, if he was still vacationing with his wife for a month every summer. And she knew now that August was going to be hell month for her, knowing where he was and with whom.

It was a heavy weight on her heart when she went back to work when he was gone. He had done wonderful things for her business, but she realized now that sooner or later, he would break her heart. And it was a price she was not willing to pay, for him or anyone else, no matter how much she loved him.

*

Izzie and Zach had a blissful honeymoon in Aspen. The house was enormous and very luxurious, and had a large staff. His father lived well off the family trust, a lot better than Zach did, who had nothing. It angered Izzie when she saw it. Why were they unkind to him? It wasn't fair.

They went for long walks, made love all the time, fished in a stream, went on hikes, and browsed through the shops in town. The restaurants were excellent, but she had to pay for every meal, and she thought it was embarrassing for him, so they cooked at home most of the time, when the help left at night and they were alone in the kitchen. Sometimes they ate naked after they made love.

They came back from their honeymoon happy and relaxed, and Izzie had to leap straight into two big projects and work late almost every night. The honeymoon was over and Zach complained about it every night when she got home. But there was nothing she could do about it. She had to work. She used it as an opportunity to try to convince him to find a job, but he didn't like that idea either. He wanted her to stay home and play and she couldn't.

"We're married now, but I never see you anymore," he said plaintively, and as the days went by, he got more and more bored and restless, and he was beginning to worry her.

She was in an important meeting with the managing partner of the law firm on one of their big projects when

Zach called her one afternoon. Her secretary said it was urgent, so she left the conference room and took the call. It was Zach, in tears. He'd been arrested, and was in jail. Her heart started pounding the minute he said it.

"I'm still on probation. They'll send me to prison for a probation violation. You have to do something."

"I can't right now," she said in a low voice so no one would hear her. "I can't leave the meeting I'm in. I'll come as soon as I'm through. Have they set bail?"

"No," he said, crying like a child on the other end.

"What are the charges?" She hoped it was something minor, or he was going to be in serious trouble, and there would be nothing she could do.

"Possession," he said in a choked voice.

"Of what?"

"Coke." He was still crying.

"With intent to sell?"

"I think so," he said miserably. "But it was very little."

"For chrissake, Zach, what did they book you for? You know damn well what the charges are."

"Okay, yes, with intent to sell. I never see you anymore. I was bored. I bought some coke from a guy I know. I wasn't going to sell it." No, he was going to use it, out of boredom, which was almost as bad.

"How did you get caught? Did someone squeal?"

"No, I ran a red light, and they stopped me. They ran my license and saw that I'm on probation, so they searched the car for drugs and weapons. And they found it. I had it sitting on the front seat." He had driven one of the cars his grandmother kept in the garage.

"How could you be so stupid?" she said in a tone of pure fury. "You know that you risk prison if you get in trouble again. Shit, I don't even know if I can get you out this time. I have to go back to the meeting. I'll be there as soon as I can. But they may not let me bail you out until tomorrow if they haven't set bail yet, and if they put a hold on you because you're on probation, we're screwed."

"Get me a lawyer, then," he said, starting to get angry.

"I am a lawyer, you idiot. I represented you last time. I'll see you in a while," she said and hung up and went back to the meeting. It lasted until seven P.M. and as soon as it ended, she flew out of the building and got a cab, and went to the jail. And just as she had suspected, they hadn't set bail, so he had to stay there for the night. She saw him in a little cubicle, and told him she'd be back in the morning. But she had a client meeting at eleven and had to prepare for it. This was a nightmare in her life.

She lay awake all night, thinking about him and wondering what they could do, so the court would keep him on probation. She'd have to pull out all the stops, call in every favor, and try all the bells and whistles she could think of to keep him out of jail, and she was not sure she could. She'd been able to pull a rabbit out of a hat before because it was his first arrest. This was different.

She was at the jail at eight o'clock the next morning, and a hearing had been set for nine A.M. to set bail. She put down her name as the attorney of record representing him and disclosed that they were married to be totally aboveboard, and they allowed him to walk into court with her. They had different names, since she hadn't had time to change any of her ID yet, so that helped her seem more credible. And thank God they hadn't put a probation hold on him yet. She was hoping to bail him out before they did.

He was established in court as not being a flight risk once again. Bail was set at fifty thousand dollars, and she had to pay five thousand of it in order to have him released, and then the judge noticed that he was on probation and asked the bailiff if there was a hold on him, in which case he couldn't leave. Izzie held her breath while they checked, and miraculously they hadn't issued one yet, and forty-five minutes later, she had bailed him out, and they were in a cab to go back to the apartment. She read him the riot act when they got there. She told him he couldn't do it again, *ever,* and that he would ruin her life and his own if he did.

"I know, I know, I was stupid . . . I'm sorry. I won't do it again," he promised, and looked deeply remorseful.

"Great. I buy it, but the judge won't." Zach went to take a shower then, and she called the assistant DA assigned to his case before, and was straightforward with him and begged him not to revoke Zach's probation. She thought it was best to be honest with him, so a sheriff didn't show up at their door.

"You're still representing him?" the assistant DA asked her, surprised. "I thought you were assigned to it pro bono last year."

"I was," she confirmed.

"So why are you back on the case? Are you a glutton for punishment?" He was laughing as he said it.

"Apparently. I married him a month ago."

"Oh, God, and you're acting as his attorney on the case?"

"I am." They both knew it was legal to do so, although unusual.

"Tell me why I shouldn't revoke his probation and send him straight to prison?" He was serious about that and not laughing anymore. He felt sorry for her, but he wasn't going to get in trouble to help her. And whatever he did, he'd be doing for her, not the defendant. She was a straight shooter and a good attorney, and he liked her.

"Because I'm begging you not to," she said in a choked voice. "Sending him to prison is not going to help anyone. He's an idiot, not a criminal." They both knew that was true too. There was a long pause at the other end. "He's willing to go to rehab," she volunteered in a moment of creativity, sounding desperate. "He's never done that before. This was a slip. Give me time to find a program.

He'll stay as long as you want." The DA was quiet as he listened.

"All right, I won't make any moves on his probation for now, while you find a rehab for him. I'll consider it, but you've got a mess on your hands." The assistant DA had brought the charges up on his computer, and he could see that the amount of cocaine was small and probably for personal use. The charge of intent to sell wouldn't stick. "They're going to send him away this time, unless you can do some mighty fancy footwork to convince the judge," he warned her. "You did a good job for him last time, getting him to plead and getting him probation. You're going to need a sympathetic judge to keep him out of prison and send him to rehab." Izzie fervently hoped the judge would let Zach do that. Rehab was their only hope.

"Do you have a time for the arraignment yet on your computer?" she asked him.

"Tomorrow. Four P.M. Can you be there?"

"I'll have to be," she said seriously. She wasn't going to ask him to change it and annoy him further.

"Good luck, counselor. I'll see you in court, if they assign me to the case."

"Thank you," she said, sounding very subdued, and when Zach came out of the shower, she told him not to leave the apartment, and that if he got in trouble again, she'd kill him, and almost meant it. She told him that he would have to go to rehab, if the judge agreed to keep him on probation and out of prison. Zach looked horrified at the thought.

"You mean like for thirty days?"

"Could be six months or a year. However long they want. It beats three to five years in prison for a second offense."

"I can't do that," he said as tears filled his eyes again.

"You should have thought of that before." She felt sick and livid, and she was about to be late for her client meeting. "And if you do it again, after this, they'll put you away for good," she told him. This was no joke.

He looked badly shaken, and she didn't say another word to him. He lay down on the bed, and turned on the TV with the remote when she left. He hadn't said a word, as Izzie closed the door firmly behind her and rang for the elevator. She just prayed the judge would agree to Zach going to rehab. If not, her husband was going to prison for several years. And she could just imagine what her family would say. She was half an hour late for her meeting, had a long day at the office after that, and when she got home that night, she expected him to be subdued, but he wasn't. He'd been drinking all day, and he was drunk and surly with her. She was angry at him for the rest of the evening, and she stayed out of their bedroom, and when she went back in he had passed out and was sound asleep. She lay awake for hours, worrying about the arraignment the next day. She needed Zach to make a good show, and she wasn't sure he was up to it.

She left for the office in the morning without saying goodbye to him, but she had already told him that she would pick him up for the arraignment. She would be there for him at three, and it was a formality for him to plead guilty or not guilty, and she was going to propose rehab to the judge. The faster they got him there, the better it would look, and it would impact if he was found in violation and sent to jail.

Izzie spent the morning in her office at her computer, looking up rehabs instead of working. There was a great one in Arizona, others in Minnesota and Michigan, a good one in New Hampshire, one in Connecticut, and one in Queens that looked grim but was close. The one in Arizona looked like a country club. But it was still rehab, which would sound like jail to Zach.

She got back to the apartment on time, and was relieved to find Zach awake, clean, shaved, and wearing a suit. And he looked scared stiff. The prospect of prison had woken him up. At last.

They rode to the courthouse in a cab, and were in the courtroom on time. Izzie was the attorney of record, and the assistant DA she had called had gotten himself assigned to the case, as a favor to her.

The arraignment was routine. Zach pleaded not guilty. And she managed to get the "intent to sell" charge dropped, because the quantity was minimal. So all he was charged with was possession of a small amount of cocaine. But it was still enough to get his probation revoked, and for him to be sent away. Zach had admitted to her that he had already used most of the coke when he got caught. The judge warned Zach that he could revoke his probation and send him straight to prison then and there. And then Izzie suggested rehab, and submitted the name of the one in Queens. She had called them that morning. They had a bed for Zach, and had several court-mandated cases. They had told her they could take him that night and she relayed the information to the judge, along with the fact that Zach had never missed an appointment with his probation officer. The assistant DA made no objection to rehab. Zach was given a court date for his case two months later in August, which Izzie planned to get postponed, and the judge mandated Zach to the rehab in Queens for three months, with a possible extension for another six to nine. Izzie felt relief wash over her like a tidal wave, as the judge banged his gavel hard and called the next case. Izzie strode across the courtroom to thank the assistant DA and he told her he was satisfied for now. He assumed that Zach would eventually plead guilty when his case came up. And then she went back to where Zach was standing, picked up her briefcase, and he followed her out. She didn't stop until they were on the steps, and he looked confused.

"Okay, explain it to me in plain English. What just went on in there?"

"You're going to rehab," she said coldly.

"When?" He looked terrified.

"Tonight."

"For how long?"

"Three months. Could be longer, up to nine months or a year. You got damn lucky in there," she said as they started down the steps to hail a cab.

"Are you crazy? Three months in rehab, and maybe a year? That's like going to jail."

"Great," she said in a fury, as they stopped a taxi and she turned to him. "Then go back inside and enlist for three to five years in prison. But don't come back to me when you're done. You need to clean up your act so you don't do this again. I can't do this with you every six months. If you don't go to rehab, I'm done, and so are you."

They rode back to the apartment in silence. She called the rehab facility and then helped him pack. He didn't want to go that night but he had no other choice. If he wasn't there by the next morning, the judge could revoke his probation and send him to prison after all.

At nine P.M., they were at the grim rehab program in Queens. Zach was looking daggers at Izzie, but by ten o'clock he'd been checked in and had a room assignment with three other men. When Izzie was informed that she couldn't see or communicate with him for thirty days, Zach looked shocked at the news. This was no country club facility, but it was an acceptable alternative to jail.

"She's my wife," he insisted.

"I don't care if she's the Virgin Mary. No calls or visitors for thirty days," they told him. Zach gave Izzie a forlorn kiss goodbye and then, with his backpack over his shoulder and a woebegone expression, he disappeared through a door. She walked out to a waiting cab and burst into tears the minute she got in. It had been a hellish forty-eight hours, but she had saved his ass. Again. And she had a lonely few months ahead of her. After a month, he could come home for visits. But until then, she would be alone. And the final blow was that the judge had sent an additional order to the rehab program, ordering Zach to wear an electronic bracelet on his ankle for the next year, so the police could monitor his whereabouts at all times.

When she got back to the apartment, she lay on her bed thinking about him, and knew she had rough times ahead. And when he got out of rehab, the probation department would want him to get a job and go to work. Zach Holbrook was about to enter the real world. But at least he wasn't in jail.

She didn't hear from Zach for a month after he entered rehab, and in some ways it was a relief. She saw him for the first time for an hour on a Sunday afternoon at the rehab with all the other visitors, and he took her in his arms and held her. He kept apologizing profusely for everything he'd done and telling her how much he loved her. They were going to let him come home for an afternoon the following weekend.

Izzie had avoided her family for the past month claiming she was busy working on a big merger, so she wouldn't have to explain Zach's absence. It had been a miserable month for both of them. But she believed him when he said he'd never do it again. Their joint life, their marriage, and her sanity depended on it.

Chapter 15

Grandma Lou left on her long-awaited trip to China with her friend Frances on the first of August. Their first stop was to be Hong Kong. Kate and Julie took them to the airport, and Louise was so excited she could hardly contain herself, while Frances was as calm and passive as ever, and might have been going to Boston for the weekend. They took one suitcase each, and each of them carried a backpack with what they needed on the plane. Kate knew that Frances always took an extensive supply of medicines with her, in case one of them got sick. Louise thought it was unnecessary and ridiculous. But they both looked spry as they strode toward the plane after they went through security.

"Grandma really is brave, isn't she?" Julie commented admiringly. She wouldn't have had the courage to travel so far away at that age, and Kate said she wouldn't either, but these trips were the greatest joy in her mother's life.

Julie and Kate chatted on the ride back into the city, and Julie said that she and Peter were going to Maine for the weekend to stay with friends of his who had a sailboat.

She was sorry they weren't driving, but were flying to Bangor. She would have liked to stop and see Justin on the way. The baby was due in less than four weeks.

"How's she doing?" Kate asked, referring to the surrogate.

"Justin says she's huge, and can't wait to have it. This one is bigger than all her other babies."

"I still can't understand how a woman can do that," Kate said with a stern look. "Rent her body out to have someone's baby, for money, and just hand it over when it's born."

"I guess the money she gets makes a big difference for her own kids." Julie thought it was strange too, but she was happy for her brother that it was working out so far. The two boys were wildly excited, and had been decorating the nursery for weeks. Richard had painted it three shades of pink. Justin and Richard had found out at the five-month sonogram that it was a girl, and they were thrilled. Neither of them was into ball sports or rugged activities and they had said they didn't know what they'd do if it was a boy.

"How's Peter?" Kate asked her.

"He's fine, busy, he just got a big promotion, so he's happy." She looked peaceful and content in the relationship. They had been going away on weekends since the beginning of the summer. Julie's whole life had changed because of him. She was much more open and social, willing to meet new people and do new things, and she wasn't constantly at work or isolated in her apartment.

"How's your French friend?" she asked her mother. She hadn't heard Kate talk about him in weeks. And in fact, Kate hadn't seen him in just over two months. They were both busy, and she was still angry about his summer vacation. He had planned to come to New York in June, but had to cancel at the last minute. She got the feeling he was avoiding her, and she needed a break, now that she realized he still spent his holidays with his wife.

"He's fine." But her jaw tensed as she said it and Julie noticed. "He's on vacation in Italy with his kids for the month. The French take long vacations."

"Are you going over to see him?" Julie asked hesitantly. Her mother didn't say much about him, and she didn't want to be nosy or rude.

"I'm too busy this month. We're expanding the website again. I need to be here to work with the IT people and figure out what we want to put on it. And I'd like to be here when Justin has the baby," she said quietly. Grandma Lou had been disappointed that she'd miss the baby's birth, but planned to see the baby as soon as she got back.

Kate dropped Julie off at her apartment in the Bowery and headed to her store. Saturday was a busy day at Still Fabulous.

*

Justin and Richard were dropping by to check on Shirley every day. They brought her fruit and fresh vegetables when they went to farmers markets, fresh eggs, or treats for her kids. They couldn't stay away and miss the thrill of watching their baby grow inside her day by day. They went to her weekly doctor's appointments with her during the last month. They listened to the heartbeat and she let them touch her enormous belly so they could feel their daughter kick. She was an active baby, and Shirley admitted that she was ready to have her. She wanted her body back. She was hoping to deliver early, and went for long walks every afternoon. Her kids wanted their mom back too. Shirley said several times in the home stretch that she wasn't sure if she'd do it again. Two of her own and two surrogate babies felt like enough to her. She had done her good deed for the world, and the two men were eternally grateful to her. No matter how much they had paid her, she was doing something unimaginably wonderful for them. They had already agreed to schedules as to who would get up with the baby on what nights. Justin was going to take care of the baby in the daytime while Richard was at work, and he'd do his writing at night when Richard got home. They had it all worked out.

Shirley's due date was two days away, when one of her boys slipped on a dock at the lake at day camp and broke his arm. Day camp was one of the advantages she could provide for them as a result of what Justin and Richard were paying her. Jack was out with the truck, and she called Justin and asked for a ride to the hospital. He went to pick her up, and one of the counselors had already brought her son Billy in to the ER. He was crying and holding his arm when Justin and his mother got there. He stopped crying after the doctor set it, and they were walking across the parking lot when a gush of water splashed onto the ground and Shirley looked surprised when she looked down. She hadn't felt anything before that, and it was totally unexpected at that moment. Her water had just broken.

"Oh my God, what is that?" Justin asked, suddenly panicked. "Is something wrong?"

"My water just broke." It was still pouring down her legs and the asphalt around her was drenched.

"Should we go back inside?" Justin said, as Billy ran around them. He was feeling a lot better with his cast, and Justin had already signed it with a funny face in bright colors.

"No, I'll go home for a while. It takes time to start after that." It had taken hours before. "I'll call the doctor when I get home. Labor probably won't start till tonight, or tomorrow." Justin looked dubious, and she had him put a towel on the seat before she got into his car. They were at her house five minutes later. She was talking and laughing as she got out of the car, and Billy ran ahead of her to show his father and brother his cast. Justin saw Shirley suddenly grip the door of the car, and she could no longer talk.

"What just happened?"

"Your daughter's on her way." She smiled at him. She was totally calm and had been through it three times before. She went inside to call the doctor and Justin called Richard to tell him that Shirley's water had broken, and she was starting to have pains. He promised to call him back after she spoke to the doctor. Shirley was talking to her doctor and saying she'd only had one pain so far but it was a good one that felt like it was ripping her guts out, as she described it, and then she stopped talking suddenly, and had another one while the doctor waited. "They're pretty strong," she admitted, as Justin and Jack watched her and she sat down. She had two more in the next five minutes after she hung up. The doctor said she was at the hospital, and to come in any time to get checked if she wanted. But Shirley said she knew what was happening and didn't need to.

"It's starting a lot faster than last time," Jack commented, while Billy played in the front yard. She and Jack had already agreed that he would stay home with the boys when she delivered. Justin and Richard wanted to be at the birth, and she had told them they could. And Jack didn't need to be there, this wasn't their baby and it wasn't a special moment for them. It was a job, albeit an unusual one, but she didn't want too many people in the room, the doctor and a nurse and the baby's two fathers were enough, and she knew she could get through it with them. She and Jack were comfortable with the plan.

Shirley told them she was going to take a shower and lie down for a while. She told Justin he could go home and she'd call him when she needed to go to the hospital, but he lingered after she went upstairs.

"Do you mind if I stick around for a while?" he asked Jack, who said not at all. He went outside to play ball with his sons, and Justin sat down at the kitchen table, wondering what would happen next and when. He and Richard had taken birthing classes so they could be helpful to Shirley at the delivery, but this was suddenly all so real. Their baby was finally on the way and would be in their arms within hours. He was thinking about it with a dazed look on his face as Shirley walked into the kitchen carrying a small tote bag. It had been ready for weeks. Her face looked pinched and she was having trouble walking and talking when he looked up in surprise and saw her.

"It's really going fast," she managed to choke out between pains. "I just called the doctor and she said to come in." Justin took the bag from her, and called Richard as they walked to his car. And she waved at Jack and her boys, and slid into the front seat with a terrible grimace.

"Is it really bad?" Justin asked sympathetically, and she smiled.

"It's the way it's supposed to be. Your little girl is in a

big hurry to come out and meet you," she said, clutching the armrest as he drove as quickly as he dared to pick up Richard, who was waiting in the street outside their house and hopped in.

"Hi, Shirley, how's it going?" Richard asked, looking nervous, and then panicked as he saw her face contort with the next pain.

"I think maybe we need to go a little faster," she said to Justin. "I'm feeling a lot of pressure," she said, but Justin was driving as fast as he could.

"We're almost there," he said, as they pulled into the parking lot of the hospital they had left a little while before. It was hard to believe she was already in such hard labor only an hour after her water had broken. Justin parked the car, and Richard ran to get a wheelchair and helped her into it, and then wheeled her inside, with Justin carrying her bag. The nurse at the desk looked up as they came in.

"Hello, everybody." She smiled at the threesome and then focused on Shirley. "Didn't I just see you here a couple of hours ago with your son?" Shirley nodded and panted through the next contraction. "Couldn't stay away from us, could you?" she said, taking command of the wheelchair and steering her rapidly toward a room. "I'll get you registered in a minute. Let's get our OB on call to see you, or do you want me to call your own?"

"My own," she said, and then gritted her teeth, and

Justin helped the nurse lift Shirley onto the examining table. Shirley told her the doctor's name, and the nurse picked up the phone, had someone at the front desk page her, and then asked for the OB in the house to come down immediately.

"It looks like things are going quickly," she explained and then turned back to Shirley and helped her undress. She was wearing a cotton dress and it came off easily and revealed her enormous belly. "Would you like the gentlemen to step outside?" she said as she put a gown on Shirley and covered her with a drape. Shirley wriggled out of her underwear between pains, and dropped her bra on the bed.

"They're the baby's fathers," she explained, through clenched teeth. "I want them here," she said, and the nurse didn't comment as a doctor in scrubs walked into the room. He told Shirley he was going to examine her, and the nurse pulled up stirrups that were attached to the bed for Shirley to put her feet in and indicated to the two men to stand up at her head. Shirley let out a scream when the doctor did an exam, as Justin instinctively reached for her hand and let her squeeze his as hard as she could. She was having one brutal pain after another, and the doctor said she was almost ready to push, as Shirley's own doctor walked into the room. She took over and examined Shirley again, which made her cry, but she didn't complain.

"I want to see where the baby's head is," she explained gently, as Shirley nodded, trying to be brave, still clutching Justin's hand. "I'd offer you an epidural," the doctor said sympathetically, "but it's gone too fast, and you're too far along. You're at nine, Shirley. If you can hang in, I think you can push in a few minutes." The baby was big, and had shifted since Shirley's last visit, and her shoulder was in the way, which made it harder on Shirley. The doctor reached in and gently turned the baby as Shirley screamed, and Richard started to look pale and sat down.

"Do you want to go outside?" Justin whispered to him, and Richard shook his head but stayed in the chair, as Justin kept a grip on Shirley's hand.

The doctor had a victorious look after she turned the baby, and told Shirley she could push, and suddenly everything was action in the room. The nurse was on Shirley's other side, telling her to push, the doctor was watching the baby's head come down, Justin was holding Shirley's hand and talking to her, as Shirley's face turned bright red as she pushed as hard as she could, and then suddenly they saw the top of the baby's head appear and a little face was looking at them, as Shirley beamed and lay back against the pillows, while the doctor delivered the baby's body easily. She was a beautiful little girl, and Justin and Richard both cried when they saw her. The doctor cut the cord, wrapped her in a blanket, and handed her to Justin. He turned to Shirley then as he held his daughter and thanked her for what she'd done. The whole delivery had taken half an hour, and their baby was healthy and normal, as Richard smiled at the sight of Justin holding the baby he had wanted so much. This was their dream come true, although a little more Justin's dream than Richard's. Justin had known he wanted children. Richard had had doubts at first, but he was sure now when he saw her. The baby looked like a little cherub.

And then the nurse took her to the nursery, to weigh her and clean her up, while Justin and Richard stood on either side of Shirley and thanked her again. She was shaking by then, under a thin blanket. It was a normal reaction after the birth.

They left Shirley to rest then. She called Jack to tell him the baby had been born, as the two men left the room. Watching their baby's birth had been miraculous and awesome, and not as daunting as they had feared, and Shirley had done so well. She was going home the next day, and the baby was too. Justin and Richard's life as a family had begun.

They went to admire their daughter through the nursery window. She had already been cleaned up and was swaddled in a blanket, with a little pink cap, sleeping peacefully. The card on her bassinet said she weighed nine pounds, fourteen ounces. She was huge. And they were naming her Milagra. It was Spanish for miracle. It was the perfect name for her.

Justin and Richard called Julie, Kate, and then Izzie, after they stood admiring her in the nursery for a while. They couldn't wait to get her out of the hospital and home the next day. There was no reason to keep her there any longer. Shirley was anxious to get back to her family too. Her mission had been accomplished. Milagra had been safely delivered to her dads.

Kate congratulated them both warmly, Julie let out a squeal of delight at the news, and Izzie sounded pleased for both of them. She had stopped lecturing them about surrogacy several months before, and Shirley was due to sign the relinquishment papers the next day. There had been no problem, and they had the final check ready to deposit in her account.

They called Willie last. He didn't answer, so they sent him a text, and then another announcing Milagra's birth to all their friends. Their entire world had been waiting for her. And now she had arrived, and they had years ahead of them to enjoy her.

When they called Izzie to tell her about the baby, Zach was a week away from finishing his three months in rehab. He had done well, and had been allowed to come home often on weekends. His probation officer was pleased, and Zach had been looking for a job but hadn't found one yet. His PO had recommended to the court that he be allowed to move home. Zach could hardly wait and Izzie had missed him too. She had been so worried about him that she had felt sick ever since his arrest. She could hardly eat, worked too hard, and had lost ten pounds in the past two months. She didn't look well, and her associates at work had noticed it too. Zach felt guilty about what he had put her through, and all he wanted was to come home and take care of her.

And when he finally moved back after rehab, it felt like a honeymoon to both of them. The only reminder of the entire unfortunate episode was the electronic anklet he had to wear for another nine months. He was confined to the city, so his grandmother's East Hampton house was off-limits, and they both missed going there. Izzie hated seeing the conspicuous anklet. It made him look like a criminal. He was wearing it for his court appearance, when Izzie asked for a continuance for another three months, and the judge granted it. Izzie knew that sooner or later, Zach would have to plead guilty to the charge of possession, but the DA had pleaded them down to a misdemeanor in exchange for Zach going to rehab. And if he got a job before they went back to court, that would help him too, but there was so little he was qualified for. All she wanted was to keep him out of jail, whatever it took. And even once he was home, she continued to feel sick. It never occurred to her until he'd been back for several days what it might be. She assumed it was all due to stress, but suddenly wondered if it was something more serious than that. Her body had been out of whack ever since Zach's arrest.

She stopped at the drugstore one night on her way home from work, and bought a test. She locked herself in the bathroom and used it as soon as she got home. Her worst fear had just come true, or her second worst fear. Her greatest terror was that Zach would go to prison, if he was arrested again or his probation got revoked. Her second worst was what she had just discovered. She was pregnant. In light of everything else going on, it was one more problem she didn't need. She loved him, but she couldn't deal with a baby on top of it. And Zach was a child himself. But it explained why she had felt so sick for the last two and a half months, and hadn't had a period, which she had assumed was from stress too. She could guess now that she was probably close to three months pregnant, almost too late to do anything about it. But even if it wasn't, how could she abort the baby of the man she was married to and loved? She sat in her bathroom for a while and didn't say anything to Zach when she came out. She needed time to think about it, and decide what to do. She hadn't expected this even though they had been careless once or twice. And now she was pregnant, and deeply upset by it.

She was still in a state of shock when the phone rang that night and it was Justin. He was calling to talk about the baby. He and Richard were ecstatic, and loving fatherhood. Shirley had signed the papers without a hitch. They had tremendous gratitude toward her.

"I'm sorry I gave you a hard time about it," Izzie said, trying not to think of her own dilemma in light of her discovery that day. She wasn't ready for a baby, Zach had just gotten out of rehab, he had a court case pending, and had been arrested on felony charges twice in the past year. He wasn't prepared for fatherhood and still had some growing up to do first.

"I'm sorry I didn't give you away at your wedding," Justin said, out of the blue. It had bothered him ever since. "I want you to see our daughter, she's gorgeous," he said proudly.

"I can't wait to meet her. I've been working like a lunatic here. I'll try to come and see you in a couple of weeks."

"We're going to bring her down to see Grandma Lou. You can meet her then if you're too busy to come up."

"Thank you." They talked for a few minutes and then hung up. She couldn't imagine being that happy about a baby, or wanting one that badly. She didn't. She had too much else on her mind, and didn't feel ready for children yet. And now she was pregnant. It was terrible news to her, and equally bad timing.

"Who was that?" Zach asked as he walked back into the room. He had heard her talking.

"Justin. They're in love with their baby," she said, looking distracted and upset.

"That's nice for them," he said casually. "What are you so glum about?" He had picked up on her mood immediately. It was hard to miss.

She gazed at him with distress in her eyes. Nothing was turning out the way she had wanted, even though he was home now. But nothing was settled yet. "I'm having one too," she said in a troubled voice as he stared at her.

"What?" He stood rooted to the spot, with his anklet in plain sight. It always was, since he was always barefoot at home, and never wore socks when he went out.

"You heard me. I'm pregnant." She looked at him as though she had just told him she was dying.

"Why didn't you tell me?" he said, as he sat down next to her and put his arms around her, obviously pleased.

"I just found out about an hour ago." Her eyes filled with tears as he held her. The timing was wrong even if they wanted children one day.

"Oh, baby, that's such good news," he said, beaming at her, as she looked at him in despair. He was thrilled, as she could feel his electronic anklet pressing against her foot. The reality of it was overwhelming, and now she was pregnant on top of everything else. She couldn't even pretend that she was pleased.

Chapter 16

The day after Milagra was born, the boys took her home and settled her in the pink bassinet in her nursery and looked at her in awe. Justin had sent dozens of pictures of their daughter to Alana, and all their friends and family. And everyone wrote back that she was the prettiest baby they had ever seen.

Kate was staring at one of the photographs as she sat in her office, trying to absorb the fact that she was now a grandmother. She was still shocked by the idea, although she was relieved that the baby was healthy and everything had gone well. Her cellphone rang as she looked at the photo of Milagra, and when she answered, she could barely hear what was being said to her. She finally understood that it was from the concierge of a hotel in Beijing, and it was about her mother. Her heart nearly stopped as she listened.

"What? . . . What? . . . I'm sorry, I can't hear you." But worse, she couldn't understand him. "Yes, yes, this is Louise Smith's daughter. Is something wrong?" They were telling her that Louise was in a hospital, but she couldn't understand the name of the hospital they gave her. She was panicked. "Is there someone there who speaks English? . . . Yes, yes . . . I know you do. But I'm having trouble understanding. Is she all right? What happened?" And why hadn't Frances called her? He was saying something about Louise's foot, but she still had no idea what had happened. "I'm sorry . . . say again . . ." A woman finally came on the line as Jessica stood in the doorway. They could hear her shouting halfway across the store, and even customers had noticed. Kate sounded frantic. She was speaking to the woman now. "Yes, Louise Smith is my mother. Where is she? May I speak to her?" She enunciated each word in an exaggerated way so the woman would understand her, and finally she was able to convey to Kate that Louise had injured her ankle, and she would be on a plane to New York the next day at four P.M. But why hadn't her mother called her? Or Frances? The woman at the hotel gave Kate their flight number, and as soon as they hung up, Kate called her mother on her cell, but it didn't even ring. And Frances's didn't either. What exactly had happened was a mystery, but at least they were coming home, and weren't stuck in Beijing. It reminded Kate that despite her mother's independence, she was of a certain age, and something bad could happen to her far from home.

Kate was desperately anxious that night and the next day, but didn't say anything to her children. Julie had driven to Vermont to see the baby, and Kate told her she couldn't get away and had a business crisis to deal with, and to tell Justin she'd come up in the next week.

It was an agonizing wait at the airport the following day, and at first she thought they hadn't made the flight, as she watched passengers collect their baggage and go through customs, and Frances and her mother were nowhere to be seen. Kate was standing on an upper level observation deck, looking down through glass windows, growing increasingly panicked, and then at last she saw them. Frances had her arm in a cast with a sling, and her mother was on crutches. They looked like they'd been through the wars, but they still managed to get their luggage on a cart and head toward Customs and Immigration. They passed out of sight, and as soon as they did, Kate raced downstairs as fast as she could to be there when they came out. They finally emerged twenty minutes later. The two women were chatting animatedly and Louise looked surprised to see her.

"I told you she'd be here," Frances said, smiling at Kate. "We told the concierge at the hotel to call you to tell you we were coming home early. But no one at the hotel spoke decent English."

"What happened to you both?" Kate asked as she took over the cart with their luggage and asked her mother if she wanted a wheelchair.

"Of course not!" she said, looking insulted. "I'm fine. I

sprained my ankle at the Forbidden City. And Frances fell in the bathroom at the hotel and broke her arm. I broke my cellphone and Frances lost hers."

"You two are a mess." Kate grinned, relieved to see how feisty her mother was. "You had me worried sick when they called."

"We are not." Louise looked even more offended, and then Kate thought of something. Since they didn't have their cellphones, they obviously hadn't heard the news.

"Justin had his baby two days ago. She weighed almost ten pounds. Milagra. You're a great-grandmother!" Louise looked mollified when she heard it.

"Is the baby all right and did the woman sign the papers?" Louise asked anxiously.

"Apparently she did, and everything is fine," Kate reassured her.

"I want to see her," Louise said as she hobbled toward the exit on her crutches, looking pleased about the baby, and refusing any help.

Louise talked about the trip on the way into the city, and Kate was relieved to know that she was all right. Frances was looking out the window as though she were grateful to be back.

"I don't think I'd go back to Beijing," Louise said conversationally as her daughter smiled. "But I would definitely revisit Shanghai and Hong Kong. They're just more sophisticated and civilized."

"They were nice to us at the hospital," Frances added meekly.

"We're not looking for a Red Cross tour," Louise said tartly, and Kate tried not to laugh.

"Are you sure your ankle's not broken, Mom?" Kate asked her.

"Of course it's not. How are the others? What are they up to?"

"I haven't seen much of Izzie, she's been busy working, as usual. Julie is still crazy about Mr. Perfect, and Willie is as elusive as ever. I never know what he's doing. He's been out of town a lot this month." Louise nodded, satisfied with the reports, and then Kate spoke of her new grand-daughter again.

"Justin said he sent you pictures, but I guess you didn't get them if you broke your cellphone," Kate commented.

"I have to get a new one tomorrow," she said matter-of-factly.

They dropped Frances off first, and then Kate took her mother home. She wanted to help her unpack but Louise insisted she didn't need assistance and wanted to go through her mail. She kissed her daughter and sent her on her way, and Kate went back to the store. And as soon as she got to her desk, she had an email from Bernard. She hadn't heard from him in almost four weeks and she was furious over it. Relations had cooled between them but neither of them had said it was over. And ever since he'd left for Sardinia with his wife and family, he'd gone quiet on her. It made his claims about how much he supposedly loved her no longer credible. He had canceled his June trip to New York, and said he had pressing meetings in London in July, which precluded his coming to New York. And he had been in Italy for most of August with his children and wife. Kate hadn't seen him since he left New York in late May, exactly three months before. It made their passionate affair seem like a farce. And suddenly he was reappearing now and said he was coming to New York. She couldn't avoid him entirely since he had invested in her business, but she was no longer a willing participant in their alleged love story. She just hadn't said it to him yet.

She didn't answer him till the next day, and then sent him a brief email reporting only on the sales figures of her online business. She said nothing personal to him about the past few months. But it was depressing to realize that his claims of having an "arrangement" with his wife had been a lie. It just made him a player and a cheater and not the person he had pretended to be with her. And he was a fool if he thought she'd ever trust him again. For Kate, it was over. It had been a miserable summer.

*

Louise called Kate the next morning, wanting to go to Vermont to see the baby in the next few days, and Kate realized that she had some problems to deal with at the store and couldn't get away as soon as she thought.

"I'm not sure I can do it this week. Let me call Justin and see what works for them." She called him shortly after, and he said Richard was feeding the baby when he answered the phone. They were taking turns so the baby would bond equally with both of them, and they were sleeping with a Moses basket between them, so they could hear her and watch her all night. They had an intercom with a video screen in the nursery, but they loved having her close to them. They were completely enamored with their daughter.

"How's Grandma Lou?" he asked her immediately.

"They came off the plane looking like a pilgrimage from Lourdes," Kate said as she laughed. "Your grandmother sprained her ankle, and Frances broke her arm at the hotel. Grandma Lou is on crutches, but as feisty as ever. She wants to go back to Shanghai," she reported, "but not Beijing. She'd like to come up and see the baby, but to be honest, I don't think I can do it this week. Things are crazy here at the store." And Bernard was coming after Labor Day, in a week, and she needed to have her latest figures and progress reports in order for him. Whatever else was or wasn't happening between them, she wanted her business dealings with him to be professional and clean. That was an entirely separate matter.

"Why don't you two relax?" Justin suggested. "We want

to bring her to New York in a few weeks anyway. You can see her then. We're all kind of adjusting to each other right now." It really made more sense than dragging his grandmother to Vermont, and Kate rushing up and back to drive her. He and Richard wanted to get the knack of fatherhood, at least for a few weeks, before they traveled with her. For now, they were barely getting time to shower and dress between diapers, feedings, changing her bedding and clothes, doing laundry, figuring out why she was crying, and getting up every two or three hours during the night. She was a big baby, so she was hungry, and neither of the two men had had more than a few hours of sleep a night since she'd been born. They had had illusions of dressing her like a little doll in pretty dresses. Instead they barely got her into one set of pajamas before she threw up, or had a wet diaper, and they had to change her again. They did laundry all day long, and ran the sterilizer night and day for her bottles.

"I wonder if it's easier when women breast-feed them," Richard said as he washed a load of bottles, after Justin hung up the phone. His mother had agreed to convince Grandma Lou to wait to meet the baby until they came to New York.

"You still have to dress them and feed them even if they're breast-fed," Justin said practically.

They were discovering that babies were a lot of work, a lot more than they thought. They had called Shirley to make sure she was all right. She was struggling with her milk coming in, and they had given her a shot at the hospital to help dry it up. But she sounded in decent spirits, although a little worn-out from the delivery and busy with her kids. She said she was happy to have her body back, and was looking forward to spending more time with her children. The pregnancy had taken over for a while. They were incredibly grateful to her, and they sent her flowers to thank her again.

Justin looked at Richard as they lay in bed that night with the baby between them. Richard thought she should sleep in the crib they had set up for her in the room that had been Justin's study before she was born. But Justin liked having her close to them, so he could see her during the night.

"So is it different than you thought?" he asked his partner, since there was no one to hear them and they could be honest with each other, as they always were. He had noticed that Richard looked overwhelmed, but she wasn't even a week old, and it was all brand-new to them.

"To be honest, it's harder and takes more organizing. We don't get time to do anything else now, and it's all about her." Justin laughed at what he said.

"Well, yes, it would be right now. Did you think it was going to be about us?" Justin seemed amused at that.

"I don't know if I thought about it before. I just figured she'd be cute and cuddly and pink and clean all the time."

Half the time, she was making messes at both ends, and Justin was decidedly better with diapers and made less of a fuss about it than Richard, who said the smell of her poopy diapers made him feel sick, so Justin changed most of them. They weren't doing much else, and hadn't been since she was born. "It'll probably be more fun when she can talk," Richard added.

"And even more work than it is now," Justin said with a smile. "We'll have to watch her so she doesn't get hurt."

"How do people get anything done? Do you realize I haven't had time to return a phone call since she was born?" Richard complained.

"Neither have I," Justin agreed, but he didn't seem to mind. He liked being a hands-on parent, although he couldn't figure out how he was going to write now, especially when Richard went back to work in a month. He was on paternity leave until then. It would be a juggling act for sure when he started teaching again. And Justin would have to write at night. He figured he wouldn't get back to his novel for many months, until they had the baby on some kind of schedule, and they weren't even close to that yet. Alana had called several times to see how they were doing, and Julie had too, but they had no time to talk on the phone. They hadn't even cooked a meal since they got home. They were living on takeout and frozen pizza, and they both were unhappy that they were gaining weight from the fattening foods they were eating, and neither of them had had time to go to the gym. But they weren't sorry. It still seemed worthwhile to them, and she was as much a miracle as her name.

"Can you imagine what it would be like if we'd had twins?" Justin said as he changed another poopy diaper. She seemed to produce them all the time. "I don't know how my mother did it, with four of us."

"Wash your mouth out with soap. I couldn't handle twins," Richard said with fervor. Realizing that that could have happened easily almost made him shudder. One baby was plenty to cope with, and Milagra was keeping two grown men running night and day. They had never been so busy or so tired in their lives.

*

Bernard called Kate from the hotel when he arrived, the day after Labor Day. He sounded as sexy and charming as ever when she answered the phone. The hotel number had come up and she didn't recognize it, which was why he had called her from the phone in his suite. He was afraid she wouldn't answer if she knew it was him.

"How are you, Kate?" he asked her, as though they were old friends and nothing more. He was feeling out the terrain, as the French said. He had hardly heard from her all summer, after their last meeting in New York, when she had made such an issue about his going on vacation with his wife. He had decided to let her cool off for a while after that. The time had stretched longer than he had intended, and it felt awkward now, after three months.

"I'm fine. Did you have a pleasant summer?" she asked coolly. "How was Sardinia?"

"Very agreeable." He kept his comments vague and subdued so as not to antagonize her further. He was still hoping to rekindle the flame of their relationship. The past three months had just been an intermission, as far as he was concerned, not the final act. "The online business is doing well?" He hadn't checked their figures recently, but her business had been booming until now.

"Incredibly." She warmed up when he asked, she was so happy about it. They had tripled the profits to the shop, and he was doing well from it too. "I can hardly keep up with the demand. And sometimes I truly can't."

"That's wonderful news. Will you be there this afternoon?" he asked in a relaxed tone. "I have a meeting on Wall Street and could stop in to see you on my way uptown." She was unhappy and angry at the thought, but she couldn't refuse him access, since his investment in her business was an important one.

"I don't think I'll be here," she said vaguely.

"Tomorrow, then? Or would you prefer tonight?" He decided to risk it, but she rebuffed him immediately.

"I'm busy. If you'd like the latest figures, I can email them to you. We just finished them for last month. We had an amazing summer."

"I'd rather meet with you myself," he said, sounding seductive and sexy. He was very French. Six months before it had enchanted her. Now she knew better. He was just another married man cheating on his wife, and she didn't find that sexy at all. In fact, it revolted her, but he hadn't understood that yet. He was expecting her to fall into his arms again. She could hear it in his voice.

"What do we need to meet about?" she inquired, sounding businesslike. "The figures speak for themselves."

"I'd enjoy seeing you. It's been too long." And then he lowered his voice to almost a whisper. "I've missed you terribly, Kate." He sounded convincing, but she knew him better now, and the many masks he wore. Devoted father, brilliant businessman, practiced lover, adoring boyfriend, and now he had added dutiful husband to the list. It was the last one that had spoiled everything for her. The other roles he played had made him appealing to her. But she had discovered that you were never too old to be played for a fool. "Will you have a drink with me?" he asked, sounding dogged and humble, and she sighed.

"I don't see the point," she said honestly.

"For old times' sake?" Although their affair had been white-hot only three months before. Very little time had elapsed, but everything had changed for her.

"You can stop by the store if you want," she conceded. She didn't want him to accuse her of obstructing his access to the business.

"How are your children, by the way?" he asked her, trying to rebuild the bridge he had burned by going to Sardinia with his wife.

"Fine, thank you," she said coldly. She didn't tell him about Justin's baby. Her personal life was none of his business anymore.

Bernard showed up at four o'clock that afternoon, looking as handsome as ever, and she felt a flutter in her stomach when she saw him. She didn't want him to affect her, and was upset that he did, but it didn't show. She kept the door to her office open when he was with her. She had a set of their figures already printed out for him, and when he tried to kiss her on both cheeks, she shifted slightly and he found himself kissing air. She kept everything on a professional level, and he finally looked at her sadly, and she had to steel herself not to be affected by him, when he lowered his voice.

"Why are you doing this, Kate? I love you. I'm sorry you were upset about my summer plans."

"I'm sorry I misunderstood the 'arrangement' you have with your wife. I didn't realize it included monthlong vacations with her, or I would never have gotten involved. I don't need that kind of heartbreak in my life, Bernard. And I assume you spend the Christmas holidays with her too. That's not the kind of relationship I want with someone else's husband," she said firmly, and he raised an eyebrow, which made him look even more handsome, much to her chagrin.

"Do you always make decisions about your heart? Why don't you let your heart decide for itself? We loved each other three months ago. That doesn't disappear in an instant, or even in a few months." He was very convincing, and he wasn't wrong, but Kate was determined not to let him sway her. She had made up her mind.

"I didn't know who you were then. I thought I did. But it turned out I was mistaken. When you make discoveries like that, it changes everything. You don't play by the same rules I do. I want an honest, loving relationship, if I have one. I thought that's what we had. It wasn't. I'm not interested in stealing someone's husband, or even borrowing you part-time."

"I'm not in love with my wife, Kate." He looked sincere when he said it, and maybe he was.

"That doesn't make you a free man. Not in my world anyway."

"You're making a terrible mistake if you throw this away."

"I don't think I am. We have a business relationship that's important for both of us. I'd like to preserve that, if we can. But as far as anything else, I'm returning you to your wife, whether you love her or not." There was ice in her eyes when she said it to him, and he looked taken aback. No one had ever been that honest with him before.

He could see that she meant it, and the door to her heart was closed.

"You're a hard woman, Kate. I never realized that before." She didn't answer him, as he picked up the print-out of the sales figures from the desk and put it in his briefcase.

"Let me know if you have any questions," she said, indicating the financial report he had just put away. "I'll be happy to answer them for you." He nodded, and without saying another word, he walked out of the store. A piece of her heart went with him, but he didn't know it. She walked back into her office and closed the door behind her. She was shaking and there was a lump in her throat. He sent her a text a few minutes later, and she read it as a tear rolled down her cheek.

"*Je t'aime*" was all it said. And as she held her phone in her trembling hand, she spoke out loud.

"No, you don't." And then she erased his message and put her phone away. Liam had been right about married men.

Chapter 17

When Justin and Richard brought the baby to New York to meet Justin's mother and grandmother, she was three weeks old, and they brought more equipment than Kate had ever seen. A folding travel bed, a Moses basket, a car seat that transformed into a carrier, a rocking seat for the baby, a quilt for the floor with toys attached to it, boxes of Pampers, formula, bottles, their sterilizer, a swing so she would go to sleep, and a stroller you could put in six different positions and fold down into the car. Their car was crammed full, and when they carried her into Kate's apartment, they looked like they were moving in.

"Good lord, how can she need all that?" Kate asked in amazement. "I used to manage with my purse, a stroller, and a diaper bag with four children."

"We have two suitcases of clothes for her in the car. She goes through an outfit every hour. She spits up a lot," Justin explained. Kate was in awe as they set everything up, put Milagra in the swing, turned it on, and set the musical mobile attached to it in motion. She was still sound asleep. They both looked exhausted, and Justin had circles under his eyes. They said they were getting about three hours of sleep a night. They hadn't gotten Milagra on a schedule yet. Kate couldn't help wondering if all new parents these days were like them, with a million different kinds of equipment, or if they were just excessive about it. They set up the sterilizer in the kitchen and washed the bottles they'd used in the car.

Grandma Lou was just as impressed when she arrived and saw the sleeping baby, surrounded by the mountain of what they'd brought.

"Are you moving to New York?" she asked, looking puzzled but enchanted by the lovely features in the tiny face. She looked like a baby in an ad.

"No, Grandma," Justin answered. "She just needs a lot of stuff."

"For what? A garage sale? No three-week-old child could need all that. How exhausting to move it all around." She looked amazed.

She was still sound asleep in the swing that ticked like a metronome, and the music was playing while little giraffes danced above her.

"You're going to need a bigger house if you've accumulated all that in three weeks," Grandma Lou said, and Justin looked faintly embarrassed at the excess, while Richard insisted that all babies had equipment like that these days, and he had bought her educational toys too. He had heard somewhere that he could teach her to read by the time she was two. They had read all the currently popular books on child development and how to have a smart baby.

Julie came to visit to see the baby, and Zach and Izzie had promised to come by. Willie was away for the weekend. They all sat around admiring the baby while she slept, and Richard enumerated all the things she could already do. According to him, she was advanced, which made Kate smile.

The baby was still sleeping when Zach and Izzie arrived. Izzie was wearing jeans and a man's blue shirt and loafers. She looked very thin, to the point of gaunt. Zach was wearing black leather pants, one of his sleeveless tee shirts, and a leather vest, and went around the room saying hello to everyone, then helped himself to a Coke in Kate's fridge, and sat down. Izzie glanced at all the equipment too.

"She has a lot of stuff," Izzie commented, and said she was very pretty. They all agreed on that, and Richard took a number of photos of her with his phone while she continued to sleep with her chin slumped on her chest. She was wearing a little pink sweater and a matching cap with tiny ballet shoes.

"She needs some black leathers," Zach said and Justin laughed, and then they chatted for a few minutes. Zach stretched out his long legs, and Izzie realized that he hadn't worn the socks she'd given him, and her mother happened to look down at the same time, and noticed the electronic anklet on his left leg. She looked puzzled and Izzie's heart skipped a beat.

"What's that?" she asked innocently, assuming it was some new trend, or one of those devices that measured your heart rate, how many steps you walk every day, and how many calories you burned.

"Oh, just something I picked up," Zach said, brushing off the question, as he crossed his legs to conceal it, but Justin had seen it and so had Richard. Justin glanced at Izzie with a question in his eyes. He knew instantly what it was.

He followed her out to the kitchen a few minutes later to get a bottle ready for the baby when she woke up, and he cornered Izzie as she got a glass of water. "What's that about?" he asked. He knew it had nothing to do with measuring steps. "When did that happen?" There was no avoiding the question or his eyes. And she was ready to kill Zach for not wearing socks. Having her family know that he had been convicted of something was the last thing she needed, particularly since she knew that to some degree they were all uneasy about Zach as a mate for her.

"It happened a few months ago," she said, looking tired as she said it. "It's nothing serious."

"They put those anklets on instead of sending you to jail," Justin insisted, and she nodded. There was no point denying it, they both knew it was true. Zach sauntered

268

into the kitchen then and his wife gave him a quelling look. "I was just asking Izzie about your anklet. How did you wind up with that?" Zach figured that there was no point lying to him now that they'd seen it. He thought they'd find out sooner or later anyway, and he didn't see any reason to keep it a secret. They were family after all.

"I got busted for possession, and I was already on probation, so I got stuck with this. It was either the anklet or prison, and it was a better deal. I only have to wear it for a year." He helped himself to another Coke, and then went back to the living room, as Justin stared at his sister.

"Are you okay?" He was worried about her all over again. More so now.

"Yes, I am," she said, looking embarrassed. "It was a stupid thing for him to do. He was drunk when it happened. I told him to wear socks today." Justin wondered what else she was hiding from them.

"He'd better behave or they'll send him away," Justin warned her.

"I've tried to impress that on him. He's like a big kid. He does foolish things. He's not a drug dealer or anything." She tried to make light of it, and Justin didn't press her, but he was very upset by what he'd heard and how casual Zach was about it. That wasn't the life he hoped for, for his sister. She deserved better than that. And she had so much faith in him, which he thought Zach didn't deserve.

No one else mentioned it when they went back to the

living room, and the baby was crying, which distracted everyone. Justin put her in his grandmother's arms, and she looked down at her with a wide smile, as Richard took pictures of them and a video. And then Justin gave Milagra her bottle, but he was still shaken by what Zach had said and how blithe he was about it.

"You'd better get some practice doing that," Zach teased Izzie as Justin changed the baby's diaper on a mat on the floor. Fortunately it was only wet.

"Why would you practice changing diapers?" Kate asked her daughter, as Izzie glanced imploringly at Zach. He was hitting all the high notes today.

"He's just kidding," Izzie said, and changed the subject, but Justin stared at the tiny bump under her shirt and then his eyes widened as he looked up at his sister.

"Oh my God, you're pregnant." There was dead silence in the room, and Izzie didn't deny it since it was true, but she hadn't been planning to tell them yet. They all stared at her for denial or confirmation.

"Yes, I'm pregnant," she said in a flat voice. There was none of the jubilation one would have expected her to express, just resignation. But given what her husband was wearing on his leg, who could blame her? "It's due in March," she confirmed. "We didn't plan it, it just happened. I didn't figure it out for a while."

"It's going to be great." Zach smiled broadly, but no one else did. Justin was thinking that it wouldn't be so great if

Zach screwed up again and went to prison, and his sister had a baby.

"Are you happy about it?" Kate asked her softly, and Izzie shrugged. She couldn't fake it. Her pregnancy had been a shock, and still was given everything that had happened since they'd been married. They'd only been married for four months and she was already three months pregnant. Nothing was happening as she'd expected.

"I'm not happy yet," she admitted. "But I will be. It doesn't seem real yet," and it was a lot less so than his anklet. "It's an adjustment." Julie glanced over at her and felt sorry for her, but tried to make the best of it.

"It'll be adorable. You'll see. Just like Milagra." The baby had started crying again, and Richard was bouncing her up and down to calm her, but instead she threw up. So he had to change her clothes, and wasn't adept at it yet. He was doing that when she pooped, and Kate went to get a towel from the bathroom so it didn't get on the rug. Her life had changed with the arrival of her grandchild. And it was a reminder of a time she had almost forgotten.

"One forgets how much work they are at that age," Grandma Lou said, watching Richard trying to change her.

"That'll be us pretty soon," Zach said, beaming, as though there were no problems in their world. Izzie looked daggers at him and snapped at him.

"That'll be you. I'll be at work. So maybe you'd better take the diaper lesson." He still hadn't found a job, and wasn't trying to. His probation officer questioned him about it every month.

"I'm not changing any diapers," he said firmly. Kate tried not to let her disapproval show on her face. He was the laziest, most self-indulgent man she'd ever met, and she hated to think he was her son-in-law.

"Do you feel all right?" she asked Izzie, with a look of concern. "You're awfully thin."

"I lost some weight. I was sick in the beginning, but I'm starting to feel better now." She looked as though she considered her pregnancy a punishment, and to her it was. The last thing she wanted right now was to be pregnant. And she worried about Zach every day when she went to work.

Kate didn't know what to say in answer to Izzie's obvious unhappiness at being pregnant, and the conversation in the room had died after Zach let the cat out of the bag. They left a little while later, and Izzie berated him as soon as they reached the street.

"Are you crazy? You don't wear the socks I gave you, so people can't see that fucking thing on your leg, you tell my brother what you were arrested for, like it's something to be proud of, and you let them know I'm pregnant, when I asked you not to. Just how difficult do you want to make things? What do you think they're talking about right now?"

"You can't hide the baby forever."

"No, I can't, but I could have for a while, so I didn't have to hear their opinions about it, and you can goddam well hide the anklet. Did you really need to tell Justin about that?"

"I'm sorry. I can't keep track of all the secrets you want me to keep from them."

"Well, getting busted for possession of cocaine is top of that list. You could have spared them that."

"So sue me. I'm sorry, it slipped." He looked miffed.

"It certainly did." They walked back to their apartment from her mother's while Justin was explaining to Kate what the anklet was and why he had it, and she looked horrified, even more so now that she knew Izzie was pregnant. She felt desperately sorry for her, and she wasn't sure if her daughter had married an idiot or a monster.

Grandma Lou saw the expression on Kate's face and wanted to know what was going on, so Kate told her, and Louise looked shocked.

"What a stupid thing for him to do, when he has everything going for him now, including a wife who loves him and a baby on the way. I hope he grows up soon, or Izzie will be very unhappy."

"She looks like she already is," Justin said darkly. "Look how thin she's gotten. That can't be healthy for the baby."

Even Grandma Lou thought Izzie's pregnancy was unfortunate and an unwanted complication.

"Do you think she'll continue working?" her grandmother asked.

"She can't afford not to," Kate said simply. "And he never will, unless he deals drugs." He was everything she had feared right from the beginning, and worse.

They were back in their apartment then, and Izzie went to lie down. It had been a horrible afternoon, and now her entire family knew about Zach's being on probation and the baby. The last thing she wanted to hear were their comments, and she was sure there would be many of them before it was all over.

Zach came into the bedroom and lay down next to her.

"Are you mad at me?" he asked unhappily. He hated it when she got angry, and she often was lately, ever since his arrest.

"I'm not mad. I'm scared and unhappy," she said sadly. "I don't like everyone in my family knowing my business," and it was all so overwhelming, the baby, his arrest, her family knowing about it now. This wasn't the way it was supposed to be.

He tried to make love to her then, and she didn't want to, but she didn't want to hurt his feelings, so she let him and just lay there. But she started to feel sick before he was through and had to stop him.

"Jesus, what's wrong with you these days, Izzie? You can't feel that sick all the time."

"Well, I do." A tear snuck out of her eye and onto her pillow.

He got up and walked around the apartment for a while, and then returned to bed, hoping she'd be willing to finish what he'd started, but when he climbed into bed next to her, he saw that she was asleep. And then he was unhappy too.

*

The next surprise Kate had was from Julie. She and Peter were inseparable most of the time now. They'd gone to baseball games together all summer, they went away for weekends, he taught her to sail, and they went to dinner and movies. He treated her like a porcelain doll and she loved it. The only thing she didn't like was that he always wanted to be alone with her, and didn't want to spend time with her family or friends. She missed them, but Peter thought it was more romantic to be alone. And she loved him, more than she had any man before. But in spite of that, the one thing she hadn't shared with him was that she was dyslexic. She had been ashamed of it all her life, and she didn't want him to know, in case he thought less of her. Even after years of tutoring, she still had trouble reading and read like a child.

And in October, after they went to a baseball play-off

game, he threw her a curve she hadn't expected. He told her he was being transferred to L.A. It meant another promotion for him and he was excited about it. She tried to be happy for him when he told her, but it meant that their romance was over. He was moving in January, and Julie didn't believe in long-distance relationships. They never worked.

"They just told me this week," he said, as he put his arms around her, and then he looked down at her as she fought back tears.

"I'm happy for you. I'm just sad for us," she said honestly.

"You don't need to be," he said softly. "Julie, I want you to come with me." She couldn't imagine it. She had a great job, she loved her family, and she had lived in New York all her life. She couldn't move to L.A. And then he took her breath away with what he said next. "Will you marry me?"

"Are you serious?" She was stunned. She hadn't expected him to propose. She'd never even thought about getting married.

"I want to do this right. I can't ask you to make a move like that unless we're married." They had been dating for seven months and it seemed too soon to her, but she knew that she loved him, and she didn't want to lose him when he moved to L.A.

"What about my job?"

"You can get another design job in L.A." But not like the

one she had. She was the head designer, and there was no fashion industry in L.A. Not like in New York. There were small California designers, but she worked for an important firm, and made good money. It was a lot to give up. But so was he. He seemed so perfect for her in so many ways.

"I can't get a job there like the one I have."

"You don't need to. I make a good salary. You don't have to work if you don't want to."

"I have friends here," she said wistfully, not many, but some she liked, people she had known and worked with for years. "And my family."

"I love you, Julie. Isn't that enough? Do you want to stay single all your life? Don't you want to get married and have babies?" She had never considered it, and had never felt ready, until she met him, but she didn't feel ready now. Not yet.

"I don't feel old enough for babies." Or marriage, she wanted to add, but didn't. She didn't want to hurt his feelings.

"I'm not ready for babies either. But what about me? We could have a great life together in L.A. I'd be the number two man out there. And I could run the West Coast office one day. I know it's fast, but I want you to come with me, and it just feels right to me."

"I don't want to lose you," she said, and as she clung to him, he pulled a small blue box out of his pocket and slipped a ring on her finger. It was a small but very pretty diamond ring from Tiffany. And her eyes opened wide when she saw it.

"I'll get you a bigger one later," he said modestly, but he had chosen a lovely ring for her. It was round with a halo of tiny stones around it. It was delicate and looked right on her small hand. She stared at the ring for a long moment, and then back at him. He had thought of everything, and she smiled. Maybe he was right, and it was time to get married. She had turned thirty-one that summer, although she still felt young. But some of her friends had gotten married, and even had babies. "We could get married at Christmas. I have to be in L.A. by New Year's. We could have a quick honeymoon before I have to be there." He had it all worked out in his head. It didn't give them much time to plan a wedding, but she had never wanted a big wedding anyway, just her family and a few friends. That wouldn't take long to organize. "Julie, let's do it. Let's start a new life together." He made it sound exciting and fun, and in the headiness of the moment, she nodded and he kissed her. When they came up for air, she whispered yes. He spent that night with her in her apartment. They made love again in the morning when they woke up, and she looked at her ring afterward and started to laugh.

"Oh my God, I'm engaged."

"Yes, we are." He beamed at her. And when he left for

work, she went to see her mother at the store. She knew Kate went in early. Julie told her the news, and as Kate looked at her, and saw the ring, she felt like she had been shot out of a cannon. Another of her children was getting married, two in a year, and she didn't know why but she still had a queasy feeling about Peter. He certainly wasn't as blatantly wrong as Zach, far from it. Everything about Peter was right, but there had always been a faint echo in her mind about him, and she didn't know what it was. And Julie would be moving so far away. Los Angeles felt like it was on another planet.

"Are you sure?" Kate questioned her. "Why is he in such a hurry?" That seemed off to her too. Or maybe she was becoming paranoid in her old age, she chided herself, and the children were right that she never thought anyone was good enough for them. Peter certainly had everything going for him, a good job, a good education, a good future ahead of him. He seemed like he'd be a responsible provider and father, and he was attentive to her even now. What more could she want? She didn't know, but Kate still sensed that something was missing.

"Everything got rushed because of his transfer to L.A. That's why he wants to get married so soon." It was either that or break up.

"What about your job?"

"He says I don't have to work if I don't want to." In many ways, Peter was the husband every mother wanted for her daughter, unlike Zach. Peter was solid, and yet Kate felt uneasy. Julie had always seemed so vulnerable, and California felt like the other side of the universe to Kate. She was torn between being pleased and terrified for her. Julie had always been her most fragile child.

"Is this what you really want?" Kate asked her, and Julie nodded and grinned like a little girl as the ring sparkled on her finger.

"Yes, Mom, it is."

"All right," she said quietly, and put her arms around her daughter. "Then I approve." She didn't want to stand in her way if he was the man she wanted and knew it was right for her. Julie had a right to make that decision. Kate held her close for a moment and then mother and daughter walked through the store arm in arm. Another of her chicks was leaving the nest, and all Kate could hope was that her wings would carry her well, and that Peter would love her forever. Whatever her initial reservations about him, he seemed like the kind of man who would.

Chapter 18

Kate had dinner with Liam to catch up on all their news. They hadn't gotten together for a while. He and Maureen stayed in their country house in Westport, Connecticut, in the summer, and he commuted. September had been busy for him, and he'd gone on several business trips, and Kate's new online business was eating up her time. In some ways, it was much more time-consuming than the store, and she had to constantly update the site with new merchandise. She was having to look at more estates, find new sources to buy from, and go to more auctions, in order to have more to sell, with a much broader base, which was exciting for her.

She reported to Liam on how well it was doing, as he had predicted and Bernard had promised. Her business had become a real moneymaker. Liam was pleased for her.

"How are things going with Bernard?" Liam asked her cautiously, not wanting to pry into her love life. They told each other everything, but there were still areas where they tried to be delicate and discreet. Although Kate usually told him when she was dating someone, and he had met several of her men over the years, he never asked for the details, nor did she give them. But seeing her with Bernard and sensing that they were involved had worried him for her, since he was married.

"I saw him when he was in New York the last time," she said cryptically, and Liam wondered what that meant. "It was fine."

"Are you still . . . seeing him?" Liam asked cautiously. "Other than for business reasons."

"Actually, I'm not," Kate said with a slightly wistful look, followed by one of resignation. "You were right. His 'arrangement' with his wife was not what he led me to believe in the beginning. When I saw him in Paris, he acted like a free agent. But I didn't realize that he still spends vacations with her. They were in Sardinia together for a month this summer."

"Maybe she dates other people too. You never know what crazy deals people make with each other, spoken or otherwise, in order to stay married."

"I don't want to share someone else's husband. I don't need one of my own, but I'm not into time shares with men." He smiled at what she said. "He's very upset that I won't agree to it, and thinks I'm too American about it. I'm too uncomfortable. It sounds like a shit deal to me." He nodded and sensed that the decision had been painful for her. She looked sad about it, and he could tell she was uncomfortable talking about him. Liam knew she was an honest, honorable woman, and given the risks Bernard's situation presented, and the potential for her to get hurt, he was glad she was out of it, even if it was disappointing for her.

He knew about Justin's baby—she had called him when Milagra was born—and he was relieved to hear that the surrogate had relinquished the baby without a problem. He had shared her concerns about that, and it was a little too brave-new-world for him. But she told him about Zach's arrest and the electronic bracelet, and about Julie's recent engagement.

"Are you happy about that?" he asked about Peter.

"I think so. He's a little too good to be true in some ways. I know that sounds crazy, but it unnerved me at first. The kids beat me up about it, and they're probably right. I just think no one can be that perfect all the time, but maybe he is. And she's happy. His getting transferred sped everything up. They're getting married on Christmas Eve, and I'm going to hate having her so far away. But I guess that's what happens. They grow up and they fly away." She didn't see much of Justin in Vermont either, and he was closer than L.A. And especially now, since she was even working on weekends. Now that the affair with Bernard had ended, she had plunged into her work more than ever so she didn't have time to think about what she had lost. She hated to admit it, but she missed him. And for her, work was always the best distraction.

"I suppose it'll happen to me with the girls sooner or later," Liam said with resignation. "Elizabeth seems to be serious about a boy in Madrid, and Penny wants to move to London when she finishes school in Edinburgh. It'll be just my luck if they stay in Europe. I thought it would be a good experience for them. I didn't think they'd want to stay. How's your mom, by the way? Where's she off to next?" Keeping up with Louise allowed them all to live vicariously through her world traveling and adventures.

"She's not going anywhere right now. She doesn't admit it, but I think finding herself in a hospital in Beijing and Frances breaking her arm on their last trip may have slowed her down a little. If she ever gets really sick halfway around the world, it could be complicated and very unpleasant. She never had any mishaps before and the sprained ankle wasn't serious, but it was a wake-up call. I think she wants to go back to Hong Kong and Shanghai next year, and they're both very civilized. She might go to Singapore too. She wants to use the Mandarin she learned, and Frances loved the shopping." Louise was more likely to come home with artifacts and local crafts, but Frances loved buying clothes anywhere, and was a frequent visitor to Kate's store.

They lingered over dinner, talking about her business again, and holiday plans. Kate was having the whole family to her house for Thanksgiving, as usual. And Julie was planning to have her wedding dinner there too, since she was going to invite so few people. She only wanted the family and a handful of friends, and Peter wasn't close to the people he'd met in New York in his brief two years in the city. And neither his brothers nor his parents were coming. It was too complicated for them over the holidays and Peter had said they preferred to visit him and Julie in L.A. in the spring. So it was going to be a tiny wedding.

Kate and Liam left each other outside the restaurant, and she went home. Julie called her that night about some of the wedding plans. There was a florist she wanted to use, and she thought she had seen a wedding dress she liked. She was going to copy it and modify it. She wanted to wear something short for such a small wedding, and she was going to have it made where she worked after she designed it. That way she could have exactly what she wanted, and she had found a perfect heavy ivory satin for the design she had in mind. The wedding was less than two months away.

*

Everyone came to Thanksgiving except Zach and Izzie. She was in bed with bronchitis, and Zach didn't want to go alone. And it was a relief not to have Zach there. But Justin and Richard came with the baby, with even more equipment since she was two months older than at their last visit. She was sweet and lively, and everyone had fun with her. And Kate was beginning to adjust to the idea of being a grandmother.

*

On the day of the wedding, the florist arrived at Kate's apartment and transformed it into a flower garden with moss and branches, small vases of white freesia and lilies of the valley, and sprays of tiny white orchids. Julie had told them exactly what she wanted, and Kate was stunned at how perfect it was. Julie always had a vision that went beyond what others would have planned.

And that night, on Christmas Eve, at eight o'clock, after the six o'clock service, the family gathered at Trinity Grace Church. Julie was wearing a short ivory satin dress with a wide belt in the same fabric and cinched-in waist, a high stand-up collar, and just enough cleavage to be enticing, but not too much so. The sleeves of the dress were long. She had added ivory satin pumps with the usual high heels she preferred. The dress had a 1950s feeling to it, and was reminiscent of Dior. Kate wore a black lace cocktail dress by an unknown designer. Grandma Lou was in emerald green, which looked well on her, and Izzie had found a loose red dress to fit over her growing belly. She was six months pregnant, and looked very pretty. And the men were wearing dark suits. Only the family was present at the ceremony. The few friends that had been invited were coming to the house at nine-thirty for a late dinner, served as a buffet. Julie had wanted seafood, and there were lobster and fresh crab on the menu. The wedding cake had been delivered that afternoon. It was a very small wedding, but every detail had been impeccably thought out by the bride.

Julie and Peter looked ecstatically happy during the ceremony. It was entirely appropriate, but Peter couldn't keep his eyes off her in the chic sexy dress. Julie looked very stylish. She wore her hair in a loose bun, with the same tiny orchids threaded into it that she carried in her bouquet, and they left the church as husband and wife.

Julie's friends who worked in fashion had dressed for the occasion, and Liam and Maureen were there, although they stayed only briefly, so they could go to midnight mass with their daughters. It was a happy and intimate evening that was enhanced by the warmth of Christmas.

The baby slept peacefully all evening in Kate's bedroom, and her fathers checked on her every few minutes, and had set up a monitor with a camera in the bedroom, so they could see what she was doing and if she woke up.

Kate noticed that Willie was texting a lot that night, but he always did, keeping tabs on his various women and his friends to see what they were doing and if he was missing anything.

"Give it a rest, Will," Justin teased him. "No one does anything on Christmas Eve."

"You never know." Willie laughed at him and slipped his phone into his pocket. Someone had just sent him an Instagram and he didn't want his brother to see it.

"Hot new romance?" Justin asked him as they went back to the buffet for more lobster.

"Maybe," Willie said noncommittally. He was twenty-five and seemed more grown up lately, and he was doing well at his job, which was so technical none of them understood it.

Izzie and Zach seemed peaceful. She sat on the couch and he had an arm around her shoulders, rubbed her belly from time to time, and brought her dinner so she didn't have to get up. He was sweet with her, and he looked respectable that night, and even wore socks and a suit Izzie had bought him. But no matter what he said or wore, he always exuded the bad-boy image that was so much his style. Julie and Izzie talked about the baby for a few minutes. Izzie had warmed up to the idea, and they had found out that it was a boy, and Zach was very pleased with himself.

"I'll come home when you have it," Julie promised. "I don't want to miss that." It was due in March, and Richard had been giving her advice about everything she'd need to buy for the baby, which made both sisters giggle when he walked away. "And a bigger apartment to put it in," Julie whispered. "Their house looks like a children's department store now." They were both still over-the-top about Milagra and the whole family teased them about it.

The bridal couple left at one A.M. to spend the night at the Plaza, where Peter had reserved the bridal suite. Everything had been packed at Julie's apartment the day before, and the movers were coming the day after Christmas to send it to L.A.

Peter and Julie were going to spend Christmas Day with Kate and the others, and fly to Hawaii that night for a week's honeymoon. Peter had to start work at the L.A. office on the second of January. And before they left on Christmas Eve, Peter thanked his mother-in-law warmly for a perfect wedding. It was just what they had wanted. He hugged Kate and told her that it meant a great deal to him to have someone so wonderful as his mother-in-law. Kate felt faintly skeptical as he said it, and then chided herself for being cynical. He was the opposite of Zach. Peter was polite, appropriate, responsible, protective of her daughter, and kind to her and Julie's grandmother. What more did she want? But she didn't know why, anytime he paid them compliments or showed respect, Kate didn't feel it was sincere.

Julie left her mother's apartment looking like she was floating on a cloud.

Izzie and Zach left shortly after the bride and groom. She said she was tired, but both brothers and Richard stayed longer in their mother's living room, and so did

Grandma Lou, who was full of energy and in great form. She was going to Santa Fe, New Mexico, after Christmas to visit friends since she had nothing else planned.

Justin admitted that he was sad that Julie was moving so far away. He wanted her to really get to know Milagra, but Julie had said they'd probably be transferred again in a few years. The firm that Peter worked for moved people around a lot. "She looks so happy," he said wistfully. "I think Peter is perfect for her. And it'll be a nice change for her not to have to work for a while and just enjoy being married, before they have kids." He and Richard had discovered how much work it was having a baby, but they loved it, even though their carefree days were over. Milagra ran their world. Their social life had ended when she arrived, which bothered Richard more than Justin. They hadn't had an evening with friends or gone to a movie since she was born.

He and Richard had been talking for the past few weeks about whether or not they wanted another one soon. Justin like the idea of having them close together, while they were already steeped in Milagra's baby needs, rather than waiting until she was older and starting all over again. And they agreed that they wanted two kids. They knew it would be tight financially, but they were willing to make the necessary sacrifices. Alana had told them she would do it again, and Shirley said she might too when they asked her, although she said she would only do it one more time. She said her body was beginning to show the wear and tear of four pregnancies, but they needed the money. If they wanted to do it, Alana had said she would start giving herself hormone shots again on her next cycle, so Justin was pushing Richard for a decision before either woman changed her mind. It had all worked so well before that Justin didn't want to have to use a different donor, or find another surrogate. They knew and trusted both, which was a major plus. But they didn't mention anything about it at Julie's wedding dinner or on Christmas because it was a decision they wanted to make themselves, without input from anyone else. They had learned that lesson the first time.

When Julie and Peter left on Christmas Day, they all went downstairs to throw the rose petals the florist had provided, and then Julie and Peter got in a cab to go to the airport for their honeymoon in Hawaii. It had started snowing and Julie was beaming. It was a scene Kate knew she would never forget, and Justin put an arm around his mother's shoulders as they went back upstairs after the couple had left.

When they got back to the apartment, Richard was holding the baby and she was crying, and her cheeks were flushed. She felt hot to the touch.

"I think she has a fever," Richard said, worried. "I think we should call the doctor, or take her to someone here."

"On Christmas Day? Why don't we wait," Justin said

practically. They had a thermometer at their friends' apartment. It reminded Kate of the days of kids sick on holidays, having to change plans every five minutes, or sitting up all night for an earache or a fever. That had been her life for many years, and Richard and Justin were just starting out. Richard looked panicked, but Justin was calm. They left a little while later, and Zach and Izzie followed shortly after. Willie took his grandmother home and then gave the driver an address uptown. He settled back in the cab, looking happy, and sent a text that said "I'm on my way. Be there in ten minutes." And then he looked out the window and smiled at the falling snow as the cab sped uptown.

*

Izzie went to lie down when they got home. It had been a busy two days, and she was beginning to feel the weight of the baby, though she'd had no problems. Zach went to watch football in the living room, and poured himself a glass of wine.

She fell asleep, and it was ten o'clock when she woke up and went to check on Zach in the living room. He had fallen asleep too, and was passed out on the couch, with an empty bottle of wine on the table in front of him. She knew he was drinking a lot these days, and he was bored. He had nothing to do, and she had been unusually busy at work for the past month, with end-of-the-year legal work to do for her clients. She still wanted Zach to get a job and was planning to talk to him about it again seriously after the holidays. He had to do something. He couldn't just sit around the house, drink, watch TV, and meet up with his seedy friends. She was afraid he'd get into trouble again if he continued doing that. His remaining idle was a bad idea.

Her law firm was closed that week between Christmas and New Year, and they spent some nice time together, but couldn't go anywhere, because of Zach's probation restrictions. The electronic anklet confined him to a specific area, which included New York City, but nothing beyond. So the house in East Hampton was out of bounds until the anklet came off. They both really missed it, and hated being stuck in the city every weekend. But it was a small price to pay for keeping him out of jail.

They had talked about going out with friends of Izzie's on New Year's Eve, but Zach thought they were boring, and it would be fun to watch the ball come down in Times Square, and go there to see it live. Izzie worried it would be crowded and cold, and she didn't want to get jostled by the crowd, but he was such a big kid about it that she agreed. She was going to make a nice dinner for them that night, and Zach went off to see one of his friends in the afternoon, and came back in great spirits. He was in a festive mood when he kissed her, and she went to shower and change before she finished cooking dinner. Then she remembered something she had forgotten to ask him, and ran back to the living room wrapped in a towel. And as soon as she walked in on silent feet, she saw him with his head bent over something, and saw that he was holding a piece of glass and snorting a line of coke. She stopped dead in her tracks and stared at him with her heart beating faster.

"What the hell are you doing?" she said in a loud voice and he jumped and turned to see her, with the powder dusting his nose and upper lip, and falling into his beard.

"Oh, for chrissake, Iz . . . it's New Year's Eve, don't be so uptight."

"Uptight?" she said, advancing on him, still holding the towel around her. "*Uptight?* Remember me? I'm the attorney who had to beg and plead and practically promise to give the assistant DA a blow job to keep you on probation, got you into rehab and kept you out of prison, with that fucking anklet you're wearing that you're so proud of. If it weren't for me, they'd have revoked your probation and put you in prison six months ago, and I'm 'uptight'? And what was the point of three months of rehab if you're doing lines?" She was horrified.

"All right, I'm sorry," he said, dusting his face off, but she saw that he set the piece of glass down carefully, so as to preserve what was left of the cocaine, and it was quite a bit. She wondered if he had more in a bag in his pocket. And she realized now that he'd been drinking too. He looked hopped up and the coke was already taking effect, or maybe he'd had some before.

"I want you to get rid of that stuff now. If you get caught with drugs again, you're dead. The cops won't even wait for a hearing, the judge will put you away on a probation violation and talk about it later."

"I'm not throwing out high-grade shit like this," he said, grinning at her. "This stuff is great."

"Get rid of it," she said menacingly. "I don't want that in my house." But she was sure he had more, and it could be hidden anywhere. "You're a fool if you keep playing with it. You're going to wind up in prison, and there won't be a damn thing I can do next time. You'll be a three-time loser. They can put you away for fifteen to life." The very thought of it made her shudder, and she could feel their baby moving inside her, as though the baby was upset too. Maybe it was the adrenaline pumping through her veins. "Don't you care about this at all?" she said, pointing to her stomach. "I don't want him to have a father in prison."

"Neither do I." Zach looked suddenly angry and aggressive. "And I don't want him to have a father who's pussy whipped either. You can't tell me what to do all the time, Izzie . . . get a job . . . go to work . . . make some money . . . be responsible . . . stay off drugs . . . Shit, that's not who I am. You knew it when you met me. I like to party.

I've never worked in my life. What do you expect me to do? Sell shoes at Macy's?"

"Maybe, if that's all you can do. You can't sit around and do nothing forever." She was fighting back tears as she saw the effects of the coke in his eyes. He was flying high now.

"Why not? What the fuck do I care about working? You make enough for both of us." It was true, but that was no reason for him to do nothing and sit around snorting coke.

"I don't want you doing drugs," she said, trying to stay calm.

"I'm not going to get caught here. What are you going to do? Call the cops?"

"You bought it somewhere. That's how you get caught."

"I bought it from my old dealer, he's cool, he knows me." Tears rolled down her cheeks as he said it. Her life felt totally out of control. He just didn't get it, and didn't want to. "Why are you always pressuring me about something? Just let me be. I don't tell you what to do. Why are you always trying to cut off my balls?" He looked vicious as he said it.

"I'm not, I just don't want you to do drugs, or get arrested. You're on probation, and I don't want drugs in our life."

"A little happy powder might do you some good. Loosen up." He was getting increasingly hostile as he said it, and he walked toward her and left the piece of glass with the rest of the coke on the table. "Get off my back," he said, as he strode past her. He wasn't usually like this with her. She knew it was the drugs. And he must have done a lot, because he was suddenly very speedy and volatile. She didn't think he'd hurt her, but he might do something stupid without meaning to, in the haze of the cocaine, and she took a step back as he grazed past her and grabbed the keys off the hall table to a truck he had rented recently.

"Where are you going?" she asked, looking frightened.

"None of your fucking business. I'm tired of being chained up like a dog in a yard, with this goddam anklet. It's New Year's Eve. I'll go wherever I damn well want to."

"You can't," she said, trying to snatch the keys from him, but he yanked them away and pushed past her as he headed to the front door. "Zach, please, it'll come up on their screen immediately if you go out of the area you're allowed to."

"Fuck them," he said in a fury, "and fuck you too." He slammed the door behind him, and when she opened the door into the hallway, he was gone. She could hear him thundering down the stairs in his biker boots. He hadn't even bothered to put on a coat, and it was cold outside. He had abandoned the line of coke on the table, which made her suspect he had more on him somewhere. He was wasted. She didn't know what to do. She couldn't call the police to stop him or find him, and she was terrified he'd drive out to the Hamptons, or someplace worse, where he'd either get caught or his anklet would set off an alarm, and they'd look for him and find him in the condition he was in.

She was sobbing when she walked into the apartment and sat down. She stood up then, took the glass with the coke on it, and washed it down the drain in the kitchen sink. Her hand was shaking so badly that she bumped the glass on the faucet, and it cut her hand. She wrapped it in a kitchen towel and went to lie on her bed. She tried calling his cellphone, and he didn't answer. She wrote him a text and told him she loved him and begged him to come home. And then she saw his cellphone sitting on the couch when she went back to the living room. He had forgotten it and she had no way to reach him. He was out in the stratosphere somewhere doing what he wanted, snorting coke and drinking, and God only knew what else. And something bad was going to happen if he didn't come to his senses. But he was high on drugs now and she knew there was no stopping him.

She went to put her clothes on. She put on the maternity jeans she had to wear now, with one of Zach's flannel shirts over them, and slipped her feet into a pair of old loafers. New Year's Eve had lost all importance. All she wanted was for Zach to come home safely. And after that, they'd have to figure out what to do next. He needed to go to rehab again. She wondered if he'd been doing coke for a while, although she thought she would have known, but maybe not. But right then at that moment, she knew he was at risk of doing something crazy, and she had to stop him, but she didn't know how. And without a phone, she had no way to reach him. And she didn't know his friends' phone numbers or his password to access them. They were all deadbeats and drug addicts, and Zach still saw them on his own time, not with her. She didn't even know who most of them were, or their right names. That part of his life was very dark. She had kept away from it, and urged him to give it up too. She thought he had, but apparently not.

She sat on the couch for hours, unable to eat or think, or even cry after a while. She just sat there, waiting to hear from him, and praying for him to come home. All she wanted was for him to find his way back, come to his senses and say, as he did when he screwed up, "Oh baby, I'm sorry." She could hear him say it in her head. She just prayed he wouldn't call her to say it from jail. If he got arrested again, or caught in possession of drugs or committing some other crime, there would be nothing she could do. If he was even caught speeding, and they searched him, they would arrest him immediately.

It was two A.M. when she glanced at the clock in the living room. Midnight had passed without her noticing it. And then it was four A.M., and she still hadn't heard from him, and finally, just after five A.M. on New Year's Day, she closed her eyes and fell asleep on the couch. She hadn't heard from Zach all night. She had called the house in East Hampton and he wasn't there. She had no idea where he was, but at least he hadn't called from jail.

Chapter 19

The sun was streaming in the windows when the phone rang and woke Izzie up just after nine A.M. on New Year's Day. She leapt toward it, and grabbed it, praying it was Zach and he was okay. He had probably come down from the coke by then, and was calling her to apologize. But it wasn't him, it was the police, and her heart sank as a Lieutenant Kelley identified himself. She knew what that meant. He had been arrested the night before. It was why he hadn't called her. Either they hadn't let him call, or he was too embarrassed to tell her he was in jail, or too stoned.

"Is it about my husband?" She sounded breathless as she asked, and the officer was startled and didn't answer for a minute.

"I . . . yes, ma'am, it is." He was serious and subdued.

"Is he in jail?"

"No, ma'am, he's not." Her spirits rose for an instant as the lieutenant said it. Thank God, Zach hadn't been arrested after all.

"Where is he?" She was smiling as she held the phone to her ear with a shaking hand. "Can I talk to him?"

"I . . . he had an accident on the Long Island Expressway last night, just before the exit to East Hampton. There was a lot of ice on the road." Izzie interrupted him before he could tell her the rest. She couldn't stand the suspense and he was speaking slowly and deliberately. She didn't care about the weather conditions. Where was Zach?

"Is he in the hospital? Is he okay?"

"No, ma'am, he's not." The lieutenant hated calls like this, but they were his responsibility as the officer in charge. The highway patrol had called him, because of the address on Zach's papers. "He was driving over a hundred miles an hour. He hit an eighteen-wheeler, went across the divider, and was killed instantly. I'm sorry." After he had said it, Izzie sat in total silence for a minute with the phone in her hand.

"He what? Are you sure?" She sounded like she was fading away and felt like she was going to die herself. How could that happen? How could Zach be dead? Lieutenant Kelley had to be wrong. "Where is he?" Not that it mattered now. He was gone. Her husband and the father of her unborn child was dead.

"He's at the hospital in Long Island where they took him. They're running some substance tests on him. We need to know if he was under the influence for our report. The driver of the eighteen-wheeler was killed too, and two other vehicles were involved. We'll be bringing him to the morgue this afternoon. You can identify the body and claim him there after six o'clock. I'm very sorry," he said again.

"Thank you," she said, shaking from head to foot. And she was aware that the baby had stopped moving too, as though he also knew that his father had just died. Without thinking, she dialed her mother's number, and Kate picked up immediately. She was planning to take Frances and her mother out to lunch. She was in good spirits, and had spent a quiet night at home. Bernard had sent her a text to wish her a happy New Year, and she had ignored it. She smiled when she saw the call was from Izzie when she picked it up.

"Hi, sweetheart. Happy New Year." She froze when she heard Izzie's voice.

"Zach is dead. He was killed in an accident last night." And then she started to sob hysterically and Kate couldn't understand what she was saying.

"Are you okay? Were you with him? The baby?"

"He drove out to East Hampton alone. . . . We had a fight. . . ."

"It's not your fault, Iz. Whatever happened, you didn't do it. He was driving. You weren't there." Kate rushed to reassure her. Izzie was blaming herself.

"But I upset him." Izzie sobbed pitifully into the phone.

"I'll be there in five minutes." Kate grabbed her coat

and purse and flew out of her apartment. She gave the cabdriver a twenty-dollar bill and told him to get her to Izzie's address as fast as he could. It wasn't far and she had just enough time to call both her sons and tell them. She didn't know the details, but she knew that Izzie would need their help, and she told Justin to call his grandmother and tell her Kate couldn't take her to lunch, but not why yet. Kate wanted to know more before she told her mother.

"Do you know what happened, Mom?" Justin asked in a shocked voice.

"No, I don't. She said they had a fight."

"Oh God. Maybe he was drunk."

"I'll call you later," she said quickly. They had just gotten to Izzie's address, and she thanked the driver and jumped out, and pressed the intercom to Izzie's apartment. She buzzed her mother in without asking who it was. Kate didn't wait for the elevator but ran up the stairs and was out of breath when she rang Izzie's doorbell and Izzie let her in. She looked ravaged and collapsed in her mother's arms with her big belly between them, and Kate was relieved to feel the baby kick. She led Izzie to the couch, and Izzie told her a disjointed, somewhat cleaned-up version of what had happened. She left out the coke at first, and then finally admitted it to her mother. But whatever he had done, however foolish and irresponsible he had been, now he was dead. And Izzie loved him.

They had been married for eight months to the day. And now she was a widow, and her son would have no father when he was born.

She cried in her mother's arms for many hours, and Willie showed up at the apartment and brought food for them. He looked shaken to see the condition his sister was in, and he sat quietly in the living room while Kate made Izzie lie down for a while, and she cried herself to sleep, and then Kate came back to sit with her youngest son.

"What do we do now?" Willie whispered.

"She has to identify the body at the morgue after six o'clock," Kate said in a grim voice.

"I can do that," Willie said somberly. He had never seen a dead body before, but at least he could do it for his sister.

They talked for a while in whispers and low voices, and Justin called his mother to tell her he was on the way. He had to bring the baby because Richard was going to work the next day and they had no sitter, but Kate was grateful that he was coming and she knew that Izzie would be too. They couldn't reach Julie because she was on a plane coming back from her honeymoon, but Justin said he'd call her that night, and he was sure she would come home. They all wanted to be there for their sister.

Izzie slept for two hours, and cried again when she woke up. They had to make arrangements for the funeral, and she wanted to call Zach's father and let him know, although she'd never met him or spoken to him before.

And his grandmother had had another stroke recently and had dementia now so she didn't think she should call her.

Kate called the funeral home while they were waiting to go to the morgue, and they said they'd make the necessary arrangements and have somebody there to get the body. And Kate had called Liam and he was stunned and sorry for Izzie and offered to do whatever he could for them, but there was very little anyone could do, except be there for Izzie.

Izzie still couldn't believe it had happened, and was hoping it was some kind of mistake, as she and her mother and Willie got in a cab to go to the morgue. The body had been brought to the city from Long Island. She had reached Zach's father on his cellphone earlier. He said he was in Sydney, Australia, on a boat, and there was no way he could come to New York. He was somber and offered Izzie his condolences, but he sounded as though Zach was someone else's son.

"I'm sorry to tell you that if your baby was already born, Zach's portion of the trust would have gone to him. But in the case of an unborn child, his share of the trust reverts to the other beneficiaries of the trust. So there will be nothing for your baby," he said clearly, as though that was why she had called.

"I don't care," Izzie said in a choked voice. "That's not why I called. I just wanted you to know, in case you wanted to come to his funeral. But you were never there for him when he was alive, so I guess it's not surprising you're not coming now that he's dead." Zach's father was shocked by what she'd said, more so than he had been about his son's death.

"I'm sorry I can't come." He attempted to sound sincere but didn't. Zach had been a headache to them all his life, and he was only surprised his son had lived that long. Zach was dead at thirty-six, and his wife a widow at thirty-three.

The hour they spent at the morgue was unimaginably grim. Two men from the funeral home were there to remove the body and take it to the mortuary Kate had called. Willie identified the body and said it was Zach, while Izzie sobbed in her mother's arms and nearly fainted, as two sympathetic policemen watched. One of them discreetly told Kate that they had removed the electronic anklet, since it was no longer needed and they thought the family would want to allow the deceased to be buried with dignity, and not as a convicted felon. Kate thanked them, and they left before Zach's body was removed, and went back to Kate's apartment, where she tucked her daughter into her own bed. She brought her a cup of soup, which Izzie refused, and then she fell asleep, before Justin arrived with the baby at nine o'clock.

"How is she?" he asked, desperately worried about his sister. He had thought her choice of husband was a bad one, but he had never imagined it would end like this.

"About the way you'd expect," Kate said, and went to make them all a salad and some sandwiches. And Grandma Lou had called to see if there was anything they needed, but Kate said they didn't, so Louise left them in peace. Kate had called her earlier and told her the news. She didn't want her to hear it from someone else.

Justin was waiting to call Julie in California. He knew their plane from Hawaii was landing at eight o'clock, and she'd be home at nine, which would be midnight in New York. They didn't know yet when the funeral would be, but Kate assumed it would be in a few days, and Julie would want to be there for Izzie.

*

The honeymoon in Hawaii had been idyllic. They'd spent three days on Maui at a fun, lively hotel, and four days on Lanai at an incredibly romantic location. Peter had planned and arranged everything. They spent hours on the beach, swimming, snorkeling, and had romantic dinners every night. It was like a dream. He was the perfect husband, and they held hands all the way to L.A. on the plane. It was going to be hard going back to real life once they landed in L.A. Peter was starting his new job the next day, and he was excited and a little nervous about it.

Julie didn't bother turning on her cellphone on the way home from the airport, and then remembered to do it when they walked into the apartment. His company had given them a furnished executive apartment to stay in until their own things arrived. Peter had already picked out a villa for them in West Hollywood, but Julie hadn't seen it yet except online. She could hardly wait to explore their new neighborhood and home. Her furniture from New York, and his from his apartment, was due to arrive in two weeks, unless there was snow on the way. But the executive apartment was very nice.

She stuck her phone in the charger and it rang immediately when she plugged it in. It was Justin. He told her the news, and she looked shocked as Peter listened to her end of the conversation. It was obvious something terrible had happened, but he couldn't tell to whom. Julie was pale when she hung up and turned to Peter.

"Zach was killed in a car accident last night," she said, thinking of her sister. Justin had said she was asleep, so Julie couldn't talk to her.

"How awful for your sister, especially with the baby." Julie nodded, thinking how terrible that would be for her. But Julie was grateful she hadn't been in the car with him.

"I have to go home tomorrow," she said, looking distracted, trying to think of everything she had to do, since they had just arrived.

"This is your home now," he said in a firm voice, sounding almost like a parent.

"I know." She smiled at him and put her arms around

him to kiss him. "But I have to go back to be with my sister."

"No, you don't." He looked completely unaffected by what she'd said.

"Of course I do. We're all very close. I can't let her go through this without being there for her." She couldn't imagine not going to Izzie.

"She doesn't need you, she has your brothers and your mother and your grandmother. That's more than enough." At first Julie thought he was kidding, but he wasn't. Peter wasn't close to his family, and he didn't understand a family like hers, and the bond they shared. They never let each other down. Their mother had inculcated that in them, that families were forever and stuck together, no matter what.

"It's not the same, Peter. I'm her sister. She's pregnant and her husband just died. Of course I have to be there for her."

"You do not. I'm your family now, and your first responsibility is to me. I'm starting a new job tomorrow, and I need you with me." She was stunned to realize he meant it.

"I don't want to argue with you about it," Julie said as gently as she could, "but there's no way I'm staying here while my sister buries her husband. You've had new jobs before. She's never buried a husband." It was crystal clear to her.

"She shouldn't have married him anyway. He was a dirtbag, and I'm not surprised. He was probably drunk or on drugs." Julie suspected that too, but didn't say it.

"That doesn't change the fact that my sister is devastated now. My brother said she's in terrible shape."

"She's better off without him. I hope she loses the baby too." Julie was horrified by what he said. It was so unlike him to be so brutal and unkind. This was not the man she knew. She didn't pursue the point with him. She took her phone into the bathroom and booked a nine A.M. flight. She'd have to leave the apartment at seven, and she was due to land in New York at five P.M. local time. You lost the whole day traveling east with the time difference, but it was the best she could do.

Peter didn't speak to her again until they went to bed. They had both unpacked their clothes from their honeymoon, and Julie had packed a small bag full of warm black clothes for New York. And he turned to her as they got into bed.

"You're not going, are you, Julie?" His voice was cold and hard.

"Yes, I am." He had to know right from the beginning how important her family was to her. This was not negotiable for her. Or for him, apparently.

"I'll never forgive you for this if you do," he said in an icy tone, and tears filled her eyes as he said it.

"Peter, please be reasonable. I have to go to Zach's funeral, for Izzie."

"This could be a deal breaker for me," he warned her in a menacing tone, and she slipped into bed feeling as though a stranger had come home from her honeymoon with her.

"Why are you so angry about it? I won't stay long."

"I don't care how long you stay. When you walk out of here tomorrow, I'll know where your loyalties are, and they're not to me."

"Of course they are. I can love my family and you," she said gently, in a loving tone.

"No, you can't, and you'd better understand that right now. Your loyalties have to be to me, always, at all times. I come first now." It sounded crazy to Julie as he said it, but she didn't argue with him. She wondered if she had tapped into some childhood issue of his. He hadn't had a problem about her family before the wedding. This was new.

He turned his back on her in bed that night, and they had been making love day and night on their honeymoon. And he treated her like a stranger when they woke up the next morning. She put her arms around his neck and tried to kiss him, and he pushed her away and got out of bed. He didn't speak to her again until he saw her dressed and ready to leave.

"You may find the locks changed when you get back," he warned her, and she looked him straight in the eye.

"I love you, Peter. And I love my family. I'll be home soon. I hope the job goes well today. I'll call you when I get in."

"I don't want to hear from you until you're back here where you belong. I'm not going to put up with this again. You'd better be damn clear about that." He had never said anything like it to her while they were dating, or during their brief engagement. He had been loving and adorable and kind to her and her family, and now he wanted to control her and be all powerful in her life.

"This isn't slavery," she said in a soft voice before she left. "It's marriage." She wanted to add that he'd better "be damn clear about that" too, but she didn't want to add fuel to the fire, and he looked furious with her when she left. She went outside and got into the cab she had called, and thought about him all the way to the airport. She had no idea why he was behaving so strangely, but maybe it was just as well that something like this had happened early. He needed to know that she had not traded her family for him. There was room for both in her life. And her going to New York had just proved that to him.

She felt better when she boarded the plane. He must have just had some kind of macho brat fit, maybe due to the stress of starting the new job, and she was sure he'd be fine when she got back. All she wanted now was to see her family. She had left them a week before, and who could have expected this?

*

When Julie landed in New York, she went straight to her mother's apartment. She knew all of them were there. Izzie had gone home to get some clothes, but she was staying with her mother. Justin was sleeping on the couch, the baby in her travel bed, and Willie at his own place. Julie was going to camp out on the other couch. They all wanted to be together, even if it was cramped. It reminded them of their childhood.

Kate had gone to the store and brought back some things for herself and Julie to wear, and she had sent Jessica to a maternity store to buy a black dress for Izzie. There was going to be a wake the next day, and the funeral the day after. And then it would be over, and Izzie would have to live the rest of her life without him. Nobody had commented on what a mistake the marriage had been, nor would they, although it had crossed their minds. Izzie had told her mother the whole story, about his arrests, his drug use, and finding him snorting lines in the living room on New Year's Eve and his storming out of the apartment. Kate had continued to remind her that it wasn't her fault, but Izzie felt terrible anyway.

Justin looked relieved the minute his twin walked in. He put his arms around her and asked about the honeymoon, and she told him it had been like a dream. She didn't tell him about Peter's strange behavior when she left. It was so atypical for him that it really didn't matter. She had sent him a text when she arrived, but he didn't answer. And Grandma Lou came over with dinner from a nearby restaurant that night. She looked appropriate in somber black, and was pleased to see her other grand-daughter.

The wake the following night at the funeral home was morbid. The casket was there and Izzie almost collapsed. No one came except the family, and Liam without Maureen. He stood close to Kate, and he talked to all of her children, and admired the baby Justin had brought with him to the funeral home, and then he left so as not to intrude on Izzie, who was distraught. He gave Kate a warm hug before he left and told her to call him if they needed anything.

They went out for a Chinese dinner afterward, and everyone's mood lifted a little. Willie succeeded in teasing Izzie and making her smile, and Justin surprised them all, while Kate held the baby.

"She's going to have a brother or sister," Justin said in a calm, normal voice, as the others stared at him.

"Who is?" Julie asked. He couldn't have meant they were having another baby so soon. It didn't make sense. She thought she had misunderstood.

"Milagra. We had to make a quick decision with Alana's

cycle. She's moving to London for a while so we wanted to seize the opportunity while we had it, since she was willing to be an egg donor again. It's not going to be easy, but we both like the idea of having two kids close together, even though it will take some juggling to do it. So they harvested her eggs the day before I came down here. Shirley agreed to do it again too. So if it all goes well, they'll be putting the fertilized embryos into her in a few days," he said, looking proud and happy. "So we're on our way again. The baby will be due in September. They'll be thirteen months apart. I'd rather do it that way. It's simpler to have everyone in diapers at the same time." This time, Kate made no comment, nor did Izzie, since the surrogacy had worked well for them before, but they were startled anyway. Two babies were going to put a huge strain on him and Richard financially, which Kate thought was unwise. But it was a decision they had a right to make. They were both intelligent men, and she and Tom had had their babies very quickly too, and Grandma Lou had been just as worried about her.

"Are you going to have a lot more?" Willie asked his brother casually.

"No, this is it. We don't want her to be an only child. Two is just right for us. Three would be too much." Everyone nodded, as though it sounded totally reasonable, which his mother knew it wasn't. Unless the novel he'd been working on was a major hit, they'd be very strapped for money, and already were. And he hadn't had time to work on the book since August, when the baby was born.

"And Richard is fine with it?" Kate asked. "It's a sacrifice for him too." Justin nodded and Izzie asked Julie when she was going back, to change the subject.

"When you don't need me." She smiled at her older sister, and Izzie squeezed her hand and leaned over and kissed her gratefully.

"Thank you for coming. It means a lot." The look in her eyes made Peter's anger irrelevant, and Julie was sure his threats were hollow. He would get over it when she got back. And since she didn't have a job, she could make her own decision about when to go back. She loved Peter passionately, but her family still came first.

*

They had made the arrangements as quickly as possible, to get the nightmare behind Izzie as soon as they could. The funeral was as horrible as everyone expected. Izzie was brave and stood strong, with her mother on one side and Justin on the other. A few people from Izzie's law firm had seen the obituary and came out of respect for her. Zach's father didn't. He had said he would notify Zach's mother, but Izzie never heard from her. Frances came with Grandma Lou, and Liam and Maureen came. Their daughters had gone back to Europe. And Richard came down from Vermont for the day. It was a small motley crew, and they drove to the cemetery in two limousines with the baby, and the burial was brief and sad. Izzie was sobbing uncontrollably as her brothers led her away, and Julie followed with Kate, after Izzie dropped a white rose on the casket. Kate thought it was the saddest thing she'd ever seen to watch her daughter mourn her husband, however unsuitable he had been, while carrying their unborn baby. They went back to Kate's afterward, and sat around as though in a trance.

Justin left that night for the long drive back to Vermont. He didn't want Richard to have to fly back, and it was cheaper if they drove, and Justin wanted to be with him. They both wanted to be there when the embryos were placed in Shirley's uterus in the next two days.

Willie went home that night, and Izzie forced herself to go back to work the following Monday. She looked awful, but said she needed the distraction and had fallen behind in her work. And once Izzie went back to the office, Julie booked a flight to California. She had been in New York for exactly six days, and Izzie was grateful for it. Julie had texted Peter every day, and he had never responded. She knew he was paying her back for going against him and defying his wishes.

Her flight from New York landed in L.A. at two in the afternoon, and she took a cab back to their temporary apartment. For a minute she wondered if Peter had made good on his threats and changed the locks, but her key worked when she got there. After she unpacked, she went to a nearby market and bought what she needed to make him a nice dinner. She was wearing an apron over jeans and a sweater and cooking when he got home, and he looked surprised to see her, although she had texted him when she was arriving. He didn't say a word to her at first and then stood stiffly in the kitchen, while she cooked a leg of lamb that smelled delicious.

"How was it?" he asked, looking stern and not remorseful.

"Very sad. It was very hard on Izzie, I'm glad I went, but I missed you."

"Did you?" he asked as he walked toward her, and for a minute she wasn't sure what he was going to do to her. There was a menacing look in his eyes, but she refused to be daunted.

"Yes, I did miss you," she smiled and said as he grabbed her hard and kissed her, and then with no warning, he picked her up, carried her easily, strode into their bedroom, and dumped her on the bed.

"Take your clothes off," he ordered her. "I want to make love to you." She wanted to make love to him too, but his suddenly harsh, commanding style was unnerving. He'd never acted like that before and it was more caveman than romantic. She did as she was told and held her arms out to him with a smile, and with that he pushed her onto the bed, grabbed her hair and pulled her head back, and entered her with no warning, with a savage look she didn't recognize.

"Hey, take it easy," she said, and he looked at her fiercely.

"Don't you ever, *ever* leave me like that again, when I tell you not to. Do you understand that?" She nodded as tears sprang to her eyes, and just as quickly he melted into the man she had married. He made love to her exquisitely, and held her in his arms afterward. The frightening new side of Peter had disappeared, but she had discovered a part of him she never knew.

They had a romantic dinner in the kitchen that night. He loved the leg of lamb, and they hurried to bed afterward. And this time, he was only slightly rougher than he used to be. Marriage had changed him. He owned her now.

Chapter 20

When Izzie returned to work and moved back to her own apartment, she left Zach's clothes in the closet. She wasn't ready to give them up yet, and she had no reason to. She never heard from his father again, nor his mother. No correspondence came for him. It was as though she had married a drifter who had existed in her life for eighteen months and then vanished. But he had left their baby behind as a memory of him. And Zach had made a profound impression on Izzie. She realized afterward that she would never have changed him, and regretted the pressure she had put on him to get a job and become responsible. That wasn't who he was. And you couldn't marry someone like that and expect them to be different. He remained true to himself till the end, drugging, drinking, in trouble with the law. She realized that he probably would have ended up in prison sooner or later. It was almost unavoidable. And they might not have stayed married, but she had loved him anyway, and it was hard to let go of the good memories, along with the bad. But her mother had been right, you couldn't win when the odds were against you. And they had been with Zach.

She had decided to continue working until the delivery. She didn't want to sit around at home thinking, and she was going to take a month off after the baby came.

The day she went into labor she had a court appearance, and managed to finish it, without letting on to anyone what was happening. She called her assistant to say she wouldn't be coming back to the office, and she called her doctor on her way home to pick up her bag for the hospital, take a shower, and call her mother. She stayed matter-of-fact about it or she knew she would fall apart, knowing that she had to go through this alone, and Zach would never see their baby. The thought of it made her cry every time it came to mind. Kate hadn't been surprised to hear from her. It was Izzie's due date. As usual, she did everything on schedule, her mother teased her.

The doctor said she could stay home for a while, since the pains were still far apart, her water hadn't broken yet, and it was her first baby. Izzie had toyed with the idea of doing it naturally but had finally decided to have an epidural for the pain. Why be a hero?

Kate promised to come over as soon as Izzie called her, and Izzie said there was no rush. Kate arrived half an hour later, having changed into jeans and flat shoes, with her own little bag of supplies for the hospital. And once she was there, as though the baby had waited politely for his grandmother, the contractions started in earnest.

"Ohhh, this is worse than I thought it would be," Izzie said as she tried to breathe through the contractions. She called Julie, and they talked for a while, and then Izzie was in too much pain, and called her doctor again. She told her to come in, and Kate and Izzie took a cab, while Kate timed the contractions.

"They're getting closer together," Kate commented, relieved that they were on their way to the hospital. It was rush hour and traffic was heavy. And the pains had gone from four minutes apart to three to two by the time they got there. Izzie looked at the nurse desperately as they wheeled her down the hall to a labor room.

"Can I have the epidural now?" she asked, panting between pains, and the nurse smiled.

"Let's have the doctor take a look at you. I think she's already here." Izzie didn't care if the president of the United States was there, she wanted the epidural *now* and she said so. "Are we waiting for Dad to get here?" the nurse asked pleasantly, as she helped Izzie take her clothes off and get into bed.

"No, Dad is dead, and I want my epidural now, god-dammit!" Izzie shouted at her and Kate smiled. She could tell that Izzie was in hard labor from her behavior and the desperation on her face. And a moment later the doctor came in and examined her. Izzie screamed as a wave of pain washed over her as the doctor checked her cervix and the nurse put a fetal monitor on her belly that constricted her and made the pains worse. "Take that thing off!" Izzie shouted at her, and the doctor looked at her calmly. She knew that Izzie was a widow, and assumed that Kate was her mother.

"The good news is that you're already at seven," the doctor told her, which was about what Kate had guessed from her daughter's outbursts. The unflappable counselor who could handle anything in the workplace was losing her cool rapidly. Izzie looked panicked. "The bad news is that it may be too late for an epidural. We'll try, but it's going pretty fast since you called me. I think you can do this without one if that's what we have to do." Izzie burst into tears as soon as she said it.

"I can't do this without one." Not without Zach, not after everything that had happened.

"We'll try to get a line in as fast as we can," she promised. The anesthesiologist showed up ten minutes later. He had been in a labor room down the hall, and a nurse was checking Izzie when he walked in. She was clutching Kate's hand, and crying from the pains now.

"We're at nine," the nurse told him. "First baby." It had gone like lightning, but the pains were overwhelming her. It was infinitely worse than she had ever dreamed it would be.

The anesthesiologist looked at Izzie apologetically, as

she let out a scream. "We can try, but I think it's too late. Do you think you can lie still on your side for me to put in the catheter for the epidural? It will feel like a bee sting," he said gently.

"Just do it!" Izzie shouted at him as she nearly broke Kate's fingers. They rolled Izzie onto her side, and she clutched her mother's arm as they put the catheter in for the epidural, and she waited to feel some relief, but there was none yet, and then she looked at her mother and the nurse in terror. Something was happening, a force was powering through her that nothing could stop. Kate kept talking soothingly to her, as the nurse went to get the doctor. Kate knew the pressure Izzie was feeling was the baby. And the epidural hadn't taken effect yet. The anesthesiologist checked the dose and upped it, and Izzie closed her eyes for a minute between pains as the doctor walked back into the room. Everything was moving quickly. Too quickly for Izzie. The doctor warned Izzie that she was going to check her again, but the epidural had some slight effect by then.

"Okay, Izzie, we're at ten," the doctor told her. "You can push now." And then she told her how to do it, as the nurse held one leg and Kate held the other. She was lying on her back, with the epidural in place, but she said she could feel the pains. The fetal monitor said they were big ones, and the baby's heartbeat sounded good. She pushed for half an hour and nothing happened, and Izzie fell back against the pillows looking exhausted. The doctor told her to keep pushing. "I see the baby's head!" she said victoriously a minute later, as everyone in the room cheered Izzie on and she pushed with all her might, and fell back against the pillows exhausted between pains. She'd never worked so hard at anything in her life. Slowly the baby's head emerged, and he gave a wail. The doctor delivered the baby's body, and laid him on Izzie's stomach, and she looked down at him and smiled through her tears. He was beautiful and he was the image of his father. She smiled at her mother in relief. It was the hardest thing she'd ever done, but it was worth it. They cut the cord, cleaned up the baby, and put him to her breast. He looked up at his mother in wonder, as Kate gazed at mother and son and cried. She was sorry about everything that had happened to Izzie, but at least she had her baby now. Izzie held him in her arms and seemed totally at peace. The agony of only minutes before was already receding as she held the reward in her arms.

"Thank you for being here, Mom," she said, her voice barely more than a whisper. Izzie looked like a Madonna as she held her son.

Kate leaned down to kiss them both, and the doctor came in to check Izzie again, and told her what a great job she'd done. Everything was fine. It had all gone smoothly, even though it had been more painful than Izzie had expected. She called all three of her siblings a little while later, and they were thrilled for her. Julie was ecstatic to hear the news and the joy and elation in her sister's voice. It was midnight in New York, and nine o'clock in California by then.

Peter listened to Julie's side of the conversation and gave her a warning look when she hung up.

"Don't even think of going back there," he said, glaring at her. They were living in their own apartment, and Julie loved it. It was open and airy with glass sliding doors into the garden, and they had use of a pool. And their furniture had long since arrived from New York.

"Of course I'm going to go back there," Julie said, trying to sound confident and not scared of him. She had discovered that he had a nasty temper when he didn't get his way, and several times recently he had made fun of her handwriting and spelling and told her she wrote like a five-year-old, which hurt her feelings. She had finally told him about the dyslexia when they got married, and he told her he didn't care. And now he was acting like the kids who had made fun of her in school. She couldn't understand the shift in his attitudes and behavior. He was often frightening and sometimes cruel, and then tender and apologetic later. He was almost like two people now. One she loved and one she feared. "My sister just had a baby, Peter. I want to see them. This is an important moment for her." She always tried to reason with him.

"I told you before, your loyalties belong to me now," he

said harshly, and as he said it, he grabbed her arm and yanked her hard until he hurt her. He had bruised her that way before. This was all new since they'd gotten married. He appeared to be an old-fashioned man who believed that he should rule the roost, and she should do what he told her to, as an obedient wife. She had mentioned getting a job in L.A., and he told her it was out of the question, a good wife belonged at home, waiting to serve her husband. She always thought he was joking when he said things like that, but in the past three months she had discovered that he wasn't. He meant it. As far as he was concerned, she was to take orders from him. She wanted to try to discuss it with him, or maybe go to a counselor, but he didn't believe in that either. "You don't need to see your sister's baby," he said tersely. "All babies look alike."

"That's not the point. I want to see my sister. This is an important time for her, especially without Zach."

"She's better off without him. It's just too bad the baby survived." He had said it before, and Julie no longer argued with him about it. But she was planning to go to New York sometime in the next week. And Justin was coming down from Vermont too.

Julie made her reservation the next day when Peter was at work. She was still happy with him at times, and loved him. But he was different, and unduly harsh. She had discovered that he was totally without compassion for anyone else. His entire world had to revolve around him and his needs, and Julie most of all. It was as though he expected her to make up for all the love he'd never had, and prove herself to him by giving in to whatever he wanted and all his demands. And he wanted to make love to her constantly now, several times a night, to the point that she dreaded it sometimes. He was so acrobatic and relentless that he wore her out. It wasn't tender and sensual the way it had been in the past before they were married. Most of the time now it was rough, and he took her anytime and anywhere he wanted to, whether she wanted to make love or not. And then he would surprise her and be gentle again.

She printed out her ticket and left it in the bedroom drawer, and was planning to tell him about it in a few days. She was going the following week. She was reading a book one night when he stormed into the living room and grabbed her by the hair.

"What is this?" he said, waving the ticket in her face.

"It's my ticket to New York," she said in a small voice.

"What were you going to do? Just sneak off without telling me?" He was livid, and his eyes were bulging with rage. He even looked different now. His face had changed. She almost didn't recognize him at times.

"Of course not. I was going to tell you. I didn't want to upset you." He was shaking with fury as he looked at her and slapped her hard across the face. She was so shocked

329

she didn't even know how to react at first, and she started to cry as a trickle of blood ran from the corner of her mouth, where his watch had hit her.

"Cancel your reservation. You're not going. You're staying here." She said nothing, but cowered on her side of the bed that night, and then he grabbed her and made love to her again, more gently this time, but not like the old days. It was all different now that they were married. He didn't mention slapping her, and didn't apologize. And the next day she didn't cancel her reservation. She was more determined than ever to go. He couldn't keep her from her family by slapping her. He was cold to her for the rest of the week, and the day before she was to leave, she told him quietly that she was going to New York the next day. They had had very little conversation since he slapped her, and she'd had a bruise on her cheek that was just starting to fade. She had covered it up with makeup, but she knew it was there.

"I'm only staying a few days," she said quietly. She had packed while he was at work. He didn't forbid her to go, but he made love to her so brutally that night that she bled afterward and could hardly sit down. She went to bed with an ice pack between her legs. She was frightened of him now, and relieved when he went to work in the morning and she finished packing. She thought about him all the way to New York, and she was tempted to say something to Justin, but she didn't know what to say. She didn't know what had happened to Peter or why he had changed. She kept waiting for him to go back to the way he'd been before. And she didn't want Justin to hate Peter. In many ways Julie thought he was a good man. He just had a terrible temper he couldn't seem to control.

Julie was staying at Izzie's apartment, and fell in love with the baby. She helped her with him, and they spent hours talking, but she never mentioned Peter's rages. She was ashamed too. He somehow always made it feel like his behavior was her fault. And she wanted to be a better wife. But Justin noticed that she was very subdued when he arrived from Vermont. She didn't need to say anything to him. He could sense that something was wrong.

"Is everything okay?" he asked her. He had never known her to be that quiet, and almost withdrawn. She had always been shy but not to this degree.

"Of course, it's great!" Julie looked falsely cheerful, and Justin wasn't convinced. His twin radar was on full alert.

"You'd tell me if it wasn't great, wouldn't you?" Justin asked her.

"Of course I would. I'm just tired from the flight." She loved holding the baby, and soaked up the love and warmth of her family before she went back. She was afraid of saying too much to Justin because he knew her too well, and might see right through her. After she left, he mentioned it to their mother.

"She seems awfully quiet, doesn't she?" he asked Kate thoughtfully.

"Maybe she's homesick. The first year of marriage is a big adjustment. And she's not used to not having a job." Julie seemed all right to her, but she hadn't spent much time with her, since she had stayed at Izzie's, and Izzie thought she was fine. And Kate was focusing on Izzie at the moment.

Julie let herself into the house in L.A. when she got home. She was surprised to find Peter waiting for her. She had expected him to be at work. She had texted him when she'd arrive.

"Well, look who's back," he said in a derisive tone. "How was your trip to see your mommy and your brothers and sister?" She could sense his anger as soon as she walked in.

"I had a nice time," she said nervously, pretending she didn't notice his tone. "The baby is very cute." And Izzie was crazy about him. She was blossoming as a mother, and very good at it.

"I stayed home to welcome you back," Peter said to her, and then forced her down on the kitchen floor, tore her clothes off, and raped her as he banged her head into the floor. She saw stars and was half conscious when he stopped. "I keep telling you to stop running home to Mommy, and you just don't listen, do you?" he said as she struggled to get up and was dizzy when she did. She couldn't believe he would do that to her. She had married a monster, and she was afraid of him now. She wished she had never come back. She went to her bathroom to clean herself up, and looked at the clothes he had torn off her. He came into her bathroom then, and turned on the water for a bath. "Let's take a bath together. I always love it when we do that," he said, in a silky tone, oblivious to what he had just done to her on the kitchen floor without remorse.

"I'll take a shower in a few minutes," she said, trying not to let him see her cry. He was worse when he knew he'd hurt her.

"No, we're taking a bath." He turned the water off when the tub was full, took off his clothes and got in, and handed her into it with him. She didn't want to be in the bath with him, but she was afraid to object. All she wanted to do was get away from him now. He waited until she sat down and tried to relax, and then he grabbed her by the neck, and held her head underwater until she was fighting and clawing at him and was sure he was going to drown her, and then he pulled her head up by her hair. "Are you going to learn your lessons now? Are you going to listen to me when I tell you that you can't go somewhere? And if you tell your family a word about this, I'll kill you." She was sobbing as she looked at him, as she coughed and sputtered the water she had swallowed. He climbed out of the bath then, wrapped himself in a towel, and walked out of the room as Julie sat there and sobbed. Julie knew then that he was insane.

*

When Justin drove back to Vermont after seeing his new nephew, he was excited thinking about their own second baby, due in six months. It was easier than the first time, because they knew what to expect. And they trusted Shirley, so her second surrogacy for them was smooth as silk. And she'd had no problems with the pregnancy. Justin had left Milagra with Richard when he'd gone to visit Izzie over the weekend, and he was glad he'd seen Julie, although he still thought something about her was strange. She seemed different to her family. Maybe his mother was right, and she was just adjusting to marriage. She said she loved L.A., although they had no friends there yet. She said Peter worked too hard to go out much, and he had a lot to learn about the office in L.A., and was tired at night.

Justin had told Richard he'd be back late that night, but he had left New York a few hours earlier than planned so he could spend the evening with Richard, and be there before Milagra went to bed. He loved playing with her. At seven months, she was a lively, happy baby, and she was crawling everywhere. They'd had to childproof every inch of their home. There were corner guards on every piece of furniture, everything was bolted, locked, or shut down, including the toilets, since they had read about near drownings with toddlers falling into them head down and getting stuck. He and Richard were the poster boys for a childproof home and were devoted parents.

Justin pulled into the driveway at six o'clock, and the lights were off. He didn't know where Richard would have gone, but he hadn't called to say he was coming back early. He'd wanted to surprise him. And as he walked in, he turned the kitchen lights on and bounded up the stairs to their bedroom, but thought he heard Milagra in her room. He found her in her crib and picked her up. She'd been having a nap, and he walked into his own room, with the baby in his arms, flipped on the light, and then stood rooted to the spot, when he saw Richard in bed with another man. Justin didn't even know what to say, he was so stunned. Richard turned to look at him and closed his eyes, as the other man leapt out of bed. Justin recognized him as one of the teaching assistants at the school where Richard taught. He looked about twenty-six years old.

"What the hell is this?" Justin said, staring at them both as the younger man pulled his pants on and looked panicked, and Richard got out of bed with a devastated expression.

"I'm sorry," was all he could think of to say, as the teaching assistant rushed past Justin and ran down the stairs and out the front door.

"You do this with our baby in the next room?" Justin said in a fury to Richard. "What the fuck is wrong with you? And how long has this been going on?"

Richard knew it was time to be honest with him. "Since Christmas. A few months. He's just a kid." Richard looked mortally embarrassed to have been caught. And Milagra was cooing at both of them.

"And you're an asshole. And you let us start another baby with Shirley while you were sleeping with someone else?"

"I told you we should wait," Richard said as he sat down on the bed again.

"Why? So you could have another baby with him? Are you in love with him?"

"No, it was just fun for a while. Everything has gotten so serious with us. We never get to have fun anymore. We're always parenting or trying to save money. I feel like we've given our whole life up for her." He glanced at the baby in Justin's arms and felt guilty for what he'd said, but it was the truth. "And now you want another one. I'm not ready to give up my whole life for kids. I feel like we've lost each other and all we have left is her." Justin stared at him in dismay.

"Why didn't you say something before you started sleeping with other people?"

"He's the only one," Richard said. "I'm sorry, Just. I feel overwhelmed. I'm tired of being broke, being a father, and never having any fun." Justin listened to him and went to put the baby in her crib without saying a word, and then came back into the room. By then Richard was dressed. The two men looked at each other in despair.

"Now what?" Justin said to him as he sat down in a chair. "We can't give her back, and I don't want to."

"Neither do I. It's just so relentless. We never get away from it."

"That's what parenthood is. It's not part-time. You either are or you aren't. And we can't afford a nanny."

"Maybe we should have waited," Richard said.

"I thought you were ready." Justin looked at him, wondering if this was the end. He was so shocked by what he had walked in on that he didn't even know what he felt. Sad, hurt, surprised, disgusted, angry. They had a second baby on the way, and Richard was already tired of the first one. It didn't bode well for their future together.

"You wanted it more than I did," Richard said accusingly.

"I guess I didn't understand that. So what do we do now? It's too late for Shirley to have an abortion. And I wouldn't let her anyway. I want the baby. You don't have to be part of it if you don't want to."

"I think we need a break," Richard said quietly. Justin had figured out that much when he had walked into their bedroom that night. "I'll move out." Justin nodded and went downstairs to regain his composure, and then returned upstairs to take care of their daughter. Justin slept in Milagra's room that night, on the floor. And the next morning when Richard left for work, he took a bag with him. He had packed the night before after they talked. Justin could hear him moving around in their room until late. Neither of them had gotten much sleep.

Richard looked at Justin feeding Milagra breakfast, and he was happy to be free of it for a while. Justin didn't know if he'd ever feel the same way about him again. He thought it was pathetic that Richard was sleeping with a young guy, instead of growing up and being the father he had promised to be. He was thirty-seven, not a kid. The kid was the one he was sleeping with.

"I'm sorry," he said before he left.

"So am I," Justin said coldly, and then burst into tears after he was gone, but that wouldn't change anything. He had decided not to tell Shirley for a while, because he didn't want to upset her and make her feel her money wouldn't be paid as regularly. Whatever it took, Justin was going to handle it all on his own. When his work sold, sometimes he made more than Richard did.

He put the baby down for her morning nap and waited till a decent hour to call Julie in California, when Peter would have left for work. He had just gone when Justin reached her and told her what had happened and what Richard had said. She was shocked and sympathetic and sounded like she had a cold. He was so upset, he didn't realize she'd been crying.

"Maybe he's just scared of all the responsibility," she said thoughtfully.

"Yeah, I guess, but he should have said something before it got to this. The baby will be born in six months."

"Are you still going to go through with it?" Julie was worried for him.

"Of course." She admired him for that. He had no doubts about it, unlike Richard.

After they talked about it for a while, he thought Julie sounded strange. Sad and subdued. "Are you okay?"

"Yeah, I'm fine. I'm just tired. We were up late last night." But he'd had the same impression in New York. She seemed different and down. They talked about Izzie's baby then. She named him Thomas Zachary, after her own father and the baby's, and Kate was pleased.

"Is everything okay with Peter?" He was just checking.

"Of course," she said blithely, but some strange ripple in Justin's gut made him wonder. He knew his twin like his own soul.

"Well, that's the news from here," he said, depressed about his own problems, and he was beginning to think he would never be able to finish his novel, especially with a new baby coming, and a toddler in the house by then. Milagra kept him running even now, crawling everywhere.

Shirley figured it out for herself three weeks later, when every time she dropped by, even in the evening, Richard was never there, and Justin was managing Milagra alone. It was mid-April by then, she was almost four months pregnant, and they would know the baby's sex at the next sonogram.

"Do you still want this one?" she asked him, pointing to her belly, when Justin finally admitted that he and Richard had split up.

"Yes, I do," he said seriously. "Breaking up with Richard doesn't change anything for me." She nodded, relieved to hear it. She had suspected something was wrong for several weeks.

"Is it over for you two?" She felt sorry for him. He was a friendly, warm person. They both were, although they had very different personalities. Richard was more frivolous and fun, and Justin warmer, more responsible, and nurturing.

"I don't think either of us knows if this is permanent or not," Justin said sadly. "For now, we're taking a break." They weren't seeing each other. They had agreed not to. Richard visited Milagra once a week, which was all he wanted. Justin hadn't said anything to his mother, or his other siblings about it, and he'd asked Julie not to. He was always closer to her and she knew all his secrets, as he did hers, or he used to. Now that she was married, she wasn't telling him anything, and all she ever said when they talked was that everything was "fine." His gut told him something different, but he couldn't put his finger on what was wrong, or even guess. And Peter was always so perfect that it couldn't be him. Maybe their mother was right and she was just homesick, or adjusting to marriage, but she sounded strange to her twin. He had an uneasy feeling, but nothing to base it on, so he ignored it.

When Kate called Julie a few weeks after that, in early May, she was worried about her. She mentioned it to Izzie, who hadn't noticed anything when she saw her, but Julie called her less often now. Kate was suddenly reminded of when Julie was a little girl and hated school because the kids were teasing her about her reading, and bullying her, and she didn't tell anyone about it. She was afraid to, and ashamed then.

"Has Julie said anything to you?" Kate asked Izzie, when she came to visit Tommy one day and have dinner. Izzie had hired a nanny and gone back to work by then.

"No, she seems fine," Izzie said, looking surprised. And the next day, Kate called Justin and asked him. He always knew what was happening with Julie even though he didn't always tell her.

"She says she's okay, but I thought she sounded down, and kind of distracted. I haven't talked to her this week. I've been working on my novel again when the baby sleeps, so she's been texting me."

"Maybe you should call her. I talked to her the other

day and she sounded odd to me. I hate that she's so far away." She liked laying eyes on her chicks, which always told her a lot more than what they said to her. And she was worried about Julie and didn't know why.

Justin called Julie the next day at noon California time and she sounded like she'd been crying, but she said she had a cold when he asked her about it. The previous time she said she had allergies.

"You wouldn't lie to your older brother, would you?" he teased her, trying to listen intently to any clue in her voice.

"You're only five minutes older, you jerk." She laughed and wiped away the tears that he had heard and she'd denied. Peter had hit her again before he left for work. He had accused her of flirting with the neighbor, which wasn't true. She'd gone swimming the day before and worn a bikini, and Peter had come home and seen it, and accused her of sleeping with him. Peter was no longer someone she even remotely knew. After four months of marriage, he had become truly terrifying. He was a monster. Now he made her read to him every day and when she made a mistake he would laugh at her and tell her how stupid she was and then hit her. It only made it worse. And Peter had hit her hard that morning. Her ear was still ringing. Her life was a nightmare and she was afraid to leave. If he found her, he'd kill her. He said so and she believed him.

After she and Justin hung up, she went to her computer

and looked something up on Google. She knew it had to be there somewhere, and it took her less than a minute to find it. She wrote down an address on a piece of paper and left the house on foot. She caught a cab in front of a hotel nearby. And twenty minutes later she was at a church in a run-down part of Hollywood. She walked inside and down a flight of stairs to the basement. She didn't know what else to do. It was an anonymous twelve-step group for abused women she had found online. Justin questioning her had made her think of it. She was afraid of Peter all the time now. Julie knew that, for now, the group was her only hope. She didn't even dare tell her family what he was doing to her. And they were too far away to help her. She had nowhere to go.

Chapter 21

After Julie started going to the twelve-step group, she got insights from the program and the other women there. Their stories were much like hers. Some of their partners had started out as loving as Peter had been, to lure them in, and then changed. All were excessively controlling, and had isolated their victims.

A sign on the wall of the dingy meeting room said "Abuse is a disease of isolation." Another said "An abuser never loses sight of his prey." Several of the women had gotten away from their abusers, and had been lured back. They were being physically and emotionally abused and were ashamed of it. Some were already out of it, but at risk for going back. Others were too afraid to leave. Their abusers told them it was their fault and they believed them. And many, like Julie, thought that if they just stuck it out, it would get better, like it had been in the beginning. It was hard for them to accept it never would. Julie couldn't understand how somebody could change so radically after they got married. This couldn't be the real

Peter. But she had no support system, no friends locally, no family, she was totally at his mercy.

The women in the group told her that men like him set it up that way, and usually chose innocent, gentle women who couldn't defend themselves against the onslaught of abuse. They also told her that 75 percent of men and women who threatened to kill their partners actually did. Peter threatened to kill her all the time. He had held her head underwater in the pool when no one else was around, just as he had in the bathtub. He slapped her now, hard, whenever he didn't like what she said. He humiliated her. He told her that if she ever told anyone, especially her family, or called the police, he would know and kill her, and she believed him. She was afraid their landline and her cellphone were being tapped. Her life had become a living hell. He rarely left marks on her except for occasional bruises no one could see, and she felt dead inside. He raped her whenever he wanted, and preferred to take her by force than consensually. Whenever she pretended to be willing, he lost interest. He had beaten her once with a whip he had bought for that purpose and tied her to the bed, and gagged her when she tried to scream. Every day she was less sure of herself and more afraid to leave.

Going to the group helped her deal with him better, and not provoke him. She tried not to let him bully her, but his punishments were getting worse. And he was angrier when she resisted his beatings or refused to be cowed by him. And she was still too afraid to leave. There was no one she could run to in L.A., and she was too embarrassed to go to a safe house for abused women, and what if he found her there? She had less money to run away with because she wasn't working, and he didn't give her any. She felt like there was a glass prison around her that no one else could see and she couldn't escape. He had told her that if she ran away, wherever she went, he would find her. He had taken her credit cards away so she couldn't buy a plane ticket to escape. He knew she would try to go home to her family sooner or later. He shamed her constantly, and her dyslexia had gotten much worse. In her constant state of anxiety, she could hardly read street signs anymore. He threatened to take away her cellphone, but he didn't so he could call her constantly and ask where she was. But he told her he would know if she called her family and told them anything about him. So she said nothing to them. She realized now that he had moved to L.A. to force her into marriage, and get her away from her family and her job. He had stolen her life from her.

Peter's behavior got steadily worse. In June she was doing some gardening in shorts and a tee shirt and he came home unexpectedly at lunchtime, dragged her into the house, and called her a whore. He accused her of trying to entice the neighbor again, who was old enough to be her father and married to a very nice woman. Peter beat her and then raped her and left her barely able to crawl across the floor to the bathroom to clean herself up. She looked in the mirror when she was washing, and saw what she had become. She remembered the stories she had heard at the abuse group. One of the women had wound up in the hospital the week before and was still in a coma from a head injury inflicted by her husband. Another woman in the group had been stabbed by her boyfriend a month before, and he was in jail. The woman had survived it but was shattered by the experience. Julie knew she was heading there and it had to stop. She knew now what was going to happen. He was going to keep beating her until he killed her.

She washed her face in cold water, put on jeans, a tee shirt, a denim jacket, and running shoes, grabbed her purse, and ran out of the house as fast as she could before he could return. He had gone back to the office after raping her.

She walked to a nearby hotel, and had enough money for a cab to the airport, but nothing else without credit cards. She called her brother when she got to the airport. She forced herself to calm down enough to read the list of flights. There was a flight leaving for New York in half an hour.

Justin answered on the second ring, and she could hear Milagra crying in the background. He told Julie to wait a minute while he handed her a bottle and put her in her playpen so they could talk. He was back in a minute.

"I'm in trouble," she said as soon as he came back on the line.

"What kind of trouble?" Justin sounded shocked. His sister had never been in trouble in her life.

"He's crazy . . . he's going to kill me . . . I've been going to a group for abused women . . . he does all of it . . . he beats me, he tried to drown me, he took my credit cards away. Justin, I'm scared." She started to cry and so did he as he listened. He wanted to kill Peter. "I have no money, there's a flight to New York in twenty minutes. If you pay for a ticket, I'll pay you back."

"Give me the flight number." He grabbed a pen. "We'll talk when you get here. Get on that flight, Julie. Get out of there. Does he know where you are?"

"No, he came home at lunchtime and beat me up, raped me, and he went back to work. That's what he always does." Justin felt sick as he listened.

"Go, get your boarding pass and go to the gate. I'll pick you up in New York."

"Don't tell Mom!" she said to him quickly before they hung up. She didn't want anyone to know.

"I won't," he promised, and hung up on her so he could pay for her flight. He had nothing left on his credit card after he did, he had reached his limit, but he had a little money in the bank. He would have used that too to save her from Peter.

Julie went to the counter and waited, and ten minutes before they closed the doors, the ticket came through. She got her boarding pass for the last coach seat left, and ran through security and to the gate to board. She held her breath until they closed the doors, and then heaved a sigh of relief. She had been terrified that Peter would appear, but he hadn't. He had called several times while she was at the airport and she didn't answer. The nightmare was over. She was safe. Or she would be in New York.

And in Vermont, Justin was throwing everything he needed for the baby into a bag. The drive from Vermont would take him as long as her flight. He backed out of his driveway ten minutes later, and twenty minutes after that, Milagra was sound asleep in her car seat, as he drove steadily toward New York as fast as he could, thinking about his sister. It was small consolation to know that his instincts about her had been right. He'd been feeling it since March when she came to see Izzie's baby, and that had been three months before. He couldn't imagine the hell she had lived through in the meantime, and he thanked God she had had the guts to get out, and had called him. What if he had killed her? Justin cried as he thought about it and kept driving.

He got to JFK Airport half an hour before she was due

to arrive. He used the men's room, with Milagra, and had a cup of coffee and a doughnut. Milagra never woke up, as he carried her around in her car seat. He was waiting for Julie where arriving passengers came out, and when she saw him she flew into his arms and clung to him as though she'd been drowning. She almost had. He saw immediately that there was a bruise on her cheekbone and another one on her neck from when he had almost strangled her the day before. It made Justin feel sick when he saw them.

"Thank you for the ticket," she said as they walked slowly out of the terminal toward the garage where he had left the car. She kept glancing over her shoulder as they walked. She was terrified that Peter would suddenly appear. What if he had followed her? Justin could see her terror. "I knew I had to get out. It's been getting worse," she said, talking quickly. "I don't know what happened. Everything changed after we got married. It made him crazy or something."

"No, he is crazy, and he hid it before. Mom kept saying he was too perfect and something was wrong, and we all thought she was nuts. When did it start?"

"As soon as we got to L.A., after I came home for Zach's funeral, he went nuts. And it just kept spiraling down after that. He didn't want me to see any of you, or come home. He said that if I told you anything, or called the police, he'd kill me. And I think he would have." She took a breath and tried to calm down.

"Thank God you had the guts to get out. He probably would have killed you." Justin's stomach turned over as he thought about it, and he looked at her when they got to the car. "Did you sleep on the plane?"

"A little. Why?"

"Can you drive if I get tired?"

"Sure." But he was too wide awake to sleep now. He wanted to talk to her and understand what had happened.

She turned her cellphone on when they got in the car, and it rang immediately. It was Peter. She jumped and didn't answer, and Justin could see the panic in her eyes.

"Don't answer it. He won't suspect where you are for a while. Don't talk to him." She nodded, and he called again a little while later. He probably thought she was hiding somewhere in L.A., but she knew that, eventually, when she didn't come home, he would guess where she was. But there was nothing he could do now. She was safe.

They talked all the way back to Vermont, and Julie told him she didn't want their mother to know where she was, or what had happened. She needed time to figure it out herself, and try to understand how she could have been so duped, and so wrong about him to let this happen, and why she didn't leave immediately. He had paralyzed her.

"He's a psychopath or a sociopath," Justin told her.

"Mister Too Good to Be True. That's what Mom called him. She's smarter than we give her credit for."

"We all know she is." Julie smiled at her twin. "We just don't like to admit it. Izzie says she knew it about Zach too. She just didn't want Mom to be right."

"Yeah." Justin grinned sheepishly. "Me too. I think she sensed that having a baby was too much for us, and our relationship wasn't as solid as I wanted to believe."

"What's happening with you two?" Julie asked him. He and Richard had been separated since March. They had seen each other a few times over baby exchanges, but they hadn't had a meal together or spent time with each other in three months.

"I guess it's over. Neither of us has the guts to say it, but it is. We keep calling it a time-out. But I think he's done."

"What about you?" Julie asked gently, as the sun came up over the Vermont hills. They were almost home, and had been driving for six hours.

"I don't know. I was so shocked when I walked in on him. I'm not sure I can get over it, or if I want to. And he doesn't like being a father as much as I do. He's a big kid. He just wants to have fun. I think having a baby and everything that goes with it was a huge shock to him. And he's not up for a second baby if he can't cope with the one we have."

"And you're okay with that?"

"I can't wait." He grinned at her. And Shirley was as big as a house. It looked like a twelve-pound baby this time, instead of ten. "Maybe I was just meant to have kids." He smiled at his sister as they drove into his driveway, and he turned off the car.

"Well, you'd better start writing again if you want more kids," she teased him, and they looked up at the sunrise. It was a magnificent day. They were both exhausted after traveling and talking all night, but they were so happy to be together. Peter had stopped calling her eventually, and must have gone to sleep, but he had sent about a dozen texts. She had read the first few, and then stopped. He was begging her to come home and telling her how sorry he was. She didn't answer, but she looked devastated each time she read one.

They had given Milagra a bottle while they were driving and she'd fallen asleep. She woke up as they walked into the house.

"Oh God, there goes my chance for an hour's sleep," Justin said. He was exhausted after driving for twelve hours and being up all night. He was running on adrenaline. They both were.

"I'll take care of her," Julie volunteered. "You drove all night, go to bed. I can sleep when you wake up." It was great having another adult in the house again, someone who could give him a break once in a while. Julie lifted Milagra out of her car seat, and went to change her, and then came back to the kitchen to give her breakfast. Justin headed up the stairs to take a nap. He looked like he was sleepwalking, he was so tired. He lay down on his bed and was asleep a minute later, and when he came downstairs at noon, Julie was playing with Milagra and feeding her lunch, and she looked half asleep. Justin was refreshed after six hours' sleep, and took over for her.

He heard another text come in on her phone, as she got up from the chair.

"What's he been saying?" Justin asked her.

"He wants to know where I am. He's starting to get nasty again." Although he was still trying to lure her back.

"Have you answered him?" She shook her head. She didn't want to hear his voice, or talk to him, or see him. She knew that sooner or later she would have to tell him that she was gone for good, but for now, she felt safer in silence. She wasn't ready to communicate with him, and didn't want to ever again.

They talked about it that night, after Justin put Milagra to bed. Julie had played with her again after a long nap.

"I assume you're going to divorce him." She nodded. "What are you going to do about your stuff?" She had abandoned everything she owned in L.A., and had left with only her purse and the clothes on her back.

"I'll have to figure that out. Maybe he won't give it back."

"You have you, that's all that matters. Everything else can be replaced. When are you going to tell Mom that you're here?"

"I need some time to chill out first," she said, thinking about it. It was humiliating to admit she had made a terrible mistake. They'd only been married for six months, and after their honeymoon, everything had been a nightmare. "I don't want to deal with what everyone thinks about it, Mom, Izzie, Willie, Grandma Lou. They'll all have opinions about it."

"I have one too," he said seriously. "He's a sociopath who should be behind bars."

"Can I stay here for a while?" she asked him, looking embarrassed. "I have some money in a savings account, not much. I have to find out how to get it transferred here. I can share expenses with you when I get it." And she was going to report her credit cards stolen, so she could get new cards. They had commingled no funds.

"Why don't you stay for the summer?" Justin suggested. "You can go to New York and get your life together after that. Maybe you can get your old job back."

"I don't think so. They replaced me with a pretty good designer from Paris. They don't need us both."

"You'll get a job."

She got twenty irate texts from Peter that night, accusing her of everything imaginable, including having run off with another man. "Did you ever photograph the bruises

355

after he beat you?" Justin asked her, and she shook her head.

"I was too scared that he'd find the pictures and beat me up again. He used to check my phone." It still pained him to think of what his sister had gone through for the past six months, and he liked the idea of her sticking around for a while. They were never happier than when they were together.

And on Friday, he invited her to come to the sonogram to see the baby. They were doing a fancy 3D one at the hospital, and he would get photos to take home. Shirley had had only one sonogram so far, at the very beginning, since she was young and healthy, and everything about the pregnancy had been normal.

"The one at our OB's office is about a hundred years old and you can barely see the baby. It looks like a weather map of Vermont. It's really cool in 3D. We did it once with Milagra too. They give you pictures afterward." He smiled at her.

"Do you have to wear special glasses like in the movies?" she asked him, laughing.

"No, you dork. It just allows you to see the baby all the way around. Milagra was sucking her thumb when we did hers, and she fell asleep."

"That sounds amazing," she admitted, as she thought how life could change in a few days. Suddenly she was safe, living with her brother, laughing and happy, and three thousand miles from the man who had almost beaten her to death, and might have, if she'd stayed. She still remembered the statistics from the group, about abusers who kill their partners. She could have been one of them, and nearly was.

*

They went to the sonogram lab at the hospital that afternoon, and met Shirley there. Julie had never seen her in person before, and thought she was nice. They went into the sonogram lab together, and the woman who ran it handed Shirley a gown and told her what to do. She had to drink three glasses of water and they'd be ready. Half an hour later, they had her lie down on the table, and her belly looked like a mountain as the technician put gel on it and moved it around with a metal wand, as they warmed up the machine.

Julie was looking at the screen intensely, waiting for the baby to appear. They took several angles, of the placenta and uterus, and then the technician looked startled and turned the screen around to face herself, and Julie, Justin, and Shirley couldn't see it. The woman smiled at them, asked about the date of Shirley's last sonogram, and left the room. She came back with a female doctor, who looked at the screen with her and smiled too. Justin was watching them, panicked that something was wrong, but he didn't want to scare Shirley by asking. She looked worried too.

"We have an interesting view for you," the doctor said to all three of them. She knew that Shirley was a surrogate from the chart, and she assumed that Justin and Julie were the parents of the baby in her womb. "This doesn't happen often nowadays with the kind of technology we have, but I gather your doctor has a very rudimentary machine, and your last sonogram was very early in the pregnancy. Once in a while, not often anymore, a fetus can be hidden by another one, and even the heartbeats appear to be one." She swung the screen around toward them then, and in 3D and living color they could clearly see two babies. "You're having twins. Two little girls." They had already said they wanted to know the baby's sex. All three of them stared at the screen for a minute, and then Justin threw his arms around his sister and lifted her off the ground, and then he bent to kiss Shirley on the forehead.

"Oh my God, Shirley, we're having twins!" Two of the fertilized ova had taken, and no one had seen or suspected it till now. It made total sense, given her size. She looked a little nervous, Justin was ecstatic, and Julie was grinning from ear to ear.

They had to take Shirley back to her OB afterward, to reevaluate the situation, measure her again in light of the fact that it was twins, reassess her due date, which hadn't changed, and discuss any problems with her, but she had had none. They told her that there was a higher risk that the babies would be premature, and at any sign of early onset of labor, she was to call them immediately. They said she might have to be on bed rest for the last month or two if there were problems. She had said this would be her last surrogacy, and she was going out with a bang. Justin was so proud he looked like he was about to burst when he walked Shirley back to the car. And Milagra was cooing happily in her aunt Julie's arms.

He could hardly wait to call their mother when he got home. He sent Alana an email in London that they had hit the jackpot, and he turned to his sister with a look of panic. "Shit, I'm going to be supporting three kids, not two," particularly with Richard not involved with the twins. Justin had given him that option with the second pregnancy, since he had admitted he didn't want the second baby, and Justin did. Now Justin was going to be supporting all three of them. It made him realize that he had to work harder than he had in the ten months since Milagra was born. He was so busy and having so much fun with her that he had been writing much less than before, and almost never worked on his book.

Kate was as stunned as he was when he told her the news. After they talked about it for a few minutes, she told him that she had been thinking of coming up for the Fourth of July weekend with Izzie and Tommy and

Grandma Lou to spend the holiday with him. There was a small hotel nearby where she usually stayed. He turned to Julie, grimacing and making signals, not sure what to say, and she looked resigned and nodded her head. Her mother would find out that she was there sooner or later, and the weekend together sounded like fun. She missed her mother and wanted to see her, and she was ready to talk about Peter now.

"Sure, Mom, that sounds great," he responded. They were going to keep Julie a surprise until then.

After thinking about it, he decided not to call Richard and tell him about the twins. Since they were not together at the moment, and he had already backed away from their second child, he didn't need to know that Shirley was carrying twins. That was Justin's problem or blessing now, not his.

*

Peter continued calling and texting Julie over the next couple of weeks. She finally took one call from him and told him she wasn't coming back. He begged her to at first, and then threatened her when she wouldn't give in to his pleas. He told her that he would find her and drag her back, that she was his wife and belonged to him now, and that he would destroy everything she owned and had left there if she didn't come back to L.A. He demanded to know where she was and she refused to tell him.

"I don't belong to you, Peter. I never did. I loved you, which was better. You can send my things to my mother, if you want. I'll get them from her sometime when I'm in New York."

"Where are you?" he asked in a wheedling tone.

"As far away from you as I can get, and if you come near me, I'll call the police. I never want to see you again." She put her wedding ring and her engagement ring in a small box that night and put them away to send back to him later. She was finished with Peter White. She was going to call a lawyer when she went back to New York and start divorce proceedings.

When her family came to Vermont for the Fourth of July weekend, Julie walked quietly out of the house with Milagra in her arms. The minute her mother saw her, she knew. Julie didn't even have to tell her. The moment their eyes met, Kate knew that Mr. Too Good to Be True had turned out to be the nightmare she had feared, and had felt in her gut he could become.

"Are you all right?" she asked as she touched her daughter's cheek and looked deep into her eyes, and Julie nodded. It was all behind her now.

Izzie was startled and thrilled to see her too. "What are you doing here? Did you come for the weekend? Is Peter here?" Julie quietly shook her head and exchanged a knowing smile with her twin before she answered Izzie.

"I've been here for a couple of weeks. I'll be here for the

summer, and then I'm moving back to New York." That said it all.

"You can come and stay with me and Tommy," she said as she hugged her sister. She couldn't even imagine what Julie had been through, but it was over now. She was home. Peter would never hurt her again.

Chapter 22

By the end of August, Julie was ready to go back to New York, look for a job, and start her life over again. And she was anxious to file for divorce. Peter still texted her occasionally, but the steam had gone out of his threats. He understood that he had lost. She looked relaxed and healthy, and other than an occasional nightmare when she woke up in the night and thought she was back in L.A., she was beginning to recover from the trauma she had lived through. She couldn't even imagine dating again, and didn't want to. But she was whole and sane and he hadn't killed her. She didn't want or need more than that, other than a divorce and a job. The rest no longer mattered to her. Peter had emailed her that he had destroyed all her clothes, and he wasn't going to return her furniture, and she didn't care about that either. She was going to start fresh, and she had accepted Izzie's invitation to stay with her for a while, until she got her life organized. Both women were looking forward to it.

Willie had come to spend a weekend with them, and Julie had been happy to see him. He suddenly seemed calmer and more mature. She told him what had happened with Peter, and he was glad that she was all right and moving back to New York.

And by the last week of August, Shirley could hardly walk. She was eight months pregnant, and had had a few contractions, but nothing to worry about. As her doctor put it, her body was getting ready for the launch. And it was going to be quite a launch. Both babies looked huge and they were talking about a Caesarian section, but no decision had been made yet. They were going to wait and see how much bigger the babies got in her final weeks, and how Shirley was doing. So far, she was fine.

Kate had offered to help Justin financially if he needed it. It was a relief to know he had that safety net under him, but he wanted to try and manage on his own. He was working on his book, and looking for an agent for it.

Justin had had dinner with Richard a couple of times. They had talked about a lot of their issues, and Richard had had time to think about it. They had been separated for five months. He had been shocked when Justin finally told him about the twins. But Justin made it clear to him that he didn't expect him to participate. Richard had a role in Milagra's life, if he wanted it, but Justin was willing to take full responsibility for the twins, and expected to. And with Julie there for the whole summer, she had babysat for him, and Justin had almost finished his book. He was trying to get it done before the twins came, because he knew his life would be crazy for a long time after that. He had hired a very nice girl who was going to help him every afternoon. She was eighteen years old, came from a family of ten kids, and had twin brothers too. She wasn't daunted by three little kids.

After the Labor Day weekend, Justin drove Julie to New York. He had just finished his book and had an appointment with an agent to give it to him to read. He was only planning to stay in New York for one night, because he didn't want to stay away from Shirley for long. He wanted to be with her when she delivered, and she could go at any minute. The twins weren't due for another three weeks, but with twins they couldn't be sure, and they were likely to come early.

Richard called him on his cellphone as they drove into the city, and Justin said he'd call him back. He dropped Julie off at Izzie's with the baby, and then he went to his appointment with the agent after lunch. They were meeting their mother afterward. And Izzie had given Julie the name of a divorce lawyer. She wanted to make an appointment with her as soon as possible.

Julie got to the store to meet her mother that afternoon, before Justin arrived. Her mother had done some remodeling over the summer, and the store looked terrific. They sat down in her office for a few minutes, and Kate looked at her with a smile. She was proud of Julie for coming through a terrible experience as well as she had.

"I have a proposition for you," she said. She had given it a great deal of thought. "How would you feel about running my online business? I don't have the time to do that and everything else, and Jessica is better with the store. I need someone to update content, keep it fresh, and pick the items they think will sell best. It's a different customer than in the store." Julie looked pensive as she listened to her mother's offer. She was a designer and had never run a business. Her mother was better at that. But in spite of her dyslexia, Julie was good with computers, and had programs that read aloud to her, which she could use when she was tired. Peter had undermined her confidence, but Julie was extremely competent, and Kate genuinely needed help.

"Can I think about it?"

"Of course. I need to hire someone. It's outgrown me. And I'd rather hire you than someone else." She mentioned a salary and Julie looked impressed. It was more than she'd been making in her old job. Kate could afford to pay that kind of salary now. And her next plan was to buy her investor out. Bernard was a shrewd businessman, and he had helped her immeasurably, but it was uncomfortable for her to work with him. And he had indicated to her that he might be willing to sell his interest in the business at the right price. Their dealings with each other had been awkward ever since the end of their affair. He no longer sent her texts telling her he loved her, since they didn't get him anywhere. He had just returned from his vacation in Sardinia, and was planning to travel to New York, but his focus was on Asia now. He had a huge deal currently in his sights in Beijing, and another one in Korea.

Justin showed up half an hour late and was pleased with the meeting with the agent. He had liked him a lot and left the manuscript with him. They went out for coffee and something to eat, while Jessica babysat Milagra at the store. She was playing with her when they left, and Milagra was having a ball. She had turned a year old two weeks before. Richard had come over on her birthday, and he and Justin had talked late into the night. Julie retired to her niece's room so they could be alone. Justin didn't say much about it the next morning, and Julie didn't press him about it.

Justin drove back to Vermont the next day, and by then Julie was settling in at Izzie's, and she played with Tommy and then handed him over to the nanny so they could go out. She was becoming a professional aunt, which was all she ever wanted to be now. Her experience with Peter had convinced her that she didn't want to get married and have kids of her own. Her siblings' children were enough for her. Marriage seemed much too high risk, and all she wanted now was to go back to work. She thought about her mother's offer all that night, and called her in the morning.

"I'll do it," she said when her mother answered the phone.

"Do what?" Kate wasn't sure what she meant.

"I'll take the job." She was excited at the prospect and had discussed it with Izzie, who thought it was a great idea too.

"That's fantastic!" Kate said enthusiastically, and meant it. She desperately needed someone to run that part of the business, and Julie had grown up in the store, and was young enough to understand business on the Net better than she did. She was enormously relieved to hear it, and Julie promised to come in the next day and get started. She was thrilled at the prospect of working again, and she liked the idea of working with her mother. They always got along, and their abilities and talents complemented each other.

"What are we doing for dinner tonight?" Julie asked Izzie when she got home from the office, and was startled by her sister's response.

"I have a date. Well, not really." She looked suddenly embarrassed. "He's just someone I work with, but he invited me to dinner, so I figured what the hell." Zach had been gone for eight months, and she said she wasn't dating, but it sounded nice to have dinner with a man for a change. "Kind of like Mom and Liam," she said benignly.

"Don't be so sure," Julie said, laughing at her, pleased that Izzie was willing to go out again, even with a friend.

"You're a lot younger than she is, and they've known each other since college. This sounds more like a date."

"Never mind," Izzie said, and went to get dressed. It was fun living together, and they were both excited about it. It was almost like being kids again, but not quite. At some point, Julie was going to look for an apartment and have a home of her own again. She was starting with a clean slate.

Izzie left shortly after to meet her friend for dinner. And the next morning, Julie left for work, and her mother was waiting for her. She had cleared an office for her, which was part of the remodel that summer. And she had a mountain of files to give her. She left her alone, as Julie looked around her new office with a grin. The walls were bare, and there was nothing on the desk. It was all brand-new and fresh, just like her life.

Kate had just gotten back to her own office when Liam called. He sounded unusually serious, and Kate started to tell him that Julie had begun her new job that morning, but he interrupted her. Kate realized that his voice was shaking and he sounded like he'd been crying.

"Are you okay?" She had never heard him sound like that before.

"No, I'm not. Maureen and I went out to dinner last night. We were crossing the street on the way back. And she was hit by a drunk driver." He started to cry then, and Kate felt terrible for him. "Kate, it was awful. I've been at the hospital with her all night. She never regained consciousness." He choked on his words then. "She died an hour ago. I just got home."

"Oh my God, I'm so sorry. I'll come over right away."

"No, I have to call the girls, and the funeral parlor to make the arrangements."

"I'll go with you," she said quietly. She had lived through that herself, and he'd been there for her. Going with him was the least she could do for him now.

"I'll call you back." He was trying to regain his composure. He had called his daughters from the hospital the night before, and they were going to come home that night whatever happened. When he called Kate an hour later, he sounded drained.

"Do you mind going with me?" he asked her. "I can't face it alone."

"I'll be there in ten or fifteen minutes."

"Thank you." He sounded devastated and numb. She called a car service and arranged for a car to pick her up, and then ran into Julie's new office.

"I'm leaving. Maureen just died, she was hit by a drunk driver last night. I'm going to help Liam make the arrangements."

"Oh, Mom, how awful." She was on her feet immediately. "Do you want me to come?"

"No, he's a mess. I'll call you. Will you hold the fort till

I get back?" She smiled at her then and kissed her quickly. "It's nice having you here."

"Thanks, Mom. I like it too." She gave her mother a quick hug, and Kate flew out the door. The car was already outside, and they went to pick up Liam. He looked shell-shocked when he got into the car and gave the driver the address of the funeral home he had called uptown.

"I used them for my parents," he explained to Kate. "I didn't know who else to call." As he said it, she put her arms around him and hugged him and he clung to her like he was drowning.

"They're fine. It doesn't matter. Did you get the girls?" she asked him as he settled back against the seat, looking exhausted. He hadn't slept all night.

"I think we're all in shock. Penny will be home late tonight. Elizabeth couldn't get a flight till tomorrow. I have to figure out when to have the funeral. Her father is going to be devastated." Maureen's mother had died recently, and her father was in his nineties and in poor health.

They went through all the steps to make the necessary choices. Burial or cremation, casket or urn. He said Maureen had said she wanted to be cremated, the only time they'd talked about it. Her family had a plot, so that she was taken care of. He had called the church they attended and was meeting with the priest that afternoon. He had to pick music and the program, and find a photograph of her

371

to put on it. He felt as though the currents were swirling around him, and Kate helped him with all of that, and then they went to the church together. Afterward, they stopped at a coffee shop and she saw to it that he ate. She dropped him off at his father-in-law's several hours later. They had done everything. She and Maureen had never been close, but she was sorry it had happened, and felt terrible for her daughters, who were so young to lose their mother. And Liam looked devastated. They had been married for twenty-five years. Nearly half their lives.

He had set the date for the funeral for three days later, and was going to write the obituary when he got home from seeing Maureen's father. Kate ordered a large cross of white roses for the funeral, from all of them, when she got back to her office, and went to see how Julie was doing. She was busy and seemed to be having fun. She looked up when she saw her mother.

"How's Liam?" she asked seriously.

"He's in shock. He's telling Maureen's father now, and the girls are coming home tonight and tomorrow. Did you tell the others?" Julie said she had, and they were all sad to hear it. They were closer to Liam because he was more outgoing and they saw more of him, but Maureen was a familiar figure in their lives too. Liam had married her around the time Tom had died, so his children were younger than Kate's, with both girls still in college. She wondered if they would come home from Europe now, and transfer to schools in the States to be near their father. There were going to be so many decisions to make.

Liam called her after he left Maureen's father, and he was crying. "It was awful. I felt as though I was killing him. He adored her, and he already lost his wife." Maureen had been their only child. It was one of the few things she and Kate had in common, being only children.

"Why don't you lie down for a while," she suggested gently. He had been through so much.

"I should write the obituary," he said, seeming flustered.

"You can do it later. The deadline is tomorrow morning. And you're going to need your strength for the girls. Rest a little."

"Maybe I will," he said, sounding vague and disoriented, which was so unlike him. Liam was always so strong and steady and sure. He had been Kate's pillar of strength and wisdom so often in the past twenty-six years since Tom died. Now she was his.

"Do you want me to come by and see you later?" she offered, and he was grateful. She didn't want to push, nor abandon him either.

She stopped by to see him after work, and helped him with the obituary and then he had to go to the airport to pick up Penny, flying in from Scotland. Kate stayed with him until he left, and then went home. She was exhausted, and her mother called her. Julie had called her too. They talked about it for a while, and Kate decided she was too tired to eat after they hung up. She didn't want to call Liam in case he was already with Penny by then. But he called her at midnight, after Penny had gone to bed.

"Oh God, Kate. This is a nightmare. Everybody's crying and I don't know what to do." Liam was a strong man, and a capable one, but dealing with other people's emotions was not his forte, which was why Maureen had suited him so well. She had never been an overtly emotional woman, which was comfortable for him. She was a quiet presence he could count on, and now she was gone.

"I know this is awful. But you'll be able to deal with this. I promise. You just have to get through the next few days. And then this part will be over," she said soothingly.

"And then what? I have to manage without her for the rest of my life." He was crying again and Kate felt desperately sorry for him. He had no idea how he was going to live without Maureen. He felt like the best part of him had died with her, and everything familiar he had relied on was gone, except Kate.

"Did you finish the obituary?" she asked practically.

"I just did. And I have to pick up Elizabeth in the morning. She couldn't get a direct flight. She had to transfer in Frankfurt." He sounded worried about it.

"She'll be fine. And then you'll all be together."

"Penny wanted to see her mother, but I couldn't let her. She was so badly damaged when she was hit." He started to cry as he said it. It was as though a lifetime of emotions were flowing out of him, and he was drowning in them.

"Don't think about it now. You have to lie down. Even if you don't sleep. Just lie down and try to relax." She was trying to talk him through it as best she could. She had been there herself, with four young children at the time. And Liam had been there for her. She had never forgotten how kind he was to her then, and to her kids. "You can call me in the morning when you wake up, or tonight, if you can't sleep."

"Kate, thank you. I don't know what I'd do without you right now. I'm so lost without her."

"You did it for me a long time ago." He still remembered how destroyed she had been to lose Tom. But she'd had time to prepare. He had been so sick that it was almost a blessing when he died. This had hit Liam like a building falling on him the night before. "Now go to bed. We'll talk tomorrow."

She hung up and thought about him, and she was drained herself. She lay down on her bed for a few minutes, still dressed, and the next thing she knew it was morning. And the first thing she remembered as she opened her eyes was that Maureen had died. She still couldn't believe it. And neither could Liam when he woke up and burst into tears.

Chapter 23

Justin checked in on Shirley the morning after he got back to Vermont after driving Julie to New York and seeing the agent. She said she was fine, and getting bigger by the hour. She was good humored about it.

"These girls are having a party in there," she said, laughing, although it was uncomfortable for her. "I think they're dancing or something. They never stop moving now." Justin thought it was a good sign, and told her to call if she needed anything, and she said she would. Justin was going to be available at every moment for her until the babies were born.

Milagra was down for a nap and he was writing when Richard called him and asked if he could come by after school. Justin hesitated but said he could. He usually saw Milagra on the weekend, but Justin had no objection to his coming by. He had made his peace by then with the fact that they weren't getting back together. They had been apart for six months. They'd had six good years together, and maybe one couldn't ask for more than that. He had accepted that it was over.

He was feeding Milagra a snack when Richard walked in, and he handed her over to the babysitter who had come so he could go back to writing for a few hours. He was working on an outline for another book, and had a magazine piece to write with a deadline. He knew he had to work harder than ever now to support three kids.

Richard looked uncomfortable when he walked in, but Milagra shrieked with delight when she saw him, and complained when the sitter took her away to play on the swing set Justin had had installed outside. And there were more toys than ever all over the house. Richard laughed when he sat on one of them, when Justin brought coffee for both of them to the living room, which seemed more civilized. The kitchen had become Justin's office.

"I miss that," Richard said, as he set the toy on the floor.

"What? Sitting on toys?" Justin laughed. "Come by anytime, we've got plenty for you to sit on." And there would be lots more soon, once the twins arrived and started moving around. Justin knew that the next several years would be chaos. He was expecting it. It would be all hard work and fatherhood for him. It was what he wanted.

"That's why I'm here," Richard said quietly, as he stirred his coffee and then looked up at Justin. He was still embarrassed at what he'd done six months before, and how badly he'd handled it, but Justin had gotten past it. He wasn't seeing anyone, but only because he hadn't had time to, between the book and the baby. And he was sure his dating life would be seriously impacted by the twins, at least for a while. "I want to talk to you. I know I was a jerk, and I had some kind of meltdown, or freak-out, or midlife crisis, or whatever you want to call it. I think I lost my bearings for a while. The baby over-whelmed me, and you're so much better at it than I am, I think I felt bad about that too. I was jealous of how good you were at it, and all the attention you gave her. I felt left out." It was a lot to admit, but Justin could see he meant it.

"I loved you, not just the baby, and I loved her because she was ours," Justin said simply.

"You're a natural mother; I'm not," Richard said honestly.

"Try saying that to someone straight." Justin laughed.

"You know what I mean," Richard said uncomfortably.

"I do, but you're a better mother than you think, and a good father. You can't be everything. Maybe my fathering skills won't turn out to be so good. You just do the best you can."

"It's taken me six months, and thirty-seven years to figure that out. And I was an idiot six months ago, but I love you, Just. I'd like to try again, if you'll let me. I want to come back." It had taken him months to get up the guts to say it, but he knew he would never be happy again unless he did, even if Justin turned him down, which he realized was a distinct possibility after the way he'd behaved. He had panicked, cheated, and run away. Now he was back, or wanted to be.

Justin was staring at him in amazement. "*Now?* You want to come back now? Are you crazy? You freaked out with one kid. You want to try again five minutes before I have twins? You're insane." Justin was grinning as he said it. It was gratifying to hear, and he was touched, but it would never work. Maybe six months before, but not now.

"Five minutes before *we* have twins," Richard corrected him.

"That's debatable. I decided to have them on my own, when you walked out," Justin said clearly. He had no expectations of him.

"But they're still ours," Richard insisted, and Justin sat staring at him.

"Do you have any idea what you're signing on for? Three girls. And I was a twin, I know what that's like. You'll be out the door in two days."

"No, I won't. And we can go to a motel for a night, and leave them with a sitter. We need some time for us too."

"Yeah, like in twenty years if we're lucky, when they're in college. Richard, we won't have a baby anymore, we'll have a family. That's a much bigger deal."

"I'm in, if you'll have me," Richard said seriously.

"Why?"

"Because I love you. In the end, it boils down to that.

I may hate this at times, and three little girls may drive me nuts. But I love you, and that's part of the deal. Will you let me come back?"

"And what happens if you hate it? You're out the door again? It took me a long time to get over that."

"Do you still love me?"

Justin took a moment before he answered and then nodded. "Yes, I do, but sometimes no matter how much you love someone, it doesn't work out." He had accepted that.

"This can work, and it will. I've grown up," Richard insisted, and before he could say anything else, Justin leaned over and kissed him. And then he looked at him seriously.

"If you want out again, just tell me. You don't have to do what you did before. If you're unhappy, just go without making a mess." Richard nodded.

"I won't leave again, I swear."

"When do you want to move back in?" He was smiling when he asked him. Justin was happy. This felt right. More so than ever before, and they had six years invested in their life together, and three children. It was too much to throw away.

"I have a bag in the car," Richard said sheepishly, and Justin laughed.

"Well, come on in. These may be the last peaceful days we have for the next fifteen years. And you thought

Milagra was a lot to deal with. Wait until we have three of them screaming at the same time." They were about to have three children thirteen months apart. It was the quiet before the storm.

Richard left and came back with his bag a few minutes later, and they walked up the stairs together. As they wandered into the bedroom, Richard thought of something.

"Where are the twins going to sleep?"

"With us in the beginning. And then in Milagra's room. When they're old enough, we can buy them triple bunk beds. Or maybe by then, my books will be selling and we can buy a bigger house. Until then, it will be five of us in this dollhouse."

"Bring it on," Richard said, grinning, and they both laughed.

*

Julie had called Justin when Kate told her Maureen had died, and Kate let him know when the funeral was, but he called to tell her that there was no way he could come down now, even for a day. Shirley was just too close to delivering, and he might not get back in time. And he wanted to be there when the twins were born. He didn't want to miss it. Kate told him she was sure Liam would understand. Especially with twins. They talked for a little while about how tragic Maureen's death was, and how devastated Liam and the girls were, and then he quietly told her that Richard was back.

"Is that what you want?" she asked him, and he said it was, and that things were better than ever between them, and they had put a lot of thought into it and had some good talks.

"Then I'm happy for you," his mother said. "Send him my love. How's Shirley doing?"

"She's getting very close. She looks like she's going to explode any minute." Kate laughed at the memory of her own pregnancy when she'd had twins.

"That's how I looked with you."

"Let me know how the funeral goes," he said seriously. "And please tell Liam and the girls how sorry I am." Kate promised to do that, and that afternoon Richard and Justin went to visit Shirley. She was happy to see them back together. Richard couldn't believe how enormous she was. She looked like she was carrying two ten-pounders this time, but nothing was happening yet, and her due date was still three weeks away, although she didn't look it, and she could barely make it up the front steps of her house without help. Jack had told her this had to be her last surrogacy, but he was good-natured about it, and happy for the boys. This time, she knew she'd never do it again. She'd done enough.

That evening there was a vigil for Maureen. Both girls were there in somber black with lace mantillas Elizabeth had brought from Spain, and Liam stood beside them looking somber and dignified in a black suit and black tie. Kate had stopped to get him the tie at Hermès, because he said he didn't have a black one. He was given to bright ties, none of which he could wear on this occasion.

Kate went to the vigil with Julie, Willie, and Izzie, and they all hugged the girls and stood with them, while the guests filed in and signed the guest book. Maureen's father didn't come that night. He was too frail, and he was saving his strength for the next day.

The funeral was as serious and proper as Maureen had been. The choir was beautiful, as was the music Liam had chosen. A soloist with a gorgeous voice sang the "Ave Maria." Liam's daughters sat with him and their grandfather. A bagpiper played, following the casket out. She had already been cremated. And the church had been filled with friends and people Liam did business with. All the details had come together with Kate's behind-the-scenes careful attention. They had paid tribute to Maureen just as she would have wanted. And after the burial at their family plot, a hundred friends of theirs and the girls came to the house. Kate had ordered an excellent buffet for their guests from one of the best caterers in the city.

"Thank you," Liam whispered to her again with a grateful look, as he helped his father-in-law back to his car, with a nurse and a walker. Kate did everything she possibly could for him and the girls. Liam's daughters left for Europe three days later since they had to go back to school, and Liam was alone in the apartment. Kate took him to dinner, and he looked awful. She knew it was going to be a long time before he got over it and would pick up the threads of his life again, particularly with the girls so far away. Neither of them wanted to transfer now, at the beginning of the semester, and they liked their schools in Europe.

Kate called to check on him every day, and took him out for lunch and dinner when he was willing. The only thing keeping him going now was his work. It was like a life raft for him in the middle of a stormy sea. Kate's calls and gentle attentions were the human touch he needed and so desperately missed.

And with the time she was spending checking on Liam, Kate was more grateful than ever that Julie had taken over her online business. She was doing a great job running it, and stayed late every night. She loved what she was doing, and was surprised to find she didn't miss designing. In some ways this was even more creative.

She was leaving the store at ten o'clock one night when she walked past a restaurant in SoHo, and was startled to see her brother Willie leaving with a striking-looking woman who appeared considerably older than he was. They looked like they were having a good time. He didn't see Julie as they talked and laughed with their arms around each other. Julie fell discreetly behind so as not to run into him. She wondered who the woman was and if it was one of his casual seductions, or just a friend. The way he went through women, she couldn't imagine that this was serious or would last long. But it was intriguing to see him with her, and then they turned a corner and disappeared. Julie thought it was funny and felt like she was spying on her brother like when they were kids, but she didn't want to intrude. Willie was always very private about who he went out with. He admitted to quantity, but never their identities. And then Julie caught a cab to Izzie's house, and told her about it, and they giggled.

"He must chase anything in a skirt from eighteen to ninety," Izzie commented. "How old was she?" Julie had told her the woman looked older.

"Well, not that old, but older than he is. I don't know, thirty-eight, forty maybe. Older than we are, and a lot older than he is. He looked like a kid with her, but she was gorgeous and they seemed like they were having a good time."

"Good for him," Izzie said. They talked about Richard and Justin getting back together then, and Izzie admitted that she liked the lawyer she had had dinner with. The two sisters enjoyed living together. It gave them both someone to talk to and to gossip with. It was just like the old days at home.

*

The weeks waiting for Shirley to go into labor gave Justin and Richard time to get comfortable with each other again, and have some peaceful times and some fun. They went to a farmers market together, which Richard had always loved to do since he liked to cook. They went out to dinner a few times, and the movies, and had the babysitter in to watch Milagra. And Justin got some work done—a series of articles on prescription drugs he had been assigned by a major magazine.

Shirley's due date was only a week away and she was hanging on, when she called them one morning while they were having breakfast and Milagra was having her nap.

"Anything new?" Justin asked her. She didn't sound any different than she did every day when they called her and she said she was fine.

"I think the ladies are arriving," she said and laughed. "I think I went into labor last night, but then it stopped, so I didn't call you. But it's getting going now. The doctor just told me to come in so she can check me. This is it." She sounded as excited as they were. The babysitter was on call, so Richard called her, while Justin put their dishes in the sink and put some snacks in a bag for them, in case it took a long time. Shirley sounded remarkably calm, so they didn't rush. The babysitter came twenty minutes later, and they left the house and drove to the hospital, parked, and walked in. As soon as they arrived, they went up to the labor room where Shirley looked like a whale lying on the bed. The OB resident had just checked her, and her doctor was arriving any minute. Shirley was panting through a pain, but smiled at them right after it stopped. They had told her it was too soon for an epidural. The doctor had suggested she not try to do it naturally this time, in case they had to do a rapid C-section if one of the babies got distressed, and Shirley had agreed. Twins were a whole different story.

"I'm only at five," she said, looking disappointed. "But they won't let me go home, in case it speeds up, like it did last time. They want me here."

"So do we," Justin said, smiling at her. "I thought I was going to have to deliver the baby last time before we got here. How do you feel?"

"Okay." But he could see that she was in pain when the next contraction hit her. They had a monitor on her that was registering both heartbeats, and her contractions.

She went on having contractions for another hour, and the doctor broke her waters to get things moving, and within minutes everything took off at a rapid rate, and Shirley was hit by wave after wave of contractions, and was begging for the epidural. It was a lot more intense than when Milagra was born, and she was clutching Justin's hand in a viselike grip. And the anesthesiologist took forever coming. He was on an emergency C-section and they said they were shorthanded that day. They had called for another anesthesiologist, but he wasn't there yet.

"Can't you do something for her?" Justin asked the nurse. He hated to see her in so much pain. The obstetrician had said it would be fast with twins, but it felt like it was taking forever and the pains were brutal. Richard had to leave the room at one point because watching her was making him feel sick, and Shirley was begging for relief.

She was screaming as the obstetrician walked in to check her, and after she did, she told Shirley she was at ten. "We're going to let you push now," she said firmly to get Shirley's attention. "We want to get those babies out," she said intently, and Justin thought he heard something different on the fetal monitor as Richard walked back into the room. Justin suddenly had the feeling they were rushing, and Shirley didn't stop screaming anymore. It was one long, continuous, agonizing wail.

"What about the epidural?" Justin asked the doctor, confused by what he was seeing. Everyone seemed to be rushing and very intense. It didn't feel right to him.

"No time," she said, as two nurses held Shirley's legs, the doctor told her to push, and another OB walked into the room with a serious expression.

"Is something wrong?" Justin tried to ask someone, but no one was listening to him, and the nurses and both doctors were telling Shirley to push. It was nothing like when Milagra was born, which had seemed under control at all times. This didn't. They were shouting at her and she was screaming, and the doctors were looking at each other over their masks. He could see worry in their eyes, as his own heart beat faster. He glanced at Richard, who looked scared too. And they had both noticed that one of the heartbeats kept slowing down.

The doctor used forceps to help her then and the anesthesiologist walked in, way too late for an epidural, but he stayed in case they needed him for a C-section. And just as Justin started to panic, Shirley made a Herculean effort and then slowly, slowly Justin could see the first baby's head appear. They delivered her shoulders, and then the rest of her, and one of the OBs took her and checked her, and suctioned her nose and mouth and she started to cry. She was beautiful, but Shirley's doctor was working hard on the next one, as the heartbeat continued to dip with each contraction. Shirley had stopped screaming and smiled when she saw the first baby girl. And then the pains intensified again. And there was still too much going on in the room for Justin and Richard to hold the baby. The doctor was trying to change the position of the second baby, which was miserable for Shirley, and it felt like a lifetime before the second twin appeared. She was even bigger than the first one, and looked at them with surprise, as though she didn't expect them to be there. And for an instant, she didn't cry. She looked almost blue to Justin and Richard. They had slipped the cord off her neck when they delivered her. The cord had tightened as she moved down the birth canal, which explained the dip in her heartbeat during the contractions. The doctor gave her a tap on the back as a resident suctioned her, and a nurse put an oxygen mask on Shirley, who was exhausted. Then, like a miracle, there was a powerful cry in the room, and the doctors looked visibly relieved, and Justin burst into tears of joy when the baby started crying.

"Is she okay?" both men asked in unison with a frantic look, and both doctors smiled at them.

"She's perfect. Her heart rate was starting to dip before she came out. She had the cord around her neck, and we slipped it off before we got her out." It had been a masterful move, and might have ended differently if they had been less adept. Justin turned to Shirley with love in his eyes.

"You did a great job, Shirley. I'm sorry it was so rough."

"It's okay," she said under the oxygen mask. The delivery had been challenging, but she had done well.

The cords had been cut and the placentas delivered. There were two placentas since they were fraternal twins, not identical. Both babies were whisked off to the nursery to be checked, and Shirley's doctor suggested that Justin and Richard go to the nursery to see them while they tended to Shirley. They gave her a shot for the pain, which made her woozy, and she drifted off to sleep. The delivery had been scary, and as they left the room, Justin and Richard were more grateful to her than ever.

When they got to the nursery to see their babies, Richard and Justin hugged each other and admitted how terrified they had been for a minute when the second twin looked blue and didn't cry. But both babies looked perfect now and the pediatrician said they were fine. Justin and Richard each held one of their daughters, and smiled at each other. They had shared another miracle that day.

"Your mothering skills have improved," Justin teased him, and Richard laughed. The babies were gorgeous, and they held them for a long time and then went back to see Shirley. She still had the oxygen mask on, and she was sound asleep with a nurse watching her and massaging her abdomen to reduce the bleeding. Jack had arrived by then, and was sitting with her. He congratulated both men in a whisper, with a smile. He was happy it was over for Shirley, and they could lead a normal life again.

Justin and Richard called everyone after that. Camilla and Charlotte had arrived. Justin and Richard had three children now. It was hard even for them to believe, as they looked at their brand-new daughters swaddled in pink blankets, with little pink hats to keep their heads warm. Charlotte had weighed just over eight pounds, and Camilla nine. They were astounding weights for twins. And they were perfect. Whatever challenges lay ahead for them, both men felt equal to the task. More so than ever. And love would carry them along.

"We're definitely a family now," Richard whispered, looking awestruck again at the miracle of it.

"Welcome home," Justin whispered to Richard as they held their sleeping daughters.

Chapter 24

Shirley and the twins stayed at the hospital for three days to make sure everyone was fine, and after that, she was grateful to go home to her own children. Justin and Richard took Charlotte and Camilla home. They had the babysitter there to help them with Milagra, and the feeding schedule was overwhelming for a while, but together they were managing it. And Justin ran it like a well-oiled machine. He and Richard took turns feeding them, and for the first few weeks that was all they did, but after a month they had the system down, and things were running smoothly.

Justin's agent called then to tell him he wanted to represent his book and thought he might already have a publisher for it. He thought the book was masterful. It was great news, and Richard was happy for him. And it was going to help provide what they needed for the children.

A week later, Richard was reading the paper for the first time in a week, and he looked horrified when he handed it to Justin. Peter White, Julie's soon-to-be ex-husband, was on the front page. He had been dating a woman in California and was accused of killing her. He had beaten her to death with a brick after torturing her for several days. She had died of head injuries, numerous puncture wounds, and strangulation. Justin felt sick as he read it. That could have been his sister if she hadn't run away and called him for a ticket to freedom. Justin called his mother immediately, and she had seen the article too. They all had and so had Julie. She felt terrible for the woman Peter had tortured and killed, but she knew how close she had come to the same fate. She told Justin the police had contacted her that morning and wanted to meet with her about her experience with him.

She had started using her maiden name again as soon as she came back from California, and the murder he was accused of made her want the divorce to be final as soon as possible. She had already seen the lawyer and filed the papers. The story in the newspaper about him sobered them all.

Kate had been right. He was too good to be true. They all hoped he would be sent to prison forever. And reading about him brought back all the memories of his reign of terror.

"Are you sure you want us for Thanksgiving?" Justin asked his mother when he called her. "We're kind of a zoo at the moment," he said, as he watched Richard put one baby down in her Moses basket and pick up the other. And

Justin had Milagra on his hip while he talked to Kate on the phone.

"Of course I want you." She had gone up to see them for two days with Grandma Lou and fallen in love with the twins, and had given Justin some helpful hints to manage them.

"You're a brave woman," he said and his mother laughed. She couldn't wait to see them again on Thanksgiving.

*

The scene at Kate's apartment on Thanksgiving was predictably chaotic, but no worse than she had expected. Liam was there, looking dazed, but she had urged him to come, since the girls didn't come home for Thanksgiving and his father-in-law didn't want to acknowledge the holiday this year. Richard and Justin brought all three babies and handed them around to anyone who wanted to hold them. Izzie was there with Tommy, who was eight months old and a happy baby who loved everyone and especially his aunt Julie. Willie came, and Grandma Lou was talking about her next trip, in the spring, to Bangkok.

And Willie stunned them all at the end of dinner, by telling them that he was dating someone. He decided to take the bull by the horns and tell them the whole story at once. She was older, divorced, and had two kids. She was a psychologist for a large corporation. He said their relationship was serious, and they had been dating for six months. There was silence in the room for a minute, and Julie suspected it was the woman she had seen him with one night a month or so ago.

"How much older?" Kate asked, trying to sound relaxed about it, which she wasn't, and Willie knew it too. He was expecting a tsunami of comments from all of them, but he didn't want to hide it anymore because they already had for months. And he said he'd like to bring her and her children to Christmas Eve dinner this year, or he couldn't come, because he didn't like leaving her for a major holiday, which shocked them even more. "She's thirty-eight," he answered his mother's question, twelve years older than he was. "And her kids are six and ten. They're really sweet. And I think you'll like her," he said hopefully.

"Here we go again," Kate said softly to Liam while the others were playing with Milagra, Tommy, and the twins, and passing them around. "They all think they can beat the odds of impossible situations, with difficult people. Can't any of them do something simple and easy for a change?" Liam smiled at what she said.

"Why would they? You didn't," he reminded her. "Their story isn't written yet. Zach is gone, and Izzie would have left him eventually. Julie escaped Peter. The boys are back together. They all have cute kids. You don't know yet what the rest of the story will look like. They'll make easier choices next time. And we all face our challenges and terrify our parents, while they try to keep us safe from our mistakes. It may look different but it's the same with every generation. Parents trying to protect their kids, and the kids taking chances and putting themselves at risk to some degree."

"But why do mine have to make it so hard for themselves on the first try? And now we're starting all over again with Willie. How do you think that's going to turn out, a divorced woman with two children, that much older than he is? The handwriting is on the wall before they even start. Do we have to do this again and again?"

"Young people are complicated. I'm sure mine will do the same thing in some form or other. They marry the people they shouldn't now, or they have babies and don't marry. It's all upside down. But sometimes it works. That's what they're counting on. Beating the odds. They think they can, even though we know better and try to warn them. They don't listen." He had summed it up succinctly.

"They can't win at these situations," she complained, and he patted her hand. "Doesn't anyone just marry normal people anymore? Do they all have to be crazy or criminals, or be the wrong ones? The ones who shouldn't get married do, and the ones who should don't."

"They play the long shots, or don't want to play by our rules. You didn't make it so easy for yourself either. You dropped out of college to marry a law student, worked your tail off to support everyone, and had four kids. Your mother must have worried too," he reminded her again.

"She did," Kate admitted, thinking about it. There was truth to what he said.

"You can't predict how their relationships will turn out. Sometimes you can win against all the odds, although not often."

"I just wish they made it easier for themselves, and for us," she said, and smiled at him ruefully.

"Give them time. Maybe they will one day," he said to encourage her. And then they went to sit with the others and play with the babies, while Grandma Lou talked about Bangkok. Kate looked over at Liam hopefully. Maybe he was right. Maybe it would all turn out right in the end. And now she had to meet Willie's woman, and see what that was all about. She could hardly wait. But she wasn't optimistic about it. Her kids seemed to be determined to scare her every time. They had done a good job of it so far. Justin and the surrogate and having three children, and now Willie with an older, divorced woman with two kids. How could they expect any of that to go smoothly?

Shortly before Christmas, Willie called his mother to confirm that he could bring his friend Zoe and her two children to dinner on Christmas Eve. He had mentioned it on Thanksgiving, but she hadn't heard anything about it since, and Kate didn't want to push it and hoped he had changed his mind. He hadn't.

"Are you that serious about her?" she asked him.

"Yes, I am. We're not getting married, if that's what you're worried about, but we're happy together. I know the age difference sounds crazy, but it works. And I really like her kids."

"Then you can bring her, if it really matters to you," Kate said quietly, wishing he wouldn't.

"I don't want to leave her alone on Christmas Eve." All of her children were kind, but also foolish about the risks they took. But they were good people at heart.

There were going to be a lot of people for Christmas this year, so Kate thought it wouldn't matter so much who they brought. With Willie's additions, there would be twelve adults and six children. Four of them were babies, and she'd have to set up a small card table for Willie's girlfriend's two children, since there was no room for them with the adults. Liam was coming with his two daughters, Willie and his group, Justin and Richard, Izzie had asked to bring her lawyer friend and Kate had said yes to that too, she was so pleased that she was dating someone civilized, and Julie and Grandma Lou were coming alone.

And when the night arrived, the apartment looked beautiful. The Christmas tree had been decorated, and Kate was wearing red velvet slacks, a white satin blouse, and gold mules, all of it Chanel from her store. And everyone stopped talking when Willie and his woman walked in. She was wearing a black Chanel suit and high heels, and looked more like one of Kate's friends than his, but she had dressed appropriately for the evening. Her ten-year-old daughter, Lily, was wearing a black velvet dress and black patent leather shoes with white tights, and her six-year-old son, Louis, was adorable in gray slacks and a navy velvet blazer and remarkably polite. Zoe thanked Kate for allowing her to come and bring her children, and she was hard to resist. She was stunning, she was smart, she had a great job, she had gone to Vassar undergrad and Harvard for her graduate degree, but she looked as though she should have been out with a forty-year-old man, and instead she was dating a kid. But Willie seemed very grown up when he was with her. It was a side of him none of them had ever seen. And she had a very interesting conversation with Liam about corporate HR policies. It was hard to find fault with her, and she loved Grandma Lou. She was cautious and respectful with Kate, who watched her all night. And Zoe was lovely with her children and loved all the babies. She was a warm, intelligent person and obviously crazy about Willie. She completely understood Kate's objections and sympathized with them, but she loved him and Willie was equally in love with her.

Justin told everyone at dinner that his novel had been sold to a major publishing house, which brought a round of applause and he took a bow. And he and Richard stole the show when they announced that they were getting married.

"I thought you didn't approve of gay marriage," Willie teased them.

"We didn't. Why should we pay alimony too?" Richard quipped.

"When?" Izzie wanted to know. And where, and how. But she had no objections to the marriage. And she loved Richard.

"We've decided to be corny about it," Justin said, looking embarrassed. It had been Richard's idea, but Justin went along with it to make him happy. "If we're going to do it, we're going all the way. We're getting married on Valentine's Day, if Mom will let us do it here." That had been Justin's only condition.

"Of course," she agreed, and smiled at them both.

"It's about time," Grandma Lou said heartily, and they all laughed. But it made sense to Kate. They'd been together for a long time, had faced their challenges, and had come back together again, with a better understanding than before. And they had three little girls to bring up, so they should at least try to stay together, if that was what their commitment meant. But she no longer felt qualified to say who should get married and who shouldn't. None of it made sense anymore. It was all a wild guess as to what would work.

Julie said that every family needed a maiden aunt who

didn't marry or have kids, and that's what she wanted to be when she grew up, which her grandmother didn't believe for a minute. She was still severely marked by her terrifying experience with Peter, and was battling her way through the divorce. The idea of being with anyone horrified her, and the role of solitary woman felt safer to her, which was understandable, for now anyway. And at thirty-two, anything she decided now could change later, although she seemed definite about staying alone, and meant it. She had been badly burned by a man who could have killed her.

Izzie added that she'd like to have more children, but would never marry again. They all liked her lawyer friend who seemed perfect for her and the kind of man she should have dated in the first place, instead of going off-track with Zach, who was so obviously wrong for her.

Willie made no comment, but smiled at Zoe from across the table. She had been a good addition to the group, and had managed five minutes to speak quietly to Kate, and said that she was sure everyone was shocked by their age difference, and she was too, but Willie was a fine man with good values and she respected him. It was hard to find fault with that. And then everyone went home, and came back for lunch on Christmas Day, as they always did. And they talked about Justin's book and his wedding in detail.

They wanted a private wedding ceremony only for

family, performed by a judge, and a cocktail party at Kate's apartment, nothing formal or too much trouble. It sounded reasonable to Kate and in good taste. And they would spend a weekend in Miami for their honeymoon, leaving the girls with a babysitter, which Kate applauded too. They needed time with each other, away from their children, if it was going to work. Kate offered to pay for the wedding and honeymoon as a wedding gift, but Justin wanted to pay for them from the proceeds of his book, and not be a burden on his mother. He assured her that they would take care of everything. The publisher had paid him well.

It had been a lovely Christmas, and Kate was exhausted when they all left. So much had happened and was happening. It was hard to keep up with them. She liked Zoe better than she wanted to, because she still thought their age difference was too great, but it made sense to them. And she was a good woman and brought out the best in Willie. Even Kate could see that. He had matured noticeably since he'd been with her, and now seemed older than his years. He said they had no plans to marry and wanted only to live together, although he commented that he wanted to have children with her one day, which would have to be soon because of her age.

*

Julie was busy at the store, working on the website between Christmas and New Year's Day, and Kate was in and out of the store but had less to do than Julie now. Julie had an appointment to meet with a new Web designer who had been recommended to her. She wanted to streamline their website and give it a more modern look. And all heads turned at the shop when he walked in. He was surprisingly handsome, but when he talked to Julie he was shy and awkward around her. He was beautiful to look at but a total geek. He came back the next day to show her some ideas, and he did very good work. Before he left, he blushed to the roots of his hair, and asked if she would have dinner with him sometime.

Julie looked horrified at the idea.

"Not if it's a date," she snapped at him, annoyed that he'd asked, although she'd liked him till then, and thought he was talented and smart. "I'm getting divorced, I never want to get married again, and I don't want kids. That makes me ineligible for most men, which is fine with me. And I can't spell, if that's a problem for you." She was like a bulldozer coming at him, and he looked terrified of her.

"It's not. I can't spell either. I've used spellcheck all my life, but I have great computer skills. And I wasn't thinking about marriage and kids, just dinner. Do you eat?" His name was Oliver, and he was handsome and blond and looked like a model, and his social skills were as poor as hers.

"Sometimes I eat, if the food is good. I don't like Thai food or anything spicy." They were like two porcupines throwing quills at each other. But there was something awkward and nervous about both of them. It was an even match, if they could get past the initial pleasantries, which they hadn't mastered yet.

"How about tomorrow night?" he suggested and she thought about it.

"Okay. I like delicatessen food."

"So do I," he admitted with a look of relief.

"There's a good deli down the street. Do you like cheesecake?"

"Yes, I do."

"Me too." He showed up the next day and they had a nice time at the deli, which seemed nonthreatening to Julie after everything she'd been through. And she told him over dinner that her ex-husband was accused of murdering the woman he dated when she left him.

"How was he with you?" Oliver asked her, as they ate hot pastrami sandwiches, after matzo ball soup.

"Not good. He tried to kill me after six months. So I left."

"How terrible for you," Oliver said and stopped eating while he said it. "I wouldn't want to date or get married again if I were you either. Maybe you'll feel better after a while. I hope so."

"I'm fine the way I am," she said defensively, and then relaxed over the cheesecake. "Do you like hockey?" she asked him, and he looked embarrassed.

"No, I don't. I hate sports. I suck at them, and spectator sports bore me. Why? Do you?"

"No, I hate them." She remembered the hockey games that Peter took her to, and a lot of other sporting events. In retrospect, they were a bad memory now, like everything else about him, after what had come later. She associated going to games with him.

"I just like computers," Oliver said innocently.

"Good." They finished dinner, and he took her home in a cab and dropped her off, and she thanked him for the deli meal.

"Maybe we could eat together again sometime," he suggested awkwardly. "The cheesecake was really good." She smiled when he said it.

"I liked it too. Thanks for dinner," she said and got out of the cab. It hadn't been as scary as she had expected it to be. But it hadn't been a date, just a meal, she told herself, which was all she needed now. And he was fine with that.

*

Justin and Richard's Valentine's Day wedding was as corny as they'd promised. The setting in Kate's apartment looked lovely, but the wedding cake was pink, and Justin and Richard wore dark suits with pink shirts and pink ties. They refused to let anyone take it too seriously, although the ceremony was, but only the family was there.

Izzie brought Jeff, the partner at her law firm that she had been dating for five months, and she admitted to her mother the night before the wedding that she really liked him. They were talking about living together eventually, but they weren't interested in marriage. They were happy as they were, and he was a responsible man and was great with Tommy.

Julie brought Oliver at the last minute, and he was awkward but adoring whenever he looked at her. Justin said he was the best looking man he'd ever seen but was a total geek. He could barely manage a conversation, except with Julie. They were comfortable with each other.

Willie brought Zoe and her children, and Kate had the sinking feeling that he wanted to marry her sooner rather than later, which she thought would be a mistake no matter how happy they were. The age difference was too great. But Kate had learned that she couldn't do anything about it if that's what he wanted. He claimed they weren't planning to marry, but she didn't believe him.

Shirley and Jack came to the wedding and were touched to have been invited. And Alana was there too. She flew in from London especially to be there.

Grandma Lou held court, and was leaving for Bangkok soon with Frances. Liam stood near Kate at the ceremony and kept an eye on her at the reception, and she finally came and sat next to him when the party was under way and everyone seemed to be having a good time.

"I like Izzie's new guy," she commented to Liam with some relief. He was normal and traditional, and good to her. Kate had no strange vibes about him and thought they were great together. "But she says she's never getting married again," Kate told Liam. "When they find respectable partners who'd be good for them, they won't marry them. And they marry all the wrong ones. We've certainly had our share of those in the last two years." It was a major understatement after Zach and Peter, although now they were all with nice people, even if Zoe was too old for Willie. But Kate liked her.

"They seem to get it right on the second try," Liam conceded. "I like Jeff a lot for Izzie, and Oliver is funny as hell with Julie. I don't know which of them is more nervous and ill at ease, but he's crazy about her, and he's harmless, and very smart." He had struggled through a conversation with him.

"She likes him too, but she won't admit it. She says they're not dating. But they go to dinner about four times a week. She says they just eat. She's terrified after Peter. But Oliver's good for her, and he's sweet." Kate agreed with Liam. "And Willie looks like he's heading for the altar like a homing pigeon with Zoe, and she's too old for him. That's a long shot that won't work," she said cynically.

"Maybe it will. She's an amazing woman and he's a great kid."

"That's the problem, he's a kid and she's a woman."

"Maybe he'll grow up with her. We all do eventually."
He sighed as he thought of Maureen. It had been a long
five months without her. And after two glasses of champagne, he told Kate something he had never admitted to
her before. "I would have married you when Tom died. I
always wanted to, but you were happily married before
that and I was too young to even think about it when you
married him. And later, I was engaged to Maureen, and I
didn't think it would be right to break it off with her and
pursue you when Tom died. So I married her. And it was
good, for both of us. And now you've been alone for all
these years. I thought you'd remarry after Tom died." She
was touched by what he confessed to her. She would never
have guessed he had feelings for her in that way. And then
he startled her again. "Would you ever marry me, Kate?"

"Now? Why?" she said, laughing at him. "It's a big
statement about the times when the most stable relationship in our family is my gay son marrying his partner. The
kind of marriages we believe in don't exist anymore." She
thought of Bernard as she said it, with his "arrangement"
with his wife.

"It still makes sense for us," Liam said quietly. "We
believe in the commitment it represents. I'm not sure they
do. With them, it's all very immediate, and they don't
expect it to last. I'd have stayed married to Maureen forever. We were best friends. It wasn't exciting, but it was
solid. I didn't want excitement. Maureen and I wanted a

stable, predictable relationship we could rely on. It suited us, and worked for all those years. And you'd still be married to Tom if he were alive."

"I was crazy about him till the day he died." She smiled at the memory. It was young love, and she was sure their marriage would have withstood the test of time, as Liam's had.

"We have a shot at a second chance too," he said thoughtfully. "And our needs are different now. We can relax and have more fun." He had been thinking about it for months, but hadn't said it to her until now. And it had upset him to see her with a man like Bernard.

"What are the odds for us?" She looked at him squarely.

"I think they're pretty good. Don't you?"

"I think you're my best friend. Why screw that up?"

"Because it would be nice to have more than that, wouldn't it?" She could see that he was serious about what he was saying, and it went straight to her heart.

"Are you proposing to me?" She grinned at him. They were so comfortable with each other that she could say anything to him, and always had. It was the best part of being friends for more than half their lives.

"Not yet." He grinned back at her. "I'm polling my constituency." He was ready for some excitement now. He liked that idea, with her. They always had fun together. And their values were the same.

"Don't rush your fences, you've only been widowed for

five months. You can't get married for a year. It would be disrespectful to your girls."

"Is that a yes seven months from now?" He was pressing her, but he had waited a long time. They were both free now, at the same time. And he thought it was right now.

"It's a maybe and that's the best you're going to get for now," she said, looking mischievous but pleased. She loved him too, and always had. Although his asking her to marry him was a surprise.

"I think the odds are pretty good," he said seriously. "If the kids can do whatever the hell they want, so can we." The thought of it made her laugh.

"What would our children say?" Kate thought about it seriously for a minute.

"They'd probably be pleased," he said gently, and she suspected he was right.

"Or surprised." She smiled at him, and the boys cut their wedding cake then. It was the most beautiful cake she'd ever seen, with pink sugar flowers all over it, chocolate inside, and two grooms on the top.

Kate and Liam stood eating their cake side by side, observing her family. They were all having a good time. And he was right. They had come through the mistakes they'd made, survived, and corrected them. Maybe that was how it had to happen. Maybe they had better odds on the second round. She hoped so for her children's sakes.

"Was that a soft maybe or a definite?" Liam asked her with a serious look.

"Ask me in September, and we'll talk about it." And with that, she disappeared among the guests, and glanced back at him. He was smiling at her. She couldn't help thinking that her children were full of surprises. Maybe it was time for them to be too. And the odds for her and Liam were pretty good. Time would tell, for them all. She had learned that sometimes all you could do was take the chance and hope. The last two years had taught her that. And all she could do was be the safety net under her children while they lived their lives, took their chances, and made their own mistakes. Every generation did it, and terrified their parents until they got it right, if they did. If not, she would be there for them.

And at the end of the day, whatever the odds, it was her turn now too.

Danielle Steel

*Turn over for more information about
Danielle's upcoming books . . .*

ACCIDENTAL HEROES

DANGER. COURAGE. SURVIVAL.

On a beautiful May morning at New York's John F. Kennedy airport, two planes have just departed for San Francisco. At a security checkpoint, TSA agent Bernice Adams finds a postcard of the Golden Gate Bridge bearing an ambiguous – perhaps ominous – message. Still grappling with guilt after a disastrous operation in which hostages were killed, Homeland Security agent Ben Waterman is also suspicious. Who left the postcard behind, which flight is that person on, and what exactly does the message mean?

Available for pre-order

PURE HEART. PURE STEEL.

THE DUCHESS

ORPHANED. BETRAYED. DETERMINED.

Angélique Latham has grown up at magnificent Belgrave Castle under the loving tutelage of her father, the Duke of Westerfield, after the death of her aristocratic French mother. At eighteen she is her father's closest, most trusted child, schooled in managing their grand estate. But when he dies, her half-brothers brutally turn her out, denying her very existence. Angélique has a keen mind, remarkable beauty, and an envelope of money her father pressed upon her. To survive, she will need all her resources – and one bold stroke of fortune . . .

Coming soon in paperback

PURE HEART. PURE STEEL.

THE RIGHT TIME

GIFTED. SUCCESSFUL. MYSTERIOUS.

Abandoned by her mother, Alexandra Winslow takes solace in the mysteries she reads with her devoted father – and soon she is writing them herself. After his death, a teenage Alexandra pursues her gift and is soon a global bestseller, writing under a pseudonym. Her secret life as the mysterious and brilliantly successful Alexander Green – and her own life as a talented young woman – expose her to the envious, the arrogant, and Hollywood players who have no idea who she really is. Once her double life and fame are established, the price of the truth is always too high.

Coming soon in paperback

PURE HEART. PURE STEEL.

Danielle Steel

Have you liked Danielle Steel on Facebook?

Be the first to know about Danielle's latest books,
access exclusive competitions and stay in touch
with news about Danielle.

www.facebook.com/DanielleSteelOfficial

extracts reading groups competitions books new discounts extracts events reading groups competitions books new extracts discounts reading groups extracts events extracts discounts events reading groups books events extracts new books interviews reading groups reading groups books extracts discounts new books events new events new books events interviews books new extracts discounts extracts discounts

www.panmacmillan.com

extracts events reading groups competitions books extracts new books